Lord of the Dark

Lord of the Dark

Dawn Thompson

𝒜

APHRODISIA

KENSINGTON BOOKS

http://www.kensingtonbooks.com

APHRODISIA BOOKS are published by

Kensington Publishing Corp.
850 Third Avenue
New York, NY 10022

ISBN-13: 978-0-7582-2180-3
ISBN-10: 0-7582-2180-0

First Kensington Trade Paperback Printing: August 2008

10 9 8 7 6 5 4 3 2 1

Printed in the United States of America

1

The Stone Garden at the Pavilion
The Eastern Archipelago, Principalities of Arcus

Gideon, Lord of the Dark, one of the four guardians of the Principalities of Arcus, stood upon the tallest phallic column in the stone garden at the edge of the amphitheater. He'd stood there for some time, observing the ritual mating of his friend and fellow prince appointed by the Arcan gods, Simeon, Lord of the Deep, and his human bride, Megaleen. He hadn't felt this lonely since the gods of Arcus flung him—the most revered archangel of the Arcan otherworld—out of paradise never to return.

The wind ruffled the silver-white feathers in his magnificent wings, and he was aroused, a cruel trick of the gods that made his wings sensitive to touch—even the caress of the wind that bore him aloft. But he couldn't fault the wind this time, not entirely. It had been some time since he'd satisfied those urges, and watching the ritual had made him hard.

Gideon glanced about. There wasn't a *watcher* in sight. The dubious-winged watchdogs of the gods that kept him celibate were conspicuous in their absence. Scarcely breathing, he opened the crotch of his skintight eelskin body garment that fitted him like it did the silver-black eels that had worn it before him and freed his thick, burgeoning cock for the air to soothe . . . or not. Then, springing from the phallic stone, he soared off over the satiny breast of the water into the dawn.

The sunrise that should have been golden shone over the water blood red—a sure sign there would be a storm before nightfall. Gideon could taste it in the salt-drenched air. Soon the innocent-looking ripples that lapped at the rocks would roil and churn, and great white-capped combers flinging spindrift would roll up the phallic columns, turning them black against a blacker sky. He would be home in his cave on the Dark Isle by then, safely out of the tormenting wind.

The stone garden was vast, encompassing the underwater Pavilion like a fence above the waves. In fair weather, the sirens would sun themselves upon the rocks and sing their haunting songs. In the center stood a little islet, a tiny spit of land, too small to build a shed upon, but large enough for a siren to lose herself among the greenery: Muriel's Isle. Gideon swooped low, his wing tips tinted pink in the fiery sun. Yes, she was there, Muriel, Queen of the Sirens, lying naked in a bed of lemongrass, pleasuring herself.

Gideon touched down at her feet arms akimbo, his naked cock hot and hard and red in the fiery dawn, the mushroom tip slick with pre-come. The wind of his motion in flight had neither cooled the fever in his shaft nor relieved him this time. The tall shadow of his enormous sex, throbbing in response to the sight of her writhing below, stretched across her naked belly. Her eyes riveted to his penis, she narrowed them to the fractured sunbeams dancing about him like a misshapen halo, for the rising sun was at his back.

Muriel smiled, still working her nipples between her thumbs and forefingers, as she undulated against the clump of lemongrass she had captured between her thighs. Grinding the grass spears into her hairless sex had crushed them and released their fragrant oils, spreading their lemony scent. She always smelled of lemongrass and ambergris, come to that. Gideon wondered if often she pleasured herself thus.

"You could not bear their mating ritual either, I see," she said, nodding toward his erection.

Gideon seized his cock and flaunted it. "Would this not better serve you than that clump of weeds you're straddling?" he said.

Muriel laughed. The sun shone red in her eyes, moist with the glaze of arousal. "At least these 'weeds' will let me rise up afterward," she said. She gestured toward his cock again. "The last time I let you put that weapon inside me I couldn't walk for a sennight."

"That was a long time ago," Gideon said.

"It's still as large," she observed. "Such a cock is wasted upon the likes of you, Lord of the Dark. Will you not face reprisals? You did the last time, as I recall."

Gideon dropped down to his knees and plucked the lemongrass from between her legs. He shrugged, and his massive wings made a rustling sound. Like a pulse beat, their motion thrummed through his body to the core. "I am hoping that the watchers are all occupied at the amphitheater gazing upon Simeon and Megaleen as they perform their nuptial rite. You cannot have him, and I cannot have her. What harm to comfort each other, um?"

Gideon didn't wait for an answer. He was a man of few words, and he'd expended what he would allow for the moment. She was ready and willing, despite the repartee, and they both were bitten sore for wanting. He spread her nether lips and lowered his tongue to her clitoris. Muriel's hips jerked forward, and she uttered a strangled gasp as he laved the engorged bud to hardness.

"You are a master at that," she crooned, moving against his mouth.

Gideon didn't answer. The citrus tang of the crushed lemongrass mingled with her salt sweetness, for she was of the sea, was like an aphrodisiac. He tasted her deeply, his tongue gliding on her salty wetness as she laced her fingers through his hair and arched herself against his mouth, begging him to take her deeper still.

When she reached to stroke his trembling wings, his head shot up, her juices glistening on his cleft chin. "*No*, not yet!" he panted, for, aroused as he was, if she touched his wings now he would come. Their sensitivity was his curse, his punishment for falling from grace with the Arcan gods who had cast him out, lest he ever forget. There wasn't much likelihood of that. His existence was a living hell, a constant torment of unclimaxed arousal, except for stolen moments like now, when the watchers looked away and he could cheat them and reach orgasm submerged in willing flesh. It had been thus for eons, and so it would be until the end of time. It was a moment to be savored, not to be rushed, for it happened so seldom. "I will tell you when . . ." he murmured.

There wasn't time to strip off his eel skin, though he did open the front, inviting her hands to reach inside and caress his broad chest; anything to keep them away from his wings. He groaned as her arms encircled his naked torso beneath the silvery black eel skin, and groaned again as her hands slipped lower, gripping his taut buttocks. Gathering her close, he feasted upon her breasts, laving her tawny nipples erect, hardening them beneath his tongue until she writhed against him, begging for his cock to enter her.

Gideon's loins were on fire. Pulsating waves of riveting heat ripped through his sex, his belly, and thighs. Leaning against her skin to skin, he savored every recess, every orifice and crevice in her salt-drenched nakedness. She was as the sea itself, undulating, cresting and eddying, spilling over with pure passion. It was no wonder so many seafarers succumbed to her wiles. She was the ultimate seductress, a mistress of libidinous lust, but that was all she was. All else was shadows. There was no love in her, unless it be for Simeon, and even that was suspect. Muriel, Queen of the Sirens, was an enigma, just the one to bring him to climax with no fear of attachment. While her loins sizzled with drenching fire, her heart was as cold as the Frozen Sea that marked the northern boundaries of the Arcan archipelago. A sea not even Simeon, Lord of the Deep would venture near.

Denied his wings, her fingers gripped his cock; it leapt in her hand, the hard, thick mushroom tip ready to explode. He could bear no more. Raising her hips, he took back his shaft and thrust into her, filling her from the thick root of its anxious bulk to the hot, smooth head leaking pre-come. A deep growl spilled from his throat as the folds of her swollen labia gripped him.

Matching him thrust for shuddering thrust, she ground her body against him to take him deep inside the dark mystery of her sex, and he cried aloud, "Now! My wings . . . stroke them *now* . . . !"

Her fingers ruffling the silken feathers felt like a lightning strike. Gideon cried out. It *was* a lightning strike! Dry lightning snaking down through the red dawn sky from the outstretched hands of a watcher hovering overhead wrenched him out of her and pitched him over in the singed lemongrass, unclimaxed.

Muriel scrambled out from underneath him, her shrill voice guttural and deep. She sprang to her feet, pounding her thighs with clenched fists, her fair, translucent skin normally tinged with green, the color of sea foam, now splotched with the crimson blush of unfulfilled passion.

"Damn you, Gideon!" she shrilled. She glanced aloft, where the creature, neither male nor female, hovered like a hummingbird, its fingers crackling with more charges showing blue-white against the red sky, as the lightning passed between them. "And you!" she spat out. "You have no dominion over *me*! How dare you hurl your missiles in my direction?" Her eyes snapped back to Gideon, attempting to right himself in the smoldering grass at her feet. "You have had your last in me, dark one!" she seethed. "Get your pleasures upon someone else. I like the flesh raw on my bones, not cooked! You see me no more!"

Still dazed in pain, though his shaft was frozen in stiff readiness, Gideon watched the smoke ghosting from Muriel's skin, where the lighting had seared her. Screaming like a banshee, the enraged siren plowed through the lemongrass, and Gideon winced at the hissing sound her body made as she dove into the water and disappeared beneath the swirling eddy her exit had created.

Surging to his feet, Gideon raised his arm and shook his fist at the asexual creature still hovering over him, fresh lightning threatening. Where had it come from? He was so sure he'd eluded the watchers this time. It did not speak. Watchers possessed no powers of speech, and Gideon spread his wings and soared off through the sky that in the space of half an hour had turned from blood red to a jaundiced yellow hue as the storm drew nearer.

Gideon didn't look behind. The watcher wasn't following. Though it wouldn't be far off, it never appeared unless, like now, he attempted to relieve himself inside a woman. His sex would not go flaccid, and he loosed a bestial howl that echoed back in his ears as he soared off over the water. The cave was his only refuge. The gods weren't completely without pity. But there was only emptiness in it, no warm, fragrant womanly flesh, no arms to hold him, no lips to receive the urgency of his kiss. It had been *so long*. Still, if he had it to do over again, he would do the same. If he were faced with the thing that had earned him his fate—cast him out and driven him into darkness—he would embrace it, just as he had that fateful night so long ago when he made the choice that had damned him only to lose the prize.

No, he couldn't think about that now. He wouldn't let his mind take him there again. *Damn the wind!* It was growing stronger, as was his need. Below, the black volcanic sand of the Dark Isle loomed before him. He passed it by. He was in no humor for a trek through the black marshes in his present state. He touched down before the entrance to his cave instead and glanced about. Nothing moved in the petrified forest that flanked the cave on three sides, except the gnarled and twisted trees, their naked branches clacking together in the wind, like ghostly applause mocking him. No foliage grew upon them, or upon anything on the Dark Isle. It reeked of death, as if the gods had cursed the isle as well as its keeper.

Gideon glanced skyward. There was no sign of a watcher, though that didn't comfort him. They were there, ready to swoop down at any moment if he should entertain any thoughts of finishing what he'd started with Muriel. There was no hope of that. Gideon was alone on the Dark Isle. He stormed into the cave and barred the towering double doors of ebony wood that shut the world out and everyone in it.

He was still aroused, still tasting the siren's salt-sweetness. Cursing under his breath, he stripped off his eelskin suit and stomped along a narrow corridor that led to a pool of dark water. Above, a narrow waterfall spilled over the cave wall through a crevice in the rock. It tumbled like a ribbon to break the surface of the pool below, where a thin mist of steam was rising. The pool was heated by an underwater current from the nearby Fire Isle, one of many in the chain of islands flung like a crooked arm into the sea east of the mainland.

Gideon flexed his wings until they furled close to his body, and plunged into the water. Even folded thus, his wings were massive, their tips touching the ground. They used to disappear, all but two nubs on his shoulder blades, lightening his load, but no more, not since his fall from grace. Now, he was cursed with their weight, and the sexual crisis they brought to bear waking and sleeping, and he would be for all eternity.

Sinking down into the warm, rippling pool, Gideon groaned. How good it felt on his sore muscles. Keeping well away from the cascade, he floated on the surface, listening to the roar of the water and the ragged beat of his shuddering heart. The tightness in his groin called his hand to his hot, hard cock. If he didn't relax, it would never go flaccid. Maybe if he just shut his eyes and floated there, inhaling the soft mist rising all about him, it would be enough. It was a pleasant fiction. There was only one way to stop the achy, drenching fire that gripped his sex, and he began to stroke himself, long, spiraling tugs on his curved shaft, the heel of his hand grazing the rigid testicles beneath.

How he hated relieving himself this way. His mind reeled back to the little islet and the brief blink in time's eye that his burgeoning cock had felt the soft, silky heat of willing flesh. Another minute—maybe two—and he would have come inside the siren.

"Damn the watcher!" he seethed, pumping his cock ruthlessly.

Beneath him, his wings were like lead, pulling him down into the water. How black its satiny breast was, with only one torch lit on the rocky wall. Calling upon his extraordinary strength, Gideon surged upward, his wings raining water. His feet found bottom, for that part of the pool was shallow. His breath was coming short, not from exertion, but from the climax that was about to rock his soul, and he plowed through the water to the fall spilling down and stood beneath it.

White water poured off him, spindrift mixing with rising steam as the flow of falling water beat down upon his wings, upon his naked skin, every pore acutely charged with the palpitating rush of orgasmic fire ripping through his loins. One last spiraling tug on his pulsating shaft, and he watched the seed leave his body in long, shuddering spurts, as the water creamed over him, spraying out from his unfurled wings in crystalline droplets.

Gideon cried out as the climax took him, the bestial howl echoing back in his ears amplified by the acoustics in the cave. When had his wings, those traitorous wings, unfurled? He flapped them now, and rose hovering over the pool, beating the water from the silver-white feathers. It rolled off them with the same ease it would have done rolling off a duck's back.

Soaring higher, he wended his way to the edge of the pool and touched down on the smooth, cold marble. He groaned again. The melancholy sound drifted over the water and became part of the roar of the little waterfall across the way. How he detested the ritual. How he abhorred that he'd once again squandered his seed thus. His cock was flaccid now, but not sated. It would never be sated. That was part of the curse. He had climaxed, but there was no satisfaction in it. Tomorrow, the wind would ruffle his feathers and he would grow hard again, with no soft hand to ease his torment, no warm, sweet, welcoming womb to receive his seed. No hand but his own would service him, and no womb save the night or the pool of dark water would have him, should he prowl the archipelago until dawn swallowed the darkness again . . . and again.

He snatched the torch from its bracket and thrust it into the water, his nostrils flared at the hissing, spitting steam and noise it made, casting the pool in darkness. Then furling his wings, he stomped back to his sleeping chamber. It had been days since he'd closed his eyes, and he was exhausted.

There was no bed. He could not lie in one long enough to sleep. On his back, pressure upon his wings would bring arousal. Were he to sleep upon his belly, the weight of the wings would crush and smother him. He stepped into the sleeping alcove, a hollowed-out niche in the cave wall that fitted him utterly. There, he would sleep through the rest of the day and night standing, hopefully through the storm, until the dawn came stealing, throwing beams of morning at his feet through the narrow apertures high in the eaves, no wider than arrow slits. He closed his eyes and crossed his arms over his broad, muscled chest. Yes, there he would remain until the dawn touched his wings with silent sound that only he could hear, setting off the cruel vibrations, making him hard again.

2

Rhiannon heard the siren's song from her cabin below decks on the brigantine *Pegasus*. The captain must have heard it, too, since he crossed the bar that separated the bay and sea and followed the sound. There, the flesh-tearing wind propelled the ship through the archipelago straits broadside in a starless, moonless night as dark as sin, fraught with horizontal rain and hailstones as large as crab apples. The missiles made a dreadful din striking the deck above, but that was the least of Rhiannon's worries then. She hadn't seen her father for hours, and she'd barred the cabin door against the first mate, Rolf, who had stalked her since they'd left port on the mainland at dawn.

What was it in the siren's song that made men run mad? Rhiannon didn't know. She had always thought legends of the beautiful sea creatures luring sailors to a watery grave were nursery tales . . . until now. Outside, the haunting music rose above the howl of the wind, and the crew had been under its spell since the storm began. The singer almost sounded angry. Why couldn't these bewitched men hear the rage in the siren's voice? Or was that something only another woman could detect?

The pounding came again at the cabin door. Rhiannon backed away, watching the seasoned wood shudder under the first mate's fist, as his hoarse voice demanded she let him in. There was no question of his intent. Fearful, though resigned that her father was more than likely dead, she accepted that she was alone. If only the siren would stop singing. It was as if everyone aboard had gone mad since her eerie music began.

The ship was being driven nearly horizontal in the water toward the shoals that marked the mysterious enchanted isles. Through the porthole, Rhiannon could see a slice of sea and sky that seemed impaled upon serrated rocks, like wolf's teeth chomping at the white-capped swells and the ship's hull as it sidled through them. Clinging to the bunk post with one arm, she groped the air in mad circles, reaching for her mantle on a wall hook alongside, for she was wearing only her sleeping shift and she was nearly naked in it. The cloak was just out of reach. Making matters worse, she hadn't finished plaiting her long, ginger-colored hair before the siren's song began. As it was, it fell down her back to just inches above the hem of her shift. It was her greatest asset, and now her greatest hindrance, for it threw her off balance.

The pounding came again. The shuddering door caved in, and Rolf careened into the cabin dripping water from his slicker. Staggering over the cabin floor negotiating the pitch and roll of the hull, he seized Rhiannon's arm.

"Little fool!" he snarled. "Do you want to die shut up in here?"

Rhiannon strained against his grip. "Let go of me!" she shrilled. "Where is my father?"

"Drowned, with half the crew when we crossed the bar," the first mate said. "And the captain's under the siren's spell. We'll never make it through the shoals. You're coming with me!"

His eyes, heavy-lidded with lascivious lust, were riveted to her breasts, to the tawny nipples straining against the thin gauze shift. Rhiannon pretended not to notice. She could feel the ship's hull shudder beneath her bare feet as it grazed the rocks. He was right about one thing. She had to get out of that cabin . . . but not with him.

"Wait, my cloak!" she cried, reaching toward it. "I will not go above decks like *this*!"

Rolf relaxed his grip enough for her to reach the mantle, but instead of wrapping it around her shoulders, she flung it over his head, kicked him in the groin, and fled the cabin just as the ship struck the rocks again, pitching it bow downward into the belly of a swirling vortex. This time it was a fatal blow. Water rushed at her from all directions. The ship groaned like a woman as it died, then nothing, nothing but the howl of the wind and the plaintive siren's song.

It wasn't the dawn that woke Gideon in the sleeping alcove, it was the lightning spearing down, reminding him of another lightning strike. Muttering a string of oaths, he left the alcove, stalked out of the cave, and went to the beach to assess the situation.

It was still several hours until dawn. The black volcanic sand was like marble beneath his bare feet, where the rain had beaten it down. Siren song rode the wind from as far off as the Pavilion. Was it Muriel's voice he was hearing? It could well be; there was anger in the sound. More than one ship would flounder on the Arcan shoals this night. Simeon would need help. On such a night as this, the Lord of the Deep would be blessing many dead. It was Gideon's custom on such occasions to see to the living, however many he could save from drowning in the sea and bays, and from the jaws of the treacherous shoals. This was one advantage of his mighty wings, and one of the ways he justified his meager existence as guardian of the Dark Isle.

He wouldn't go back to the cave for his eel skin. It was still sopping wet, and he only had one dry one. The prospect of struggling into a wet eel skin was not a palatable one; neither was soaking his only dry one in such a maelstrom. He was not Simeon, Lord of the Deep, whose natural state was being wet. Gideon relished his creature comforts, for he was permitted so few. His skin could be dried a great deal quicker than eel skin. Besides, there was something very sensual about flying naked through the wind and rain. It stirred his feathers, making him hard, and the punishing hail scourging his erect cock was excruciating ecstasy, prolonging the only climax he was allowed—that which did not involve the sweet, willing flesh of a woman, or any other entity, for that matter. He was cursed with a solitary existence. He was, being immortal, impervious to lightning, the watchers' weapon. It could inflict great pain, but it would not kill him.

Without a second thought, he spread his wings and soared upward into the stinging rain splinters, instantly aroused. A hot, hard cock was a difficult thing to ignore, but the sight that met his eyes once he'd gotten aloft was enough to rival the curse that kept him in a nearly constant state of arousal. More than one ship had been impaled upon the shoals thus far. The wreckage was spread clear to the Forest Isle already, and the eye of the cyclone hadn't yet passed over. It would reach Lord Vane's Fire Isle by dawn at this rate. If only the siren song would cease, but it seemed louder still, and Gideon felt somewhat responsible for that. If only he hadn't provoked Muriel's ire, precious lives might have been saved. That it was the watcher's lightning that set the siren off mattered not. Gideon had a conscience, and as he saw it, if it wasn't for the curse he'd brought down upon his own head, there would have been no watcher.

He was over the Forest Isle, and he circled low. It was moon dark, but he could clearly see Marius, Lord of the Forest, in the clearing at the edge of the strand, lit in the lightning's glare. Marius had become the centaur again, just as he always did during the dark of the moon. That was the curse of the Prince of the Green, a strikingly handsome man until the moon went dark. Then, the creature would emerge, with all of Marius's dark good looks and broad, muscled trunk and arms, but the body and legs of a feather-footed black stallion. And thus he would stay for the three-and-a-half days of moon darkness until the new cycle moon appeared in the indigo vault and set him free.

With the help of what looked to Gideon like a vine lasso, the Lord of the Forest was trying to drag some who had washed up on shore to higher ground and the protection of the great enchanted forest, no mean task for a man who was half horse.

Gideon touched down alongside. "Let me," he said, taking over the chore.

"Thank you, my friend," Marius said, pawing the ground with his feathered forefeet. "I am not at my most powerful for such a chore in my present state."

Gideon grunted in reply. He never wasted words. One by one, he turned the bodies that had washed up on shore over, seeking a pulse. He shook his head. "Do not waste your pains," he said of the ones nearest. "These here are dead."

"And those others?" Marius asked him, pointing several yards off.

Gideon stalked over the strand to several more bodies sprawled on the beach. "This one in the slicker here lives," he observed, "these others, no."

"We cannot leave them here to rot on the strand," Marius said.

"By your leave, I will load them on your back and help you consign them to the deep, that Simeon might bless them for their journey to the afterlife."

"As needs must," the centaur said.

Between them in the teeming rain, they put the dead back

into the bay, and Gideon lifted the lone survivor. "Looks like a crew member," he observed. "Where do you want him, at the cottage?"

"No," Marius said. "We shall put him in the sod house. My faun will tend him. I do not take strangers into my home. These are dangerous times, old friend."

Hefting the inert seaman, Gideon strode into the forest with the centaur following. There, the rain did not penetrate so severely, though the trees' fragrant pine boughs and leafy arms reached out to stroke and caress him as he passed. For these were ancient tree spirits to whom he had always been friend.

Gideon hadn't visited the Forest Isle in some time. As he passed among the trees now, their embraces grew stronger. They leaned toward him narrowing the forest path, encroaching upon it as the trees genuflected before him. They all but rose up out of the ground tethering him with their roots and vines and tendrils. The forest was lush with burgeoning species clinging to the trees' trunks and branches. When several leafy arms began fondling his wings, Gideon stiffened.

"Do *not* touch my wings!" he admonished the trees. He was aroused to begin with, and the fondling was driving him mad.

The centaur laughed. "They worship you," he said

"They waste their worship," Gideon grumbled.

Marius gestured toward the obvious. "That there is long sore for wanting," he said. "It's virtually purple with unshed come. They know your curse. What harm to let them pleasure you?"

"What? And have the watchers shear off their limbs with great lightning bolts?" What the centaur was suggesting was something Gideon had never done, though he'd seen the Ancient Ones pleasure others over the years.

"They are *spirit*," Marius reminded him, "not women, and they seem willing to take the chance. What harm to let them relieve you?"

"While you stand there pawing the ground with those great hooves grinning like a satyr, eh?" He slung the dead weight he'd been carrying in the person of the unconscious sailor over the centaur's back none too gently. "Enough!"

"You need to take what harmless pleasures come your way when they are offered, old friend," the centaur said, prancing in place with the added weight on his sleek black body.

"Oh? And I suppose you let these overgrown weeds pleasure you?" Gideon scorned.

Marius shrugged. "Sometimes," he said. "I am not so different than you in that the gods have cursed me also. Where am I to get a willing mate like *this*?"

"Ahh, but you are not like 'this' every hour of every cursed day, only three days out of a month. My curse is perpetual, and I am growing tired of dodging the watchers' fireballs."

"Umm," the centaur hummed. "I take it back. We are not so alike after all. I have not forgotten how to smile. I often wondered what it is about that handsome face of yours that spoils it. You have no laugh lines by your mouth! A smile would likely shatter it like glass."

"And what, pray, have I to smile at, Prince of the Green? The wind blows on my wings and my cock grows hot and hard. The slightest touch upon those damned feathers and I am on the verge of climax, but no climax comes! Stubble that look! They *are* damned, these traitorous feathers. That is no blasphemy, 'tis *fact*! Look at me! And you want me to go about with a stupefied smile on my face?" He slapped the centaur's rump, setting him in motion. "Get on with you, before that crewman you're carrying expires as well. Go find your faun. Where the devil is he anyway? *He* should be helping you here, not me."

"You know fauns are a lazy lot," the centaur called over his shoulder. "They always wander off when there's work to be done. Remember what I said . . . You have championed these spirits since time out of mind. There is no sin in letting them repay the favors in kind . . . ."

If Marius said more, Gideon didn't hear. The forest lord's constant companion, a great, noisy magpie, with a long tail and black and white plumage, swooped down and followed the centaur into the forest, where they both disappeared among the trees.

"Aggh, *sin!*" Gideon ground out in disgust. "Smile, indeed!" But when he turned back toward the strand, he was surrounded by leafy branches and graceful pine boughs.

"Ancient Ones . . ." he addressed the tree spirits, "you must let me pass. I am needed elsewhere." But the trees hovered still, edging closer. "No," Gideon protested. "You do not understand. What you propose could bring lightning bolts from the gods down upon you. I am *cursed.* You cannot . . . help me . . ."

Pine and ash, rowan and oak formed a canopy above Gideon's head in reply to that. He was cocooned beneath a virtual bower of different species of tree, both sapling and ancient.

"Damn Marius and his lecherous trees!" he muttered under his breath, regretting it at once, for they were not lecherous at all. They were reverencing him, wanting naught in return but the privilege of his release. Of all the curiosities in the enchanted isles, the Ancient Ones and Marius, their enigmatic keeper, were the most mystifying.

Fully expecting lightning strikes, Gideon groaned. Soft, fragrant pine needles brushed his hard, muscled chest, lingering upon the turgid nipples. He had always liked his nipples stroked, but this experience was new. Pinesap from the needles mingled with the misty rain leaking through the entwined branches overhead and sent riveting tongues of searing fire coursing through his loins. The intoxicating scent had his pulse racing, the blood pounding through his temples to the rhythm of the throbbing in his rigid cock.

The ground shifted beneath his bare feet. Something gripped

his ankle, then the other, and his eyes flashed toward them. In the eerie green darkness capturing reflected light from some unknown source, he watched the hairy tendrils of young roots that had broken through the mulch on the forest floor creep up his legs. Like gentle fingers, they groped higher, and he gritted his teeth, fully expecting the watchers' missiles to cancel the delicious sensations riveting his loins as the tendrils gripped his shaft.

At first the tenuous threads seemed only to explore, like curious fingers, touching the distended veins, thick root, and pronounced ridge that wreathed the mushroom head of his penis. The sensations those fingers caused were like none he had ever experienced before. It was as if silken threads were seeking the sexual stream that knitted him together and had joined with it. The effect was almost more than Gideon could bear.

Another tendril flicked over the purple head of his engorged cock. How cool it felt against his hot, moist flesh. Instinct made him reach to replace the roots with his hand, but sturdy branches held his arms, and he was at the mercy of the tree spirits, as another root tendril seized his testicles and squeezed them gently.

Gideon's breath was growing short, and his heart felt as if it were about to leap out of his breast. The first root tendril began to tighten around his shaft and pump him in a spiraling motion that nearly stopped his heart; meanwhile, the delicate pressure of foliage-laden branches began stroking his magnificent wings. Folded close against his naked body until then, the silvery white appendages now began to steadily unfurl. It was happening. Gideon's pulse pounded in his ears. He gave a bestial growl that he scarcely recognized as his own voice. His hips jerked forward and the riveting climax ripped through his loins. He was helpless to prevent the steady stream of his pearly seed spurting out of him as the root tendrils glided up and down his shaft, milking him dry.

Shuddering aftershocks of involuntary contractions buckled Gideon's knees. After a moment, the ground shifted beneath his feet once more, and the tenuous roots receded back beneath the mulch as if they had never emerged from it. For a moment, the leafy branches covered him. It was a tender embrace, before the trees returned to their natural places, and the vaulted ceiling their uppermost branches had created parted, letting in the rain and the wind and the siren's song again.

Gideon raked the dark hair back from his moist brow and drew a ragged breath, spreading his great wings wide. A quick glance about at the trees standing silent now in the rain showed him that the spirits had receded deeply inside their ancient shells as if they'd never left them.

Sketching a silent bow, Gideon sprang into the air and soared skyward. He'd scarcely cleared the treetops when the lightning bolt hit him, pitching him out of the forest and onto the wet packed berm at the top of the strand. He'd struck it hard. Loosing a string of expletives, he dragged himself upright and spread his smoking wings only to be hit by another fireball, like a writhing snake stabbing down from the watcher's outstretched hands. It lifted him off his feet and flung him down in the crashing surf at the water's edge.

Gideon shook himself like a wet dog in a vain attempt to clear his vision. He would pay for his moment of ecstasy, but the Ancient Ones had been spared, for they were powerful beings and had the sanction of the gods. They were as gods themselves in their domain, and all who visited the Forest Isle were duty bound to pay them homage or suffer the consequences. It had been thus since time began. But it wasn't until that moment dodging towering waves and lightning bolts that Gideon really understood their power or realized how great a privilege it was to have received their favor.

Raising his fists toward the hovering watcher earned him

another lightning strike, which spiraled him into the rearing head of a high-curling comber racing toward shore.

Roaring like a lion, Gideon soared straight toward the watcher, but the entity had vanished when he reached it, and he roared again, spinning off to disappear in the fast falling curtain of rain.

3

Rhiannon wasn't a strong swimmer, and she was terrified of deep water, but she was determined not to die in the roiling tempest of sea and razor-tooth rocks that had torn the *Pegasus* apart. The current was driving the wreckage toward the isles, and once she'd passed the jagged shoals, she grabbed fast to a plank and let it buoy her toward shore.

Aside from a few superficial cuts and bruises, she'd come through the treacherous rocks relatively unscathed. The most difficult trial she faced was navigation. The elements and the sea itself had taken that out of her hands. The difficulty was in letting go. She had always been able to control her destiny, chart her own course. Whether it was right or wrong, the way of it had always been hers to choose. Now, her future had been taken out of her hands. She was no longer able to decide her fate; the gods would do that for her. She would either reach land or perish in the salty sea.

All that was left was prayer, and it was a long time since she'd asked the Arcan gods for anything. Would they even hear her after so long a silence? She glanced about. All that met her eyes was inky blackness. But for an occasional tuft of white lacework on the distant waves, it was impossible to tell sea from sky, and she saw no land, for it blended with both. All edges were blurred, and for the first time in so long she could scarcely remember, she was afraid.

Still, divine intervention seemed to be steering her course. At least the first half of her journey had been providential. She had been slated to become a priestess on Shaman's Isle, until it was destroyed in a similar storm. It would take years to rebuild, and her father couldn't wait years. He needed the tribute now, and she was his only hope of riches. He had nothing else to sell. The next logical choice was an arranged marriage. Her father was taking her to meet her betrothed when the storm took his life and spared hers. Again, the winds of change had blown her off course. Hoping that there really was such a thing as fate and that the gods designed it, she picked her deities carefully, and prayed.

"Lord Zaar, god of land masses," she began breathlessly, for she was tiring, and her grip upon the timber was weakening with each relentless swell, "let my feet once more touch dry ground . . . if it be your will. Lord Mer, god of the seas, of the bays and all waters, release me from my terror of the deep . . . if it be your will, or let death be quick and merciful, for . . . I tire. Lord Mica, god of all . . . if you have a purpose for me, stay the angry hand of Mer, and let me live to know it. . . ."

The Arcan Otherworld was populated with many gods. Aloud, Rhiannon had picked the three who might best address her situation, and prayed to the rest in silence, her lips barely moving, for it seemed as if she'd swallowed half the bay. Nearly an hour later, she washed up on a spit of black sand. It stretched to a petrified forest at the edge of steaming marshes, whose bubbling quagmire could be heard belching above the wind and rain. Coughing and spitting out mouthfuls of salt water, she lay in the frothy surf until she caught her breath, then crawled out of the backwash, her sleeping shift in tatters, and staggered toward the shelter of the trees.

Giving the marshes a wide berth, she stumbled upon a small clearing and what appeared to be a cave formed in a rocky tor. Tall double doors marked the entrance. They were ajar, and she didn't bother to knock.

Reeling inside out of the storm, she sagged against the rocky wall to catch her breath. Only then did she call out: "Is anyone here?"

There was no answer. Relieved, Rhiannon padded along the sparsely torch-lit corridor and let the strange warmth embrace her. The air smelled of honey and sweet flag; the rich, pungent aroma, like incense, rushed at her nostrils, and she breathed it in deeply.

She called out again, but still no answer came. She ventured deeper into a labyrinth off which rooms were carved in the rock, strangely well appointed with furniture, most likely gifts of the sea from wrecks like her own. This was not the natural cave she'd hoped. It was someone's home, but whose? She'd seen no sign of life since she crawled out of the sea on the black volcanic strand below.

Rhiannon shuddered. Everyone knew the archipelago was enchanted. What creature lived in this strange primeval place? She should run and never look back. She would do just that, after the storm, when the dawn cancelled fearsome shadows and made all things real again. But now, no one seemed to be at home, and that played to her sense of curiosity. That such had always been her undoing never crossed her mind. She was safe and warm in a place that smelled of honey and sweet herbs. After what she'd just been through, it felt safe enough . . . at least to explore.

One room she entered boasted a fine elevated bed so neatly made it was as if it had never been slept in and a fine teakwood wardrobe. Rhiannon peeked inside. A whiff of the sweet wood ghosted past her nostrils, mingled with the stale sent of disuse. She opened the door wider. Clothes were hung inside, men's clothes and women's. Rhiannon walked her fingers through them. Some were very costly, especially the women's togs. Many were even embellished with threads of gold and silver.

She glanced down at the remains of her shift barely hanging on her body. The skirt was in tatters, and the bodice barely held together by an inch or two of braid at the neckline. Her breasts were practically bare. She fingered a mulberry shift of the finest homespun, and after a moment, snatched it from the wardrobe. Even the most hard-hearted creature couldn't deny a woman the decency of covering her nakedness, she reasoned. She couldn't very well go about as she was, with her sex exposed, and her nipples peeking through the threadbare gauze. But it would be a shame to slip such a fine kirtle on over sand and mud splatter from the marshes; perhaps if she could find some water to wash with first . . .

Looping the kirtle over her arm, she stepped back over the threshold and continued along the corridor that took her deeper into the cave. Another, larger chamber caught her attention on the opposite side of the hallway and she looked inside. It, too, was well appointed, a sleeping chamber surely, but there was no bed. A strange heart-shaped niche was carved in the rocky wall, with great hollowed-out sections at the top and sides that almost looked like wings. She padded nearer, running her hand along the curious indentations, but try as she would, she could make no sense of it, and left the chamber with a shrug.

Continuing on, a sudden rush of herb-scented warmth enveloped her. It was drifting along the corridor from deeper in the cave. Drawn to it, Rhiannon followed the wraithlike ribbon of steam obscuring what lay beyond, for the torches set in their rocky brackets stopped here. She was too short to reach one to carry with her, and she almost turned back, fearing to do herself a mischief blundering about in the dark, and would have done just that if the welcoming sound of rippling water music hadn't changed her mind. Had she found a means to wash the filth of her ordeal from her body? Inching her way along, her hand groping the slimy wall bleeding with dampness, Rhiannon moved with the stealth of a cat, mindful of every cautious step where the corridor spilled into what looked like the perimeter of a sunken pool.

Once her eyes became accustomed to the dark and rising steam, she found that there was enough reflected light filtering in from the last torch along the corridor for her to define the pool quite well. Her breath caught in her throat. Had the gods answered her prayers? Well, all but one of them, but she wouldn't complain. Zaar, the god of land masses, had let her reach the isle, and Mer, god of the seas, had not only spared her life, he'd given her the use of a fine, fragrant pool to clean and soothe her aching body; miraculous, indeed, considering her apostasy. What Mica, god of all, had in store for her didn't signify. Zaar and Mer had blessed her, and if she were to subscribe to the theory of Divine intervention, she had to assume Mica would show her his plan in due time. With that thought to give her confidence, she stripped off her ragged shift and dove into the pool.

The water felt like silk against her skin, rushing into every crevice, every orifice in her aching body. On the far wall a narrow cascade of falling water spilled into the pool in a froth of lace and spindrift. How soothing it was to listen to. How beautiful it was to watch in the dim glow of reflected light from the distant torches. They gave it an ethereal rose-gold glow tumbling down, and she floated on her back to give herself a better view of the spectacle.

What looked like a small dish resting upon the marble edge of the pool caught her eye and she backstroked to it. It was a large scallop shell with a cake of soap inside. Rhiannon lifted it to her nose and inhaled deeply. The soap had an herbal scent, not unlike the honey sweetness she'd smelled when she first entered the cave. It was spotted with flecks of brilliant blue that reminded her of sea holly, and it smelled similar as well. A sea sponge lay beside it, and she took both soap and sponge, and floated on her back again, working up a rich, fragrant lather. It felt so good, as she smoothed it over her throat, over the firm globes of her breasts. When the sponge grazed her nipples, something tugged at her loins. Working the lather into the hardened buds, she moaned as rippling waves of drenching fire spread through her belly and thighs.

The fragrant steam rising from the mineral-rich water was like an aphrodisiac. She inhaled the moist honey sweetness. How cleansing these mineral salts were after the abrasive sea salt water she'd breathed in earlier. She floated, buoyed gently on the surface of the water, her long hair fanned out wide about her like a cloud of sea grass. Her whole body throbbed like a pulse beat, as the lapping ripples laved her from head to toe. Working in slow, concentric circles, she massaged the thick, rich lather the length of her body, over her belly and thighs, lingering when she reached the tuft of ginger-colored pubic curls shielding her mound.

Probing beneath the silken V, she found the hardened bud of her female erection and rubbed it until it grew harder still. Working the lather into the tender, sensitive flesh of her nether lips, she stroked the virgin skin beneath until waves that felt like liquid fire arched her back and raised her sex, white with undissolved suds, above the surface of the water.

The urgency of her arousal was such that it broke the concentration she had summoned to keep her balance floating there, and she sank beneath the water momentarily. Adrenaline surged, and she struggled to rise. When she broke the surface again, gulping and thrashing and brushing her hair back from her face, suds and silken water slid the length of her in random rivulets and sheets of fragrant soapy bubbles. They collected upon her breasts, calling her hands there to sweep them away from her turgid nipples. They had grown so hard she could barely stand the delicious pain of her caress.

Working her legs scissor fashion to keep herself afloat forced the mineral-rich water and soap suds to flood her vagina, laving her sex until her hips jerked forward, her whole body tensed with unclimaxed sensation. She spread her legs and the water laved her deeper, the heat of it penetrating. All around her, bubbling white water from the little fall at her back nudged her, heightening the achy sensations roaming over her flesh like a thousand anxious fingers, spreading through her sex like ripples in a pond when a pebble disturbs the smooth, still surface.

Rhiannon sank down in the water and flipped over on her back, smoothing the rest of the silky lather from her breasts and belly. Twirling through the ripples, disturbing rising steam and spindrift, she swam to the fall and floated underneath it, spreading her legs to the pulsating flow crashing down. It beat upon her sex, upon her clitoris as she floated there, calling her hands to her breasts and her fingers to her nipples. Strumming the hard buds, she groaned as the cascade took her, as the creaming froth of falling water found her sexual stream and took her like an overzealous lover.

The climax was like nothing she had ever experienced before. She'd touched herself in the dark, in the bath, and her touch had brought release, but never this. It was as if she had mated with the waterfall, and it was a passionate lover, indeed.

The very air around her seemed to sigh as she lay beneath the flow, her legs spread wide, savoring every last shuddering contraction of her release until the orgasm drained her weak and breathless. Once the palpitations began to subside and she could bear no more of the excruciating ecstasy, she swam away from the cascade, for her hard, distended clitoris was swollen, as were her nether lips, and pleasure quickly turned to pain in that tender, virgin flesh.

Her pale skin rouged with the blush of climax, she swam to the marble edge of the pool and climbed out of the water. Leaving her tattered shift where she'd dropped it, she padded around the perimeter, looking for something to dry herself with. Where there was soap, there had to be towels. She'd traveled halfway around to the waterfall without finding anything, but she did notice a little alcove carved in the jutting rock behind the fall that seemed warm and dry. It was fairly deep, but narrow, a low fissure Nature had provided, scarcely wide enough for her to squeeze through. Stepping inside, her breath caught at the spectacular sight looking through the falling water from behind it. It was like seeing the dimly lit pool of dark water through a beautiful lace curtain, and the sound it made amplified by the acoustics in the cave was soothing to the ear.

There were no towels here, and she moved on following the edge of the pool almost to the point where she'd begun, when she spied another alcove, where many towels were stored. They seemed to have been woven of spun lemongrass judging from the scent as she lifted one to her nose. A satisfied moan escaped her as the citrus fragrance filled her nostrils; she quickly scooped an armful, snatched the borrowed kirtle she'd left at the edge of the pool earlier, and padded back to the little alcove behind the waterfall. It seemed as good a place to rest as any. If whoever lived in the cave were to return, she would be safer there than if she curled up in the sumptuous bed she'd seen in one of the chambers earlier.

Safely inside behind the cascade, she dried herself and slipped on the kirtle. It fitted her as if it had been made to order. Then arranging the rest of the towels to cushion her on the floor, she curled up in the warm, fragrant womb of her waterfall lover and drifted into a deep, dreamless sleep.

4

The storm raged on all day before the wind finally died, and it was on the verge of a spent and breathless twilight that Gideon returned to the cave exhausted. He and the other guardians had done what they always do in such emergencies. They'd worked tirelessly to carry the stranded to safety, rescue those who could be saved, and reverence the dead consigned to the deep on their passage to the afterlife.

Gideon felt not a little responsible for the many ships the sirens' songs had run aground. If he hadn't been responsible for Muriel's rage, the casualties might have been lighter. Would there be no end to the burdens weighing upon his soul? Would he never cease causing them? If he hadn't in all the eons he'd been thus cursed, it didn't bode well.

Standing on the threshold, he examined the double teak-wood doors. He distinctly remembered leaving them ajar when he went to the strand to assess the storm. He'd worried about that. Could the wind have closed them? Not likely. Maybe he was mistaken. Maybe he'd closed them after all. He'd been out of sorts over the incident with Muriel at the time. He entered with a shrug. He was alone on the Dark Isle. It must have been the wind.

The moment he crossed the threshold and closed the doors behind him, Gideon felt a tremor in the atmosphere. Something was . . . different . . . out of balance. Both his sensory and extrasensory perceptions flagged caution, yet everything seemed as it should be, as he prowled through the chambers. The musical sound of the waterfall called to him, and he followed it to the pool. The rippling breast of the water looked inviting. It beckoned like sultry black satin in the misty semidarkness, but he was too exhausted to take up the invitation. Exhaustion always heightened arousal, and he was too tormented to go through that again now.

Something under his feet nearly tripped him up as he was turning to go. Bending, he snatched up what looked like a pile of rags. At closer inspection, he saw that it was some sort of women's shift. Giving a start, Gideon glanced about but saw nothing. His night vision was infallible, still he strode back through the corridor and snatched the torch from its bracket. Holding it high, he returned to the pool, his narrowed eyes snapping around the perimeter. Nothing untoward met them, only the waterfall, and the pool of satiny black water, with steam from the mineral spring ghosting over the surface.

Gideon raised the torn garment to his nose and breathed in deeply. It smelled of sweet clover, and he stood for a long moment, staring into the pool, as if he expected its owner to rise up out of the water. But she did not, and he strode back the way he'd come, taking the shift with him.

Storming into one chamber after another, he searched every one and found them empty. But someone *had* been there—a woman. He wasn't alone on the island. He *had* left the door ajar, and she must have entered. But who was she? Where did she come from, and where was she now? Could she be a refugee from the storm? She must be.

Bolting out into the bleak semidarkness, Gideon took flight. There wasn't much shelter aside from the cave on the Dark Isle. Nothing but rubble too shallow to conceal anyone remained of his original keep after the watchers demolished it eons ago. The petrified forest that hemmed the strand offered the only place someone might hide, and he made a pass over it heading for the strand, for he had decided to start from there.

The black volcanic sand at the water's edge was littered with wreckage, none of it human, though he flew the length of it and back before combing the forest itself. But there was no sign that anyone had been there. The evening tide had come in and fore-shortened the beach, obliterating any footprints that might have been amongst the assorted debris.

It was full dark when he abandoned the search. Nothing living moved on the Isle of Darkness. Aside from the sighing, crashing thunder of the waves beating upon the shoreline, all was still. Perplexed, Gideon returned to the cave. He would search again in the morning. If there was someone abroad on the isle, they could go nowhere without a vessel, and he threw the bolt on the double doors, made another search of the rooms without success, and went to his sleeping chamber.

Unfurling what was left of the shift, he examined it in the light of a rush candle in its hanging bracket beside his sleeping alcove. Whomever it belonged to was small in stature, and slen-der, young as well, for it was of a style worn by maidens. He raised it to his nose again and breathed in clover. Something ur-gent stirred in his loins, and he dropped it on the little table alongside as if it were hot coals, wiping his hands on his naked thighs, half expecting a watcher's lightning bolt to find him even there, in his private sleeping chamber, the only refuge he had from the diabolical winged watchers of the gods.

He almost laughed. He had never brought a woman there for lustful purpose. Not after what had happened what seemed a lifetime ago when he'd tried to secret one into the keep. He'd never brought a woman to the cave at all, except for Simeon's Megaleen once, when she was in need of refuge, while he fetched the Lord of the Deep to her. The watchers never let him get that far. They'd always hurled their lightning bolts well before any courtship he might have instigated came to bed sport.

All at once he broke out in a cold sweat. What would happen if one did get in and he could keep her? Could he cheat the gods of their harsh punishment and live in the arms of a woman at last? Suppose one did wash up on the shore below and sought refuge from the storm in the cave. The watchers wouldn't have been watching her, they would be watching *him*, and he was nowhere about. He was off with the other guardians, trying to salvage something of the ravages his lust had caused, bringing the sirens' wrath to bear.

It was a pleasant fantasy, but not very probable. Still, in all the eons he'd been outcast, nothing like it had ever occurred before . . . and there was that shift on the table calling his eyes, proof positive that someone had been there. . . . If only she still remained. Impossible! He would have found her. He'd searched every inch of the cave—*every inch*. Hadn't he?

Wearily, Gideon stepped into the sleeping alcove, folded his arms across his hard, muscled chest, his taut abdomen beneath corded as if steel bands roped it. He shut his eyes in a desperate attempt to beat back the arousal finding that shift had caused. But he would not sleep the sleep of the dead his sore, tired body demanded, not while the scent of sweet clover drifted past his nostrils and his mind was racing with possibilities. What dreams may come would be dreamed with one eye open until he's solved the mystery.

As he drifted off, from somewhere on the periphery of consciousness, hushed voices echoed in his mind. He'd heard celestial murmurings before, but they had never become so clear that he could understand them. He had always thought them to be long forgotten imprints upon his soul from that other life before the fall. As ever, they were strange whispers, like pieces of dreams that made no sense, but still he listened. . . .

Shall we wake him? one voice said. *There is one place he has overlooked . . .*

No, another voice replied. *It is too low and narrow for him to enter in. Leave him.*

But what if . . . The first voice trailed off, then said, *Shouldn't we warn him—tell him?*

Leave him, I say! said the other. *We may not have to . . .*

On the verge of sleep, Gideon could make out no more though the disembodied voices droned on and on as he drifted off to the meter of their mumblings.

Rhiannon had no idea what time it was when she yawned and stretched awake in her little niche behind the waterfall. Peeking through the lacy cascade that barred the entrance, there was no way to tell if it was day or still night, with no window to show it to her.

Attempting to rise, she groaned. Every muscle in her body ached from her ordeal in the bay. The warm, steamy water beckoned. How good it would feel to soothe the pain that seemed to be coming from everywhere at once. She gazed through the falling water with narrowed eyes. Everything seemed as she'd left it. Without a second thought, she struggled out of the mulberry homespun kirtle, stepped out on the ledge, and dove into the water. It was just as warm and soothing as she remembered, and she let the steamy spindrift caress and titillate every pore.

The sea sponge had floated to the far side of the cascade, but the soap had vanished. It had sunk like a stone the minute she dropped it when arousal called her to the pulsating flow of the waterfall. Hoping it was hard milled and that the warm water hadn't melted it, she ducked her head beneath the surface. An eerie phosphorescence caused by the miniscule organisms living in the water showed her the soap, in better condition than she'd supposed, on the bottom. The pool was shallow there, and though she would have never attempted it in deep water, she swam below and snatched it only to drop it again when she broke the surface. Her breath caught in her throat and a strangled gasp escaped her when she came face-to-face with the towering figure of a naked man, with massive silver-white wings. He was standing on the marble edge of the pool staring down, arms akimbo, his dark eyes all but hidden beneath the ledge of his brow. The stiff muscles in his handsome jaw were ticking an angry rhythm, and his sensuous mouth had formed a hard, lipless line above the shadowy cleft in his chin. He was aroused, and like everything else about him, his erection was gargantuan.

"W-who . . . *what* are you?" she breathed, for that was the first thought that rushed into her mind. She regretted it the moment the words were out. His posture clenched and seemed to expand, and his wings unfurled halfway. His sex had grown larger, if such a thing could be, and when he took a step closer to the edge of the pool, Rhiannon put more distance between them, treading water to stay afloat, for it was deeper there.

He flashed a smile that did not reach his eyes. "I will ask the questions," he said. "You trespass! Where did you come from? How did you get in here?"

Rhiannon swallowed audibly. "The doors were open," she defended. "The storm . . . my ship came apart on the rocks and I washed up on your dreadful beach. I did not think whoever lived here would be so rude as to deny hospitality in such a tempest."

"This gives you leave to invade my bath?"

"How was I to know it was 'your bath'?" she fired back. "There was no one here. For all I knew this cave was abandoned, like the rest of this godforsaken isle. I was covered with bruises from the rocks and mud splatter from those horrible marshes, and this bath seemed sent by the gods."

"Nothing here is a gift of the gods," he said succinctly.

"I beg your forgiveness for the intrusion," she returned. "If you will kindly step outside, I shall try to find the shift I came in and leave. I borrowed one from a wardrobe in one of your chambers. I will return it."

"That will not be necessary. You cannot go about in the shift you came in, it is in tatters."

"Oh? So you've taken it, have you?" Rhiannon cried, her voice echoing, amplified by the water.

He nodded, turning to go. "Keep what you've taken. Leave at your leisure."

"Wait!" she called after him bravely. She'd gotten out of it nicely. What possessed her to antagonize him? He was still aroused, and decidedly angry. Would she never learn to hold her tongue?

He turned from the threshold, his erection even more pronounced in profile. "Yes?" he grunted. The man had no modesty! Had he forgotten he was naked, and erect? It was almost as if it were his natural state.

"You have not told me who you are," she reminded him. "One of the fallen angels, I take it? I've heard the tales. I thought them myth."

"Believe me, I am no myth," he snarled at her, his handsome face spoiled by a riveting scowl. "I am Gideon, Lord of the Dark, guardian of this isle, prince appointed by the gods." He thumped his chest with a scathing fist. "And there is only one of me. No other 'fallen' reside in this hemisphere."

Rhiannon was so taken aback she lost her rhythm and nearly floundered. Recovering herself, her breasts rose above the surface of the water, calling his eyes like lodestones. She quickly hid her nipples in the water.

"But Gideon was an *archangel*!" she breathed. "I know the tale. Even in the polar hemisphere they tell it—"

"Is that where you come from, then?" he interrupted her. "You are a long way from home."

"No, it is not!" she snapped. "I have no home." It was the first time she realized she was homeless. She was completely on her own; saved from being sold to the shamans by another storm, now saved from a dreaded marriage by this maelstrom. The gods were known to possess a warped sense of humor at times. What did Mica, god of all, have in store for her next?

"Did anyone see you enter here . . . anyone at all?" Gideon asked her.

"I saw no one."

"Have you eaten?"

Rhiannon hesitated. It was too bizarre. Here she was without a stitch on her body in a pool of steamy mineral water, staring at what had to be ten inches of erect, hard male flesh, casually discussing the Arcan polar hemisphere and food! She couldn't help but stare. His thick, veined shaft was so engorged it was nearly blue, and the mushroom tip was slick with precome.

"I . . . I haven't been thinking about . . . food," she said, swallowing hard.

"How do you propose to leave the island?"

"I . . . I don't know," she stammered. "I . . . I haven't thought that far ahead. I've just been shipwrecked. I thought I might stay here . . . for a little. Surely you cannot object to that. Aren't angels supposed to have compassion and offer hospitality to those in distress . . . ?"

"Not this one," Gideon pronounced.

For one terrible moment there was silence. Rhiannon scarcely breathed. He looked as if he was about to spring from the edge of the pool, and she swam farther away.

"Then I will leave at once," she said haughtily.

"Where will you go?"

"Somewhere that my host is not an ill-mannered cad," she shot back.

He laughed outright then, and she got the distinct impression that he didn't do it often. In a blink, he spread his wings, plunged into the water, and seized her in his arms.

"Good," he ground out close to her face, water dripping from his massive wings. They were skin to naked skin, his hardness between them, leaning heavily against her belly; how hot it was, throbbing against her. "It had best be soon," he panted, "because if you stay, this is what you can expect..."

Thrusting his hardness between her thighs, he swooped down and took her lips in a hungry mouth, his silken tongue entwining with hers as he deepened the kiss. Paralyzed with a heart-stopping mix of desire and alarm, she trembled against him as he parted her pubic curls with his shaft and undulated against her nether lips.

Cupping one breast, he took the nipple in his mouth and laved it to hardness with his tongue as he rubbed himself against her vagina. His hot breath puffing against her wet skin silkened by the mineral water sent shockwaves of drenching fire through her loins, and she sucked in her breath as the distended veins in his thick, hard member ground into the swollen nub of her clitoris.

She should resist, push him away, but she couldn't. She should strike out with all her strength, but it felt so good to straddle the hard, throbbing penis that seemed to know exactly where to touch her to cause sensations she couldn't resist.

She was beyond the point of no return. His scent rushed up her nostrils, his sweet, musky male essence was like a drug taking her under, bringing her to the brink of orgasm. His groans grew rhythmic. His body hardened like steel as it clenched against her, his corded thighs rippling.

Yes, she'd heard the legend of the handsome archangel of the

Arcan gods, who lusted and fell from grace, condemned to live out his eternity as a solitary being, neither creature nor man. She almost gasped aloud. This *was* his natural state!

All at once, his gigantic wings began to fully unfurl. Rhiannon did gasp then, for the massive appendages nearly spanned the width of the pool. They seemed to be arching forward, as if to embrace her. Her heart leapt inside. The thought of being cocooned in the embrace of those silver-white feathers was both exhilarating and terrifying. This was the legend himself come to life. She could scarcely believe it, but it was so.

Self-preservation moved her now, for she feared smothering, and she pressed firm hands against the iridescent feathers, though the fire racing through her belly and thighs betrayed her. She shuddered as his posture clenched again and his deep sensuous voice assailed her ears at close range.

"Do *not* touch my . . . wings," he groaned, but too late. The gravelly sound reverberated in her very soul as his wings closed around her, and she felt the hot rush of his seed leave his body in hard, shuddering spurts between her thighs.

Rhiannon tried to forestall it, but it was too late. The friction of his sex grinding her pubic curls into her clitoris brought her to climax, and he groaned again as her contractions riddled him. There was no question that he'd felt her release, and her breath caught as he let her go, spread his wings, and rose out of the water.

He was still erect when he touched down on the marble rim of the pool, and when he spoke, the acoustics in the bathing chamber made his voice boom like thunder.

"I will bring food," he said. "Once you have eaten, I will take you where you wish to go. I cannot help what I am. I am cursed by the gods. I cannot help myself, and you are too great a temptation. You cannot stay here, for if you do, our next . . . encounter may not be so . . . external, if you take my meaning." He stood staring down through the mist, his hooded eyes glazed with unshed tears and the dregs of desire. The look in them turned Rhiannon's away. "Dress yourself," he charged her, stalking toward the corridor beyond. "I shan't be long."

"You do not even know my name!" Rhiannon marveled. Again he stiffened, the furled wings stretched across his broad back shuddering. She bit her lower lip. Would she never learn to hold her peace?

"I do not wish to know it," Gideon said. "If I have your name, you become real to me . . . a reminder of what I can never have."

Rhiannon's lips parted to reply, but before she could speak again, he had disappeared.

5

Gideon dragged himself back to his sleeping chamber and put on his eel skin. What had happened in the pool was only meant to be a demonstration, to warn her away. Why didn't she resist? He could still feel the soft pressure of her breasts flattened against his hard, muscled chest, silk against iron, her nipples, like two acorns, hard and peaked, boring into him.

Something rumbled in his loins again as the whole bizarre incident came flooding back across his mind. Heat rushed to his temples, and cold sweat beaded on his brow. He relived the touch of her small hands roaming over his steely roped torso, and the excruciating ecstasy of those tiny fingers embracing his wings.

A soft moan escaped him as he recalled the little V of hair that felt like swan's down caressing his cock as he slid it between her thighs nestling his hardness against her soft virgin flesh. The sensation was like a lightning strike. *A lightning strike.* Beguiled, it wasn't until that instant that he realized that *there was no lightning strike!*

Excitement at the thought that he had defeated the watchers

overwhelmed him. It hit him like a crashing comber pounding the strand. Had he been right in supposing they were monitoring *him*, not her, and thus she had come there unseen? Had he finally eluded them?

His mind was racing with possibilities. Had he finally found a way to escape the watchdogs of the gods, and if he had, could he let her go? Could he live without the ecstasy he'd experienced in this exquisite creature's arms? He didn't even know her name, but he knew every inch of her body. Could he bear to let her go? Could he dare to try to keep her?

He collected bread, wine and cheese, and some dried beef from the larder, and returned to the pool chamber. At sight of his strange houseguest, his breath caught and escaped his throat in a little moan. She was standing beside the waterfall, drying her hair on one of the woven lemongrass towels. He gasped again. He had never seen such hair, the color of honey kissed by the fire of the setting sun. It was so long it nearly challenged the hem of the mulberry homespun kirtle. Stepping into the shadows, he watched her collect the length of it over her shoulder and work several plaits before tossing it back. It fell from a center part, framing her face in soft waves before the plaits tethered it.

She was fair, though her translucent skin glowed with the blush release had left behind, and her bowed lips were bruised from his kiss. He had never seen a creature so beautiful, and if he had any sense he would stick to his original plan and take her as far away from the Dark Isle as his wings would carry her. But temptation had damned him long ago, and some things never changed, especially since the gods had cursed him with libidinous lust—cursed his wings to cause his cock to rise, as it was rising now, straining against the tight eel skin. But his wings weren't to blame this time. He was hard from the sight of her alone!

Moving out of the shadows, he approached her. Wary, she

stopped ministering to herself and arranging her hair and kirtle, her eyes riveted to him as he approached; they were the color of an angry sea.

"Come," he said, gesturing with the tray in his hands. "There is a more comfortable chamber."

He led her to a small anteroom off the corridor and set the tray down on a drum table at the edge of the carpet, motioning her to take a seat beside it. Striding to the opposite side of the room, he climbed a dais and sat on a high curved bench that allowed for his wings, for few chairs did.

"Eat," he said, in his inimitable brusque manner. It was never more necessary.

"Will you not eat also?" she asked skeptically.

"I have not just been . . . shipwrecked," he replied. "You must be ravenous. It is simple fare, but satisfying. I do not entertain here."

Should he apologize for what happened in the pool chamber earlier? Why? He wasn't sorry, and neither was she. Best to ignore the whole episode, it wasn't ever going to happen again, he'd decided. She would eat, he would take her wherever it was she wanted to go, and that would be the end of it. It was the only way. It was best to have it over and done now . . . before things went any further . . . before he formed an attachment. It could only end badly otherwise. Yes, he'd decided.

"This bread is fresh," she observed. "Have you a cook?"

"No," he said. "Supplies are ferried over from the mainland. We are quite alone here."

"How is it that the noble archangel Gideon must live in a cave?" she asked, nibbling on the cheese. "Is this part of your punishment, then?"

Gideon hesitated. How much should he tell her? Enough to frighten her away, he decided. "Yes," he pronounced, "I once had a fine keep on this isle. The rubble still remains beyond the forest. I lost it."

"How?"

"I lusted," he hurled at her. She froze with a morsel of dried beef halfway to her mouth, and he answered the expression as part of the conversation. "I am not allowed to lust, you see," he said. She flashed him a skeptical look, no doubt considering what they'd just done in the pool, and he spoke to it. "Oh, I fully expect to lose this fine cave here one day as well," he said. "It is only a matter of time." That should be enough to deter anyone . . . Anyone but this exquisite creature whose name he didn't even know, but who had orgasmed with him in a pool of steamy mineral water not an hour ago.

"Can you not rebuild your keep?" she asked him.

He shrugged, setting his furled wings ajar. They opened halfway. He was aroused again. The sight and scent of her was enough to grow balls on a eunuch. "What would be the point?" he blurted. "It would only be taken from me again."

"You want me to go," she said, answering her own question.

He nodded. "You must."

"Yes," she said demurely, her eyes cast down as she returned a bit of cheese to the tray.

Gideon steeled himself. The look of her then would melt the polar ice cap. "I will take you wherever you wish to go," he said, avoiding the eyes that shot up pleading.

"That is just it," she said. "I do not know where to go. My father was drowned in the shipwreck. I am . . . alone."

"Where were you going?" he probed her.

"West," she said, "to the hills of Thurgia, to meet my betrothed. It was to be an arranged union, not of my choosing."

"Umm," Gideon grunted. "You do not wish to go there, I take it?"

"No! I do not!" she cried. "My 'betrothed' is an odious creature old enough to be my father! We have never even met."

"Where, then . . . back to where you've come from?"

She shook her head. "I cannot go back," she said. "There is

nothing for me there. My father lost all his properties and fortune. Were I to return they would imprison me for debt. I can never go back."

"Where, then?"

Her eyes misted. "When the sea spat me out on your strand, I foolishly thought the gods had favored me," she said. "You see, I prayed to Zaar when the ship broke apart to see me safely to dry land. I prayed to Mer not to drown me in the water. Then I washed up here, on your isle, and I thought both prayers had been answered. I also prayed to Mica, god of all, to show me his plan for my future. If this is it, here, now, I like it not. I have been cast out *everywhere*. Father and I were run off our land in the north country steppes, then the shipwreck, and now you would cast me out as well. . . ."

"I must! You call what is said of me 'legend.' It is *fact*. Because I lusted I am cursed to ever lust and be denied that which I lust after. I do not know a more delicate way to put it, but what happened in that pool before is a good example. Stay and it will happen again, and worse. I am allowed no companion here."

"Is this island not large enough to house us both?" she pleaded.

"Have you heard nothing I've said?" he snapped.

"We need not be companions if I remain on this isle," she said. "Surely it is large enough to accommodate the both of us . . . at least until I am sure it is safe for me to leave."

"Why wouldn't it be safe for you to leave? Hah! It is not safe if you stay!"

"The mainland in these parts seems a likely place," she said. "But first, since I am on my own, I would be certain none there mean to harm me."

What was she trying to tell him? How could he abandon her to danger, if such existed? It was times like these that he wished the gods had taken his conscience, when they stripped him of his privilege.

"Who means you harm?"

"I do not know that anyone does ... for certain," she replied. "But the first mate on the *Pegasus* was stalking me, and would have had his way with me if the ship had not split in two when it did and cast us all into the sea. I was no match for his strength. He had been after me since the voyage began, and I strongly suspect that he *helped* my father drown so he could pursue me unopposed. I would wait until I knew what has become of him before I show my face hereabouts. But if you insist that I must go, so be it!"

Gideon cursed under his breath. "What is this person's name?" he said.

"Rolf," she told him.

"Very well," Gideon said. "I will seek word of this 'Rolf' on the isles and on the mainland. You may remain until I am satisfied that he is no longer a threat to you. Then I will see you to safety and leave you in the hands of those who will care for you."

Her face brightened, and she rose to her feet and rushed at him. "How can I ever thank you?" she cried.

Gideon vaulted out of the chair, his wings menacing. "Come no nearer!" he warned her, his voice echoing off the rocky walls. "There are conditions."

She halted in her tracks. "O-of course," she said. "Name them."

He hesitated. What was he doing? He should snatch her up and take her to the mainland. Any delay was dangerous for them both. One could not cheat the gods. He'd learned that lesson firsthand over time. This was what his brain told him. What came out of his mouth was something entirely different.

"You must keep your distance, for one thing," he began.

"Fair enough," she said with a nod, her hands raised in a gesture of acceptance. She was so excited then, he was certain she would have agreed to anything.

"You must never touch my wings," he said. She blushed at that and lowered her eyes with a nod. He hesitated. Should he tell her about the watchers? No. Why frighten her for naught, though he weighed it over and over in his mind before he spoke again on an audible breath. "And while you are my guest here"—he didn't want her to think she was his prisoner—"you must remain inside the cave."

"Why?" she asked him warily.

"Because I wish it."

"I thought to take the air in the daytime," she said.

"There are dangers in the air," Gideon responded. "Besides, if your Rolf has washed up on these shores as well and I am not here to protect you, you could put yourself in great danger."

She considered it. "Not even in the courtyard or the gardens if I stay close by? You keep such a dreary house. I thought perhaps I might pick some flowers."

"You 'thought,' " he said, arms akimbo. "There is no courtyard, and there are no gardens. Nothing grows upon the Dark Isle. Did you not see the trees in that wood out there? They are as dead, bearing neither fruit nor foliage. *Flowers!*" He spat out the last in disgust. "I see you had this all planned out. Well, miss, I have resided upon this isle for many ages. It is fraught with pitfalls where you might do yourself a mischief. I have valid reasons for my conditions. If you cannot abide by them, we leave for the mainland straightaway."

She nodded. "I don't suppose you will tell me what those reasons are?" she murmured.

She would not leave well enough alone, this enchanting, outspoken beauty the sea had left on his shore. She was passionate and innocent, virginal and seductive all at once. He had never met the like, or her equal. Yes . . . there was great danger, indeed, for he was passionately intrigued.

"My reasons are not important," he said. "Suffice it to say they are very good ones, and have done."

"Are there more conditions?"

He breathed a sigh that flared his nostrils. "Those three shall suffice," he said. "That you will keep your distance from me and not touch my wings will protect you from my curse—"

"And what if I do not wish to be protected from your curse?" she interrupted him boldly.

Gideon stared. This was the last thing he expected her to say, and he froze for a moment. "That would be very unwise," he finally said in his most casual voice. He went on smoothly, "Remaining inside this cave will keep you safe from any who might see you . . . unless you want your Rolf to find you?"

She stamped her bare foot. "He is not *my* Rolf!" she shrilled. That struck a chord. She had a temper too. He was impressed. He'd seen enough insipid females in his time. This could be quite a pleasant interlude if things were different. He shook himself, disturbing his wings. What was he thinking?

"A figure of speech," he said, "nothing more."

"Why wouldn't you let me tell you my name earlier?" she snapped. "Oh, I heard what you said, but there is more to it, I think. If you won't tell me the rest of your valid reasons, will you at least tell me the real reason for not wishing to know my name?"

"I had a valid reason for that then as well," he grumbled dourly. "No more. Tell it if you must. It no longer matters." Indeed, it did not. Had he been alone, he would have scourged himself for it. He'd told her the truth. He hadn't wanted to personalize her in his mind with the familiarity of her name. He didn't want to risk the consequences of an attraction. He had never risked that. Considering the conditions of the curse, such a thing as love would have been a catastrophe he could ill afford. Those consequences were encroaching upon him without the intimacy of first names. It was too late for preventative measures. Now he must find a cure.

"I am called Rhiannon," she said.

He gave a start. "You are named for an Otherworldly goddess of myth?" he marveled. "No one remembers such deities anymore. They have faded into the mists of time. How did you come by such a name?"

"My mother gave it to me," she said. "She loved the old myths. My namesake endured much suffering. I think my mother knew I would suffer also."

"You are too young to have suffered the sorrows of your namesake," he said. "A poor choice, though somehow it suits you."

"I am four and twenty summers," she said with pride. "And although my namesake suffered, she was strong enough to surmount her trials. I will surmount mine also."

Gideon climbed down from the dais and strolled toward the doorway. "What does this Rolf look like?" he asked her.

"He is tall, with angular features. His hair is dark, but not as dark as yours, or as long. He has the eyes of a snake . . . they shift as if he sees beyond you when he looks at you . . ."

"What was he wearing when you last saw him?"

Rhiannon shrugged. "Seaman's garb," she replied, "and a yellow oilskin slicker."

Gideon gave a start. It was only a brief tremor in his steely demeanor. He had become a master of concealing his feelings. "My home is at your disposal," he said without missing a beat. "You may claim the chamber with the bed as your own during your stay . . . the one with the wardrobe where you found that kirtle you are wearing."

"Where will you sleep?" she asked.

"That is not my chamber."

"Oh . . . I assumed . . . that is, I looked at all the other rooms. That chamber is the only one with a bed."

Gideon had to pass very close to her to leave the room. How very lovely she was staring up at him. Her scent drifted past his flared nostrils, sweet clover rising from her hair and moist skin. He was aroused; he had been since the pool—in spite of the pool. There was no hope for it. He was so hard against the skintight seam in his eel-skin suit he was in pain, so much pain another moment and he would have to open the crotch and expose his aching cock to relieve the pressure, just as he had done when he left the Pavilion.

Who was he fooling? If she stayed—even for a day—he would have her. It was inevitable. He could feel her body heat. He could almost see it. He *could* see her aura. That ability was one of his gifts. She was on fire for him, the halo of color around her a shimmering crimson. If only she would resist. Why wouldn't she resist?

He recalled, as he did so often, how it was before the fall, when he had control of his urges, before the gods cursed him and made him a slave to lust. He had defied them ever since, and managed to steal what pleasures he could, only because they were nothing more than lascivious need, an itch to be scratched out of the watchers' view. Sometimes it worked; for the most part, it failed, but that didn't matter because the passion was purely physical, the way it was with Muriel. Heart and loins were separate segments of his complex makeup. He could just as easily pleasure himself; that was allowed. But this! This had all the potential of a nightmare of epic proportions. The attraction was more than physical. He recognized it all too well. Only once before had he felt such an attraction. It had been the reason for his fall, the reason he was cast out of Paradise. There was no mistaking that feeling now. He had lived eons avoiding the wonderful, terrible thunder in the soul, the unquenchable ache in the heart that had damned him. Yes, he knew the feeling well. It was like an old ghost come back to haunt him.

He stepped over the threshold. "I cannot sleep in a bed," he told her. "My wings prohibit me. Feel free to avail yourself." He hesitated. "Remember our bargain," he reminded her. "I shan't be gone long. . . ."

6

Rhiannon followed Gideon out of the anteroom and watched him stride down the corridor. How tall he was. He nearly filled the span, his magnificent wings all but sweeping the ground. If his posture wasn't so clenched, they would have done just that. The legend of the fallen archangel condemned to live out his eternity in solitude upon the Isle of Darkness in the enchanted Archipelago of Arcus wasn't exaggerated. He was a force to be reckoned with, and one she could not resist.

She had become as two people inhabiting the same skin since their encounter in the pool. Where had her innocence gone? She had never seen a naked, fully aroused male before. She should have resisted, but she couldn't. He had awakened something deep down inside, at the very core of her sexuality that commanded her. His touch was pure ecstasy, his kiss sublime, his passion irresistible. He had aroused her to pleasures of the flesh she never imagined, pleasures that demanded consummation. What was happening to her under this enigmatic creature's spell? Where had the shy, virginal, proper young lady she had always been gone?

A flash of bright sunlight beaming along the corridor as the double doors opened caught her eye. It was all too brief. The door slammed shut, casting the cave in bleak semidarkness again, with only the torches in their iron brackets on the curved walls picking out the turns and twists in the labyrinth.

Rhiannon breathed a weary sigh. She could certainly understand his first two conditions, but why she must remain in the cave on such a beautiful sunny day, when she would surely see any of the pitfalls he was so worried over, was beyond her. He said they were alone on the isle, so there was no threat of harm from anyone. It made no sense.

She started down the corridor with a shrug. How could he sleep without a bed? She was halfway to the sleeping chamber he had allowed her when she remembered something she had thought odd earlier. Taking a turn, she went to the largest chamber and entered it. Glancing around the room, she spied the strange, almost heart-shaped alcove recessed in the rocky wall and gasped. Stealing close, she traced the shape of the niche with her hands. Was this carved to fit him, to accommodate his wings? Yes, it must be. It was filled with his scent, and she breathed him in deeply.

Rhiannon stepped inside the niche and appraised its size. She was lost in it, but he would not be; it would fit him utterly. How could he sleep standing up? She couldn't imagine it. But it must be so. She folded her arms across her chest and closed her eyes, standing thus to test it. It wasn't long before she grew restless and finally left the alcove.

Retracing her steps, she returned to the chamber with the bed and flopped down upon it trying to imagine herself in Gideon's arms atop the eiderdown quilts. His scent was still fresh in her nostrils, and she whispered a moan writhing there, her arms stretched over her head. Lowering them, she palmed her body through the homespun kirtle, sliding her hands over the mounds of her breasts, pausing upon the nipples hardening at her touch. Her hands slid lower, following the contours of her waist, her belly and thighs. As if they had a will of their own, her fingers began to inch up the skirt of the kirtle until she'd exposed herself.

Parting the tuft of pubic curls with her fingertips, Rhiannon probed for the spot Gideon had found, then groaned when she touched the hard bud of her clitoris. Closing her eyes, she called the dark lord's image to mind. She relived the hot, thick hardness of his engorged shaft thrusting between her thighs, parting the pubic curls. She felt it leaning against the erect bud she was fondling now, until her whole mons area felt swollen, and a rhythmic throbbing began deep inside at the epicenter of her sex.

Warm rushes of orgasmic fire teased her belly and rippled through her thighs as she writhed against her stroking fingers. Arching her back, she leaned into the friction, reliving his kiss, the hot touch of his massive hands cupping her breasts in the steamy mineral water, the unstoppable ecstasy of their bodies rubbing together naked skin to naked skin. She could not get enough of it—of him.

A troop of husky pleasure moans escaped her throat on the verge of climax. Hot blood thrumming through her veins rushed to her temples. Her whole body throbbed like a pulse beat as she imagined his shaft gliding between her legs, igniting her sex like a lit torch as he brought her to orgasm.

Opening the neck of her kirtle, she spread it wide and strummed her nipples erect, first one and then the other. Something tugged deep inside her, something ravenous, gnawing at her senses until she could bear no more, until every nerve ending in her body screamed for release that only he could give.

Guilty pleasure overwhelmed her, but the guilt was only in that she celebrated such ecstasy alone. She may be able to conjure his image, but there was no substitute for the man or beast, creature or celestial being, for she did not know how to call him. Still, oh, still, her hips jerked forward, her fingertips, dampened with her juices, glided over her sex. Her breath came short and labored, and she was his again. . . .

The orgasm pounded through her in great, wide-reaching ripples that nearly stopped her breathing altogether, or was she holding her breath to savor every last delicious dram of sweet sensation? She had touched herself many times before, but it had never been anything like this. But then, never before did she have an image to conjure while she pleasured herself, or a guide to pleasures unknown and unexperienced. Gideon, Lord of the Dark had opened her like a flower to what could be, and he hadn't even come inside her. What would that be like? Palpitations fluttered through her at the thought of it, and she curled on her side, like a babe in the womb, and let her rapid breathing become shallow and deep again.

Release was sweet, but there was no warm, fuzzy feeling of fulfillment, no contentment in her solitary satisfaction. She felt empty—hollow inside, ashamed—as if someone else had crawled inside her body, and at the same time she felt as seductive as any siren. She was definitely not herself, whoever that was. She hardly knew anymore, nor was she brave enough to find out . . . at least not then. It was all too new to her.

Swinging her bare feet over the side of the bed, she climbed out of it and padded to the wardrobe in search of shoes. There had to be something . . . yes, a fine pair of soft leather slippers just her size. Slipping them on, she made a mental note to ask him who all these fine clothes belonged to, when they spoke again.

She went to the door and flung it wide. No trace of the storm remained. The sun was shining brightly down, and there wasn't a cloud in the sky. The air smelled salty sweet and inviting. She breathed it in deeply. What harm to take a brief stroll about? She would stay close to the cave just in case, though she was certain his concerns in that regard were a bit excessive. Without a second thought, she stepped out into the sunlit morning.

She had already seen the strand, and the strange petrified forest that edged the marshes. She decided instead to go north beyond the wood, where the land sloped down toward the remains of the keep Gideon had told her about. Taking this tack, she could keep the cave in sight, and reach it quickly if needs must.

There was a narrow footpath winding through the dark, rolling meadow that led below. When she reached the little valley, she saw that the hills were carpeted with black heather. Its bloom-filled stalks had withered on the stem, much like the trees in the petrified forest. What had blighted the Dark Isle to cause such death and desolation? She shuddered to wonder. Not even the sunshine could brighten the place. It was a land of sorrows forgotten by time; nothing grew upon it, and no living creature, neither rabbit nor squirrel, scampered over the ground. Whatever had cursed the Lord of the Dark had evidently cursed the isle he lived upon as well.

Stalks of black heather encroaching upon the little path groped the hem of her kirtle and snagged her long hair, like pinching fingers. Were they trying to capture her attention, like curious children? Or was there nothing Otherworldly about them at all?

It was well known that the Arcan Archipelago was enchanted. Tales abounded of Simeon, Lord of the Deep, the selkie prince, who ruled and guarded the oceans, bays, and seas for the sea god, Mer. And who hadn't heard of Marius, Prince of the Green, on his forest isle, where nymphs and fauns, centaurs and unicorns cohabited with ancient tree spirits. Then there was Vane, Lord of the Flames, on his volcanic Isle of Fire. It was said his touch would turn a girl to ashes! And of course, her enigmatic host was certainly under a spell if he was condemned to live a solitary life of unclimaxed lust in such a desolate place.

Rhiannon wasn't frightened. She would never admit to that. Just a bit uneasy and quite relieved to reach the ruins. At the sight of them, all other thoughts fled her mind. The remains of the keep were as black as the landscape, no more than a heap of char and slag. It had been an awesome structure, judging from the foundation, which was all that remained. It would have supported a keep at least four stories tall, with a round tower, from what she could tell. Here, there could well be pitfalls, especially in darkness, but she was certainly no ninny, and it was broad daylight.

Hoisting her skirt high enough to climb over the rubble at the edge of the foundation, she stepped inside and began to walk the perimeter. What a magnificent place it must have been. Halfway around, something caught her eye, something round and iridescent gleaming in the sunlight wedged between what appeared to be two bricks. It was caught there in such a way that it could be turned by someone with a small enough hand to slide between the rubble.

Rhiannon assessed her hand in comparison to the fissure. The last thing she wanted was to get it stuck between the bricks. It seemed wide enough to accommodate her fingers, and she eased them inside the crack, turned the object on edge, and slipped it through the fissure.

Wiping it on the hem of her kirtle, she assumed it to be an amulet of some kind made of fine opalescent glass that had clouded in the fire. It was too symmetrical to be random window or tableware glass. How many centuries had it lain there at the mercy of wind and weather? She would never know. That hardly signified. It was a pretty thing, and she had liberated it. It would be her relic of the Dark Isle, and she slipped it inside the pocket attached to her kirtle without another thought.

Continuing around the perimeter, she raised her eyes to the

sky, trying to imagine the tower spearing the clouds, and froze in her tracks. Her heart leaped so violently inside, she feared it would burst from her breast. Something was flying overhead, circling at a great distance. She couldn't quite make it out, but it was much too large for a bird, at least any bird she'd ever seen. Had Gideon returned so soon? Maybe he had searched the Dark Isle first and was just now leaving to search the other isles. Had he seen her? There was no way to tell, but that he was hovering over the keep so long did not bode well.

There was nowhere for her to hide. The black heather hills were open ground, offering no shelter between the remains of the keep and the cave. There was nothing for it. She had to go back. Deciding not to run like a fugitive, she ambled toward the cave at a leisurely pace, trying not to look at the winged creature soaring overhead, half expecting the dark lord to swoop down and chastise her for disobeying one of his "conditions." But he did not. She wasn't certain how long it was before the winged one soared off, but the next time she braved a glance aloft, the beautiful azure blue sky was vacant.

Rhiannon scarcely breathed until she'd reached the cave and gotten safely inside. Half expecting Gideon to fly at her the minute she entered, she made her way along the corridor to her appointed chamber. It was just as she'd left it, with the indentation of her body in the feather bed. One by one, she checked the other chambers, beginning with Gideon's, but they were vacant too. She must have been right. She had probably glimpsed him just as he was leaving to check the other isles. Whether he had seen her or not she would learn soon enough the moment he returned.

She went to the pool chamber last. It, too, was vacant. The sultry steam rising from the surface of the water beckoned. Her exposed skin was smudged with dirt from her ramble in the ruins. He would surely know she'd been out of the cave were he to set eyes upon her now, if he didn't know already.

Stripping off the kirtle, she shook it out, then folded it neatly and set it aside. Plunging into the water, she let it take her under, hair and all, for the soft plait had collected bits of dead scrub and black heather, and she swam beneath the cascade to remove all traces of her outing while she awaited Gideon's return.

After searching the Dark Isle first for any other survivors who might have washed up on shore in the night, Gideon flew to the Forest Isle for an audience with Marius. The man he had helped the Lord of the Forest carry up from the beach bore a striking resemblance to the description Rhiannon had given him of the crewman Rolf. He touched down in the forenoon and was met with row upon row of genuflecting tree spirits as he made his way to Marius's rambling lodge at the edge of a little clearing skirted by pines. It was customary to leave a tribute to the Ancient Ones when passing. Little statues with outstretched hands holding basins to receive herbs, flowers, seeds, and the like peppered the wood for just that purpose, and Gideon never shirked his duty to them. It wasn't just an idle gesture. The rain would eventually wash the tribute into the ground, where the trees' roots could drink in the benefits of the offering.

Gideon always carried such tributes when visiting the Forest Isle, for unlike the gods, the Ancient Ones had not rejected him. He had knelt to say a blessing and sprinkle dried herbs into one of the statue's dishes, when something lightly touched his wings, and he spiraled up swirling the dried leaves at his feet into a whirlwind to face one of the forest's wood nymphs.

Gideon scowled. He knew the exquisite creature well. Many a time he'd dodged the watcher's lightning bolts attempting to submerge himself in her willing flesh. Her flowing gown of spun spider silk with jewels of dew was fashioned with a sprinkling of tiny leaves that hid none of her charms. Her long chestnut hair was likewise decorated. Her skin, as white as marble with a greenish tinge, showed through the spider's creation, as did her tawny upturned nipples, inviting his touch. Instead, he balled his hands into white-knuckled fists, his hooded eyes spitting fire.

"You know better than to touch my wings, Vina," he said.

"Ahhh, but I love to watch that magnificence rise," she crooned, sidling closer, meanwhile giving his bulging cock a cursory nod.

"Do not waste your pains," Gideon returned. "You above all should know the futility of that. Don't you remember what happened the last time?"

The nymph nodded. "I'm worth a try," she purred, sidling close.

"Do *not* touch my wings!" he warned her. "I'm beginning to believe you are in league with the damnable watchers!" It might not be a bad idea to take his pleasure in the wood nymph. In all the years, he'd only had her once, and she was a skilled lover. If he did, he might just sate himself enough to keep from ravishing Rhiannon, which somehow seemed paramount. He almost laughed. He must be going mad. The sexual stream that flowed through him was always at high tide. It wouldn't matter who he penetrated or how many. His cock was ever hard and at the ready, thanks be to the gods who had decreed his fate.

That thought was scarcely out when he realized he was surrounded. Wood nymphs converged upon him from all directions, backing him against a tall oak tree, whose branches tethered him while they fondled and caressed him. That was most excruciating of all, for the branches were rough and unyielding against his tender feathers, and his arousal was acute.

Vina opened the front of his eel skin and freed his cock. One wood nymph would have been torment enough. He counted six, two wearing spider silk, one draped in silkworms' gauze, the others naked, or nearly so. Twelve hands were upon him, stroking penis, nipples, wings, and testes, massaging his corded thighs and ridged middle.

Gideon groaned and steeled himself against the watchers' missiles. It didn't matter what the wood nymphs did to him. The damnable harpies of the gods would make an end to pleasure before it began.

When the trees' leafy branches formed a canopy overhead, Gideon laughed. "Just what good do you suppose that will do?" he said. "Just yesterday the Ancient Ones tried that. The minute I flew aloft, the watcher hurled his thunderbolt."

"We will make it worth the price of thunderbolts," Vina murmured, inching up the skirt of her garment.

"I did not make the rules," Gideon said.

"And we need not abide by them," the nymph countered.

"It matters not that I would not be enduring this if it wasn't for the curse?" he asked her.

Vina shrugged. "We are wood nymphs, Lord of the Dark. We take our pleasures where we may, especially when they are a gift of the gods . . . and so generously endowed."

"Then take, and have done!" Gideon snarled. "This is not a social visit."

"Yesss," she hissed. "I will take it, and when I've done, thanks to the curse, there will be plenty left over for my sisters."

They covered him then, like a living quilt, lifting Vina up within his reach, until she was able to take him inside her. Gideon groaned. It was beyond his control, so many hands exploring him, so many dainty fingers playing with his skin, with his sex and his senses. Tethered as he was by the great oak's branches, the last thing he needed then was to tear his wings. He had to get back to Rhiannon, and as traitorous as the appendages were, he needed them to fly. Besides, to move a hairsbreadth then would have brought him to climax before she'd had her fill. The only thing deterring it thus far was the pain.

As if they'd read his mind, the nymphs began stroking his wings as well. It was beyond bearing. Gideon seized Vina's buttocks and took her deeply. She was a skilled lover, as were all the nymphs. Their prowess was legend, and few could resist it. The climax was swift and riveting, but the others were not to have their turn. The twang of a bowstring and the rush of displaced air stopped the orgy, as an arrow sliced through the foliage and struck the tree, tethering Gideon.

The thunderous racket of heavy horse's hooves shook the forest floor as Marius pranced through the trees. He had reloaded his longbow and held it at the ready. At sight of him, the squealing wood nymphs fled deep into the forest.

"That's right, run, my beauties!" the centaur shouted after them. "As well you ought! You overstep your bounds!" He pranced close and yanked his arrow out of the oak tree. "And you!" he thundered at the tree. "Stop your puling! Your bark is thick enough to bear my arrow without harm. You have forgotten who rules here, I think. I shall deal with you later. High time your branches were pruned."

Gideon ordered himself and strode away from the tree. "Do not fault him," he said. "The wood nymphs are quite irresistible, and 'tis my fault in any case. If I hadn't stopped to pay homage—"

"He tethered you while you were paying homage?" Marius interrupted him. He turned to the tree. "Mica's toenails! I ought to cut you down!" he seethed.

Gideon had rarely seen his friend and fellow guardian in a rage. Marius, Lord of the Forest, was rarely in a good humor at the dark of the moon, when he took the form of the centaur, but this was different. Marius's eyes were glowing iridescent green. This was not a good sign. Even the magpie, always close enough to the forest lord to qualify as his familiar, kept his distance, opting for an upper branch in a nearby pine instead of its customary perch on the centaur's back.

"Leave him," Gideon said, gesturing toward the chastised tree. "No harm has been done. I cannot stay. We need to talk."

"Come," Marius said, leading him out of the wood toward a little clearing, where his lodge stood at the edge of the forest.

No sooner had they cleared the shelter of the trees than the watcher's lightning bolt seared down pitching Gideon over in the meadow. Stunned, the dark lord righted himself and raised his fist toward the hovering creature.

"I will not be held responsible for being *ambushed*!" he railed.

Muttering a string of blasphemies, Marius raised his longbow, taking dead aim upon the watcher who had struck Gideon down, for there were more than one aloft.

Staggering to his feet, Gideon arrested Marius's arm, but Marius shook himself free. "Eeee*nough*!" he trumpeted, letting loose the arrow. It hit its mark, for Marius rarely missed his target, and Gideon groaned. What would be the punishment for *this*?

The watcher the centaur shot shrieked, then spiraled off, his companions with him. "They have no jurisdiction here!" Marius shouted, loud enough for the watchers to hear. "This is *my* isle, and I will have no truck with harpy watchers of the gods! My quiver is full—moon dark or no. They come here again, and they will all carry my arrows back to Mica in their bony arses!"

"There will be reprisals," Gideon said dourly. "I'm sorry, my friend."

"Reprisals?" Marius seethed. "You have not begun to see reprisals! When a man cannot have guests to his home without them being set upon by sex-obsessed wood nymphs, it is time for reprisals!" He brandished his longbow, shaking it toward the sky in a white-knuckled fist. "He who seeks refuge here has sanctuary!" he thundered. "I, too, have the favor of powerful gods. Zaar, god of land masses, protects this isle."

"And I have brought discord down upon it," Gideon regretted. "Let me state my business and be away before those damnable creatures return. Something is amiss. They rarely come in pairs or larger numbers. I counted three. Something untoward is happening here; I feel it."

Marius nodded, waiting.

"A female washed up on my shore in the storm," Gideon began. "She cannot stay on the Dark Isle, but she is in danger from one of the crewmen on her ship. From her description, I believe it to be the very one we brought up from your beach. I would have a word with him."

"He is gone," Marius said. "He left on the supply ferry from the mainland at dawn."

"Did he tell you his name?"

"He called himself Rolf."

"Mica's beard!"

"He's the one?" Marius queried. "If I'd known . . ."

"Did he say where he was going . . . anything at all?"

Marius shook his head. "He wanted to know if anyone else had come ashore. When he learned that no one had, he became anxious to leave. I did not see him go myself. While bringing the supplies up from the beach, Sy, my faun, watched him board the ferry."

Gideon unfurled his wings. "I have to go," he said. "Rhiannon must leave the Dark Isle, and my conscience will not let me turn her out if she is not safe."

"'Rhiannon'. . . she is named for a powerful goddess of lore. Is she like?"

"How would I know? I do not follow the legends of Otherworldly deities. She is too tempting, and I could hardly keep her hidden in that cave, though, Mica forgive me, if I asked her to, she would stay."

"So keep her!" Marius trumpeted.

"That is easier said than done, old friend," said Gideon.

Marius was accustomed to taking what he wanted, and keeping what he'd taken. The Lord of the Forest would not understand conscience. He was Lord of Fertility, a creature of the land and all its bounty, ruler of the wood nymphs, guardian of the Ancient Ones, and he had control of his urges. He had no watchers monitoring his every move. He was ruler of his domain. "It is only a matter of time before the watchers discover her," Gideon went on. "This one is different, Marius. I have not felt thus since I fell into darkness. The gods have also cursed me with a conscience. It is best that she go now, before the attachment becomes something . . . more, something I could not bear to lose."

"Women! Curse of the gods!"

Gideon smiled. "You only say that because you have not found your soul mate," he said.

"Perhaps so," the centaur conceded, "but I know one thing, my horny friend, if I ever do, I will not let her go for any price, least of all *conscience.*"

7

Rhiannon had bathed all traces of her outing away. She had folded the mulberry homespun kirtle neatly and placed it on a curved bench in her appointed chamber. It had grown late, and Gideon hadn't returned. She saw no reason to sleep in the fine kirtle with so many other garments at her disposal. She chose instead a gossamer gauze night shift she'd unearthed from the wardrobe, so fine it looked as if silkworms had spun it, and crawled beneath the feather comforters on the fine raised bed.

It wasn't long before she drifted off to sleep. At first, it was deep and untroubled, but it wasn't long before her guilt at having disobeyed Gideon's condition bled into her slumber, bringing dreams. They were fearsome, frightening visions. Oddly, she could not make out what was happening in them, only the nagging splinter of ill boding and unease that always comes with guilt. That it had bled into her dreams was telling.

Rush lights in their hanging lanterns were suspended from chains beside the bed. She hadn't extinguished them. The flickering, fat-soaked rushes gave off a glow that colored the darkness behind her closed eyes a rich golden hue. It was comforting somehow, until a shadow fell across her dulling the warmth to dusk.

Rhiannon's eyes snapped open to Gideon standing over her and gazing down, his wings half unfurled. How handsome he was in the soft golden light, with it playing upon his silver-white feathers and slick eel skin. It picked out warmer lights in the dark hair combed by the wind, waving about his broad brow and earlobes.

"I didn't mean to wake you," he said. "I see you've bathed again. . . ."

Rhiannon stretched like a cat and sat upright. There was nothing in his demeanor that suggested anger, though she took no comfort in it. Her enigmatic host was as changeable as the wind, and could, no doubt, be just as deadly. She would not draw an easy breath until she'd observed him longer. He was aroused, but that had never prompted anger. He was always aroused.

"What hour is it?" she asked him.

"Nearly dusk," he said. "I've prepared us some food in my chamber. As I've said, I do not entertain here, and my own rooms are more . . . comfortable for me. Will you join me?"

Rhiannon climbed out of the bed and reached for her kirtle, meaning to slip it on over what she was wearing, since the gauze shift was as thin as a moonbeam.

His quick hand arrested her. "Leave it," he said. "That frock will neither spare you nor deter me. I already know what lies beneath." Rhiannon hesitated. "Come," he urged. "We need to talk."

Rhiannon's heart was thumping in her breast. Could he see it moving the gossamer gauze that barely covered her charms? He must be able. The shift was trembling visibly, and his eyes were feasting upon her upturned breasts and tawny nipples straining against the gauze.

She feared the lecture to come. Was it a good sign that he hadn't come charging into her chamber roaring like a lion because he'd caught her out? Or did he have some other punishment in mind? She couldn't tell by looking at him. His dark, silvery eyes were hooded with desire gazing down at her, and arousal had heightened his male essence. It ghosted all around her in the close confines of the cave. She could feel—almost see—his body heat rippling through the air around her, and in the guiding pressure of his massive hand against the small of her back as they turned the corner that led to his chamber.

Yes. Her suppositions were correct. She recognized the room at once, with its strangely carved alcove. Now she could see how well it was designed to accommodate his massive wings. And then there was the elevated chair, like the one in the anteroom next to the pool chamber. These things almost didn't need an explanation now, though she would ask him just the same.

He had dressed a table with an exquisite cloth of linen embroidered in white work, and set it with fine china and silver. The fare was hearty, but simple, consisting of a marvelously fragrant soup, poached fish, and cucumber chutney, and an aromatic green vegetable unfamiliar to her that resembled seaweed. There was also a bowl of roasted beach plums and a crock of honey mead that had a sweet nutty flavor. He motioned her to sit, then served them both and took his own seat in the elevated chair, setting his plate upon a tall pedestal table beside it.

"Forgive my distance," he said. "My wings make sitting in an ordinary chair most uncomfortable—impossible, really, without cramping."

Rhiannon tasted the fish. She hadn't realized how hungry she was until her taste buds reacted to the delicious food, and a soft moan escaped her lips.

Gideon smiled. "Simeon, Lord of the Deep, keeps me well supplied with fish," he said around a mouthful.

Rhiannon ate in silence, wishing he would get to the lecture and have done. She was uneasy, not knowing how to handle the situation. Each moment that passed was a lost opportunity for her to confess what she had done and would count against her when he got around to the real reason for their little talk here in his sleeping chamber.

She nodded toward the hollowed-out niche in the rocky wall. "This is where you sleep?" she asked.

He nodded. "Considering their . . . sensitivity, I cannot lie upon my back, and I can only lie face down for very short intervals. The weight of the wings would smother me otherwise, not to mention the weight they would impose upon my body. The alcove was a viable solution. The one I had in my keep was much grander, but this one suffices quite well. I have been sleeping thus since my 'fall,' as it were."

"And how did you sleep before you fell from grace?" Rhiannon asked.

He smiled sadly. "You put it so . . . diplomatically," he said. "I was flung out of the Paradise of the gods, exiled to the Arcan Archipelago, and given this slag heap of desolation and death to tend for all eternity. My wings used to retract when I did not have need of them, sometimes partially and sometimes completely. Then, I was like any other man in the eyes of others. It was this gift that allowed me to walk among humans as one of them on occasion. On one of these outings, I met a human woman. We fell in love. This is my punishment."

"These clothes I'm wearing, and the rest, they were hers?"

"No," he said. "The clothing—everything you see here, furniture, carpet, even the plate you eat from—were washed ashore after storms not unlike the one that has just passed. It is so with all the isles."

Rhiannon hesitated. He had become thoughtful suddenly. She was reluctant to probe him deeper, but she might not get another opportunity. After a moment, she spoke on an audible breath.

"How is it that you are not with her?" she finally asked him.

"If we had wed, I would have been cast out and become mortal as she was. I would have lived with her and died when my time came just as all mortals die. I would no longer be . . . immortal, as I am now."

"What happened?"

"She died," he said. "You mortals are fragile . . . susceptible to all manner of disease that we are not. A fever took her, and the gods punished me for erring, with immortality and a constant state of arousal that rarely reaches climax without emptiness and pain. They took away all privileges of my wings and made them a constant reminder of my error, and a perpetual torture, for the slightest touch wreaks havoc in my loins. . . ."

There was more, Rhiannon was certain, but she did not probe him further. It was clearly a subject that pained him, and she was anxious to get to the real issue of this invitation.

"You said we needed to talk," she said warily, glad that she still had food on her plate to focus upon. Fearing the lecture, she did not want to make eye contact with him.

He clouded suddenly. "I was not altogether honest with you earlier," he said.

What was this? She stared at him, her fork suspended.

"During the storm, I helped Marius, Lord of the Green, save a seaman who had washed up upon his Forest Isle. When you spoke of the crewman Rolf, he fit the description of that seaman. I wanted to be certain before discussing it further with you, so I went there straightaway this morning. . . ."

So that was why he didn't want her to leave the cave, in case Rolf should find her in his absence. "So that is why you—"

"Let me finish," he interrupted her. "I was right. It was Rolf, but I was too late. He had left the Forest Isle on the morning ferry. I was ... detained there a while, and when I reached the mainland, the ferryman had already gone out again. I wasn't able to find your crewman anywhere in the immediate area. The ferry will not arrive here again for a sennight. I will go again in the morning and speak with the ferryman before he makes his rounds. If it is safe, I will take you to the mainland, or wherever you wish to go. If it is not, I will see you to somewhere that you will be safe until I can sort this out. You cannot stay here, Rhiannon. It is not safe for either of us if you do."

"But why?" she persisted. "Who is to know? I don't understand." This was not at all what she expected. Could it be that he didn't see her outside earlier after all? Had she been steeled against a lecture that wasn't coming? If so, she would have rather had a lecture than *this*. An ache had started inside at the mere thought of leaving him. By the look on his face, he felt it too. There was a mutual attraction between them that went beyond mere lust; there had been from the start. Was he trying to deny it?

"You do not need to know why," he said. "You do not have to understand. You just need to do as I ask ... for both our sakes."

Exasperating female wouldn't let it go. Suppose she was right. Suppose they both could live together on the isle. Suppose the watchers couldn't reach him in the cave. They had never done it before, but he had never hidden a woman there before either. It would require a test.

He climbed down from the elevated chair, and returned his empty plate to the table. Rhiannon had finished eating also, and Gideon took a succulent roasted plum from the bowl and raised it to her lips.

"Taste," he said. "I have removed the pits."

He watched Rhiannon's sensuous lips close around the skin of the plum and suck out some of the pulp. Raising what remained to his mouth, he finished it, licking the sticky juice from his fingers. Some traces remained on Rhiannon's lips, and he wiped them away with his fingers and licked them clean.

"More?" he said, taking another plum from the bowl.

Rhiannon nodded, and he offered a second plum. Juice squirted out, when she bit into the shiny black skin of the fruit and began sucking on the translucent pulp inside. In one swift motion, he raised her to her feet, seized her in his arms, and covered her mouth with his own, sucking the sweet juice from her lips, drawing them into his mouth. Pulling back, he gazed deep into her eyes; they were glazed with arousal.

"You know what will happen if you stay," he murmured.

Rhiannon nodded. "I don't want to go. I don't know where to go. I don't want to leave here . . . to leave you."

Gideon stared. "You see the life I must lead. You cannot hope to remain here indefinitely. There are dangers . . ."

"So you keep saying," she said as his words trailed off. "But you won't tell me what dangers, Gideon."

"I am not permitted a . . . consort. It is not allowed," he said. Now was not the moment to tell all and have her run screaming from the cave before he'd had a chance to test his theory. What had already happened between them was no criteria. The gods always let him suffer—for that is what it was—foreplay before meting out their justice. If he could have actual sex with her here without a lightning strike from the watchers, there might just be hope. It was consensual, that was obvious from the start, and he had told her the truth . . . just not the truth entire. "There will be reprisals that may extend to you," he said.

"What kind of 'reprisals' "?" she asked him. Would she never leave things lie?

"The gods do not like being disobeyed, Rhiannon. Look what they've done to me already! Their retribution is far reaching. I would hate to have their wrath visited upon you over a moment's pleasure. I never should have taken advantage of you in that pool. I meant what happened to warn you away. It would be best if you go."

"You didn't take advantage of me, Gideon. I believe the gods led me here apurpose. And what if they didn't? It isn't as if they will strike us dead."

Gideon's breath caught at that. She was so beautiful. Why did she have to gaze at him like that? If the test worked, could he keep her? It wasn't as though anyone knew she was there. No one but Marius knew, and the Lord of the Forest would never betray him.

Scooping her up in his arms, he strode out of the chamber and down the corridor. "Trust me," he said. "There will be less pain in the water . . ."

He set her down on the edge of the pool and stripped off his eel skin, while she discarded the night shift. How golden she was in the nimbus of torchlight flickering over the chamber. He stood transfixed watching her dive into the misty water, watching her surface, rivulets running over her body, over her firm, up-tilted breasts and tawny nipples, over her narrow waist and belly before she disappeared beneath the surface again.

Gideon laid a lemongrass towel at the edge of the pool, then sliding into the water, he reached her in seconds and seized her much as he had the first time, skin to naked skin. She was like silk in his arms as he molded her to the contours of his body, his hard cock leaning heavily against her belly. The touch of her tiny hands caressing his body was sheer ecstasy without the feel of them caressing his wings, for she avoided them.

Raising her out of the water, he laid her on the towel he'd set there earlier, slid her hips to the edge, and spread her legs. Rhiannon groaned as he lowered his mouth to the soft, swollen nether lips and sought her hard, erect bud with his tongue. Her primal sound, guttural and rich, resonated through his body, as he laved the little erection as hard as steel, tasting her honey-sweet juices.

His tongue probed deeper, gliding over the length of her virgin skin, the barrier he must penetrate. She shuddered with pleasure at his touch, and his fingers quickly replaced his tongue. Gently at first, he stroked the barred entrance to her sex, long, languid strokes that made her groan in involuntary spasms. He was holding back to prolong her pleasure, while finding the most painless way to open her to his anxious cock. Desire starred his vision and quickened his breath. Grazing her hard, erect bud, the rhythm of his fingers working the barrier skin grew faster—deeper—more urgent until the friction heated his fingertips. She sucked in her breath as the skin gave, admitting one finger, then two. They came away smeared with the blood of her virtue, and Gideon pulled her back into the water and wrapped her legs around his waist, pressing the hot, hard tip of his cock against her broken virgin flesh, until the mushroom head entered her.

Rhiannon's pleasure moans heightened his need. Lying back in the water, his wings became a flotation device that buoyed them as she straddled him, taking him deeper and deeper in slow, tantalizing increments until he filled her. The water laving his wings as he floated there had brought him to the brink. His need was so great the pain of holding back was nearly more than he could bear. White pinpoints of blinding light starred his vision again as her vulva gripped his cock. He could feel every vein in his engorged sex boring into her virgin silkiness as he raised and lowered her on his shaft, feel the ridged head strike her womb again and again. She was his, and there was no lightning bolt, no watcher to torment and deny him. Could it be? It was too good to be true.

Gripping the firm, round globes of her buttocks, he held her fast as he righted himself in the water. Climax would no longer be denied. Every inch of him—every pore—every cell in his skin had a pulse of its own beating to the same meter throbbing through every feather in his silvery wings.

"Hold on to me," he said huskily, leading her beneath the waterfall.

He had reached the point of no return. Backing her against the moss-covered wall beneath the cascade, he took her lips in a ravenous kiss as he undulated against her in an unstoppable frenzy, thrusting into her again and again to the rhythm of the pounding in his blood. Deep, spiraling thrusts wrenched a troop of moans from Rhiannon's throat and shot hot blood through his temples the more he pistoned into her.

Holding her beneath the fall, he let the water pour down over them, over their bodies, over his sexually sensitive wings, and groaned into her mouth as he came inside her. Gripping his pulsating shaft with her vagina, she milked him dry until he'd filled her with his hot, thick seed, until it overflowed her body and mixed with the great, diaphanous clouds of spindrift sifting down over them.

Gideon groaned again. He could feel her release. It heightened his own. Her hands fisted in his hair unleashed sensations he'd never felt before, and her sweet mouth taking his tongue deeply tasted of her own essence and the honey mead she'd drunk at dinner. Yes, she was *his*. How could he ever let her go, but how could he keep her?

His heart was hammering against her, as he held his breath through the final orgasmic ripples coursing through his shuddering body. At the last vibration of drenching fire, his enormous wings bent forward and wrapped around them, cocooning Rhiannon against him as he withdrew himself and crushed her close against him.

Tears and the falling water misted Gideon's vision as he led Rhiannon out from beneath the pulsating flow. Cupping her face in his hand, he gazed into her eyes. They were dilated with desire—desire he had awakened in her. What had he done to her, this beautiful creature whom the storm had cast up on his beach? What had he done to them both?

Swooping down, he gathered her hard against him again, as if his life depended upon it, and took her lips in a smothering kiss. It was volatile, but brief, before leaving her there veiled in spindrift, like a bride, without speaking the words his heart was screaming, but he dared not speak, not now—not ever.

8

Rhiannon remained in the pool a while. He had left her so abruptly, but he had loved her so well. Did this mean she could stay? He hadn't said a word. But then, neither had she. He had rendered her speechless. His dynamic body, so powerful and anxious, had opened her like the petals of a rose, layer upon silken layer to pleasures she never dreamed imaginable. And yet, he had taken her tenderly, for penetration had been difficult. Her virgin skin was thick, the slit beneath narrow, and his sex was enormous, not only in length, but in thickness. The gods had endowed him well. How they could have done that and then punished him for using it was unfathomable to her.

Stroking through the steamy mineral water, Rhiannon spiraled on her back; working her legs like scissors, she opened them to the spindrift, rather than the pulsating flow, to let the fine, luminous mist soothe her sore vagina. But something unexpected happened. Thinking of Gideon, and how he had pleasured her, she became aroused all over again.

She closed her eyes as she floated there. The pulse beat deep inside at the core of her sex and began to thrum a steady rhythm, calling her hand to her mons area, where the root of his rock-hard sex had bruised her. Needing to explore, for he had changed her, and she wanted to see how, her fingers crawled through the V of honey-colored pubic curls and delved deeper, finding the hard nub of her clitoris. Probing deeper still, she parted her swollen nether lips, so sensitive to the touch after Gideon had loved her, and touched the place where her virgin skin had been. Her breath caught in her throat as her fingers slipped inside. How hot the flesh was, still slick with traces of his seed and the dew of her release.

She could see him gazing down at her, his dilated eyes hooded with desire. Her fingers remembered the tactile feel of his soft, silver-white feathers, and what happened inside her when she touched them—how he exploded, pumping her full of his seed—his primitive, bestial groan resonating through her body as he kissed her so deeply, their tongues conjoined.

She was touching places he had touched, places no one else had touched—not even herself until he made it possible. She was his. She was *all* his, but did he want her? She beat those thoughts back trying to duplicate the ecstasy of Gideon's embrace, trying to feel what he'd felt as her sex seized the fingers she'd slipped inside her.

Groaning, Rhiannon moved closer to the little fall, opening her legs to the flow as she'd done once before. The clouds of diaphanous mist covered her body. Creaming white water suds played upon her breasts, her belly and thighs, stinging, seeking the pleasure points, hardening the tawny buds of her nipples to tall, dimpled peaks as she opened herself to the flow. On the verge of climax, she let the water lave her, let the cascade take her as Gideon had done. The water was her lover then, and she embraced it, just as she'd embraced Gideon. But it wasn't lover enough. It wasn't *him*. Nothing would ever be enough again—nothing but him.

Did he want her? Would he keep her? Or would he send her away? Rhiannon had to know, and she had to know right now. Climbing out of the pool, she dried herself on the soft towel, wriggled into the nightshift, and went straight to Gideon's chamber. But his sleeping alcove was empty. Gideon was gone.

Gideon didn't go to his chamber. He needed to be alone then. The gods only knew he was certainly conditioned to that. It was the presence of a certain passionate little female, part tigress, part virgin still, that he'd just deflowered and left naked in his pool that drove him out of his cave. He couldn't trust himself not to turn around and ravish her again, and again, until he'd sated himself. But that was the trouble. He could ravish her for eons and not have his fill. Already he was hard again. And he had just emptied himself in her—filled her with the life of his body to overflowing.

He hadn't stopped to collect his eel skin when he left her, or to fetch his spare. Half expecting to be struck down the minute he stepped outside, he'd burst out into the darkness and soared off. The night air was like balm upon his damp skin. A pity it turned his traitorous wings into instruments of sexual torture.

He should have said something to her when he left her. But what could he have said, that he had conducted a little *test*, and that he had passed it, but it made no difference? Could he have told her he'd ruined her for naught, spoiled her for a mate who could keep her—love and cherish her? Could he have told her that it would be only a matter of time before a watcher would find out and banish him yet again? Could he have warned her that such a watcher would surely mete out some dreadful retribution he couldn't imagine that might well overflow onto her as well? What would happen to her then, alone, her virtue gone, cast out among strangers? They would make a whore of her. What else could she be, the castoff consort of Gideon, Lord of the Dark, fallen archangel of the gods, condemned to wander the Arcan wilderness alone forevermore—even to *Outer Darkness*? For that was what he was courting, what surely would be the next plateau of his punishment, to be cast into the Netherworld abyss, where night prevailed and there was no light of day. No fallen ever returned from the halls of Outer Darkness, or human either, come to that. On his present course, it was only a matter of time.

The wind whipped tears in Gideon's eyes as he streaked through the starry night sky. How good it was in Rhiannon's arms. How warm and sweet and willing she was under his caress. If she had only fought him from the start, it might have been easier. But no, she wanted him just as he wanted her. They were perfectly matched, and already he did not know how he could ever bring himself to part with such an exquisite woman who surrendered so totally to his passions and shared his same appetites.

He had awakened her to pleasures of the flesh unknown to her. Could he have become so calloused as to have done such a thing with no promise of a future in the offing? No, never that, but it is just exactly what he'd done nonetheless. He hadn't thought it through. All he wanted was to see if it could be done, if he could dupe the watchers and have the love of a woman— *this* woman. Now that he knew he could, he dared not, else what was blossoming between them become full blown, making separation unbearable. And yet... there was that little voice at the back of his brain reminding him Rhiannon was a gift of the gods and telling him to have what he'd taken while he could.

Flying through the clouds, his cock grew harder as the wind grew stronger, sighing through his wings like a woman in coitus. Other voices were speaking then. He'd heard them before, but never in a conscious state. They had always come to him before in dreams, or on the shadowy edge of consciousness . . .

What say you now? the first voice said. *Shall we take him before more harm is done?*

Not . . . yet, the other replied. *That option will always exist if needs must. The runes have been cast . . . the fates decreed. It must play out as it is designed.*

Gideon strained his ears to hear more, but all he heard was the wail of the banshee wind. "Who are you?" he called out. "What do you want? Take me where?"

Now look what you've done, the first voice said. *He heard you! No more while he wakes . . .*

"Who is there?" Gideon demanded. "Speak!"

But there was no answer. The voices had stilled, but for a rumble of incoherent mumbling, though he called to them again and again.

Gideon lost altitude straining to hear, and began to spiral downward out of control. The wind ripping through his wings as he plummeted toward the bay beneath him tugged at the chord rooted deep in his sex. The climax was riveting, throwing him off balance even more, as his seed left his body in involuntary spurts. But there was no pleasure in it happening so swiftly, only pain.

He had nearly reached the surface of the water when he finally pulled out of the tailspin. That hadn't happened to him in eons, but then he hadn't been this distracted in eons. He needed to touch down somewhere and rest a while. Already the tingling had begun as new currents buoyed his wings. He raised his fist to the heavens in a silent blasphemy. He *needed* his wings. If only the gods had left him that, but they had not. They had turned his very *anatomy* into his enemy when they cursed him with libidinous lust.

His head ached from the sudden spiral downward. His heart was pounding in his chest. It felt as if it would burst through his ribs and fall into the bay. His throat was parched and dry from gulping rapid air that dried his throat and nostrils, not to mention the unbridled sensations ripping through his cock all over again.

What had the voices said? He wracked his brain trying to remember what he had heard before self-preservation took over his senses and he lost the thread of their strange disembodied speech. *The runes have been cast . . .* That was all he could remember. *The rune caster!* Maybe she was the answer. Gideon hadn't visited the rune caster since before he fell, when the woman he loved was so gravely ill. The rune caster was always a last resort, for she did not have the favor of the gods, since they took a dim view of divination. Visiting her again would bring back those dark times, but there was no other alternative. He'd heard those words: *The runes have been cast.* And whether a real voice had delivered them or his subconscious, he had to heed them, and he changed direction.

The rune caster's dwelling stood on a rocky little islet swathed in mist on the edge of what the Arcans believed to be Outer Darkness, for no man had ever gone beyond it and returned. Tales abounded about the Netherworld, about the Poison Sea that bordered it, and about the gateway beyond the last of the archipelago's string of enchanted islands. But Gideon knew well what lay beyond the great stone arch that marked the channel. It was the gateway to hell.

Halfway there, he wondered at the wisdom of making the visit. The rune caster was a woman to be reckoned with, and he had no tribute to bring her, naked as he was. That had been enough the last time, but who knew what would be expected now.

The worst of it was no one ever knew what incarnation they would find her in when they visited her rocky islet. She was a shape-shifter, able to transform into many guises. No one really knew which incarnation was her true one, and some were terrifying. The last time, he found her in the form of a beautiful, voluptuous woman, and seduction was her price for augur that was true enough but brought him sorrow. What would her price be this time? And how would she extract it?

Thinking these thoughts, he almost turned back. What good would it do to visit her? What could she tell him that he didn't already know deep down in the depths of his soul? He was doomed to suffer the wrath of the gods through all eternity, unless there was some way for him to have what he had just tasted with Rhiannon.

A she-wolf met him on the rocks when he touched down, a sleek, black wolf, with eyes like fire. Was it a minion or the woman herself? There was no way of knowing. It disappeared in a fog pocket as Gideon scaled the rocky islet and made his way to the rune caster's thatched roof cottage in a little hollow, steeped in mist. The door was open. Stooping down, for he was much too tall to pass through it upright, Gideon entered, his sharp eyes darting about the perimeter.

At first, he thought the one-room cottage was empty, until a great raven strafed him soaring past to disappear in the mist outside. Sorceress glamour, he had no doubt. The formidable creature left a mark upon his cheek when whizzing past, drawing his hand to the wound. His fingers came away smeared with blood.

"Mica's arse!" he trumpeted, wiping his cheek again.

A burst of giddy laughter from behind spun him around to face the woman he'd come to see, Lavilia, the rune caster, in a different incarnation than she'd appeared to him so many ages ago. This time she was old and withered, her sour-smelling hair, a matted snarl of wiry gray matter that resembled frayed hemp, fanned out about her head like a misshapen halo. She wasn't naked now. Instead, she wore a metal collar, from which long ropes of seaweed hung, sparing him the sight of her grotesque body beneath.

"You ought to cage that vulture!" he snapped at her, still soothing his face.

"He doesn't like intruders," the woman cackled.

"I am hardly that," Gideon said.

"You may as well be, Lord of the Dark." She nodded toward his wound. "That there is your punishment."

"Will there never be an end to punishments?" Gideon railed.

"Is that a question," she returned. "You may have only three, and it wouldn't be wise to waste them. That I even ask is a courtesy I need not extend. You are too long a stranger, Gideon."

"It is a complaint," he sallied, "nothing more."

She nodded. "Very well, then . . . To what . . . or whom do I owe the honor of this visit?"

"Three questions, you say?" he queried. "Cast your runes then."

She drew a leather pouch from the folds of her seaweed costume, flashing glimpses of her faded nipples, which he was certain was not accidental.

"Your price?" he asked, nodding toward the gray sagging breasts.

"Not this time, dark lord," she said. "What I want from you is far more precious than that cock I see there standing at attention, but we will get to that."

"Just cast your runes, old one," said Gideon. "I want none of your riddles."

The woman sank to the floor cross-legged and emptied the bag of small carved pebbles on the floor in front of her. "I knew you would come," she said. "I saw it here. I have been waiting for you. You have met another . . ."

Gideon nodded. "I have met one I would keep . . . if I can. Is it possible?"

The crone studied the runes. "It is possible," she said at last, "but not the way you wish."

"And what does that mean?"

"Another question, dark one?" She asked. "You only have two left. . . ."

"No, damn you!"

"You haven't the power to damn me, dark one. Take care. You can ill afford to evoke my wrath. You do not know what you deal with in me."

"I have precious little left to lose," Gideon said. "Do your worst!"

"You have your *soul!*" she shot back, rising to her feet. "Come!"

Gideon followed the woman out into the prevailing mist, for he had never seen the islet other than as it was now, cloaked in white. They climbed upward to a pinnacle that gave a panoramic view of the vista beyond through rocky shoals. There, a gateway was marked by phallic stones rising from the rockbound ledges. The standing stones were joined by a capstone that bridged the span. Some said the gods had fashioned the arch, and that it led to Outer Darkness. Others said the shamans of old raised it to hold sway over the Arcan Isles. There was no way to know, since the shamans were no more. Custody of the key to whatever lay beyond the gateway had fallen to the rune caster.

"The gateway?" Gideon queried. "Passage to the Netherworld, or shamans' folly, eh? I fear it not. After the way the gods have cursed me, I have no fear of Outer Darkness, old woman. I carry *inner* darkness with me waking and sleeping. I am *Lord of the Dark*, remember?"

"You are a fool, Gideon. You have much to fear. Please the

gods you see it soon enough. I keep the gate, dark one. Those whom I send through it never return. The gods cursed you, yes, but spared you *this*. Take care how you anger them now."

"I have two more questions," Gideon reminded her, changing the subject. "I've left her alone too long. I must get back before she grows impatient."

"Oh, it is far too late for that," the woman tittered.

Gideon's scalp drew taut, and cold chills riddled him until he nearly lost his footing. Something in her coal-black eyes and odious cackle smacked of catastrophe, and his heart began to pound.

"Why did you come?" she queried. "What made you risk leaving her to come here now?"

"I heard a voice," Gideon said. "I've heard voices before, when I'm drifting off usually, but what they say makes no sense . . ."

"What did it say, your voice?"

"It said 'the runes have been cast . . . the fates decreed . . .' "

The woman's posture clenched. "You must get back," she said. "That much I tell you for free."

"Your price?" he urged.

"Three feathers from those magnificent wings of yours, dark one," she said. "They hold great magic for one such as I, and you shan't miss a one."

"Have them, then!"

The rune caster approached and plucked three feathers from the soft underside of Gideon's wings. A thrill coursed through his body as she pulled them out, and the places she'd plucked them from remembered their presence for some time after, punishing him with stinging, pulsating waves of orgasmic fire. He shrugged the feeling off as best he could, though it called his hand to his burgeoning cock. No one had ever pulled his feathers out before. It was not a comfortable thing.

"You will have them back one day . . . when needs must,"

the woman said, tucking the feathers beneath her seaweed garment.

"What of my other two questions?" he asked her.

"Another time," she said. "I'll not cheat you, dark one. Now, get thee gone, lest you have your answers before you can ask your precious questions!"

9

Gideon reached the Dark Isle in the wee hours and burst into the cave, the rune caster's words ringing in his ears, and went straight to Rhiannon's chamber. To his great relief, she lay curled on her side sound asleep. One rush candle flickering in its bracket cast a golden aura about her pale face and shone in the long, ginger-colored hair fanned out about her from a loose plait. How beautiful she was lying there so peacefully—so still. The rune caster must have been mistaken. Everything seemed as it should be.

Her mulberry kirtle was neatly folded on the bench alongside, and he raised it to his nose and inhaled her deeply . . . sweet clover and her own natural essence, sultry and mysterious, yet innocent, just as she was. He held it for some time, staring down at her nestled in the feather quilts, and it wasn't until he started to fold it up again that something rolled from the pocket; something round and iridescent that had once been shimmering blue caught his eye and held it.

He recognized it at once, one of the medallions from the stained glass windows that used to adorn the keep before the watchers destroyed it. "Mica's beard!" he seethed. She had left the cave.

Gideon began to pace, his mind was racing. Should he wake her? No, not yet. Raking his hair back damp with the evening mist, he groaned in spite of himself. He should have known the rune caster hadn't been mistaken; Lavilia, keeper of the Gateway to Outer Darkness, was never mistaken.

Folding the kirtle as he'd found it, he stalked out into the corridor and went to the pool chamber, where he struggled into the eel skin he'd left there. Then returning to Rhiannon, he waited, pacing again, until a shift in the rhythm of her breathing called him to her bedside. The sight of her alone aroused him. It must be love, if he could stand there bulging at the seam, meanwhile roiling in anger that she had disobeyed one of the conditions—very possibly the most important one. He should have told her why, but he feared frightening her. Evidently, that is just what was needed. It didn't matter now. Mesmerized by the look of her, he couldn't help but reach out and stroke the silken length of plaited hair tumbling over the counterpane.

Her tremulous breathing drew his eyes. Could she be dreaming? Were the dreams that moved her so of him? The rapid rise and fall of her upturned breasts stretched the gauze tightly over them, showing him the tall, tawny nipples beneath. The wide areola had puckered, bringing one hardened bud dangerously close to escaping the neck of the night shift with each deep, shuddering breath she drew. The tall, hard nipple teased him unmercifully, catching on the lace that edged the shift as those exquisite breasts rose and fell, almost, but not quite, exposing it to his eyes, hooded with desire.

Gideon licked his lips in anticipation, fighting a primeval instinct to swoop down and take that nipple in his mouth, to lave it with his tongue until she arched herself against his sucking, tugging lips. His wings began to unfurl, the pain in his cock pressed so tightly against the eel skin called his hand to relieve it. He tore open the crotch and exposed himself, gazing down at the hard, veined shaft and ridged, slick mushroom tip, and stifled a groan. What had the gods done to him? A moment ago, he was ready to throttle her, and now . . .

Evidently, the lace scraping her nipple had aroused her, for she writhed there momentarily, but it still wasn't enough to free the tawny bud. Gideon could bear no more. He had to feast his eyes upon it naked in the golden lamplight. Deftly, he flicked the fabric as she moved and freed the trapped nipple to his hungry eyes. It was enough. Sight of the dark, hard puckered bud, which he fantasized had come to life because of dreams of him, sent waves of drenching fire coursing through his loins.

Wave upon wave washed over him, they would not stop. No matter how he prayed to stay the lava flow of his seed, it came still. He seized his shaft and turned away as the orgasm struck him like cannon fire, spewing his thick, hot come over the hard-packed dirt floor with each involuntary jerk of his pelvis.

Staring down, he watched his life spew from him, seed of his body spurting out of the ridged mushroom tip of his cock from the look of her alone. It wasn't the gods. Not this time. It was this breathtaking creature so innocently asleep in the bed alongside. What had she done to him? Even in her sleep she had the power to seduce him. No one touched his damnable wings this time. They fluttered on their own at the mere sight of her laying thus, her breast half exposed to torment him.

Enough! He must stop trying to make sense of it, or it would happen again! Seizing a towel from the nightstand, he cleaned his penis and stuffed it back inside his eel skin none too gently. Maybe that would curtail his passions. Such a notion was myth! He would be hard against the seam as long as Rhiannon was in sight.

Anger was returning now, at the gods, for he truly believed they were enjoying his punishment; at himself, for the blame because the damnable curse always came back to haunt him;

and at Rhiannon, for breaking their bargain and making him angry in the first place! He was going mad. He had to be, and when she moved and he called her name in a voice he scarcely recognized as his own, he was certain of it.

"*Rhiannon!*" he gritted out through clenched teeth. "Wake! We need to talk."

She woke with a start, then lurched erect covering her naked breast. Dazed, she sought him with sleep-glazed eyes. For a moment, he thought he saw fear in them, but mercifully that passed. He could have borne anything but her terror of him.

He whipped the glass medallion from an inside pocket in the eel skin and brandished it. "What is *this*?" he seethed. "Where did you get it—when? Answer me, Rhiannon."

She paled as gray as a ghost before his eyes, and his heart sank like a lead weight in his breast. She *had* been out of the cave. He'd been hoping against hope that she'd unearthed it from some hidden crevice he'd overlooked in the cave itself, since the explosion the gods performed on the keep so long ago had scattered debris for miles in all directions. It had killed what foliage still lived back then, blackened heather and tree, creature and grass to petrified char, slag, and death, and had given the *Isle of Darkness* its name.

"You left the cave?" he said to her silence.

"O-only for a little," she murmured. "It was such a beautiful day, and there was no harm done. You were worried that I would do myself a mischief, but I could see the pitfalls, and—"

"There were conditions!" he interrupted. "We struck a bargain. I told you I have valid reasons for my directives!"

"But you didn't say *what* reasons, Gideon. Your 'directive' made no sense to me."

"It wasn't supposed to make sense. It was supposed to be honored. There are dangers here for both of us. This wretched place has been my home for eons. I ought to know where dangers lie. I trusted you to keep the bargain!"

Rhiannon swung her feet over the side of the bed and stood to face him. "Why are you just getting around to chastising me for it now?" she asked him. "I would have thought you would have done it the minute you returned. Why wake me out of a sound sleep now to rail at me over it?"

"I didn't know about it until this!" he said, brandishing the glass medallion again.

"What do you mean you didn't know about it? You *saw* me out there. I know you did. You couldn't possibly have missed seeing me in the open as I was."

"Saw you? What are you talking about?" he asked her, non-plussed.

"I walked to the ruins, where I found that bauble. It is a pretty thing, and I saw no harm in keeping it . . . as a relic of this place . . . and of you . . ."

"Go on," he murmured, his voice like gravel.

"Walking over the open hills returning, I saw you circling overhead, very high in the clouds. For a moment, I thought you were about to swoop down and confront me then and there, but you soared off instead, and I came back here straightaway . . ."

"Ye *gods*! You don't know what you've done!" he thundered. His wings snapped open wide, as they always did when he was in the throes of any form of passion. Anger moved him now, and he took a step toward her, fists clenched at his sides. "You foolish, foolish child!" he groaned. *"That wasn't me!"*

"What do you mean?" she shrilled, padding down from the platform. "Of course it was you. There are no other 'fallen' on the isle. You told me so yourself! Maybe you didn't see me after all, but I know what I saw, and it *was* you!"

"I never should have trusted you!" he raved. "I should have told you, but I didn't want to frighten you away, and now you've damned us both!"

Her eyes were wild and wide-flung at his outburst. His

words reverberated from the vaulted ceiling, ringing back in his ears as if they were coming from an echo chamber. He hadn't meant to frighten her, but he had. She stood staring up at him, like a startled doe caught in a hunter's sights. He could not think beyond that he had put that terrible look in those haunting eyes that had always viewed him with such awe and adoration.

Bolting like that very doe, she ran then, into the corridor and out through the double doors at the end of it, leaving them flung wide behind her, the diaphanous night shift billowed about her like a ship's sail in the starry darkness before dawn. There were pitfalls now, and all he could think of was having her back before she hurt herself running barefoot over the slag and rock and sharp black heather carpeting the hills.

"*Rhiannon, wait!*" he called after her, running over the uneven ground on long, sturdy legs. There was no need of wings. Those legs would carry him well enough, or so he thought until she missed a rut and tumbled down a little incline into the belly of a hillock. That took him aloft, for the wind to seduce ruffling his feathers unmercifully until he touched down alongside her and gathered her into his arms. But it was too late. He was aroused, and she was prostrate beneath him, the hem of her night shift hiked up about her waist caught on a stalk of petrified heather.

"Don't ever run from me again!" he said huskily, crushing her close.

Her arms flew around him then and he was undone, as intoxicated by her closeness, by the very feel of her satiny skin, as a drunkard in his cups. In that moment, there was no one in the world but the two of them, nothing mattered but filling her with his hard shaft and coming inside her just as he had in the pool. Raising her hips, he thrust into her, feeding upon her throaty moan as he filled her, spiraling deep. He swallowed the sound with a hungry mouth, tasting her deeply, his skilled tongue dancing with hers, releasing her honey-sweet essence, until his lips came away from hers trembling.

"Never . . . run . . . from . . . me . . . again," he panted against her eager mouth. "Touch my wings, Rhiannon. If I must bear them being touched, let it be your touch—no other. Stroke them . . . do it . . . Make me come."

The words were scarcely out, when the lightning bolt struck him hard, wrenching him out of her, pitching him into the sharp black heather, where he doubled over and rolled as a second bolt drove him down again.

Rhiannon screamed. The sound ran him through like a javelin, but it kept him from losing consciousness. He was grateful for that, for he feared what might happen to her if he did. Dazed, he saw and heard through a haze. His singed wings were smoking. The smell of burnt feathers rushed up his nose, and the pain in his cock was almost more than he could bear.

"What is happening?" Rhiannon shrilled, crawling to his side, but another lightning strike snaked down between them, stopping her.

"*No*, stay back!" he charged. "Come no closer. *Run!* Get back to the cave. Do not stop until you are safely inside."

"But what *is* this?" she pleaded. "What is happening?"

"This, my love, is the reason for the third 'condition' of our bargain . . . that you not leave the cave. It is my curse. I *told* you . . . what you saw in the sky on your outing . . . was *not* me! Go!"

Screaming uncontrollably, Rhiannon scrambled to her feet and started to run back toward the cave, when the watchers hurled down lightning bolts in her path preventing her. She screamed again. The sound nearly stopped Gideon's heart. All at once a rumbling in the ground beneath them shook the hills and caused a split that stretched before them to the cave.

Clutching his groin in pain, Gideon staggered to his feet and seized Rhiannon as the fissure widened underneath their feet. "Hold on to me!" he commanded. "We cannot stay here. The cave is gone, and I cannot fight the three of them as I am."

"Gone? How, gone?" Rhiannon shrilled. "Who are these creatures? What is happening here?"

She was terrified, and he couldn't still her fears while great flashing bolts of lightning streaked across their path. The watchers seemed to be sparing her their missiles, unlike what they hurled at him. Instead, their volleys aimed at her seemed cast down more to warn than strike her, but he dared not place his trust in supposition, since this had never happened before.

More lightning bolts widened the fissure as they danced about trying not to become caught in the cracks and swallowed up by the gaping holes forming around them. More lightning bolts touched down, and the crack in the ground rushed straight for the cave, widening as it went as if it were alive. As if it were a ravenous monster with a will of its own, it gobbled up all the black heather, rock, and dead scrub in its path.

Rhiannon clung to him, her tiny hands digging into the rock-hard muscles of his biceps, as before their very eyes the ground opened up and swallowed the cave, as if the hungry beast had gulped it down until all that remained was a crater and choking clouds of thick rock dust. It rose in great profusion, blotting out the stars and the watchers as well. There wasn't a moment to lose.

"Do you trust me?" Gideon asked her, though he couldn't imagine how she could in such a circumstance.

"Y-yes, I . . . y-yes . . ." she sobbed, trembling against him.

"Good, then hold on to me," he charged, ignoring her hesitation. "We cannot remain here. I know a place, but we must go now, while dust and debris cloak our escape."

"Go . . . how?"

"Put your arms 'round my neck and *hold fast!*" he said, as he spread his wings and lifted off through the dust and smoke and flames that now shot up where the cave had been. Gas pockets having exploded deep underground sent great columns of flame belching skyward, turning the dust cloud they soared through an eerie shade of pink.

Once he'd become airborne, Gideon wrapped one strong arm around her, as she buried her face against his broad shoulder, the eel skin stifling her cries. They were hardly safe and away. The minute they cleared the dust cloud the watchers were in pursuit, and Rhiannon cried out as snake lightning streaked past them.

"Gideon, please!" she sobbed. "Take me back down, I beg you! I fear I'll fall!"

"We will both fall if one of those missiles hits us," he said. "You must trust me. They cannot fire their lightning bolts upward. I must take us higher, out of their range until we reach the Forest Isle. My friend Marius, Lord of the Forest, is the guardian there. He will help us if we can reach him. He gave me refuge once before when they destroyed my keep."

"But who *are* they?" Rhiannon sobbed.

"They are the watchers of the gods who torment me for finding pleasure in the body of a woman. You know the legend. This is what it means. This is what I am condemned to suffer through all eternity for the lust that they have cursed me with, Rhiannon. Their missiles will do bodily harm, but they will not kill me. They enjoy my torture too much to end my misery. Thus far they have visited none of it upon you, save by way of warning. Please the gods their leniency continues. We are not out of this yet. . . ."

"But why am I spared? I should think I would share in your punishment."

"I cannot presume to get inside their heads, but it may well be that when they saw you, your reaction convinced them that you were unaware . . . an innocent. I do not know. Hold fast to me now . . . there is no time for speculation."

Mercifully, she said no more. Gideon, being a man of few words, had run out of them, along with breath enough to speak them. He'd spoken more since he'd met Rhiannon than he had in thirty eons. Besides, he didn't want to tell her that the watchers would be waiting for them when they made their descent, and Marius was already under threat of reprisal for firing upon them when he made his last visit to the Forest Isle.

His wings were still smoking in places, and his eel skin was torn at the shoulder. Though his groin was still in pain, the wind whistling though his wings was playing havoc with his sex. He longed to soothe it, but he didn't dare, not while he was carrying such precious cargo. She was so brave. Terrified though he knew she was, she made no protest, nor did she voice a complaint. She held her peace and clung fast with all her strength. If he didn't know it before, he knew now that he loved her, most ardently, and in a way that he had never loved another, with a passion unknown to him.

It wasn't long before they neared the Forest Isle. They had lost the cloud of smoke and dust and ash long ago, and just as he'd suspected, the watchers were circling below, waiting for him to make his descent. There was nothing for it but to do just that. They couldn't stay aloft forever. Still, he was reluctant. He wouldn't have been if he didn't have Rhiannon to worry about. He was not opposed to taking risks. He had taken many over the ages. But this was different. He held the hope of his future in his arms. If anything were to happen to her because of him, he would never be able to live with it, not after all that had gone before.

He drew her closer, soothing her rigid back, for every muscle in her body was tensed against him. "We must descend," he said. "It must be swift. The watchers wait." There was no use to sugarcoat the thing, nothing to be gained in keeping the danger from her. He'd learned his lesson in the folly of that. "If we can reach the isle below we will be safe . . . at least for now."

She stifled a cry. "I . . . I see them!" she shrilled.

"Do not look down!" he warned her. "Close your eyes, and hold tight to me. No matter what occurs, do not let go!"

The last was said with wasted breath, for her arms were strung so tightly around his neck he feared he'd strangle. Pulling his singed wings in close, he plummeted downward, heading straight for the three-winged creatures circling over the Forest Isle below. Down, down, he hurtled through the first wan streamers of a fish-gray dawn at a speed that flayed moisture from his eyes. The dawn breeze mingled with the wind his motion created tearing through his wings literally wrenched the seed from his body. He'd scarcely opened the crotch of his eel skin and freed his sore cock in time to let the wind take him. How he could come in such pain he couldn't imagine, but this was the nature of the very curse that had put him in such a predicament. He could do naught but give in to the demands it made upon his body, but not his life, he decided. There had to be a way to take back his sexuality, a way to free himself from the curse of libidinous lust. And he made a vow as he streaked through the clouds like an arrow toward the Forest Isle below, that if there was a way to cheat the jealous gods of their delight in his torment, he would find it or die in the attempt.

Below, lightning danced between the watchers; a deadly ring of crackling death they must pass through to reach sanctuary with Marius. It did not bode well until missiles of a different kind began zipping past them, so close they disturbed Gideon's feathers, and in one case, tore two loose.

Arrows! Marius was firing on the watchers from the strand. The creatures' lightning bolts turned toward the centaur then. Marius had drawn their fire just long enough for Gideon to soar through the winged circle of arcing, snapping snakes of blinding light.

Gideon heard the shriek of a watcher who had taken one of

Marius's arrows. He watched the creature soar off with the aid of another, while the third still hurled down snake lightning until the twang of the forest lord's longbow string released an arrow that came too close for comfort, sending that watcher off as well.

Losing consciousness, Gideon aimed for the protection of the trees that edged the strand, and fell from the sky with Rhiannon clinging to him into the open arms of oak and rowan, ash and pine that cushioned their fall and cocooned them in their lush foliage.

Gideon's vision blurred and he groaned, as from the back of his mind a voice said, *What say we take him now? He has nowhere else to go.*

No, said the other all too familiar voice, *his trial has just begun.*

He'll never last, the first speaker said.

Did someone laugh? Gideon strained his ears to overhear more, but all he heard was the joyful sighing of the Ancient Ones' foliage as they cradled him to sleep.

10

"Are you sure he is all right?" Rhiannon pleaded, giving the centaur a wide berth, "He doesn't look all right. He is so very pale, and his lips are blue. Why are they stroking his wings like that? They shouldn't be stroking his wings. I like this not!"

"Come away, my lady," the centaur said. A *centaur*! Whatever next? She'd heard of the lecherous beasts, half man, half horse in legends, but never thought them real.

"I'm not a lady," she corrected him. "Well, yes, I am a lady, but not a *lady*, you know, a society lady."

"That matters not," he replied, nudging her toward a clearing and a rambling lodge, with a barn and paddock behind. "I address the lady who is not a *lady*, yet is. It is perfectly acceptable for me to call you 'my lady.' You see, we have no class distinctions here."

"I can see that," Rhiannon said, casting a backward glance toward the forest, and the trees that had all but swallowed Gideon whole. She could scarcely see him at all now. "Forgive me, but are all the prince guardians . . . cursed?" she asked him.

"Not all," he returned. "Simeon, Lord of the Deep, is the only true prince. He rules the water for the sea god, Mer. The rest of us are princes appointed by the gods; a token served with our curse, and because they needed guardians for these godforsaken spits of land formed in the great cataclysm, and couldn't get them any other way but by coercion. We live out our sentences here as it were, you see. All things come at a price with the gods, my lady. They are a jealous lot, demanding much. I much prefer the Ancient Ones, like those who cradle your beloved. Their justice is swift and pure."

"How many . . . guardians are there?" Rhiannon queried.

"One more, aside from Gideon and myself," said the centaur. "Lord Vane, guardian of the Isle of Fire. But there are more who occupy other hemispheres." He stopped in his tracks, prancing in place, his feathered hooves clopping on the forest floor. How ruggedly handsome his human half was, with his dreamy amber-colored eyes and wavy mane of shoulder-length chestnut hair kissed by the sun. His face was all angles and planes, a study in light and shadow. His was a raw, primeval beauty, a true creature of the wild. The other half of him was frightening to view, like a horse that couldn't be broken, a hulking feral beast. It seemed to be under control, they were one entity after all, but she gave it a wide berth nonetheless.

"Look here," he said. "I am called Marius, and since Gideon is indisposed at the moment and cannot give us a proper introduction, mightn't you do the honors?"

"My name is Rhiannon," she murmured.

The centaur clouded. "Named for a goddess of Otherworld legend," he reflected. "A lovely name, 'tis true, but it will not serve you here. The wood nymphs will be jealous."

"I can hardly do anything about my name!" Rhiannon said in a huff. What sort of fellow was this centaur to speak to her thus?

Marius threw up his hands in a gesture meant to unruffle her feathers. "You take me wrongly," he said, "'twas meant as a word of warning. Wood nymphs are jealous creatures by nature. When mortals take on the names of gods and goddesses— even, and especially, Otherworldly deities of myth—the nymphs are envious, because such privilege is forbidden them. Your name is known throughout all the kingdoms, and revered. I mention it to put you on your guard."

"I thank you for the warning, then," Rhiannon said.

"Eh . . . there is just one more thing," Marius continued.

"Yes?"

"The nymphs are quite smitten with Gideon. They have been since time out of mind. Oh, there's nothing to it . . . nothing serious. Again, I mention it only to give you fair warning. You are very beautiful, and as I say . . . they are very jealous creatures. But I rule here, so all is well, eh? Just keep your distance from them. It would be best."

Rhiannon nodded. "Forgive me," she said. "Have you always been . . . thus?" She was still finding it difficult to believe she was conversing with a centaur.

Marius laughed, causing handsome lines to form on his angular face. "Since I was cursed by the gods," he said. "Oh, but I am not always the four-legged beast you see before you now, only at certain phases of the moon. I'll be quite myself tomorrow, with the rising of the new moon."

Rhiannon was dying to ask him how he came to be cursed, but thought better of it. That would hardly be polite. Besides, she was worried over Gideon, and that odd business about the wood nymphs didn't sit too well either.

"What is wrong with Gideon?" she insisted. "He isn't going to . . . ?" She couldn't form the words.

"No, my lady," the centaur said. "The watchers haven't

killed him. He has been lightning struck. It isn't the first time, believe me, and if I know Gideon, it shan't be the last."

"But his wings . . . they are very . . . sensitive, and the trees . . . Are they enchanted? I have never seen trees move like that."

Marius nodded. "They are the Ancient Ones. Spirits have inhabited trees since the beginning of time. They will not harm your Gideon. There task is to nurture, to heal, and to protect. The oaks will give him strength; the ash will give him continuance. The rowans will boost his faith, for it is threatened, and the pines are perhaps the greatest healers of all. Pinesap will soothe his singed feathers and set him to rights. Let the ancient ones minister to him. All will be well. "

"*My Gideon?*" she said, having heard little past that. How good it sounded. She needed to hear more.

Again, Marius smiled. "He loves you," he said flatly. "Oh, he may not know it yet, but he does. I know him for eons, my lady. What's needed now is rest, for both of you. Let me make you comfortable out of the watcher's view. I shall keep vigil. No harm will come to either of you in my keeping. Then once you've both had your rest we shall see what is to be done."

"What do you mean?" Rhiannon asked him.

"You cannot return to the Dark Isle," Marius said. "I saw the flames, the clouds of dust and smoke. The cave is gone. There is no more shelter there, no place for you to hide. It is a barren wasteland; it always was. The cave was his last refuge, and when the aftershocks come, it will likely sink into the bay altogether. You are left without shelter, and as long as you are together, you are fugitives from the watchers who enforce the curses of the gods."

Rhiannon accepted the Lord of the Green's hospitality, which included a delicious cup of sassafras root tea beside the hearth in the centaur's cottage kitchen, prepared by Marius's mute faun, Sy, since Marius could not enter himself in his present form. On such occasions, he told her, he either kept to the forest or availed himself of accommodations in the barn in dirty weather. Sy was an engaging creature, well-mannered and eager to please, though he wasn't the cleverest entity she'd ever met, and it was no great feat slipping away from him after a time. It wasn't that she didn't trust Marius. There was no question that he had saved their lives, but something untoward was going on in the forest with Gideon—something the forest lord didn't want her to see—and she meant to find out what that something was.

Marius was absent most of the day making his rounds, for the isle was quite large, and he was a skilled hunter no matter what the quarry. This time, watchers were on the agenda, and he wouldn't return until he was certain none lurked about. It was a small matter to send Sy off on an errand to pick her some wildflowers, for he was a simple sort, and she had totally beguiled him. The minute he was out of sight, she went back to the wood in search of Gideon.

The sun was sliding low, and it was cool and dark in the forest. The mingled scents of bark and fern, pine and mulch, with overtones of mushroom and herb, and rich, fertile soil rushed at her as she padded deeply in. The very air was like an aphrodisiac, with a pulse all its own, tantalizing the core of her sexuality, binding her to Nature and the sultry wood. She breathed it in deeply.

Rustling among the trees stopped her in her tracks. Straining her ears, she listened for the author of the noise, but there was only silence. She resumed her cautious pace, and a tittering stopped her again. She hadn't imagined it. Disembodied voices, buzzing like bees and giggling musically, drifted toward her from all directions. Again, the sound ceased the minute she stopped and continued the minute she moved on, padding deeper into the wood.

All at once, the tree trunks gave up different sorts of watchers, as from behind each one close by, pine and oak, rowan and ash, a wood nymph emerged, trailing yards of filmy spider silk spangled with the evening dew. Their leader reeled to the fore, her every motion seeming a dance step, a voluptuous, though lithe creature with diaphanous chestnut hair, and eyes the color of mercury that had a way of changing color. Meanwhile, the others gathered around, but kept their distance as their obvious leader whirled and spun and danced around Rhiannon, who had stopped in her tracks. So these were the wood nymphs who were so "smitten" with her Gideon. They were exquisite. Rhiannon couldn't imagine any male resisting any one of them, least of all a fallen angel cursed with ravenous lust. The pang of jealousy those thoughts sired was far worse than the glancing blow she'd taken from the watcher's lightning bolt earlier.

"So, you are his new love, then?" the dancing nymph said. "A mite thin for his taste, but then, considering his situation, I imagine he settles often."

Her sugar-sweet voice dripping venom made the wounding crueler. "Let me pass," Rhiannon said.

"I am called Vina," the nymph said, sweeping her arm wide. "These are my sisters . . . figuratively speaking, of course. We shan't hinder you. We only want to have a look. Gideon won't mind. He sleeps. What are you called?"

Rhiannon was clever enough not to answer that question so readily. This was a dangerous enough situation without inciting a gaggle of wood nymphs to jealous rage. She was hopelessly outnumbered. Where was Marius? Even the faun, Sy, would have been a comfort then, neither were anywhere about. She knew where Gideon was, but she needed to pass the nymphs to reach him.

She kept walking. "I really need to pass," she said. "Excuse me . . ."

Vina seized Rhiannon's long, loosely braided hair and fingered its texture. "Lovely, this," she purred, "and so long! Wouldn't the lower forms have a grand time snarling this! That's what they do, you know, the lower fay . . . snarl hair. We nymphs, on the other hand, do not sink to such childish levels for our . . . amusements." She twirled around Rhiannon, wrapping the tresses around her like a rope. "See what a fine cocoon it makes," she tittered on. "Or a blanket even"—she gave the braid a sharp tug—"or a *leash!*" she triumphed, jerking Rhiannon to a standstill.

"Let me go!" Rhiannon cried, trying to loosen the braid that the nymph had cinched in tightly around her neck. "I cannot breathe!"

"Oh, be still!" Vina said, giving the braid another sharp jerk that all but closed Rhiannon's throat. "We shan't kill you, foolish chit. But we are what we are, and we will have our bit of fun!"

One by one, the nymphs took their turn swinging Rhiannon about by the tether they'd made of her long hair. Her arms were bound to her sides by the rest of the braid, and twice they'd brought her to her knees before she was able to work her forearms and hands free, and take hold of the hair rope that was choking her. It was no use. It was cinched so tightly she couldn't budge it.

"Let me go, I say!" she got out through clenched teeth.

But the wood nymph danced on, while her sister nymphs followed, twirling Rhiannon about until her head reeled dizzily. Familiar hands groped her body. Rhiannon beat them away as best she could with her motion curtailed, but they groped her still as the nymphs led her off in the opposite direction. The undergrowth was thicker there. A tangled snarl of briar, thorn, and woodbine carpeted the forest floor. Sharp nettles snagged the hem of her sleeping shift rending tears that left her nearly naked, openings for the groping hands to enter and finger her pubic mound and turgid nipples. They knew exactly where to stroke and what to seize, these she-wolves of the wood. In spite of the nagging concern that they were taking her farther away from Gideon, and in spite of the anger and fear roiling in her, Rhiannon could not stay the waves of scorching fire that spread through her belly and thighs. What enchantment was this?

When the nymphs closed the circle they'd formed around her and their caresses became more urgent, Rhiannon groaned, straining against the tether her own hair had become. Everything seemed so far away, as if the fringes of her peripheral vision were closing in on her. She saw nothing but a foglike swirl obscuring Vina and the others. Their tittering voices ringing in her ears seemed to be coming from an echo chamber. It was a coarse, mocking sound that raised wave upon wave of cold chills along her spine. At the same time, pulsating heat rushed though the epicenter of her sex as the nymphs stroked and laved and probed and fondled.

They had taken her to a little clearing and backed her up to an ancestral oak that stood in the center of it. There, they circled her again and again, taking sexual liberties with her in their turn, and with each other. Each outcry Rhiannon made in protest caused the noose around her neck to tighten, for indeed it was a noose, and she'd begun to fear that it would soon cut off what scant breath still remained in her lungs.

"P-please," she choked, pushing them away. "Why are you doing this? I beg you . . . let me go!" But it was no use, they were too many, and when Vina spread her legs and probed her nether lips feeling for the hardened bud of her clitoris, Rhiannon's breath caught in her throat in spite of herself.

The nymphs had slipped her shift down over her shoulders exposing her breasts to their collective touch. Rhiannon had freed her arms, but the gauze now tethered them, and she uttered a dry sob, trying to twist away as two of Vina's deft fingers penetrated her.

"Hmm, still sore from your deflowering," the nymph observed. "I shouldn't wonder. His sex is enormous. We have all known its magnificence, and we will again." She shrugged, plunging her fingers deeper into Rhiannon's vagina. "You have nothing we do not have," she said. "You are a curiosity for him now, but we will have him again. He is one of us. No human female can outshine the fay when it comes to the sexual arts."

Rhiannon shut her eyes. Vina knew what she was doing. There was no way Rhiannon could beat back the orgasm. Vina's rhythmic thrusts inside her had brought her to the brink. When one of the others began to lave and suck her nipple, Rhiannon was undone. She couldn't see which nymph had taken her breast. The circle of swirling fog had nearly closed completely, blocking her vision as wave upon wave of orgasmic fire ripped through her sex with the release. Everything seemed so far away all of a sudden. The hands fell away from her body, and the tether Vina had made of her braid slipped away from her neck. Her hair, come loose of it plaits, fell about her near nakedness like a silken waterfall. Rhiannon was grateful for the warmth of it, for cold rushed at her from all directions with the nymphs' body heat removed.

Their constant tittering now seemed like disembodied voices sharing secrets. It had grown distant, and Rhiannon took a deep breath as she sagged against the tree at her back. She had just begun to relax when Vina's sultry voice assailed her at closer range. Though she couldn't see the nymph for the fog, Vina's warm breath, earthy sweet with the scent of herbs, puffed hot against her moist cheek.

"Foolish chit," the wood nymph whispered. At the sound of her voice, Rhiannon cried out and vaulted away from the tree trunk as if she'd been shot from a catapult. "He wants you so badly?" the nymph went on. "Let him see if he can find you!"

"Wait!" Rhiannon cried out as Vina's voice began to fade. "What do you mean if he can find me?"

But there was no reply except for the distant titter of the nymph's triumphant laughter that soon faded to nothingness.

"He won't have to find me!" Rhiannon called out after the vanished nymphs. "I shall find *him*! I took notice of the way we came to this place, and I will find him, I say!"

All at once, the fog lifted, and Rhiannon stood alone and shivering in the little clearing. She glanced about, but all she saw in any direction was ground-creeping mist ghosting over unfamiliar terrain. Where had the forest gone? Where was the ancestral oak she'd leaned against? Gone—all *gone*!

Rhiannon sank to her knees sobbing, as the last of the fog drifted away showing her what lay beneath her. Tethers of a different nature held her now. These would not be so easily removed. The wily wood nymphs had tricked her. They had led her to a place where Gideon might never find her, for she sat in the middle of a faery ring. Once a human entered into one and become captive of the fay, it was said they would never return, that they would live forevermore in Otherworldly captivity.

Rhiannon raised her face to the heavens and screamed her heart dry. Spread out wide around her in a ragged circle, was a ring of mud-brown, lace-edged toadstools. Their earthy scent rushed up her nostrils, mingled with the forest smells of mulch and bark and rich fertile soul. *Forest smells?* Had she brought some of Marius's world with her into this Otherworldly limbo? Was there hope she might escape?

Rhiannon surged to her feet, her eyes riveted to the toadstool ring, but in a blink it was gone, carried off on the last wisps of mist as they fled over the thicket like living things.

"Nooo!" she cried, groping the ground. Sobbing in spasms, she stepped outside the place where the faery ring had been, but doing so changed nothing. It was too late. She had crossed over.

11

It was full dark when Gideon stirred awake under a lush canopy of leafy boughs that cradled him, soothing and nurturing him deep in the forest. This had been a particularly painful encounter with the watchers; he didn't usually have to battle them, three against one. They would have killed a mortal, or a lesser form entity, with their lightning bolts. Consciousness was returning slowly, and with it, arousal. He groaned. It wasn't the gentle petting of the leafy boughs that made him hard. Their ministrations this time were purely therapeutic. It was the wood nymphs.

They were purring like a litter of contented kittens as they danced around the tree that had embraced him, their familiar hands flitting over his naked skin through the opening they'd rent in his eel skin. They seemed in a celebratory mood as they stroked and caressed and fondled him. Despite the ancient tree's attempt to keep the nymphs at bay, a rogue wind ruffling its foliage made a hissing sound that bespoke warning. Cracked and twisted branches were the ancestral oak's reward for that, and the hissing soon changed to something more akin to cries of pain.

Vina had hold of Gideon's penis, while the others stroked his wings despite Gideon's protests and the tree's valiant attempt to prevent them. These vixens of the wildwood had mastered the art of seduction. They had no compunction about mauling Gideon when he was conscious. It was no surprise that they would take advantage of him in a vulnerable state. It had happened thus many times before.

Rubbing up against him until she'd trapped his cock between her legs, Vina took his face in her hands. "Awake, my lord!" she whispered, her voice sultry and urgent. "We hunger for you . . . favor us . . ."

Gideon struggled toward consciousness. What was that scent, that sweet, musky herbal redolence ghosting past his nostrils? He'd smelled that scent before. It had overtones of sweet clover that set his heart racing. His dry lips parted, emitting a soft moan.

The nymph, quick to seize the opportunity, ran her hand along the angular planes of his cheek and slid her index fingertip into his mouth. It tasted familiar, evocative, and mysterious, and he moaned again.

"R-Rhiannon?" he murmured, for it was her savory-sweet juices he tasted and her essence he smelled.

Gideon's eyes snapped open, but not to the sight of Rhiannon. Instead, he looked into the iridescent green cat's eyes of Vina, whose rage was palpable as she withdrew her finger from his mouth and lowered the flat of her open palm hard across his face.

"*Rhiannon,* is it?" she shrilled, backing the other nymphs up apace. She flung his turgid member aside. The motion stung, and Gideon quickly covered his sex with his hand to prevent more damage done. "So that is her name, your human!" the wood nymph snapped. "No wonder she was reluctant to tell it! A mortal—a piddling *human* endowed with the name of a deity of the forgotten realm? *Sacrilege!* I am not sorry now!"

"Sorry?" Gideon queried, shaking his head like a dog in a vain attempt to clear his head. Voices were mumbling inside it again. "Sorry for what? What have you done? Where is Rhiannon?"

The name seemed to send Vina into a blind fury. The moment he uttered it, she began beating him about the face and chest with her clenched fists and shrieking like a banshee. When she began pummeling his wings, Gideon let go of his cock and seized her upper arms shaking her to a standstill. That left his erection unprotected and the wood nymph seized it in a savage hand and gave a tug that doubled him over in pain.

Well? said an all-too-familiar disembodied voice in Gideon's mind. *Do we step in now, then?*

No, the other voice he'd heard before said, almost angrily. *It is begun, his rite of passage. It must play out as it is designed.*

Even if . . . ?

No matter what . . . if we are to save him . . .

The voices faded then, swallowed by the vibrating pain in Gideon's bruised sex. White pinpoints of blinding light starred his vision. His head was still reeling from the lightning strikes. That Vina had attacked him when he was aroused had nearly cost him his consciousness again. Seizing her hand, he raised it to his nose and sniffed it through flared nostrils. Recognition drew his scalp back, and his jaw muscles began to tick. It was Rhiannon's essence. There was no question.

He seized the wood nymph's wrist. "Where is she," he demanded, wise enough not to call Rhiannon by name. There was no need. Vina knew exactly who he meant. "What have you done with her?"

Trembling with rage and the still lingering effects of the watchers' missiles, Gideon didn't feel the tremor in the ground beneath his feet. He didn't hear the clopping of heavy horse's hooves approaching either, but Vina evidently did, for she wrenched her hand free and vanished in a blink, evaporating in the mist as if she had never been there, her sister nymphs with her.

Gideon knew she'd been there, however. The taste of Rhiannon's juices still lingered on his tongue from Vina's fingers. "Come back here!" he thundered at the absent nymph, but his words echoed back emptily.

Marius crashed through the underbrush and ranged himself alongside. "What is it?" he asked.

Gideon spun to face him, raking his hair back roughly. "Rhiannon," he said. "Is she at the lodge?"

"No," the centaur said, "I was hoping to find her here with you."

Gideon stared. "What do you mean?" he demanded. "I counted upon you keeping her safe while I could not!"

"And my priority was keeping *you* safe from the watchers," Marius defended. "I left her with Sy, while I made a search to be certain those damnable harpies weren't lurking somewhere about, ready to hurl down more lightning bolts. Yes, yes, I know he is simpleminded, but I had no choice. She tricked him into going on a foolish errand so she could slip away and go in search of you. She wasn't too thrilled with the nymphs' ministrations. Where have they gone? I could have sworn I heard their voices when I approached just now."

"I was hoping you could tell me!" Gideon said darkly. "They just vanished before my eyes. They've done something with her. Her essence was all over Vina. I have to find her, Marius!"

Gideon unfurled his wings, and the centaur halted him with a quick hand. "No," he said. "Where they have gone, you cannot follow, my impetuous friend. They have crossed over."

"Get them back!" Gideon raved, spinning in all directions, as if he hoped to make them materialize out of thin air.

"I cannot," Marius said. "I have no dominion over the nymphs; you know that. They do not dwell on my island. They frequent it, yes, but they live in the Otherworld. They are creatures of the wildwood. They come here to play . . . and to catch a glimpse of you. If they have fled from you, you haven't a prayer. What did you do to anger them?"

"*Anger them?*" Gideon trumpeted. "Haven't you heard me? Rhiannon's sexual essence is all over Vina. How could you let this happen? You know how jealous the wood nymphs are. You never should have let Rhiannon out of your sight!"

"That's gratitude," Marius bellowed, rearing back on his haunches as Gideon's wingspread threatened to knock him down, for unfurled, the dark lord's wings were massive and strong. "Wait! Where do you think you're going?" the centaur shouted, for Gideon was already in flight. "You cannot follow them. The Otherworld is entered by invitation only. You cannot storm those bastions. Wait, I say!"

"If she returns, *keep* her here!" Gideon thundered back. "Lock her in if needs must. Do not leave her side until I return."

Marius said more, but Gideon paid him no mind. The centaur's voice was bleeding into the disembodied voices that had begun mumbling in his mind again. He couldn't make out any of it, but that didn't matter. There was no time for chasing shadows. He needed answers, and there was only one who could supply them . . . the rune caster.

Gideon approached the rocky little islet on the edge of Outer Darkness on the cusp of midnight. His instincts told him that. It was still moon dark, and there wasn't a star in the sky, dense cloud cover had swallowed them.

A stiff wind had risen, ruffling the feathers in his wings, making him hard, when he shouldn't be hard, bringing him to turgid arousal, when he needed his wits about him. There was no help for it. This was his curse. He had learned to live with it, but not to like it.

He touched down on the rocks in a cottony fog bank too dense for the wind to chase that challenged his intuition again. Gideon's sense of direction was infallible. Over the ages, his aerial observations had carved indelible maps of the Arcan terrain in his mind, automatically updating them as the geography changed over time. None in the hemisphere had such an advantage. Often he was sought for his navigational skills. He tapped them now, for he could scarcely see a handbreadth of distance ahead of him.

Stepping down off the rocks, he started in the direction of the rune caster's cottage, when her voice assailed him at close range—so close, he made wide circles in the fog ahead of him expecting to touch her odious, misshapen form, or the comely seductive image she presented him with on occasion. He felt neither.

"Back so soon, Lord of the Dark?" Lavilia said, her voice a curious meld of seduction and mockery.

"Where is she?" Gideon blurted out. "Where are the nymphs? Where have they taken her?"

"Take care, dark one," the woman warned. "You have but two questions left. Are you certain you want this to be one of them? Ah-ah! Take care! Do not speak too soon. You have posed *three* questions. Choose!"

Gideon raked his hair back wildly. This was no time for her games. "Where are you? Show yourself! I have no time for this. There are enough voices echoing about in my brain. I do not like jousting with shadows!"

Lavilia cackled. "I am here," she said. "And I am wise

enough to keep my distance when such a madness takes you, dark one. Choose, but remember, once you speak it, you will have but one question remaining."

Gideon needed no reminders of that. He was in a blind passion with worry over Rhiannon, but she was right, he had posed three questions, and he wracked his brain to decide upon the most frugal one.

"Where is Rhiannon?" he finally said.

"Well done, Lord of the Dark!" Lavilia said. "The wood nymphs are of no use to you. She is not with them. They have abandoned her to the Otherworld."

"How do I get there?"

"Is that your final question, dark one?"

"Yes . . . no . . . wait . . . you are confusing me!"

"I am not the one who has confused you," she warbled. "But take your time. It will not count unless you say it. I will not trick ye, dark one."

"That would not be wise," Gideon said, his voice like edged steel.

He gave her directive thought. Marius said he could not cross over unless it was by invitation. That wasn't likely. But how had Rhiannon been invited? And how had the wood nymphs abandoned her? The rune caster said they'd abandoned her *to* the Otherworld, not *in* the Otherworld. Could it be that they had not gone with her after all? And should that be his last question? He was reluctant to ask it. Who knew but that he would need that final precious question in the future? The way things were going, he was loathe to ask it. Could he trick her into telling? It was worth a try.

"No," he said, "I shall save my last question if you please. Besides, being overanxious I've already wasted one. Marius told me she had crossed over."

"Marius told you the nymphs had crossed over. You drew

your own conclusions, dark one. If you've wasted one of your questions, credit love madness, it is no fault of mine."

"No, not," Gideon said. "But I shall be more careful with my last one if you please." He still couldn't see her for the fog. That made him uneasy. He always held that fog hid deep secrets. What secrets were Lavilia holding back from him, for she surely knew all. "How did you know the Lord of the Forest told me the nymphs had crossed over?" he asked her, a light having gone on in brain. It was as if the fog had seeped inside and clouded that as well. "And that is not a question, sly one. It is a clarification."

"I know much, dark one," she said smugly.

Praying that mind reading was not one of her talents, he took another tack. "Marius also said one cannot cross over into the Otherworld unless it be by invitation," he said as casually as he could manage with a screaming need playing havoc with his loins, and a hard cock begging to be relieved, to say nothing of the madness she so rightly diagnosed in him.

"It is so," she returned.

"I've also heard that one could be tricked by the fay and taken captive," he said cautiously. "I've heard that if one tastes fay food, or blunders into one of their land traps, they could be lost in the Otherworld for all eternity. Rhiannon is a strong entity for a human. She has come through shipwreck, faced the watchers' lightning bolts, and *me*. She is no fool. They would have to have tricked her in some way or used force in order to cross her over. I need ask no question to come to that conclusion, but . . ."

The rune caster sighed through his hesitation. "I tell you one thing for free," she said.

Gideon scarcely breathed. Had she taken pity upon him? He could only hope. "Tell it, then!" he said, with as much restraint as he could muster without diving into the fog and throttling her.

"They did trick her," she replied. "I will tell you how, but that will cost you, and you will still have your final question in reserve. What say you, Gideon, Lord of the Dark? Are you game?"

"Name your price!" Gideon said without blinking.

"It is what you thought my price would be on your last visit, dark one, that cock of yours inside me again. I have a need, and you have the means to fulfill it."

Gideon was silent apace. Her image at their last meeting ghosted across his mind, and he shuddered. Sight of her halo of foul-smelling, matted hair and gap-tooth grin, of her sagging breasts and faded nipples poking through the flimsy shift of stringy seaweed was enough to make his cock go limp as a noodle despite the curse.

"Come now," she said through his hesitation. "Does she mean that little to you, then, your Rhiannon, that you cannot suffer your cock in the likes of me for a brief blink in time's eye? It isn't as if I am a human—a threat to her. I am not even real by your standards. We are all of us cursed by the gods, doomed to our different fates. Think of me as spirit, with no more substance than one of the Forest Lord's trees if it eases your conscience. And being spirit—and feared—the watchers will not strike you down for penetrating me ... in case you have forgotten. It has been a long time, Gideon."

"I have no conscience, old one; the gods have driven it out of me with their lightning bolts. I do have self-respect!" That was wishful thinking, for he dearly regretted that the gods hadn't taken his conscience, too, or that it evidently couldn't be driven out of him; for in spite of everything he'd lost in all the eons since his fall, he hadn't lost that.

"As well you ought, but it will not buy you your Rhiannon. Decide! Embrace me and have the means to find her, or be gone and bungle about on your own. The choice is yours."

"You drive a hard bargain," Gideon growled.

"You will accept it, then?"

"How do I know you will keep your part of it? I've not had much good fortune with bargains of late." He was thinking of the pact he'd made with Rhiannon to stay inside the cave.

"If I tell you beforehand what proof have *I* that you will keep your part of the agreement?" she countered. "Foreswearing is no good. You have renounced the gods you would swear upon."

"I have not renounced them, old woman, they have renounced *me*."

"So we are at loggerheads?"

"We have a bargain," Gideon conceded, with more than a few misgivings. "I will take you at your word."

The fog parted then, but the wizened old hag of recent memory did not emerge from it. Instead, a specter from the past stepped forward, young and voluptuous, with hair like spun gold that teased the firm, round globes of her buttocks.

"Your reward for trust," she crooned, sidling up to him until her body heat radiated against his damp skin. She seized his cock. "Remember how it was the last time, dark one?" she crooned as she ran her soft, warm fingers the length of his shaft, tracing the distended veins and bulging mushroom tip. "Remember, I am but spirit, a succubus," she soothed, pumping him rhythmically, meanwhile running her free hand over his torso through the open front of his eelskin. He'd forgotten it was open thus. When had that occurred? He had to be mad. "Coitus with me," she went on smoothly, undulating closer, "holds no more stigma than a wet dream in the night, dark one. Take me, and I will tell you how to find her . . . if you dare . . ."

Her hand riding his shaft inched lower, her deft fingers strumming his sac, gently squeezing until his testicles puckered with the gooseflesh of excruciating ecstasy. He groaned, his breath coming short as she found his lips with a hungry mouth and plunged her pointed tongue inside, past his teeth to the silken warmth along the inside of his cheeks.

Parting her nether lips, Gideon slipped his finger between them, spreading her wetness. When he withdrew it, it came away slick with her juices, which he smeared on the head of his aching cock. Her pleasure moans ringing in his ears, he spanned her slender waist with his hands and lifted her upon his shaft, penetrating her in one swift thrust that filled the tight fissure of her sex as it gripped him.

Wrapping her legs around his waist, Gideon backed her up against a moss-covered phallic stone poking though the fog and thrust himself again and again, deep pistoning spirals as he undulated against her, grinding the root of his sex into the hard bud of her female erection until she cried out in her rapture.

"That was no . . . spirit's cry," he panted, as she clung to him.

"Be still and take me, dark one," she whispered.

Fisting her hands in his hair, she drove his head down until one hard nipple entered his mouth, and held it there while he laved and nipped and sucked, tugging at the pebbled areola until she writhed against him. He could feel the involuntary contractions build toward her release. The grip of her sex upon his was more than he could bear, but he would see her come first. She was holding back for maximum pleasure, but time was short. Every second wasted here put more distance between him and Rhiannon.

His cock was aching for release. Thanks be to the traitorous wind, he was aroused before her seduction began. He was dizzy with need now, his shaft on fire, steeped in the hot, moist seat of her sex. Would she never come?

Balancing himself against the stone with Lavilia impaled upon his member, he cupped her breasts and stroked both nipples with his thumbs as he quickened his rhythm. Thrusting into her in mindless oblivion, he took her until she ground out a deep, throaty groan, holding him fast as the rapid pulsations of her orgasm riddled his cock with drenching fire.

"My wings . . ." he panted. "Stroke my wings! Stroke them *now*!" For while he held a beauty in his arms, his mind's eye saw the wizened crone, and for the first time in so long he could not remember, he was in difficulty.

Lavilia did as he bade her, ruffling his feathers, and his release came in shock waves like cannon fire until she had drained him of every drop of his seed.

Clinging to him fiercely, her hot breath puffing against his skin running with sweat, she murmured, "They took her to a clearing northeast of where the Ancient Ones were ministering to you. Look for a tall ancestral oak whose branches touch the ground. It stands alone. There is a ring of toadstools at its base. You must step inside the ring and—"

"That is all I needed to know," Gideon interrupted as he withdrew himself and staggered back from her. "You will forgive me if I do not linger," he said, unfurling his wings. "Rhiannon's very life could well depend upon my haste."

The rune caster seized his arm. "You must listen . . ." she cried. "You cannot just cross over on your own. You must be led or aided. Notoriously, the fay lead their captives to a faery ring and cross them over. There must be an invitation or magic intervention to breach the span between the worldly and the Otherworldly. I can do this for you, but you must think it through . . . there are choices!" she cried. "Possibly the most important choices of your life . . ."

"There are no 'choices'! I must have her back!" Gideon thundered.

"Then listen well and pay attention, impetuous one," she returned. "You paid me three feathers upon your last visit. If you recall, I told you you would have them back when the time was right."

"So?"

"I must cast one through the portal to gain you entrance to the astral realm," she explained, "but there are limits. You must reach your Rhiannon and carry her back through the portal before that feather touches the ground on the other side, or the opening will close to you."

"Do it then! We waste time, old woman!"

"Wait, dark one!" she called after him, for he was already in flight. "Those three feathers are critical to your life, Gideon. Once used, they cannot be had back. If I do this, you will have only two feathers left and much yet before you. Wait, I say! I have not finished! There is more! You need to hear me out and *think* before you—"

"Work your magic," Gideon shouted, for he was out of earshot. "I have heard all I need to hear. Another time, Lavilia, when I return to collect my due . . ."

She was shouting something, but he had flown too far aloft to hear. It didn't matter. She had told him what he needed to know. It only remained to find the faery ring, cross over, with the help of her magic, and bring Rhiannon back.

The wind whistled in his ears, stirring the strange disembodied voices again. Gideon strained to hear what they were saying as he soared toward the Forest Isle.

You still do not think we should intervene? one was saying. *I should think it would be the perfect time. He should have let her finish.*

The other heaved a gusty sigh. *If Lavilia could not prepare the impetuous young fool, what chance have we? No, nothing worth having comes without as price. He will pay his.*

The other voice sputtered, *It comes too dear, I think, the way he squanders feathers.*

Cheap or dear, he pays it, and soon . . . the other said, and said no more.

12

Rhiannon staggered back from the place where the ancestral oak had stood, wracking her brain for any long-forgotten lore of the astral realm that might help her return to her own world. She'd been told many a tale at her mother's knee. Why couldn't she remember them now?

She glanced about. Though she could feel a thousand eyes upon her, there wasn't a soul in sight. Her mind was a blank. There was nothing for it but to rely upon common sense. She wasn't comfortable in the open, but—not even knowing why— she felt she needed to be able to find her way back to the spot in the clearing where she'd crossed over. Without the oak tree or faery ring, she had no landmark to guide her, and she searched the ground for something to leave in their place. Several small rocks nearby sparkling with metallic flecks caught her eye, and she snatched them up and placed them as near as she could re- call to where the oak had stood in the physical world. Strange voices riding the breeze began to whisper in her ears as she arranged the stones. Several times she stopped to listen, but the whisperers hushed the minute she stilled, and when she resumed her chore and the whispering continued, what they were saying wouldn't come clear. No, she definitely wasn't alone. Whoever these entities were, why wouldn't they make their presence known? Surely, they knew she didn't invade their realm voluntarily. What possible threat could she pose to the dwellers of the Otherworld—a frightened, half-naked woman lost in a fold in time and space, sobbing for her sorry predicament?

Straightening up from her chore, Rhiannon noticed a darker green swath in the grass taking shape. It was leading in the direction of the forest that flanked the clearing on what appeared to be the south, judging from the position of the sun. It seemed like an invitation, and though she was wary of accepting anything from the fay, she began to follow where it led. There wasn't much choice. She wasn't comfortable in the open, and so fixing her position in her mind, she began to follow the faery trail.

An eerie green darkness not unlike that which prevailed in the copses in the physical world enveloped her the instant she stepped inside the lush, dense foliage. Strange spangled light filtered through the trees, and the whispering grew louder. It seemed to be rushing at her from all sides. All around, the trees began to take on shapes within their towering trunks. Their bark began to shift and pulse and undulate as human-like figures became visible that almost seemed trapped in the bodies of the trees. Rhiannon blinked as the naked forms of men and women came clear, writhing seductively, their gray-green bodies never touching, for they were one with their host trees, and yet their seduction was the most powerfully erotic display she had ever seen.

Rhiannon took in her surroundings. Brilliant specks of buzzing white light flitted all around her. How happily they danced, some coming so close they nearly grazed her long hair. One by one they took living form, human-like, but not, for they were winged, and naked, flying all around her, like curious children.

At first glance, she would have taken them for butterflies. Other creatures materialized. Fay of all shapes, sizes, and descriptions appeared before her eyes. They indeed seemed to be performing some ritualistic dance, but at closer inspection . . . no. They were *mating*—openly, without a shred of modesty.

She was mesmerized by the spectacle, and it began to trigger the long-forgotten memories of the fay she had been trying to conjure from her nursery days. The worst had already occurred. She had crossed over. There was nothing to be done about that but try to make the best of it and, if possible, find a sympathetic entity willing to champion her release. These seemed to have accepted her to make so free in her presence, but she saw no champion among them. They seemed content to satisfy their lust en masse for her to view. What had begun as bold pinpoints of glaring light darting about among the swaying boughs of trees whose spirits had come to life had become an orgy of unbridled passions. The innocent-looking spangles had merged into conjoined fay creatures mating in flight, while on the ground other entities had paired off cavorting in like lascivious manner.

But it was the trees that that took her breath away. Was she actually seeing their inner selves, their ancient spirits, or were these naked male and female entities mere faery glamour, staged to raise the fever in her blood? Whatever the case, they had succeeded. Her loins were on fire, her sex throbbing like a pulse beat. Hot blood rushed through her veins, thrumming through her temples, setting her cheeks aflame—calling her hand to her pubic mound. As if they had a will of their own, her fingers parted the honey-colored curls that hid her clitoris and began rubbing it to steely hardness. She was on fire, caught up in the sultry rhythm of the ritual. There was no turning back.

Beguiled, Rhiannon parted her nether lips and let her fingers glide in and out of her vagina on the cream of her juices. She probed deeper. How warm she was inside, like hot silk. She shut her eyes. Even the fiery darkness behind her closed lids had a pulse to it, a pounding, throbbing, shuddering, blood-red rhythm begging for release as she swayed to the beat of the strange orgiastic dance. The climax came quickly, riddling her with wave upon wave of achy orgasmic fire.

A sudden breeze brought her eyes open. The wind hadn't risen. Two winged dryads were spinning around her. These were nearly as tall as she was, their wings so fine all Rhiannon could see was the iridescence of their motion, like a silvery veil the color of rain. Their garments were just as sheer, hiding none of their charms, as they circled her in a blur of twinkling motion, their tittering like the tinkle of bells to her ear. Each carried a thread from the ragged kirtle that barely hung on her body. Giggling and whispering as if they were sharing secrets, the two doe-eyed, long-haired beauties were unraveling the threadbare shift from top to bottom.

One had begun with several threads from the shredded hem, while the other had begun at the neck. As tattered as the garment was, it did provide some shred of decency, and Rhiannon's hands flew in all directions in a vain attempt to preserve what little coverage remained over her private parts.

"No!" she cried. "Please, don't! I am not one of you. I am human. I—we prefer to remain clothed . . ."

But the dryad's tittering laughter only grew louder as they spun and danced and flitted around her, now and then bestowing a playful pat, like a butterfly kiss, with their wings as they passed by.

Rhiannon couldn't see the others any longer. The whole forest had become a whirling, spinning blur of motion. She had begun to spin now as well into a void of pitch darkness. The dryads' voices seemed to be coming from an echo chamber, then finally grew distant, and the breeze of their motion stilled. Something as featherlight as eiderdown touched her skin from her neck to her ankles. She felt it glide over her breasts, over her belly, hips, and thighs. But vertigo starred her vision and she fell to her knees too dizzy to stand.

On the edge of consciousness, Rhiannon's heart began thumping against her ribs, and her breath was coming short. After a moment, her eyes came open to a twilight mist drifting over the forest floor, but the mating creatures had vanished. It wasn't even the same forest. These trees showed no human-like shapes in their blackened trunks. These were bent and twisted, like the trees had been in Gideon's petrified forest on the Dark Isle.

Gideon.

His image ghosting across her mind stabbed her through with the most excruciating pain. Where was he? Had the wood nymphs won? Was he with them, loving them—living inside them? Had he forgotten her in the arms of those treacherous creatures? Would she never see him again? No. She wouldn't think about any of that—couldn't think about it or she would run mad.

Glancing down, Rhiannon gasped. Her threadbare kirtle was gone. In its place she wore a garment so fine it seemed spun of pure moonbeams, just like the gowns the dryads wore. So that was what the playful creatures were about. They had replaced her kirtle with a fine new one—a gift. What had she heard about accepting gifts from the fay? It was forbidden in the physical world, but what about here, in their world? Were the rules different here? Why couldn't she remember? The garment was enchanted, surely, and she'd had no real choice. The flimsy stuff it was woven of scarcely sufficed to preserve modesty, but it was better than going about wearing nothing at all among such highly sexed creatures that went about naked and had no compunction about mating in public in full view of all.

Rhiannon shrugged those thoughts off. It was too late in any case. She was wearing the dryads' gift, and they were nowhere about even if she wanted to return it. Instead, she concentrated upon the lay of the land around her. It had a decidedly sinister feel to it, not warm and welcoming like the other copse. She glanced about looking for the ribbon of darker grass that had led her to the other forest, but it was nowhere to be seen. The land was draped in darkness, like a shroud—a living, breathing darkness, where a thousand eyes lurked in wait. She could feel them boring into her, and she shuddered so violently she misstepped making her way among the slimy tree trunks she reached toward for support.

Another bit of fay lore ghosted across her mind. It was common knowledge that the dryads had the favor of tree spirits. The enigmatic beauties ministered to the trees, petted, groomed, and reverenced them. In return, the ancient spirits that lived within the trees' rough bark and leafy branches gifted them with knowledge of their innermost secrets. It was said that the dryads taught the druids what magic the tree spirits were willing to impart, and often even bestowed such knowledge upon worthy mortals. Dryads could always be found in the company of trees. They were conspicuously absent from these Rhiannon found herself among now, and she shuddered again. There was great danger here. She could feel it in the marrow of her bones.

Surely the dryads knew this would be. Why had they left her among such as these after helping her so kindly? Just another evidence that the fay could not be trusted, she surmised. She had followed the rules. She hadn't thanked the dryads for their gift of the garment, for that was strictly prohibited. The fey neither expected nor solicited thanks for their deeds. In fact, they considered such displays rude. Still, for all their fickle reputation, she would have welcomed their presence here among the blackened branches rheumy with malodorous sap that seemed to be closing in on her. But that was ridiculous. They were only *trees,* rooted to the ground. Nevertheless, she gave them a wide berth as she continued on, anxious to be out of that forest.

There was no path, but there was only one way she could go. The spongy ribbon of flattened mulch winding through the trees was narrow, and even if she had wanted to go back in the opposite direction, one glance over her shoulder showed her that this was not an option. The undergrowth and trees behind her closed the path with every step she took, and what had once been a lane wide enough to accommodate a horse and rider, was fast becoming a tangled snarl of jungle-like impenetrable growth nipping at her heels.

Rhiannon quickened her pace. The pearly twilight was fading all around her. It was suddenly full dark. The forest seemed to be breathing in and out in rhythm with her footfalls. She could see the blackened trees in silhouette against a blacker sky expand and contract with every step she took.

An insidious murmur of disembodied sound rushed at her ears. Her eyes flashed in all directions in a vain attempt to pick out the authors of the noise from the misty shadows, but nothing came clear. Whoever—*whatever*—these creatures were, they were not anything she wanted to be alone with in the night, in the dark, and she quickened her pace again until she was nearly running; evidently, so were they. Their monotone buzzing had grown louder, and it was coming at her from all directions.

Covering her ears, Rhiannon ran on, dry sobs welling in her throat. The petrified trees' bony arms reaching across the narrow path groped her familiarly as she passed among them, or was it the invisible creatures hidden in the mist that plucked at her long plaited hair, pinched her breasts, and tugged on the hem of her gown? Rhiannon didn't stop to make an assessment. The trees thinned ahead, and she ran sobbing through the bog toward a clearing, where shafts of moonlight lit the meadow as light as day. Clapping her hands over her ears, she screamed at the top of her voice to drown out the hideous misshapen sound of the disembodied laughter mocking her flight.

The minute she reached the meadow, the dark swath of grass reappeared, and she spilled out onto the ground, her breath coming short, and collapsed in a bed of marigolds.

"Here now!" a woman's voice croaked from nearby. "Watch where you're goin', missy! Ya' nearly trampled me poor lost lamb."

Rhiannon scrabbled to her feet, a startled cry on her parched lips. It was a wizened crone wearing a green shift, her hunched body bent nearly parallel with the ground. She was carrying a shepherd's crook, and the lamb in question whose bleating was a welcome sound after the blood-chilling laughter still echoing in her ears from the forest behind. It, too, had disappeared now, like the first forest had. It was passing strange.

There was nothing threatening in the woman's countenance. In fact, she had a pleasant face, the apples of her cheeks glowing with the rosy blush of good health, though her body was twisted and grotesque. Her smile was most pleasant, and the way she petted and crooned to the little lamb in her arms was reassuring. Could she be a *gruagach*? If so, there was nothing to fear. According to legend, such creatures, though simple-minded and prone to mistakes, held no ill will toward humans, but were reputed to be quite helpful. If that was the case, this woman might just be the one to help sort out the situation. But still, Rhiannon was wary.

"There now, my pet," the crone sang to the lamb. "The lassie didn't mean ta hurt ya'." She winked at Rhiannon. "*Cead mile failte!*" she said. "A hundred thousand welcomes to ye', missy."

Rhiannon nodded. "I fear I've lost my way," she said. "Can you tell me where I am?"

"Where is it ya' want ta be?"

Tears welled in Rhiannon's eyes. She blinked them back. It wouldn't do to show emotion to any here. "I want to go home . . . to the physical world . . . to Arcus," she got out through a dry sob despite her resolve.

The old woman clicked her tongue. "Well ya' shouldn't have crossed over then, should you?" she scolded.

"I didn't do it apurpose," Rhiannon defended. "I was tricked . . . the wood nymphs, they—"

"Oh, that lot was it?" the crone cut in. She wagged her head. "Ya' want ta have no truck with the wood nymphs."

"There was a clearing, and a huge ancestral oak, with a ring of toadstools around it," Rhiannon explained. "The nymphs took me there and disappeared, and now I'm here and I cannot find my way back. Can you direct me? Everywhere I've been keeps disappearing just as they did."

"You've been took, that's what," the woman said. "There's nothin' ta be done."

"I need to find that clearing where I left the stones to mark the spot where I crossed over. Please, I beg of you, show me the way."

"There is no 'way,' missy. You've been *took*, I tell ya'. They cast a glamour over ya'. No use ta fret. You'll like it here. Stay outa the bogs, keep your thoughts to yourself, and stay on the path till you're absolutely sure ya' want ta leave it, and you'll be fine. Me name is Maribelle. What's yourn?"

Rhiannon opened her mouth to say her name, but thought better of it. Recalling the effect it had upon the others in her own world, it wouldn't do to test it here. "There has to be a way back," she pleaded instead.

"I'd like ta stay and chat, but some of us have chores ta tend to," the woman said. "We'll meet again I have no doubt, the way you're goin', missy. 'Tis my job ta see ta the lost, ya' know, and care for the livestock." She turned her attention to the lamb then, crooning and petting it profusely, and waddled off.

Rhiannon was right. The woman *was* a gruagach, and she started after her. "Maribelle, wait!" she called.

"Mind the path, missy!" the crone reminded her, clicking her tongue again.

Rhiannon glanced down just in time, for she had nearly stepped off the dark green swath. When she looked up again the woman was gone.

Rhiannon's heart sank with her posture. She glanced behind. A sheer-faced wall of granite three times her height now stood where the bog had been, and she heaved a sigh. There was nothing to do but to go forward, and she followed the dark path through the meadow to a parklike clearing whose central feature was a maze sculpted in the center of well-manicured grounds. The faery path of lush dark grass led right into it.

Almost at once, she saw a faun seated cross-legged on the ground just inside the first tall hedge, his elbows braced upon his hairy, goatlike legs. His pipes had his full and fierce attention, and he didn't seem to notice her. *Sy!* Could it be? Rhiannon's heart leapt.

"*Sy!*" she cried, starting toward him. "Is that you?" Of course it wasn't. The satyr paid her no mind. Seeming mesmerized by the music drifting from his flute, it was as if she wasn't even there, and she checked herself just in time, for she'd nearly left the path.

For one split second, she'd had hope only to have it dashed. The creature looked so like the Prince of the Green's simpleminded faun, she was certain she'd found her way home. How could the gods be so cruel? The satyr looked right through her as she passed him by, and Rhiannon trudged on, her eyes peeled for any sign of movement ahead, but there was none. Was she invisible? It wasn't likely. Maribelle had no trouble seeing her. There was no time to waste puzzling it out. She needed to return to the spot where she had crossed over, and she pressed on, begging Mica, god of all, to show her the way.

Tears stung behind her eyes. Under any other circumstances, she would have been awestruck at the breathtaking shadowlands she passed through, burgeoning with all manner of wildflower, moss, and fern, and silvered with dappled moonlight. It was a sight to behold, but it was tainted with thoughts she could not help but think of what had brought her there. If only she had respected Gideon's conditions. If only she'd stayed in the cave, none of this would be happening. But no, she had left it, and now there was no cave. There probably was no island. She had angered the gods and cost Gideon his home, and very likely his life.

His handsome image flashed before her mind's eye, his striking angular features, the dark mercurial eyes that spoke with more articulation than his handsome lips had ever done, his long dark hair, combed by the wind, teasing the broad ledge of his brow. She could almost feel his strong, well-muscled arms around her, and the hardness of his sex throbbing deep inside her, pumping her full of the warm rush of his seed.

Rhiannon groaned. Would she never feel him come inside her again? Would she never again touch the soft, silky feathers of his wings? Would she never feel them fold her close to his magnificent body, skin to skin, or know the freedom like no other as those appendages carried her aloft, to what had to be the very gates of Heaven? It mattered not that they were denied entrance to Paradise. Her Paradise was in Gideon's arms. It would have been enough to live and love, and end her mortal days cradled in those voluminous wings. She could almost feel the way they furled around her when he came, the way they shuddered against her as she milked him dry of every drop.

Her arousal was deep and demanding, her sexual pulse throbbing a steady rhythm, her breath coming in thick, short puffs that rumbled up from the epicenter of her sex, begging to become deep-throated pleasure moans. Her need was great, a burning, aching demand of body and soul that only Gideon could satisfy.

She slowed her pace and shut her eyes, calling his image to appear in the velvet blackness behind her closed lids. How clearly his shape took form—every line in his face, every brooding furrow in his brow. How odd that he had no laugh lines to speak of. She couldn't recall ever seeing him laugh. What torments had he suffered over the ages? She was just beginning to realize what she had done to him—to them both— and an agonized cry poured from her throat. She had lost him, and now she was lost herself.

All at once a rustling sound to the east of the path disturbed her reverie and her eyes snapped open. Blinking back the tears, she searched the mist in the direction of the sound, her heart pounding in her ears. What entity, what creature of the fay had her outburst attracted? Adrenaline crippled her, rooted her to the spot as a shape slowly materialized out of the mist. Her breath caught in her throat. It couldn't be, but it was. *Gideon,* in all his winged splendor, standing like a statue as the mist faded around him. He was naked and aroused, his eyes riveted to hers. Their message was clear. Despite all she had done, he wanted her still.

The gruagach had warned her not to stray from the path unless she was absolutely certain she wanted to leave it. There was no question. He reached out his arms, those strong, muscled arms, and she stepped off the path and rushed into them.

His rock-hard body collided with hers in a volatile explosion of pent-up passion. His hands, roaming over her curves, explored every inch of her through the gossamer gown the dryads had given her. It hid nothing from his hungry eyes; they devoured her.

He didn't speak; there was no need. She was in his arms, his engorged penis leaning heavily against her belly, his need evidenced in his rapid breathing, in the runaway heart hammering against her through the gossamer gown. His touch was a little rougher than she remembered. Where was the gentle strength, the power of a passion that married tenderness to the lust that had damned him? He was angry. That was understandable.

Hadn't she just cost him everything, his home, the very island it was built upon—nearly cost him his life, for though he said not, the lightning strikes had done damage; she had no idea how much. Yes, he had every right to be angry, but he had never caused her pain before, not even when he took her maidenhead, and she had never felt fear in his arms, like she did now.

His kiss had become smothering. His hand twisted in her hair tethered her cruelly. His bruising hardness forced against her caused her to pull back.

"Stop . . . Gideon . . . *Stop!*" she gritted out past the hard mouth grinding against her lips. She pushed against his massive chest, and when that didn't work, she began pounding it with her tiny hands balled into white-knuckled fists. "Stop, I said! You're hurting me!"

But he didn't stop. He tightened his grip, his arms like a vise, his fingers pinching her breasts until she cried out: "*Gideon* . . . let me go!"

This wasn't the Gideon she knew. What had happened to him? She couldn't break his hold, and she screamed as he drove her down in the tall grass in hopes that she would shock him out of the madness that had evidently overtaken him. She screamed again as he spread her legs and attempted to struggle between them.

Overhead, the stars twinkled innocently in the indigo vault, like spectators to her struggles. It all seemed so unreal, and yet the pain, the pressure of rock-hard flesh, and pinching fingers was very real, indeed. She fought against them, her eyes flung wide to the star-spangled sky winking overhead like faery dust, from which a single white feather slowly floated down. Where did it come from? Fascinated by the languid progress of its un-expected fall, she gasped, and gasped again as a tear was sud-denly rent in the vault itself. Yet another scream spilled from her throat while watching the sky seem to peel back as through the hole—feet first—a white-winged figure plummeted down on a mercurial surge of displaced energy the heat of which spread its wavy aura wide.

In a blink, the creature pinning her to the ground dissolved before her eyes, and Gideon scooped her up in strong arms and soared skyward at a dizzying speed she would have thought impossible for any creature. Past the treetops he zoomed, past the feather still drifting down, the wind of his motion spinning it upward momentarily before it once again began its spiraling descent.

"Hold fast!" he charged. "The portal is only open until that feather hits the ground!"

Rhiannon shut her eyes. The rest was no more than a blur.

13

Gideon streaked through the tear he'd rent in the cosmos crossing over and left the Otherworld behind not a moment too soon. He'd scarcely carried Rhiannon through the portal, which had rolled back like a tightly furled scroll, when it nearly snapped shut on his heels. His heart was pounding so violently, it nearly threw him off balance. He had all but run mad. Rhiannon was precious cargo, and he clutched her so close to his hard, muscled chest the pressure of his fingers chased the blood from her shoulder, bared by the loose-fitting shift she was wearing. Where the deuce did she get such a garment? Anger flared at sight of her all but naked draped in such flimsy stuff.

"Have you been harmed?" he got out through clenched teeth.

"N-no," she said. "It was quite pleasant . . . except for the last. What was that creature? I thought it was *you*! Are we still in the astral, or have we come . . . home?"

"We have no home," Gideon said flatly, glancing down at the gaping hole in the archipelago, like a missing tooth, where the Dark Isle had been. It wasn't much, but it had been his—all that he had. The gods had stripped him of his privilege. They had taken his keep, and then his cave. Now, they had driven the land it had stood upon beneath the sea. He was hunted like an animal because he dared to seek the pleasures of the flesh, because he dared to *love*. That was how it began. Where would it end?

Gideon was well aware of his failure in falling from grace, but how long would he have to suffer for it? It had been eons. When would the reparation be enough? It was a never-ending nightmare, and now it wasn't just himself that must suffer. There was Rhiannon. If he had any sense, he would take her to the mainland and have done, but it was much too late for that. Their hearts beat as one. Their souls breathed as one. He was on fire for her—even now, when jealousy and rage roiled in him. He was in love with her. The minute he thought she was lost to him was when he knew. It wasn't a comfortable thing.

"Where will we go?" she murmured, to his silence.

Gideon's eyes darted every which way, scanning the midnight blackness for some sign of watchers. He saw none, but he knew they were there. They were always there. "For now, we go to Marius," he said. "The Ancient Ones will protect us until I can find a better place."

"They did not protect me!" she cried. "The wood nymphs, they—"

"They are banished from the Forest Isle ... at least for now."

"They tricked me! They crossed me over!"

"I know," he said. "Hold fast! We go below. I see no watchers, but that does not mean there are none nearby."

Rhiannon stiffened in his arms. He knew she feared flight. He would end it as swiftly as possible. They were far from out of danger.

"Who was that impostor?" she persisted.

They were over the Forest Isle, and their descent would

have to be swift if they were to avoid any watchers lurking about. Gideon covered her eyes with his hand and plummeted below, where the trees formed an instant canopy over them. Carrying her deeply into the ancient wood, he set her down in a velvety moss bed.

"That creature was a *thought stealer*," he said, dropping to his knees beside her. "The stealers probe your mind and take the form of whomever you trust most from the images stored there, so that they can seduce you off the path."

Rhiannon gasped. "Maribelle warned me to keep my thoughts to myself!" she said. "I wish she'd made herself plainer."

"Maribelle?"

"A gruagach, I think. I met her on the path. She said to keep my thoughts to myself, and not to leave the path unless I was absolutely sure I should."

"Why did you?" he snapped.

"Because I saw *you*!" she defended. "At least I thought it was you."

"You couldn't tell the difference?" Was he jealous of his own effigy? He was surely going mad.

Rhiannon pouted. "Not until it was too late," she said.

"You would have been safe if you had stayed on the path."

"I wouldn't have been there in the first place if your nymphs hadn't—"

"They are not *my* nymphs," he corrected her.

"Perhaps you need to tell them that," Rhiannon said frostily. "They seem to think otherwise."

"I have existed as I am for a very long time, Rhiannon, since the great cataclysm—a time incomprehensible to you, a mortal. Considering my . . . situation, I have taken my pleasures where I could find them over time. And yes, the nymphs have been my consorts. I shan't deny it, but that is in the past, and I will not be damned for things that happened before I met you. You have no reason to be jealous of that lot."

"*Jealous?*" she returned in a huff.

"Call it what you will, that's what it amounts to, and we have no time for childishness. We have serious issues that needs must be resolved—"

"I am no child!" she interrupted.

"All right, then, I can play the same game," he responded, his voice like gravel. "Where did you get that frock? Did the nymphs give it to you? You have no right to admonish me, while you parade yourself thus before every creature in the astral!"

"No, your nymphs did not give it to me," Rhiannon fired back. "They shredded the fine shift you provided, violated me, and left me far more naked than you see me now to fend on my own in a strange and hostile place."

"Who, then? Who dressed you thus?"

"Now who is jealous?"

"Never mind! I told you I, too, could play this ridiculous game. Who gave you that shift?"

"Two dryads," she replied. "They unraveled my torn kirtle and spun me this." She slapped the skirt of her frock. "It is just like the ones they wore. They evidently thought they were giving me something fine. I suppose they were your consorts, too?"

"Probably," he pronounced. "As I told you, since the gods cast me out, I have taken my pleasures where I could, with any who were brave enough to risk the watchers' lightning bolts. Now, enough! All that is in the past; we have serious dangers in the present to contend with, and we need to spend our energies upon those."

She looked so forlorn that he raised her up and took her in his arms. "We will find a way," he murmured against her hair. The last thing he needed now was physical contact with her. He was already aroused, the bulk of his hardness leaning heavily against her belly—throbbing to life, like a separate entity be-

tween them. It lived for her. It remembered gliding on the silk
of her wetness as it plunged deep inside the sweet musk of her
sex. Every memory was indelibly fixed in his mind, every shudder and thrust etched in the sexual stream flowing between
them.

"Rhiannon," he murmured, his husky voice savoring her
name as it rolled off his tongue like honey. "Do not ever leave
me. When I thought I'd lost you . . ." He couldn't finish the
thought much less put it into words.

He found her lips with a hungry mouth and teased her
tongue deeply. Lacing his fingers through her hair, he drew her
closer to his need, to the rock-hard cock challenging the seam
of his skintight eel skin. When their lips parted, she reached for
more. Dare he free the anxious penis and take a chance that the
leaf-laden boughs the trees had formed into a canopy overhead
were dense enough to fool the watchers?

"How did you ever find me?" she said. "How did you ever
cross over?"

Gideon was glad she'd broken the spell for the moment. He
wasn't ready to test the inevitable. Instead, he held her close,
soothing her through the gossamer shift with gentle hands.
What glorious torture to hold back. What exquisite agony to
live on the brink of ecstasy. "I visited the rune caster," he said.
"It as not the first time I've solicited her aid over you."

Rhiannon's breath caught in her throat. "Her services come
dear," she said.

Gideon frowned, remembering. "Once, her fee was three of
my feathers, which she plucked from my wings. She said I
would have them back when needs must."

Rhiannon gasped again. "The feather that floated down?"

Gideon nodded. "She hurled it through the portal. It opened
to me, and I had only the space of time before it reached the
ground to retrieve you and cross back over before the portal
closed. Where there is enchantment, all things come at a price,

often above gold. To tap the rune caster's magic is like looking into a cracked mirror. There is never a true image. Things are not always what they seem."

"I don't understand . . ." she said, her brows knit in a frown.

"The rune caster said one true thing when she took my feathers. She said I had no inkling of the power in them. What she has given me is three chances."

"Like three wishes?"

"Not . . . exactly. She has given me three chances to tap into her magic. I must choose wisely. Once used, those chances cannot be had back. Meanwhile, she extracts some beneficial element from the feathers for her own use."

"And you used one of those chances bringing me back?" she asked.

Gideon nodded. "Yes," he said. Two chances remain."

"All this is my fault," she sobbed.

Gideon smiled. "Actually, the fault is mine," he said. "And all that happened a long time ago. Leave it. We need to talk. We cannot stay here. For one thing, we wouldn't be safe, for another, I cannot put my friend in danger. . . ." All at once a rustling sound in the undergrowth pulled Gideon up short, and he laid a finger across his lips. "Shh!" he whispered. "Someone comes!"

"Your friend can take care of himself," said a deep resonant voice, as a tall, muscular man parted the brush and joined them. He was bare chested, his long hair tethered with vines, wearing skintight buckskins that revealed hard, muscled thighs and left nothing to the imagination between them. His penis was clearly outlined, long, curved, and thick, straining the stitching in his breeches, which were tucked into fringed buckskin boots. One muscular arm was threaded through a longbow, with arrows at the ready in a quiver on his back, sharing the space with his very vocal magpie perched on top.

It was a moment before Rhiannon gasped, and Gideon almost laughed outright. She had never seen Marius, Lord of the Forest, Prince of the Green, in his natural state. The moon had begun to wax, and he was no longer trapped in the body of the great black centaur.

"Well met," Gideon said, gripping the forest lord's forearm. "I am relieved to see that the watchers haven't done you harm."

"They tried," Marius got out through a throaty chuckle. "They do not like my arrows overmuch."

"Do they know we are here?" Gideon asked.

"Oh, they know, my friend," Marius returned. "It is far too still in the wood. Listen . . . not even a chipmunk chirping."

Gideon frowned. There wasn't a sound. The forest was steeped in deathly silence. The watchers were there all right, lurking in wait, and cold chills raised Gideon's hackles. "We will not linger," he said. "You have done enough for us."

"I am not chasing you," Marius said. "I merely want to warn. You need to be on your guard. These harpies of the gods are relentless beings. I have never seen the like." He turned to Rhiannon, dosing her with a deep, dark-eyed stare. "Are you well, lady?" he said. "We did not part well, and I fear I have been lax in my hospitality. I should have stayed with you. Sometimes I tend to forget how simple Sy is. He is quite enamored of you."

"My fault again," Rhiannon said low-voiced. "I never should have tricked him and left your cottage." Gideon stared at her, and she couldn't meet his eyes. "I tricked the faun into picking me some flowers so I could steal away and come in search of you," she confessed.

"No matter now," Gideon said. "We will leave before more harm is done."

"Where will you go?" the forest lord queried. "The Dark Isle is no more, and Simeon's underwater palace would not suit. Vane would take you in a heartbeat. He is your staunch supporter, is the Fire Lord."

"Fighting fire with fire, eh?" Gideon said.

"You've had to do it before," Marius reminded him.

"And will again, no doubt," said Gideon. "I will give it thought. We were just deciding when you came on just now."

Marius took Rhiannon's measure. "I have interrupted something," he said. "Take some time with your lady. I shall keep vigil. I have noticed that the watchers are particularly active in the wee hours before dawn. We are approaching that now. The Ancient Ones have granted you protection. You will be safe as long as you remain under the canopy they have created for you. I cannot vouch for what will be once you leave it, but I will cover you when you do."

"I do not want to bring the watchers' wrath down upon you, Marius. Do not put yourself in harm's way. The gods are quick to anger and slow to forgive. I do not want your chastisement on my conscience. I will deal with this."

The Forest Lord ignored him. "There is a spring at the end of this path that feeds a rock pool. Refresh yourselves." He turned to Rhiannon. "All the isles of the archipelago have warm springs fed by the Isle of Fire, like beads in a chain," he explained. "I'm sure you know that, Gideon, but what you do not know is that mine connects to Lord Vane's isle directly. It is for the most part cloaked—a discreet means of travel among the isles—but I shall reveal it to you. I trust you will keep its whereabouts to yourselves—"

"That goes without saying," Gideon cut in.

Marius nodded. "I have my reasons," he said. "Take some time with your lady. "You do not know when you will be able again, if you take my meaning. I will make my rounds. When you are ready, you need not take to the air and draw the watchers' fire. You will need to swim beneath the surface of the water for several yards to reach an underwater tunnel with air pockets, like a bathing tub, quite pleasant. Follow it in an easterly direction, and it will lead you to a similar rock pool at the foot of Lord Vane's volcano. You will need to take shelter once you emerge, and there are precious few hiding places to be had on the Isle of Fire. At least this will buy you a little time. I wish I could offer you more."

"I am in your debt, Marius."

"There is no 'debt,' old friend, just keep my secret hideaway to yourselves. Now then! I go to lead the watchers on a merry chase. Hail and farewell, Lord of the Dark. When we meet again, let us hope it is in less dire circumstances."

The Lord of the Forest melted into the shadows as mysteriously as he'd emerged from them without a sound, and Rhiannon uttered another gasp.

"What a strange creature," she murmured. "I mean no disrespect calling him that, but what *is* he, human or fay?"

Gideon pulled her close in his arms, brushing loose tendrils back from her face in the stray flashes of defused moonlight seeping through the canopy of boughs above. "Marius is a creature of Nature, neither man, nor beast, nor mortal, nor fay. He is like all of us lords of the archipelago, a plaything of the gods. He serves Mother Nature and the Ancient Ones, tending all things green and burgeoning. He is fertility. He *is* Nature, the keeper of all grounding balance in the land. His sentence was lighter than mine. He only must take the form of the centaur for three days each month."

"But why? What did he do?" Rhiannon persisted.

Gideon hesitated. "He forgot who he was," he said. "He killed a creature he was duty bound to protect, and the gods have suffered him to walk the land in the body of that creature as punishment each month at the dark of the moon for all eternity."

"He is . . . immortal then," Rhiannon murmured, answering her own question.

Gideon nodded. "We all are," he said.

"I see," she replied so softly he scarcely heard.

"Enough of Marius!" he said, pulling her closer still. "It matters not to me what he has done. He is my friend, and yours. He has just proven that. We are safe here for the moment. The gods alone know what will be when we leave the forest."

She clung to him, and he found her lips with a hungry mouth. How soft and sweet they were. They felt like velvet and tasted of honey as he deepened the kiss, his tongue inviting hers to join the mating dance. It was a swift thrust, extracting a moan from her throat that resonated through his body, igniting flames only she had the power to kindle. He was aroused, his loins on fire, his penis swelling to life against the soft cushion of her belly.

Gideon's wings unfurled halfway, grazing two ancestral pines that seemed to sigh awake and stretch, their fragrant needles caressing them as their boughs swayed to an erotic rhythm that moved the ground beneath their feet. Rhiannon stiffened in his arms, and he soothed her gently.

"There is nothing to fear," he murmured. "The ancient spirits in these trees would bless us."

The words were scarcely out when the mulch-covered forest floor began to shift. One by one, roots and tendrils began to break through the groundcover. Like curious children, the roots began exploring their bodies. Rhiannon cried out as one root lifted the hem of her shift and began inching it up along her thigh. Another reached to stroke her hair, still another joined with the first, and together they unbound the loose plait and spread the long tresses wide.

Gideon had never seen anything so beautiful as Rhiannon with her hair free of its tether falling over the creamy expanse of her shoulders. Where had her gossamer shift gone? It didn't matter. The flimsy thing hid none of her attributes. The dryads had robed her well, in the filmy gauze of spider silk spangled with what seemed like shimmering stardust. She was more provocative in that shift than she was naked, for it rested upon the turgid peaks of her firm, young breasts and pubic mound, and clung in shadowy seduction to the voluptuous hollows and valleys that defined her narrow waist and sculpted her curvaceous buttocks. It now lay puddled about her feet sparkling in the half-light before dawn. Gauze of the gods, for it truly was too fine to have been spun by mortals.

Gideon opened the front of his eel skin, shrugged it down, and freed his anxious cock, soothing it from thick root to ridged head. Slow, pulsating waves of achy heat spread through his loins as her hand replaced his gliding along his thick, veined shaft. Her long, languid strokes made him harder still.

His wings unfurled wider, caressing the trees that had joined boughs and formed a ring around them, like a fragrant cocoon, their needles running with sticky sap leaving little trails upon their naked skin. It was an intimacy like no other as roots, vines, tender shoots, and tendrils of other plant life stroked them both relentlessly, tethering their ankles to the ground, binding them to Nature and to each other.

Shuddering waves of drenching fire ripped through Gideon's penis as tender shoots of the climbing vines that had made their home on the great pines' trunks wreathed his erection and snaked their way between the globes of his ass. He could have sworn he heard one pine sigh under the umbrella of rustling branches, as the two trees began to stroke each other.

Gideon recalled what happened the last time the trees had relieved him thus. He might be able to get away with coitus beneath the Ancient Ones' canopy, but the minute he left the protection of the trees, the watchers would descend and hurl their lightning bolts. How long before their wrath extended to Rhiannon? How long before their retribution threatened her? Their missiles could not kill him, but they could kill her. Could he live with such as that burdening his conscience? He dared not linger over such fears. He needed to remain focused. No mean task, while gripping waves of smoldering heat, the slightest touch of her hand, the merest puff of wind, or flutter of a pine needle threatened to riddle him with a climax that would rock his soul. The curse was working in him now unlike it ever had before, because love had become a factor. He had reached the point of no return, but he wasn't the only one to consider any longer. Now there was Rhiannon.

Tender shoots were strumming her nipples, and ivy runners had crept between her thighs. Leaning her against one of the swaying pines, Gideon spread her nether lips and thrust his penis into her from mushroom head to thickened root not a moment too soon. Shudders of orgasmic contractions gripped his shaft as her vagina tugged at his penis. Slow, fluttering tugs at first, then faster, more urgent pulsations as he rode her silken wetness.

Rhiannon called out his name as the climax took her, milking him dry as she rode the firestorm of their simultaneous orgasm. Gideon groaned. The shuddering timbre seemed to bubble up in his throat from the very depths of the enigmatic fiber that knitted him together. Could this climax be his last? Had his time finally run out? His cock was burning with unbridled need as she stroked his wings. With the last shuddering thrust, they furled around her, releasing the trees, for they were no longer touching.

Roots and tendrils, tender shoots and climbing vines crept over them returning to the ground, burrowing back beneath the mulch of dead leaves, fallen needles, sap, and wildflowers. The pulse beat beneath them faded as the ground cover returned to its solid form as if the trees' roots had never left it. The whole forest seemed to sigh as the canopy shifted overhead, and Gideon withdrew himself, snatched up Rhiannon's shift, and scooped her up into his arms.

"We must go," he murmured, stalking deeply into the lush, dense underbrush along the path Marius had pointed out. "It is no longer safe here. The boughs soon part and the watchers lurk in wait."

"I fear the Isle of Fire," Rhiannon confessed, gripping him tighter. "It is said that everything Lord Vane touches bursts into flame, even people—even *himself*, that he has the power to self-combust!"

"It is not Lord Vane's fire you need fear," he said. "It is the watcher's fire that threatens, and it is Marius, who needs to fear those lightning bolts more than either of us. The gods are patient with the Ancient Ones, but these ancestral spirits are not exempt from their wrath. I saw fire consume an Ancient One once. I wish never to see such as that again, nor could I live with myself if I were the cause of it. Hold fast and make no sound. I hear dawn breaking. It is time to go."

———————

14

He cannot fight the watchers single-handed, a familiar voice ghosted across Gideon's mind.

There is nothing we can do, said the other. *Besides, he is not alone.*

We could spare him much, the first voice argued.

The other uttered something akin to a growl. *What, and bring the watchers' wrath down upon our heads?*

Just because the gods employ the watchers does not make the watchers right, which is why the gods employ us also, the first voice spoke up.

When the gods want us, they will let us know, the other said. *They also employ the rune caster. The winged one has sought her counsel, and I want no truck with that one.*

The first speaker hesitated. *I still think—*

Shh! Be still! He hears us. You forget his powers. He would have heard us long ago if he was not blinded by love madness. You forget, he can hear night fall and dawn break. He hears the music the sun makes, and the sighing of the moon—the very symphony of the universe when he is not bewitched like now, by

*such as she. He has not lost that gift, it just lies dormant. But
enough! We wait on the gods. It is in their hands now....*

Gideon did hear something, but only fragmented bits that
made no sense. There was no time to trouble over disembodied
voices. His way was clear. He was a fugitive, hunted like an animal, and now Rhiannon was a fugitive as well. He could not
think past that he had put her in such a position. He could not
rationalize beyond that his selfishness in that he would keep
her may be the very thing that damned them in the end. For he
felt the chill of the angel of death's icy breath puffing down his
spine this time; something he had never felt before. It raised his
hackles and riddled him with cold, clammy chills.

They found the mineral spring and reached the rock pool in
an unexpected clearing deep in the wood, as first light began to
chase the shadows. It was just as Marius had described, like a
little oasis in the midst of lush vegetation. The prospect of submerging himself in the warm mineral spring, having the silky
water lave his tender wings in Rhiannon's arms, was almost
more than he could bear. The thought of it alone made him
hard as he hesitated on the brink of the pool.

"Must we swim under the water?" Rhiannon asked, hesitant.

"Only for a short distance," Gideon replied, slipping his
arm around her waist. He had just come from her steamy embrace, and his member was throbbing to life again. His skin had
begun to tingle in anticipation of those lapping ripples of dark
water lifting—separating each feather in his traitorous wings,
missing no crevice; it was sheer torture. Water was his enemy
now. It would bring the libidinous drive, the unstoppable passion, which would be bad enough if he were alone, but with
Rhiannon in his arms, he would be perpetually hard against the
seam, and there was no help for it.

"I don't swim underwater well," Rhiannon confessed.

"Take my hand," Gideon said. She did as he bade her, and together they plunged into the rock pool.

Gideon groaned as the steamy mineral water cascaded over his wings. He remembered that submerging himself in the warm water of just such a pool, or standing under a waterfall, or swimming off the shores of Simeon's Pavilion had soothed and relaxed him. But that was before his fall from grace, before the gods turned his own body against him and made it an instrument of sexual torture.

Rhiannon clung to him, and he stiffened as her hands came too close to those recreant appendages for comfort. "Do not touch my wings!" he cautioned. "I need all my wits about me now. Let your body become accustomed to the water temperature. When you're ready, take a deep breath, and hold on to me."

Moments later, they were moving underwater. His wings were like lead weights, the surge to sexual readiness almost more than Gideon could bear. He could feel her fear. He could also feel her trust, and he held her closer, sifting through the phosphorescent glitter in the water with narrowed eyes searching for the opening Marius described. It seemed like an eternity, but it was only a moment before he saw it, like a burst of ethereal light, and he streaked upward through the water to the underwater cave.

Defused light from anonymous chinks in the rock formation above showed him the labyrinth with air pockets supplied by the same source. The air smelled strongly of pine, rosemary, and cress. The water was only waist deep as they began treading toward a glimmer of daylight at the far end of the cave, but the constant laving of his wings had taken its toll, and Gideon loosened the crotch of his eel-skin suit and soothed his aching penis.

Rhiannon took him in her arms. "Is it . . . Am I worth all this?" she murmured, searching his eyes in the half-light.

Gideon could no longer mask the pain and the desire that lived in his shuttered gaze. He hesitated. Of course she was worth it, but did he have the right to risk putting her in harm's way?

"Worth it?" he breathed. "My love, you are worth any torment the gods can hurl at me, but nothing is worth putting you in danger; this is what troubles me."

Rhiannon laid her soft hand against his cheek. "Several times you have asked me never to leave you," she murmured. "Now I ask the same of you. Whatever comes, we face it together."

He found her lips with a hungry mouth and pulled her against his anxious hardness. Her body heat excited him as hot steam rose around them from the mineral springs that fed the corridor they traveled. His wet wings shuddered, unfurling halfway, and his breath caught as her pleasure moan resonated through his body.

Taking his penis in her hand, she guided it between her thighs until it glided the length of her slit, riding her wetness, a different wetness than the water that rushed to lave their genitals. It was as if his cock had been ensconced in musky hot silk and at long last found its home.

"Do you remember how it was the first time we met . . . in the pool in your cave?" she asked. "You did this to me then. I was a virgin, and you were so masterful, trying to frighten me."

"I was trying to warn you away."

"Yes, well, you will never know what an opposite effect it had upon me, how often I dreamed of what it would be like to have such as this inside me." She undulated against the unsuspecting penis trapped between her thighs. It was enough—more than enough.

Gideon seized her, and in one thrust plunged into her. Wrapping her legs around his waist, he backed her against the smooth wall of the cave in a mindless explosion of carnal oblivion. His need was unstoppable, his passion inexhaustible, fed by the fuel of her breathless moans. The climax was swift and riveting, like cannon fire, paralyzing them both.

Finding her lips, he took them eagerly, and she melted against him. How soft and fragrant she was. Hers was a palpable passion. He could feel it in the eager abandon of her response. He could taste it in the desperation of her kiss, as if it was their last. It was then that he realized not all of the drive, the unstoppable frenzy of desire, was due to the curse that left him in a perpetual state of some level of arousal. He didn't feel this way relieving himself in the wood nymphs, or in the siren Muriel, or in the shape-shifting rune caster. Those occasions were mere bodily functions, desperate acts performed to relieve the pressure the curse brought to bear. This was different. He had never felt this way before—not even when it all began. The remotest possibility that this embrace could be their last had opened his eyes to a poignant truth: He had come back from the others, when they were taken away, but he would not come back from Rhiannon. He had found his soul mate, and he would keep her no matter the cost.

Light trickling in at the end of the tunnel had grown brighter. The sun had risen. There was no more time. How much help evading the watchers of the gods Lord Vane could offer remained to be seen. The relentless creatures stalking him with their lightning bolt seemed set upon his destruction this time, and the gods had closed their ears to his pleas for mercy.

Pulling Rhiannon close in his arms, he tilted her face toward his. "I won't lie to you," he murmured. "This has never occurred before, Rhiannon. I have always had a refuge, a place of sanctuary; no more. We are fugitives, and my greatest fear is that the gods will try to get to me through you. It is not too late for me to carry you to the mainland. For all we know, Rolf is long gone by now aboard another vessel. I must offer you the option. There are places there where you could easily blend in. It would be impossible for me, but you—"

Her finger across his lips silenced him. "I will never leave you, Gideon," she said with passion.

He crushed her close and offered up a prayer he prayed hadn't fallen on deaf ears like all the others, and led her toward the glimmer of light in the distance. "Come," he said. "Lord Vane already knows of our coming. Marius will have seen to that. He will be waiting. You have nothing to fear in him. He is not the ogre you expect. He is, I think, the most tragic of us all."

The cave opened onto the foot of a towering volcano. A lone figure stood at the base of it raking volcanic coals onto what looked like a litter drawn by an enormous black draft horse, its white feathered feet pawing the steamy ground. It whinnied at their approach, and the figure straightened up, his eyes like molten amber taking their measure.

Rhiannon's breath caught in her throat. How striking he was, tall and well muscled, his hair a thick mass of chestnut waves tinged with copper and gold in the sun curling about his earlobes and combed by the wind across his brow. He was naked but for a scant leather loin cloth, the sunlight gleaming off his sweat-slicked biceps, roped torso, and corded thighs. He was ruddy complexioned, but Rhiannon couldn't tell if that was a natural phenomenon or due to the exertion of his chore. He threw down the rake and strode toward them. Gideon was right. Nothing in the Fire Lord's demeanor fostered fear, there was something rather tragic in it.

"Well met, Gideon," he said, sketching a bow, and turned toward Rhiannon, "and Gideon's lady," he said. "You will forgive me if I do not shake your hand, my dear. I am sure Gideon has told you that would not be . . . wise."

Rhiannon offered a nod.

"What the deuce are you about with that?" Gideon asked, gesturing toward the litter and the nervous draft horse prancing in place.

"Something that can wait," Vane replied. "Let me get you two inside. It isn't safe to linger here. The watchers have been flitting about since sunup." He turned to the horse, stroking its neck and withers. "Hold, Eli," he whispered to the animal. "Do not move from the spot. . . ." The horse whipped its head around, gave the Fire Lord a playful nip on the shoulder, and bobbed its head, spreading its silky mane.

"One might think that beast understands you," Gideon observed.

"Oh, he does," Vane returned. "He will stand thus until I return. First, I get you inside, out of the watchers' view, while Marius draws their fire. Then, I will return and bring the lava rocks I've collected to your chamber for your bath. You shall stay in my spare rooms. They are seldom used, since I rarely entertain, and the rocks will heat the pool there. Meanwhile, everything will look quite natural, to the watchers' spying eyes. Come . . ."

"We shan't stay, Vane," Gideon said. "We will not bring the watchers' wrath down upon you. It's bad enough that Marius is involved. We just need time to form a plan and slip past the watchers. If we can manage that—"

Lord Vane threw his handsome head back and loosed a mighty guffaw. "Look around you!" he warbled. "What harm do you suppose the watchers' missiles could inflict upon me here, hm?" He swept his arm wide. "What damage do you think their piddling lightning bolts could do against this sleeping volcano of mine?"

"They could wake it!" Gideon pronounced in his inimitable manner, scanning the sky for any sign of the watchers.

"You have a point, my friend," Vane said. "Follow me . . ."

He walked ahead then, motioning Gideon and Rhiannon to follow, and skirted the foot of the volcano, their feet crunching in the slag that wreathed it below the hot lava rocks Vane had been collecting. Waves of heat rising from the slag gave the volcano a dizzying aura. The air was steamy hot, which was why Lord Vane's burnished bronze and all but naked body glistened with sweat. So this was how the Lord of the Fire passed the time on his volcanic isle, mining lava rocks and laboring beneath the hot Arcan sun. *It must be like living in hell,* Rhiannon opined.

Judging from the evenness of his tan, the Fire Lord labored thus scantly clad regularly. His bronzed skin showed no lines of demarcation from his neck to the heels of his bare feet. He walked with a graceful swagger, the sun beaming off the round, firm globes of his bare buttocks and muscular shoulders, defining his waist and arrow-straight spine.

Why was the legendary Lord of the Fire doing manual labor? Were there no lackeys to take on such chores? Were there no other inhabitants on the isle, come to that? She hadn't seen any since they'd arrived. Questions flooded her mind. Things were definitely not as they seemed, but there was no time to address that then. Gideon's eyes were trained skyward, and she'd had enough experience with watchers to know that just because one didn't see them didn't mean they weren't there.

Outcroppings of lava rock jutting from the base of the volcano were flung like a casual arm eastward into a stand of scrub pine. *Poor dwarfed-looking things,* Rhiannon thought.

"Do spirits live in these pines as well?" she asked of neither of them in particular.

It was Gideon who replied. "No," he said, "those who once occupied these trees are . . . gone now."

Both Gideon and Vane stopped in their tracks. Rhiannon didn't miss the strange sidelong glance that passed between them. She had evidently touched on a topic that was forbidden, and she said no more.

After a moment, they resumed their pace and came upon a rock formation that at first look seemed like something an eruption had left there. Following Vane through an opening that was virtually invisible to the untrained eye, they found themselves inside a well-appointed chamber.

"Rest here," Vane said. "I shall go and bring the lava rocks I was gathering when you arrived. They are to warm your pool." He gestured toward a small archway. "It's through there. This dwelling is separate from the rest, and therefore not fed by the volcano directly. I repair here often. It's cooler. The lava rocks will heat it pleasantly. Remain inside during the day. I will join you later with food and we will see what's to be done."

"You are too kind, my friend," Gideon said, "but we cannot stay here. We shan't put you to the hazard. The watchers are relentless this time. I haven't seen them like this since they destroyed my keep. I won't have you suffer reprisals for helping us. We will leave when the sun sets."

Vane nodded. "As you wish," he said. "Meanwhile, whatever I can do, consider it done."

Lord Vane left them then, and Gideon took her in his arms. "I can battle the watchers on my own easily," he said. "I've been doing it for eons. It is your safety that troubles me. I would leave you here. You would be perfectly safe with Vane, but I also left you in Marius's keeping and look what occurred."

"You mustn't fault Marius. I should have stayed where I was safe. I shan't make that mistake again, but I don't want you to leave me, Gideon—not for moment. If they separate us and play to our weaknesses, they could win. Whatever we are facing, we need to stay together."

"I can't get enough of you," he murmured against her hair. "It started out as the curse that has damned me to perpetual lust and turned my own body against me, but now, oh, *now* . . . it's not that at all. Every breath I take is for love of you, Rhiannon, and I fear only that I could well be putting you in danger because of it."

Rhiannon silenced him with a finger across his lips. He drew it into his mouth, and she moaned as he laved it with his tongue. The sound of his wings rustling riddled her with expectant fire in anticipation of ecstasy to come. The magnificent appendages had unfurled halfway, just as they always did when he was aroused, and when he pulled her close, the bruising pressure of his hardness leaned heavily against her belly. The soreness would linger long after they made love, reminding her of the power of his passion and the magnificence of his member.

All at once, she stiffened in his arms. "Wait..." she murmured. "I heard something..."

Gideon hesitated, his ears pricked, listening. "I don't hear anything," he said, pulling her close again.

"There! I heard it again... a rustling sound."

Gideon smiled. "Field mice, no doubt," he said. "It's too soon for Vane to be returning with the lava rocks, but not if we waste it." He reached for her lips, but she resisted still.

"Is there a rear entrance to this place?" she said. "The noise I heard sounded like it was coming from beyond that arch, where Lord Vane said the pool was."

"I am not certain," Gideon responded. "He's virtually alone here, though. Few will risk the threat of an erupting volcano, or the company of one whose touch could turn them into a human torch."

Rhiannon gasped. She'd heard the legends, but she'd never had it explained so vividly before. "His touch did not set that horse on fire," she pointed out.

"No, but if he had been aroused or in a rage, it would have, along with anything or anyone he touched."

"Well, I doubt he was aroused or in a rage when we met. Why did he refuse to take my hand?"

Gideon laughed. "Your innocence delights me," he said. "For all your loss of sexual naïveté, you have not lost that wide-eyed childlike innocence that so often is lost with it. Silly goose, the Lord of the Fire is a *man* after all, and the mere sight of you—especially as you are now, in that flimsy veil that hides nothing—is enough to make a dead man's member rise! He was merely being cautious, and well he ought. Now, enough of Vane! *I* am on fire for you. Let us deal with that."

He began sliding the frock down over her shoulders, but again Rhiannon hesitated. "Shouldn't we wait?" she asked. "What if he comes back and catches us?"

"Trust that such a thing shan't happen," Gideon said, circling one hard nipple with the tip of his finger and then his tongue as he sucked it through the spider silk frock. The sensual wetness remained, pebbling her areola, laving and scraping her nipple through the gauze long after he lifted his lips. She had never felt the like. "Lord Vane has given us this time together," he went on, nipping at the other hardened bud. Besides, worry over that happening should heighten our pleasure. There is something very erotic about being caught in the act, as it were."

She melted against him, no longer able to resist the pull of the fiery sexual tether crackling between them. It seemed enhanced since they arrived on the Isle of Fire, with its visible heat and sultry atmosphere. The whole isle seemed to pulsate like a living, breathing entity, its steamy pink breath rising from the volcano looming above. The very air smelled of brimstone and felt hot to breathe, like the heat of a scorching day in summer, when no breath of a breeze is stirring and there was no relief in sight. It was the kind of heat that scorched the nostrils inside and out, paralyzed the senses, and ignited sexual desire. It had consumed them both with its magical fire.

All thoughts of rustling sounds, of watchers, and of the peril they were in melted in the blistering heat of that moment. Her gown floated to the floor and puddled at her feet. Gideon had opened the front of his eel skin. Driving her to her knees, he offered his aroused sex. Rhiannon took it in her hands and guided it into her mouth.

Gideon groaned as she laved his shaft from root to tip. Rhiannon felt it harden like steel beneath her tongue, felt his blood pumping through the distended veins. They were standing out in bold relief through the silken skin as she took him deeply in a swift, spiraling motion that brought his wings fully open, stirring in the steamy air.

She had avoided the sensitive tip of his penis as she sucked. Tasting the salt of his pre-come, she slowed her rhythm. She could feel the pulse beat of his passion through the tip of her tongue as it circled the rim of the head of his sex. The anxious rhythm of his desire vibrated through her body and soul.

Groaning again, Gideon took back his penis and raised her to her feet. Seizing the globes of her buttocks, he hoisted her up and plunged into her to the base of his shaft, grinding himself against her, undulating from side to side as he raised and lowered her in an unstoppable frenzy of carnal oblivion.

Rhiannon cried out as she clung to him. The root of his sex was grinding against her clitoris. As he pistoned into her, the curve of his shaft found that innermost spot—that hidden mystery of succulent sensation that opened her to him like the petals of a rose. One layer at a time, his passion peeled away the layers until, full blown, the flower of her sex, wet with the juices of her climax, exploded in wave upon wave of orgasmic fire.

Rhiannon felt as if her bones were melting. Her breath was coming short, her heart hammering against him in a shuddering rhythm that captured her breath and held it. She could feel his climax building through her fingertips, through the pores in her skin, slick with the glistening patina the sweat of raw sex had left behind. When she stroked his wings, a cry like nothing she had ever heard him utter poured from his throat. It mellowed into a shuddering timbre, a gravel-voiced supplication in the shape of her name that rang from the rafters of the little chamber that neither of them had even noticed for the urgency of their coupling.

Surges of drenching fire ripped through Rhiannon's loins as the climax lifted her out of herself. The involuntary spasms of her release gripped his penis until she'd milked him dry of every pearly drop of his come.

As if she floated on cresting waves of the sea, Rhiannon let the rhythm of his climax take her again. Oh, how he filled her, even now. Fused to his dynamic body, she was powerless against the riveting surges of climactic sensation that riddled her mercilessly. His enormous wings folded around her, cocooning her to him in a whoosh of eiderdown softness, and she burrowed into them like a child snuggles beneath a comforting blanket. How safe she felt under the protection of those wings.

Gideon didn't withdraw himself. Instead, he dropped his head down to her shoulder, groaning as the hot breath puffing from his nostrils ruffled his feathers. His evocative scent rushed at her laced with the piquant musk of sex, stirring her senses awake again. Now she did begin to fear that Lord Vane would return and catch them out. Gideon was right. There was something erotic about the prospect that someone might see them thus. It made her heart race and her sex thicken with arousal.

Neither spoke. There was no need. Like dancers, their bodies moved and swayed and undulated as one, their moans resonating in the breathless air like living things. Gideon found her lips and slid his skilled tongue between her teeth, tasting her deeply. She could taste his arousal and feel the palpitations fresh erection brought to bear. It was even more powerful than the first, and her heart began to race with new ecstasy.

From somewhere far away, she could have sworn she heard that rustling sound again, and her heart leapt. Had Lord Vane returned? Was he hidden in the shadow-steeped umbra that surrounded them, watching? A strange thrill surged through her at that prospect, but it soon passed. In that one perfect, suspended blink in the eye of time, there was no danger. Lord Vane didn't exist—no one did. The moment was theirs alone, and Rhiannon surrendered to his kiss, and to the urgency of a need that took her again and again.

15

"You are sure your lady won't go prowling about on her own?" Vane queried of Gideon. They had repaired to the Fire Lord's sanctum sanctorum in the base of the volcano. From there, Vane could monitor the pulse—the very heart of the fiery mountain, which was vital not only to the Isle of Fire, but to all the isles in the Arcan Archipelago, as Gideon knew well from past catastrophes. For it was an eruption eons ago that had turned the Dark Isle into a virtual slag heap.

"She will not venture forth," said Gideon, who remained standing, his wings being prohibitive. "She did that in Marius's keeping, and I had to enlist the aid of the rune caster to have her back from the astral realm when the jealous sprites crossed her over."

"I wish I had your confidence," Vane returned. He had dressed as appropriately as one could dress in such a steamy climate. He was stripped to the waist, over tight-fitting raw silk leggings and high-top buckskin boots of the same type Marius wore. Gideon could see he was uncomfortable in his finery. But for company, the Lord of the Flames would be going about quite contentedly in the altogether.

"I needed to have this conversation with you in private," Gideon said. "We are in far more danger than Rhiannon imagines, and I do not want to frighten her any more than she is already."

"Umm," Vane gargled around a swallow of grog from his goblet.

"How can you drink this stuff?" Gideon wondered, eyeing the contents of his cup dubiously.

Vane lifted the ruby glass goblet to the rushlight flame as in salute. "Liquid sanity, my friend," he said, twirling it to and fro between his thumb and forefinger. " 'Tis what makes life bearable here in the bowels of hell." He dipped his finger into the glass and stirred the brew. Steam rose from the goblet and the grog began to bubble. "Tastes better warmed," he said, raising his finger. "Allow me?" he offered.

Gideon's eyebrow shot up. "Thank you, no," he declined. "Mine is . . . fine as it is." He hadn't visited the Fire Lord in some time, and the sight of him thus was painful to view. He couldn't imagine the loneliness of Vane's existence, but neither could he have imagined his own, if it were happening to someone else, and he lived that on a daily basis.

"There isn't much chance for socializing here on my isle," Vane drawled, "but then, I'm sure you know all about that."

"At least you have an isle," Gideon chortled. "This last escapade of mine left me homeless. Are there no others here with you now?"

Vane shook his head that there were not and took another rough swallow from his goblet.

"I ask," Gideon resumed, "because Rhiannon thought she heard something moving about in the pool area of our chamber. I know it couldn't have been you, you'd just left us . . ."

"No, it wasn't me. I wanted to give you two some privacy. The gods only know when you'll get another opportunity as things stand."

"And I thank you for it. I didn't hear anything, but she seemed so certain. Is there a rear entrance to that chamber?"

"Yes," said Vane. "It isn't easily accessed, but there is a way out. I should have shown you. I will when we return." He hesitated, twirling his goblet. "What are you going to do?" he asked.

Gideon sighed. "I can't impose upon Marius further. I fear for the Ancient Ones he protects. He is a fearless sort, is Marius. He fired upon a couple of watchers—hit them, too!"

"Did he?" Vane warbled. "I'd have loved to have seen it."

"There are bound to be reprisals, and I won't have them on my conscience. Simeon would shelter us in a heartbeat, but neither of us could exist beneath the waves. And I cannot impose upon you. Your situation here is volatile enough without my adding to it. I fear this respite you've allowed us may have already brought the retribution of the gods to bear."

"Suppose you let me worry about that," Vane said. "What about the mainland?"

"Too close, and I would be too conspicuous there, though Rhiannon would fare well. That is what troubles my conscience. I love her, Vane. I should have let her go long ago, but I waited because there was one who was a threat to her on her ship when it ran aground in that storm. I wanted to be sure he'd moved on before I left her unprotected . . . and now it's too late. I'd rather die here now than lose her."

"What about the nomads in the hills?"

"The watchers can reach the nomads. They can reach everywhere in the twelve hemispheres."

"But they won't bother you as long as you're not . . . in the company of a woman . . ."

"No, they won't—at least they never have before."

"Will you hear advice?"

"I will hear," Gideon said, "but I make no promise to heed it."

"Fair enough," Vane said, refilling his goblet from a decanter on the table alongside his Glastonbury chair. He offered more to Gideon, but Gideon declined, still nursing the drink Vane had given him earlier, and wondering what the Fire Lord saw in the dreadful stuff. "There is something you are overlooking," Vane went on cautiously. "You are immortal; she is not. She will age and she will die, and you will not." Again, Vane hesitated. "There are . . . other . . . women, Gideon. There have been in the past, and there will be in the future . . . but not if you force the gods to end your existence at last—or worse yet, force them to end *hers* to punish you, which would be more likely."

"What makes you the sage in these matters all of a sudden, old friend?" Gideon snapped. The mere thought of losing Rhiannon in such a horrific manner was more than he could bear. "Are you drunk? Are you in league with them, too—the damnable watchers—with the gods themselves, perhaps? What have they promised you to bring me low?"

Vane vaulted out of his chair as if he'd been launched from a catapult. His startling amber eyes glowed like molten lava in the lamp light. Gideon could see the Fire Lord's aura—blood red—rising in heat waves from his body. He seemed to have burst into flame. Rage flared his nostrils, and he brandished the goblet.

"This damnable stuff makes me a sage in these matters, Lord of the Dark!" he seethed. "You think that I am in my cups?" He loosed a spate of raucous laughter and heaved the goblet—grog and all—across the room. It landed against the wall with a clang that echoed, its contents dripping down the chipped plasterwork. The sound ran Gideon through. "*You* are the drunken one—besotted upon the fruit of the vine called *love madness*! How dare you accuse me of such disloyalty? By the gods, you go too far!"

Gideon set down his goblet and raised his hands in a gesture of truce. "Forgive me," he said, raking his hands through his hair as if he meant to keep his brain from bursting. "I am half mad with this. You think I have not thought of what you say? You think it does not haunt me waking and sleeping?" His cock was hard against the seam of his eel-skin suit, and he struck it a harder blow than he'd intended with his fist. "Bad enough the curse keeps me in a state of perpetual hardness!" he raved. "Bad enough that I cannot bear the touch of the wind that carries me aloft without an attack of libidinous lust—bad enough that my own body betrays me, but now the mere sight of her drives me mad. It isn't only the curse of the gods that keeps me hard any longer. I need her, Vane, and I mean to have her!"

Vane's anger was palpable. Gideon could feel the heat of it reaching toward him from across the room. He had no idea why he'd said what he'd said. It wasn't like him at all. He must be running mad. There was no other explanation. After a moment, the Fire Lord's breathing sought a calmer level, and he began to resemble something other than a fire-breathing dragon. Gideon was well aware that Lord Vane, Prince of the Flames, took his loyalties seriously. He had little left but his fierce integrity. Gideon could not imagine what had possessed him to challenge it.

"Very well," Vane said. "If you must have this woman, would you be willing to give up your immortality to do so?"

"Whatever I must do," Gideon said before the Fire Lord's words were barely out.

"Then that is where you begin," Vane said. "You know what you are willing to sacrifice if needs must—"

"If the gods will allow me," Gideon corrected him. "Judging from the events of the past few hours, it does not bode well."

Vane poured himself another goblet. He heaved a mammoth sigh. "I have no right to advise you," he said. "I do not know the lady. But from the light in her eyes when she gazed at you earlier, it is clear that she loves you, Gideon. I would give my eyes to see a woman gaze at me thus . . . just once. And if I had such a love, I would destroy it. That is *my* curse, my friend."

"When I leave here at sunset, I have no idea where I will take her," Gideon said, attempting to change the subject. It needed changing. His dilemma had brought the Fire Lord's own situation to the fore, and that was the last thing Gideon wanted. "I need to see her to safety. I fear the watchers will use her to get at me, and I cannot let that happen. I do not presume to imagine I have reached your isle undetected. You said you saw them hovering this morning. That is no accident. They lurk in wait. I know them well."

"Then we must find a way to spoil their strategy," Vane said buoyantly. He had come out of his dark reverie suddenly. "I will pour us each another goblet and we shall see what we shall see, um?"

Rhiannon fell asleep the moment she curled up in the mahogany sleigh bed where she waited for Gideon in Lord Vane's guest chamber. It was made with sheets of the finest silk, and quilts of eiderdown, no doubt gleaned from the sea after shipwrecks like the one that had claimed the *Pegasus* and begun her strange odyssey among the enchanted isles.

Her eyes had no sooner closed when dreams came, soft, tender visions of gliding airborne in Gideon's arms on zephyr winds high above the cottony clouds that hovered over the archipelago. She could hear the air whispering through the Dark Lord's wings, feel the kiss of those silvery white feathers against her bare skin, for she was naked in his arms, and he had cocooned her against his likewise naked body as he soared higher still.

His hands roamed her curves, finding all her pleasure points, lingering upon the ones that set her heart racing and turned her bones to jelly. She felt him grow hard. His thick shaft bruising her belly sent waves of silken fire through her loins. She undulated against him, making him harder still, wrenching a husky moan from his throat as he took her lips in a fiery kiss that stole her breath away. Literally.

She had dreams before when she couldn't open her eyes, when she couldn't scream, or run, but she had never had one where she couldn't breathe. Making matters worse, Gideon's flight pattern changed abruptly. All at once he was spiraling downward. She could feel the rush of air from the wind his motion created. Why wouldn't her eyes open? Why couldn't she breathe? It felt as if something thick and hard was clamped over her mouth. That was why she couldn't breathe! *A hand!*

Rhiannon's eyes snapped open. She was in motion, but not soaring through the air. He was carrying her through the doorway out into the twilight. His arms were strong, but they weren't Gideon's arms. His long-legged stride was surefooted, but it wasn't Gideon's stride. The hand clamped over her mouth was powerful, but it wasn't Gideon's hand. This hand was foul. It smelled of strong spirits. It pinched her cheeks and prevented her scream as her eyes focused. Blinking back the last veils of sleep, she stared, not into Gideon's mercurial eyes but into Rolf's dark glare instead, and it wasn't a dream! The nightmare was real, and she struggled against his hold upon her with all her strength.

"Stop that!" he snapped, carrying her through the scrub at the base of the volcano. "You thought you could escape me? I know what you've been up to with that . . . creature. Don't think to deny it. I've *seen* you fornicating with him, and he isn't even human! Well, that's ended now, my pretty." Kicking her feet wildly, she wriggled out of his arms, but his hand over her mouth remained firmly in place and he dragged her along instead, a good grip on her hair wrapped around his arm. "I used to want you for myself," he grunted, "but no more . . . not after what I've seen! You wouldn't spread your legs for me, but you spread them wide enough for whatever that creature is. . . ."

Rhiannon's trapped screams sounded more like squeaks trying to escape her throat. His hand forced over her mouth pressing up against her nostrils as well had cut off so much air she'd become lightheaded and feared she'd lose consciousness. She clawed wildly at his hands, wrists, and arms, but her hair was wound around them and she couldn't get a good grip.

"We might have had a good life together if you'd been . . . willing," he panted, for she was putting up a valiant struggle. "Now I have a much more lucrative plan in mind. I visited your intended—the gentleman your father had sold you to—and he is willing to pay handsomely to have me deliver you to him relatively unscathed. Oh, but that's not to say I won't take a little of what that winged creature's been getting before I turn you over. Hold still! I've a skiff in the cove waiting to take us to the mainland . . . for starters . . . He won't mind my sampling your wares, as it were, along the way, but I shouldn't want to leave too many marks on you in the process. He was most particular about that."

Terror gave Rhiannon strength, and she bit down upon the hand Rolf had clamped over her mouth with all her strength, drawing blood. He jerked his hand away and cried out, lowering the back of it hard across her face. Raw fright loosed a troop of screams from Rhiannon's throat that reverberated off the steep sides of the volcano, rupturing the twilight silence.

While he soothed the bite on his hand, some of her hair fell away from his arms where he'd wound it to secure her, and she snatched it back, raised her foot, and struck him a brutal blow to the groin.

Doubled over in pain, Rolf let her go, and Rhiannon ran

screaming through the darkness. Overhead, the stars had just begun to show in the indigo vault. The moon had not yet risen, it was blocked by the volcano, tinting the issue rising from the cone with an eerie pink glow. Great tufts of the smoke belched into the sky. It wasn't until then that Rhiannon noticed the sparks and bits of burning matter spewing from the mouth of the fiery mountain. Neither had she realized until then that she was climbing upward over the hot gritty slag that made up the face of the volcano. There was really no other direction open to her with Rolf in close pursuit, hurling blasphemies after her as she fled.

Her gossamer gown was torn in spots and trailing tatters at the hem. It hung off her shoulder, baring more than she wanted Rolf to view. Her bare feet scarcely touched down long enough between steps to feel the heat of the slope she climbed. Her entire focus was escaping Rolf, and praying that her screams would bring Gideon.

By the time she neared the summit, her stamina was flagging. Rolf was gaining on her, and her screams had reached fever pitch. It was one thing when he wanted her for himself. Now, she had monetary value, and Rolf was obsessed with money. He would never give up until he'd had his way with her, until he'd delivered her to the odious individual her father had sold her to, and collected his handsome bonus.

Rhiannon had been hoping against hope that Gideon would come, that Rolf would back off when she reached the summit, but her strategy failed her on both counts and Rolf seized her just as she teetered on the brink. She was caught in her own trap with nowhere to go but down into a roiling pit of molten rock. They struggled on the edge, not only with each other, but with a sudden wind that had risen, and with the intense heat of the volcano that had changed the shape of the archipelago many times in the past about to erupt again.

Just when she feared she could struggle no more, another wind arose, and the flapping sound of a thousand birds rushed at her from all sides. But it wasn't birds, it was Gideon's massive wings, and a surge of new strength broke her free of Rolf's grip, with another blow to his groin.

"Get down!" Gideon thundered.

She needed no encouragement to follow that order. Exhausted, she dropped to her knees on the rim of the volcano. Below, great explosions of molten lava rising slowly challenged the sides of the cone. Bubbles spat from the surface, blood red and white hot. It was about to explode.

Rhiannon dropped to her knees as another flash of light caught her eyes. Rolf had a knife. Hovering on the brink in the steamy air, half hidden in the plumes of smoke belching from the volcano, he was slashing at Gideon. All at once, the Dark Lord surged upward avoiding a swipe of the blade that nearly met its mark. He had no weapon to fight with but his body, and to Rhiannon's wide-eyed horror for fear it wouldn't be enough, he spun and shot back down, striking Rolf a blow to the chest with his feet that pitched him over the edge and into the boiling lava below.

Screaming at the top of her voice, Rhiannon scrambled to her feet as Gideon seized her in strong arms and lifted off with her cocooned as she had been in her dream.

"Get you down!" he called to Vane, whom Rhiannon hadn't even seen until that moment. The Fire Lord had climbed up as well and stood on the brink of the angry volcano, its roar and burning breath ruffling his hair and billowing his shirt tinted crimson in the moonlight. "*Now*, Vane!" Gideon commanded, spiraling away from the intense heat rising from the lava flow. "It has its sacrifice. The gods alone know if it is enough."

They soared off then, leaving Vane on the brink. There was

no danger. The fire lord had tended his volcano for eons. He would know what to do and when the risk was too great to put life and limb to the hazard. Looking on, Rhiannon gasped. It was almost as if Lord Vane was baiting the fiery mountain—as if he challenged it to bury him in the lava that he had battled since time out of mind.

"Do not fear," Gideon whispered in her ear, as she craned her neck watching Vane in the distance. "Vane knows what he is about. You are safe now. Hang on to me!"

Streaking through the night sky, Gideon swooped down and set her on her feet in a patch of scrub pine in lee of the fiery mountain. Evidently, for all his reassuring words, he wanted to be certain Lord Vane was safe before leaving him at the mercy of the elements.

He no sooner touched down, when he seized her, his trembling hands flying over her body. "Are you harmed?" he said. "Has he . . . molested you? *Answer me!*"

Rhiannon's breath caught in her throat. Gideon was like a wild man, his eyes flashing mercury-tinted red in the glow of the volcano. They flitted over her body from head to toe again and again, as if he didn't trust them to present him with a true image.

"N-no," Rhiannon stammered. "He was hiding in that chamber. He was stalking us! I told you I heard something!"

He crushed her close. "I never should have left you alone," he murmured. He was aroused, his hardness forced against her as he crushed her closer still. His wings were half unfurled. Hot breath puffing from his flared nostrils scorched her cheek, and his heart was hammering against her. His feathers were practically standing on end from passion and ordeal. Rhiannon longed to smooth them, but she dared not. When such an unstoppable frenzy came upon him, the merest pressure upon those magnificent wings would bring him to a riveting climax.

Instead, she threw her arms around his neck and wrapped her legs around his narrow waist.

Seizing her buttocks, Gideon rushed her against the slender trunk of one of the taller scrub pines and opened his eel skin, exposing his thick, hard penis. His mouth was hot, like liquid silk, as he took her lips in a fiery kiss. It buried a trail from the deep recesses of her throat to the innermost depths of her womb, spreading wave upon wave of achy heat through her belly and thighs. The firestorm of insatiable need peeled back layer upon layer of her innermost folds, like petals opening for him from the inside out, until her clitoris hardened like steel, begging to be touched.

Overhead, the sky glowed with an eerie blood-red hue as great plumes of belching fire shot from the volcano into the night. The heat of the eruption was visible in waves rising from the heap of slag that rose to the top of the inferno. Neither Rhiannon nor Gideon noticed. Their oblivion was such that all they could see was each other, the visible waves of their own body heat rising from their skin, and the desire in their eyes devouring each other. All they could feel was the drenching fire of their volatile embrace.

This was the curse of the gods at its worse, for it not only used his own body against him, it was in league with the palpable passion of their love. It blinded them both to all that went on around them. It made them oblivious of the danger of lava spewing out of the volcano, oozing down over the mountain of slag to the shore, where it emptied in a hissing, spitting rush into the bay. It rendered them impervious to the imminent threat of earthquakes and tidal surges it would spawn. But worst of all, it blinded them to the two silhouettes hovering overhead, their wings tinted blood red against the indigo vault.

Rhiannon guided his shaft along the rim of her nether lips.

Riding her wetness, Gideon undulated against her, going deeper with each thrust, but not enough to penetrate. Excruciating ecstasy. There was almost a feeling of desperation in their embrace, as Gideon's wings slowly unfurled. Rhiannon leaned into his gyrations. She could feel the hot silken head of his penis as he moved deeper along the curve of her opening. She could feel the rim that defined the mushroom tip, and the distended veins, feel the blood pumping through them to the rhythm of his ragged heartbeat as his shaft rubbed against her from clitoris to anus.

His hot hardness was more than she could bear. Lost in the power of a passion that had captivated her from the very start, the infectious urgency that had joined them soul to soul, she melted against him. Unable to hold back any longer, he raised her buttocks and plunged into her, grinding the thick root of his sex against the bud of her clitoris until she cried out in a rush of husky pleasure moans.

The lightning bolt hit them both directly this time, stunning Rhiannon and pitching Gideon over in the smoldering patch of scrub pine the missile had ignited. Gideon's agonized groan ran her through like a javelin. She tried to rise but fell back down, the heat of the ground rushing at her now that awareness of her surroundings was trickling back. Glaring white pinpoints of light starred her vision. Her head reeled dizzily. Gideon's groans bled into the fringes of her fast-fading consciousness, and she called out to him, the sound of her voice so desperate she could scarcely believe it was coming from her own throat.

Then all at once she felt herself lifted into the air, felt it bear her up above the volcano spewing great streams of lava skyward, above the radiant heat rising from the holocaust the Fire Isle had become, above Gideon writhing in the smoldering scrub pines. *Gideon!* For one wonderful moment, she'd thought it was he who had hold of her, but no. Sight of the Dark Lord lying doubled over in the undergrowth below, his crumpled wings tinted red by the lava flow as if they were bleeding, all but stopped her heart. He lay so still. It was as if he were dead, and she screamed his name at the top of her voice as the watcher who gripped her none too gently carried her high above the fiery mass of lava and slag, and spirited her away.

16

*H*e *is gone*, a disembodied voice ghosted across Gideon's mind. *It is too late. We should have intervened long ago.*

The other sighed. *He will rally, watch . . .*

The first speaker heaved a gusty sigh. *And what of the other?*

Lord Vane is not our concern, the second voice said. *He has dealt with far worse than this in eons past, and will again, so my scrying tells me. The Prince of Flames has the power to self-combust to fight the volcano. Look! He makes of himself a human backfire to stay the lava flow when, like now, sacrifice is not enough to appease the gods who live within the fiery mountain.*

The first speaker sighed again. *These accursed islands are the playgrounds of the gods.*

And the lords who tend them are their pawns, the other observed. *See? He stirs, the dark one. There will be hell to pay now.*

Where has the watcher taken his lady? the first speaker asked.

The other hesitated, then said, *Into Outer Darkness.*

But I thought the watchers could not enter Outer Darkness! the first speaker said a little too loudly.

Shhh! the other warned. *They cannot.*

Then . . . how?

The other grunted, clearly out of patience. *They have their minions who can. Enough now! See? He wakes, and he has heard us . . . !*

Gideon groaned awake, the words *Outer Darkness* ringing in his ears. He tried to rise and failed. Searing pain ripped through his crimped left wing, trailing smoke where the watcher's lightning bolt had struck it. Blood was seeping out between the feathers. He groaned again, shaking his head like a dog to clear his vision, but the motion only grieved his wing and made his head ache.

A watcher still hovered overhead, making flamboyant gestures with his hands as if he were juggling with the snake lightning passing between them. The creature's intent was plain. The moment Gideon slithered into position to rise, the watcher aimed his missile with intent to hurl it. Gideon roared like a lion, pounding the slag beneath him with clenched fists, but blinding pain doubled him over with the effort, and he couldn't lift off. His wing was too severely damaged.

"I know where you've taken her!" he thundered, his fist raised against the watcher poised overhead. "You think I won't follow her to hell itself if needs must. What? You think I fear darkness?" He loosed a mad, misshapen laugh. "Fool! I am *lord* of it!" he cried.

Watchers never spoke, at least they never had to him, and this one was no exception. The lightning was their voice, and the creature hurled another searing white-hot bolt down, missing him by inches, though he felt its heat and shrank from it.

Gideon roared again. Not only was the pain in his wing

more than he could bear, he was aroused, just as he always was when his wings were touched; it mattered not whether the caress was one of passion or of pain. The wound was deep, and his cock was throbbing in an erratic rhythm, his heart pounding so violently, he feared it would burst through his chest. This is what the nymphs and the Ancient Ones that lived in their ancestral trees had helped him overcome in Marius's forest. This was what they soothed, with their carnal ministrations, relieving the pressure in his cock that the watchers' missiles had set loose upon him, pressure that he had been too weak to relieve himself.

He could almost feel the softness of their hands stroking his shaft from root to tip, and the fluttering of their anxious tongues laving him, the deep, dark mystery of their sex gripping him each in their turn, milking him, making him come to relieve the terrible agony and ecstasy the lightning bolts inflicted upon him. Time was when he used to look forward to their ministrations, for there had been sexual pleasure in it. Lately, since Rhiannon, their tending had become more therapeutic than sexual, like it had been the last time in the forest, when the Ancient Ones had cradled him so the nymphs could perform their services. That episode had begun the current nightmare. If only it had been Rhiannon's hands upon his engorged penis. If only it had been her lips laving him instead of the jealous nymphs', and her sex milking him of every drop of the damnable come the age-old curse had brought to bear, none of this would be happening.

But the nymphs were a clever lot. They had spirited him away before Rhiannon ever realized what they were about. Unconscious, Gideon had no idea what was happening either, until it was too late. And now, for all his brave words earlier, he feared he might never see Rhiannon again.

Overhead, the watcher gloated, pacing in the steamy red air as it flitted back and forth, toying with its lightning bolt.

Gideon had no doubt that it would hurl the damnable thing at him if he made an attempt to rise. But time was passing. Every second was carrying Rhiannon farther and farther away from him. She had already disappeared from sight. The last glimpse he had of her struggling in the watcher's arms as it soared off into the fiery, smoke-filled sky had left an indelible stain upon his memory that threatened to drive him mad.

What sort of obscene test was this that the gods had inflicted upon him? What depraved deity had devised this torture of tortures? In total aberration, he screamed Rhiannon's name at the top of his voice. It echoed back in his ears above the rumble of the volcano spewing lava, above the crackle and roar of flaming slag, and the echo of the bay, for it had risen from its bed in a tidal surge that brought towering waves nearly as tall as the fiery mountain itself crashing toward the shore.

Hissing, steaming waves gobbled up the shoreline foreshortening the strand, sucking the sand back into the water until it lapped relentlessly at the very foot of the volcano that had spawned the devastation. The sounds of Nature at its most powerful raised gooseflesh over Gideon's spine, for he above all knew the power of the elements enraged. He had seen it all before and become one with it—an elemental of the air that carried him aloft, a plaything of the gods, and of the mother of all that was and is and ever would be in Nature, the essence of his being, and his curse.

He was not near the lava flow, and yet the heat of it was suddenly fierce enough to scorch him. Glancing about through eyes narrowed from heat and pain, he searched for the cause of the sudden rush of blistering discomfort, only to stare slack-jawed at what was generating it. A blazing column of what could only be described as white-hot rage was streaking down the mountain. Lord Vane was in the middle of it, his arms raised in an attitude that expanded his already gargantuan posture enhanced by the radiant glow rising from his fiery body.

The heat of the Fire Lord's approach was almost unbearable. The rush that preceded it all but closed Gideon's eyes. Shielding them from the glare, he watched in stunned amazement as Vane's raised arms hurled shafts of flame skyward that singed the watcher's wings and sent it careening off into the night. A troop of agonized shrieks pouring from its otherwise silent throat trailed off on the sudden wind that had risen. The sound ran Gideon through to the core.

"A moment, old friend," Vane said from the midst of the fiery column that had all but consumed his image. "That fellow won't be returning anytime soon. Give me a moment and I will help you . . . I cannot touch you yet. . . ."

Gideon could do naught but stare. He had heard of this, but he had never seen it as he did now, up close, only at a distance. He had never felt the heat of Lord Vane's combustion or seen the power it generated. Staring in rapt awe, he couldn't help but wonder how Vane made love to a woman in such a state.

"By all the gods," Gideon stammered in spite of his better judgment. "How do you . . . eh . . . that is . . . with a woman . . . how . . . ?"

"Not without reducing her to cinder and ash," Vane replied. "And you thought you had problems, did you, my fellow plaything of the gods? We keepers of the Arcan Isles are all of us damned to our own special darkness."

"There is only one darkness that concerns me now—*Outer Darkness*. That is where they have taken Rhiannon."

"I know," Vane said. "I saw. I need to see how badly that creature has hurt your wing. You will need both of them if you would follow after her."

"It bleeds badly," Gideon said. "The pain is scarcely bearable."

"Can you stand?"

Gideon made a bold attempt, then fell back down in the scrub pines.

"No matter," Vane said. "I can heal you there. Lie still for just a little longer. . . ."

Gideon tried to do as Vane bade him, but the pain in his wing and the anxiety of knowing each minute ticking by put more distance between him and Rhiannon were beyond bearing. As hard as granite, his cock was bursting, throbbing—begging for the achy heat of release. The watcher was gone, but he had left his punishment behind, just as they always did since time out of mind. There was no besting the watchers of the gods.

"How can you heal me?" he asked Vane. He couldn't imagine it.

"Once my flames have cooled enough to touch you without setting you afire, I will cauterize that wound there," Vane replied. "Then, a few days' rest and—"

"No!" Gideon cried out, his eyes trained upon the eerie blood-red sky above. "I haven't got a few days. I haven't got a few hours. Every moment I delay, she is in mortal danger. I haven't a moment to lose!"

"Outer Darkness will be there once you're fit, believe me," Vane said, reaching toward Gideon's wing. "Forgive me, old friend," he said. "But I must inflict pain if you would mend. Steel yourself . . ."

Lying on his side in the scrub, Gideon gritted his teeth against the pressure of Vane's fingers beneath the bent and crumpled feathers on the curve of his left wing. Writhing as the gut-wrenching sensations he had steeled himself against challenged his consciousness, the Dark Lord stiffened. Smoke acrid with the stench of burnt feathers rose from the ragged tear, oozing blood as Vane probed it and finally applied the pressure that seared the wound and closed it, ceasing the blood flow.

Gideon groaned. Vertigo starred his vision. Cold sweat beaded upon his brow as the stink of burnt flesh and singed feathers rushed up his nostrils. Vane almost looked like himself again, though the heat waves still rose from his naked skin, and his eyes still glowed like the molten lava that had finally ceased to slow crawling down the mountain.

"Why do you stare at the sky so?" Vane queried. "That watcher won't be back, believe me. The smell that's caused that grimace is not all from your fine feathers, Gideon. I singed a few of his as well."

"It's not that," Gideon confessed. "When this began, the rune caster took three of my feathers as payment for her auger. She said I would have them back when needs must. One floated down when I needed help bringing Rhiannon back from the astral. I was hoping . . ."

"Evidently, you have a greater trial to face before that time comes, my friend," Vane said. "Rest . . . I need to assess the damage now that the lava flow has lessened."

"Watchers cannot enter Outer Darkness," Gideon said. "How can I rest when I do not know what creature they have bribed to take Rhiannon through the gate?"

"Suit yourself," said Vane, with a shrug, "but do not ever say I didn't warn you."

"Thank you, my friend," Gideon murmured. "I am in your debt, and I have brought enough hardship down upon you tonight. I must away before more harm is done, before that watcher you just fried brings reinforcements and prevents me. I have always been the pariah of these islands, but never more than I am right now, stripped not only of my privilege, but of my home, and in grave danger of losing the woman I love. Yet I have always tried to serve the isles and those who dwell upon them for the good, because despite the curse my lust has brought to bear, I am still the creature I always was . . . an angel devoted to the gods that have cursed me. I have to find the place that will let me be that creature again . . . or let it end here. But I will do that with Rhiannon or not at all—immortal or mortal. It matters not. That is for the gods to decide."

"It amazes me that you still trust the gods!" Vane said through a rough chuckle. "I don't—not anymore, not until they let me take a woman in my arms without turning her into a human torch. I wish you well, my friend, in your quest. If you find such a place, let me know. What heaven if it could be the polar ice cap, eh? Hale and farewell, brother prince . . . until we meet again."

Gideon watched Vane stalk off then, and waited until the Fire Lord was out of sight before he attempted to rise. He felt like a wobbly-legged colt taking its first step as he rose gingerly to his feet and squared his hunched posture. He flexed his wings and took a deep, ragged breath. He'd been in worse shape. Praying that his wings were still operable, he tested them rising only a few feet off the ground before soaring off into the night.

There was no sign that watchers were near, but Gideon put no trust in that. Vane's mend in his wing was holding, but for a few bloodstained and crimped feathers it seemed as good as new. This had been the worst. Never in his memory could he recall a lightning strike drawing blood. There was no question that the punishments were becoming more and more severe. He could put an end to them by letting Rhiannon go and embracing celibacy for the rest of his eternity, but he could not—would not do that. He would have Rhiannon no matter the cost, and judging from the watchers' last reprisal, that cost may well be his life.

He was aroused. His hardness was acute between the wind his motion created rushing at his wounded wing, the residual sexual heat a lightning strike always inflicted, and the perpetual curse triggered by the merest pressure upon his feathers. Vane was right, he needed time to regenerate his strength, or barring that, he at least needed a means of release.

He rubbed the bulge in his groin in an attempt to cancel the inevitable, but it was no use. The achy fire in his loins would not be denied, and he opened the front of his eel skin and exposed his throbbing penis to the cool midnight air. Groaning, he let the night wind take him, like he had done so many times in the past. He let it caress the fiery flesh of his shaft, stroking the distended veins, bearing down upon the sensitive mushroom tip. The slightest touch of his hand would make him come, but he resisted the urge to seize his swollen penis in his fist and pump himself dry. Surrendering to the elements, he threw back his head and took the night as his lover, for he was Lord of the Dark.

And what a lover Mother Night was, with her thousand eyes winking down from the indigo vault, and the waning moon tinted red in the aftermath of the volcano's fire. She took him slowly, for he was her liege lord, and she serviced him often, and well. In the arms of Mother Night, he found solace. In her dark embrace, he escaped where the watchers could not harm him, for she was illusion, and in her dark womb he found a glimmer of peace.

The gentle wind that was her breath stroked his face, ruffled his wings, and petted his shaft as he soared through the air until his cock grew harder still, the sensitive head glazed slick with pre-come. He couldn't help but wonder, since he came to Mother Night so often for comfort, if the watchers would take this carnal fantasy from him too. But they had not interfered in all the eons she had been his lover, for she had no corporeal substance, earning no more notice than he earned relieving himself. The only trouble was, for all the comfort of the night's dark fantasy, for all the mystery of her passion, she was not lover enough.

Gideon called Rhiannon's name as the climax came, for hers was the image he saw in the wind, in the clouds massing thickly overhead, cloaking the stars and darkening the moon. Gripping his throbbing penis, he glided on a zephyr above the weather, watching the seed of his loins pulse out of him in a steady stream, watching it slow to spurts that milked him dry, blessed release from the ravages of the watchers' missiles earlier. It was all part of the curse.

Roaring like a lion, Gideon dove toward the breast of the sea below, through the heavy clouds massing steadily, through the starless darkness toward a little patch of mist that cloaked the rune caster's isle on the brink of Outer Darkness. She would know what creature had carried Rhiannon through the phallic gates that barred her captors, and he sped through the sky with the velocity of one of the watcher's missiles and touched down in a fog bank not far from the succubus's cottage.

All at once he loosed a bitter laugh. For all he knew, the watchers could have taken Rhiannon somewhere else. All he had was the word of disembodied voices whispering across his mind on the edge of consciousness that they had banished her to Outer Darkness. He didn't even know to whom the enigmatic voices belonged, only that they had served him well in the past and never misled him before. Taking a positive stand, he liked to think that they were of the gods, or gods themselves, for all humankind had guardian angels appointed them at birth to guard and protect as needs must. Even angels had such protectors, himself included. At least he had before his fall from grace, when all privilege had been stripped from him and he was cast out—cursed and alone—his light snuffed out, to serve his eternal sentence in solitary darkness.

Shaking those thoughts loose like a dog sheds water, Gideon plowed through the fog in the direction of the rune caster's cottage. No creature met him. No occupant of land or sea crossed his path or whispered across his ears pricked for just such a sound—something to tell him he was not alone on the tiny spit of land on the brink of Outer Darkness that time had forgotten.

"*Rhiannon . . .*" he called out in desperation. She was not there. If she was, his extraordinary senses would have detected her scent or picked up her aura. Nonetheless, he called out her name again, but still no answer came. It was a desperate fantasy, and he wasted no more of his breath. His lame wing was beginning to pain him again, exertion having stressed Lord Vane's mend, and he dared not soothe it and risk lust rearing its ugly head now. He was already aroused again from the rush of wind that played havoc with his wings, driving his traitorous body landward.

He plodded on, causing the ground-creeping fog to flee in little whorls as his feet disbursed it. Then the shape of a thatched roof emerged from the mist, and the cottage underneath it loomed before him, its windows, like blind eyes, blinking vacantly from some mysterious reflected light in the shadows.

Gideon's heart sank. The rune caster was gone.

17

Rhiannon curled on her side in the stern of the little punt as it glided down the river. It was a narrow ribbon of dark water, whose satiny breast danced with reflected light, from where, she could not fathom, for all around the land the river sidled through was steeped in shadow. Would it be thus when dawn broke? She had heard tales that the sun never shone upon the land beyond the phallic gates of Outer Darkness. She couldn't imagine it. The prospect chilled her to the bone.

Between her and the bow, a tall, robed figure manned the pole that moved the punt forward toward a thick, dark fog bank that stretched across the lake. She could not see the ferryman's face. The deep hood on his garment hung down in front, preventing her from viewing a sight she knew she would not welcome.

There had been a tense moment when the watcher touched down with her at the gate and deposited her in the punt. Neither spoke aloud, but their posture was easy to read. The ferryman did not want to take her without tribute, and Rhiannon had no coin to offer him. All she possessed was the tattered garment the sprites had made. An argument ensued, and Rhiannon was just about to take advantage of it, slip over the side, and swim for shore, when one of the watcher's lightning bolts cast alongside the little boat made an end to her dreams of escape. The fiery missile hit the breast of the lake in a hissing, spitting rush of angry steam, and the water began to boil. The threat of another missile drove Rhiannon back down into the bilges of the boat, while the watcher renegotiated with the ferryman.

The little punt was moving again now, toward the thick, black fog stretched across the lake ahead. Beyond that point lay Outer Darkness. Once they entered the eerie fog, the watcher could not follow, though the winged creature hovered overhead, his missile at the ready, and would, Rhiannon had no doubt, hover until the very last second.

Rhiannon blinked back tears. What lay beyond that foggy wall of drifting mist ahead too thick to penetrate with the eye? She knew what lay behind; the watchers' deadly missiles and Gideon. Would he be able to penetrate the eerie fog and follow her? Had he even survived the watchers' lightning strikes? She had taken comfort from his insistence that the watchers' missiles couldn't kill him, but he was bleeding so, and he hadn't looked conscious when the creatures carried her away. How would he know where to find her if he had survived?

The punt glided into the fog, and Rhiannon could taste her fear; it was like a separate entity, a living, breathing presence in that little boat, alive as she was. The watcher was gone, and she was almost sorry. At lease that creature hadn't meant to kill her, only to punish Gideon by taking her out of his reach. The gods alone knew what lay on the other side of the fog bank, so thick she feared it would suffocate her.

Brave with the threat of lightning bolts removed, she decided to appeal to the ferryman. "I beg you take me back!" she pleaded. "I've been brought here against my will!"

The ferryman made no reply. Scrambling to her knees, she

tugged at the end of his robe. His posture clenched, but he did not break his rhythm with the long pole as he punted along. Rhiannon scrabbled closer and tugged harder. This time the boat rocked, challenging the ferryman's balance. He turned halfway. There was no mistaking the anger in his bearing. He didn't speak. Yanking his robe out of her hands, he turned back to his chore, and the punt began to move again.

They were still inside the bleak fog bank. Gripping the ferryman's arm, Rhiannon pulled herself up alongside him. "Please . . . I beg you," she sobbed. "Take me back! Don't leave me here alone . . . in the dark . . ."

Again, the ferryman's posture clenched, but he did not respond as he dug the pole into the sandy bottom and kept his pace.

"*Please!*" Rhiannon cried. "I am nothing to you. The watcher is gone. Let me go. He will never know! Look at me! Why won't you answer me?"

But the ferryman continued to pole the punt forward, ignoring her pleas.

Not to be thwarted, Rhiannon ranged herself in front of him. No mean task, for the punt was very narrow, and it swayed in the water with her weight displaced. She could not see his face. It was veiled in shadow. Reaching up, for he was very tall, she tore the hood away and froze, a scream trapped in her throat, for there was no one inside it. The cloth she gripped fell away to puddle at her feet in the bilges.

The scream growing in Rhiannon's throat did escape then. Loud and shrill, it echoed over the breast of dark water that suddenly started to rise, taking the punt under; then it was gone—ferryman, pole and all—and she was floundering in deep, dark water.

Panic gripped her like an iron fist. This was no place to test her lacking swimming skills. She'd even been somewhat uncomfortable bathing in the deep end of Gideon's pool when she first attempted it. She'd gained more confidence once she realized there were sections of the pool where her feet would touch bottom. That didn't seem likely here. She could feel the water rushing beneath her feet and she dared not test it and confirm her worst fears. It was cold . . . so cold, not steamy warm and welcoming like it had been in the pool chamber, and it was in motion, taking her breath away, making her hyperventilate when she tried to scream again. A rush of the frigid water poured into her mouth, choking her instead. The cold, salty flow flooded her airway. Adrenaline surged through her body. Her strength was flagging. The weight of her long, thick hair was dragging her down. She couldn't catch her breath. She was drowning!

All at once, the fog began to lift, not a moment too soon. Had she drifted beyond it? Frantically, she scanned the drifting mist in search of a direction—a spit of land—a glimpse of shoreline—anything that would give her hope. She was struggling with what she was certain was her last breath when she saw it, a dark silhouette against a darker sky—*land!* But it was too far away to reach by swimming, even for a strong swimmer.

Gingerly, she stretched one leg, feeling for the bottom, praying that something firm would touch her toes, but there was only water, dark and murky black beneath her. With all hope gone, she lost the balance she'd maintained and slipped beneath the surface. Once, twice, she sank, then rallied one last time, screaming Gideon's name at the top of her hoarse voice before she sank a third time and then came up no more.

Gideon paced back and forth in front of the rune caster's vacant cottage, troubling the mist with his heavy footfalls, and long wings sweeping the ground. Where was Lavilia? She must know he had need of her counsel. He hated the way she toyed with him, like a cat toys with a mouse. He paid tenfold for whatever information he managed to pry out of her. It had always been thus, and he'd gone along with the game, but not this time, not when Rhiannon's life was in danger.

He had one question left, and she still had two of his feathers, which she'd promised to return when he needed them. Three opportunities? Possibly. He needed answers now. Lavilia had those answers. She must have known he'd come seeking them. Where had she gone? Or, *had* she gone? She was a shapeshifter after all, and she had been too afraid to face him the last time as well, until the very last.

One had to be very careful how one handled the rune caster. Emboldened by hope that the mistress of illusion was hiding again in plain sight, Gideon chose a direct approach. *"Lavilia!"* he thundered. "I know you're here. Show yourself! I have no time for your games tonight!"

"Bravo, Lord of the Dark!" her disembodied voice echoed. "Your sight is improving. What brings you here this time, eh? Have you come to ask your last question? Well, speak up! You haven't all night. Time is wasting . . ."

Gideon spun in all directions, his wings half unfurled, but nothing except the mist met his eyes. "Still afraid to face me then?" he observed. "I wonder why? Are you in league with the watchers? I've long thought it."

"You have no one to blame but yourself for your predicament, Gideon," she said. "I tried to help you on your last visit, but no, you were in too much of a hurry to listen, and now here you are again. Well, that resolution is no longer available to you. The opportunity has passed. A funny thing about opportunities, once missed they cannot be had back. Now, you must suffer what your impetuous nature has bought you."

"You make no sense. Show yourself! They have taken Rhiannon into Outer Darkness, and—"

"And you wish to know the way?" she interrupted. "Right through those gates, you know that already."

Yes, Gideon knew the way, but he wasn't absolutely certain

that is where the watcher had taken her. He only had the whispers of strange voices ghosting across his mind to go on, and he didn't want to waste his last question upon speculation, hoping her reply would confirm the voices' banter.

"I know the way," he said.

"Then why waste time here?"

"Because you are the keeper of that gate," he said. "Unless the gods decree it, you must admit me. There is grave danger in tampering with Outer Darkness, and you know more than you are telling. You were trying to tell me something more when I left so abruptly last time. I would know what that was."

"You would pay for useless information with your last question? That is hardly practical, I dare say."

"Why should I pay for something you offered freely?" Gideon said slyly.

"One day I shall tell you, but this is not that day. Get ye gone! And watch your back. The winged ones know your mind. They put her there, and they will try to prevent you from tampering with their decree. Once you leave this isle of mine, you are under siege until you enter through that gate. Just be sure it's what you want before you enter. That much I tell you for free."

"I have no choice." Gideon said. "The watchers have decided my actions for me. Punishing me is one thing. Punishing Rhiannon is something else entirely, something I cannot allow. I am aware of the danger. I will be careful."

"You have no idea of the danger in tampering with what lies beyond that gateway, Lord of the Dark. The gods have cursed you, but they have spared you much, for you are not lord of *that* darkness, nor would you want to be. Well? What are you waiting for? The gate is open. *Go!*"

Gideon hesitated. Should he ask that final question? What would it be? There were so many questions banging around in his brain. No . . . he had already squandered one. It was best to wait, but there was one thing she hadn't made clear, and he couldn't leave without knowing.

"This is not one of your damnable questions, Lavilia," he said. "You never clarified the feathers, only that I would have them back when needs must . . ."

"You have had one back already," Lavilia said, from deep in the mist. She was slipping away, and Gideon's posture clenched, his wings expanding wider.

"Do not think to leave before you explain!" he warned her.

"Ours is a special bond, dark one," she said, her voice sounding back amplified by the fog. It had a ghostly ring to it that turned Gideon's blood cold. "Impaling me upon that magnificence between your legs has earned you the privilege of *mind melding*. We have always had it, you and I, but you have always been too preoccupied to see it. I do not expect you to understand the mysteries of my magic, but please pay attention! You will know when you are in need of your feathers, just as you knew the first time. All you need do is reach me with your thoughts, and your feathers will come back to you. Do not squander them. You have only two left. Think carefully before you summon me, Lord of the Dark, for one of them is life . . . and death. That is all you get for free. Now, steel yourself and *go*! And the gods be merciful, my rash young fool . . ."

Her voice trailed off then, and Gideon dismissed her from his thoughts. Only one thing mattered now, getting past the watchers he was certain massed between the isle and the gateway to Outer Darkness. There was only one way to do it, and that was by employing the element of surprise. He would soar into their midst at great speed in hopes of confusing them long enough to get past their number. Already aroused, the velocity wreaking havoc upon his penis as the wind attacked his feathers would be unbearable of itself, not to mention the tenderness of the wound that needed more time than he could spare it to mend.

Spreading his wings, Gideon leaped into the air and surged up out of the stubborn mist that cloaked the rune caster's isle into the night sky. Lavilia hadn't exaggerated. It was a gauntlet, two lines of watchers flanking the way to the phallic stones that marked the Outer Darkness gate. He counted eight, no ten of the winged creatures, snake lightning crackling between their outstretched hands.

Thunderbolts ripped through the sky. Gideon spiraled above them. More lightning speared down, exploding in the crossfire as he sidled in and out among them. There was only one way to enter the dark world. One had to pass between the columns. He could not go over or around them, which meant Gideon had to risk the lightning bolts at close range to achieve it. His cock was on fire, the weight of his motion bearing down upon his wound dizzying. He'd nearly made it halfway dodging the watchers' missiles when one glanced off his wounded wing, wrenching a cry like nothing human from his parched throat, and he spun off momentarily to regain his strength, trying to draw their fire away from the gate. Several did leave the gauntlet line flying after him. Enraged, Gideon struck them feetfirst, sending them spiraling off out of control. He was clearly beyond caring.

He was nearly to the gate when he heard it, a woman's shrill voice—*Rhiannon's voice*—calling his name. Was he imagining it? Was his desperate need to find her causing cruel hallucinations? It came again, so loud and shrill it pierced his soul. His heart leapt. No, it wasn't a hallucination. Amplified by the fog, her voice was echoing from beyond the Outer Darkness gate, and he streaked through the air dodging missile after missile toward the tall phallic stones that marked the entrance to the dark unknown and careened through the gate, feathers smoking.

Lightning bolts glanced off the columns Gideon passed through, but no watchers followed. Gideon gave the display only passing notice to be certain the tales of watchers being barred were true. Searching for some sign of Rhiannon, he strained through the eerie half-light of perpetual night that existed in Outer Darkness. It took him a moment to become accustomed to the atmosphere. Then he saw it, her head breaking the surface of the water, her arms flailing wildly. Scarcely thinking, he dove into the lake, seized her in his arms, and soared skyward with her cradled against his hammering heart, and the thick bulk of his aroused penis. His wings, still hissing and crackling from submersion in the icy water of the lake, trailed steam now instead of smoke. It felt so soothing, he groaned, but it was almost a subconscious outburst. Nothing mattered then but his Rhiannon. He had her in his arms again, and he flew straight for the shoreline and set her down in a marshy tangle of reeds and rushes at the edge of what could only be quicksand from the way it belched and undulated, set ajar by their untimely presence.

His hands roamed over her body frantically, searching, begging for reassurance that she was sound. What met them was soft, trembling flesh; hard, firm breasts; and nipples like two rigid acorns against his trembling palms. Fire raced through his loins, warming his flesh beneath the torn eel-skin suit clinging cold and wet to his body.

Rhiannon threw her arms around his neck. "I do not swim well in deep water," she sobbed. "I tried to reason with the ferryman to take me back, but he disappeared—boat and all—and I fell into the water!"

"They gave you to the *ferryman*?" Gideon seethed. "The whoresons! There is no return from the ferryman's punt."

"He didn't want to take me without a tribute, but they made him. He was not happy, believe me!"

Gideon swallowed dry. "The ferryman is Death's alter ego, Rhiannon," he said. "You are fortunate to be alive. That you

are my soul mate is probably why you still draw breath. We are
. . . old adversaries, the ferryman and I, and on several occasions . . . friendly enemies."

"Does he rule this place, then?" Rhiannon queried.

"No," Gideon returned, "would that he did." He clouded
suddenly. "If that were the case I might have reasoned with
him."

"Who is the keeper here, then?"

"An entity you do not want to meet," Gideon told her. "A
great horned satyr, half man, half goat, in the manner of a faun,
who metes out hideous tortures upon those whom the gods
banish here. He is called *Ravelle*. Never say his name, for to
speak it thrice will summon him and open a pit of eternal fire."
All color drained from her face, and he quickly added, "But
you needn't fear. We rest here only till the watchers tire of waiting. Then we will leave this place forsaken by the gods and find
some corner of this world that will accept us."

"You're bleeding," Rhiannon cried, stroking his bloodied
wings.

Even the faintest touch to wings already charged with the
curse of sexual arousal was more than Gideon could bear despite the pain ripping through those wounded appendages. The
last thing he needed was a distraction now, but those hands . . .
those gentle hands stroking, smoothing, sliding over aching,
throbbing tissue and sexually charged feathers were weaving
their magic, and he fell back in the snarl of tangled weeds and
let her minister to him.

It was a bad position, for the weight of his wings held him
down, but he scarcely thought about anything then but the ravenous lust her fingers ignited. This was hardly wise in such a
dangerous place, where he needed all his wits about him, but
the curse was running rampant in him then, compounded by
the libidinous need her touch had unleashed.

He groaned. "I have bled before," he said, "and I will bleed again. I will not die of the injuries. The gods would not grant me that blessing. I will rally and mend to live and bleed another day as long as there are watchers to make certain of it."

"You haven't begged me to stop," she murmured, still straightening bent feathers.

Gideon shrugged, and loosed a bitter laugh. "It is too late to stop now, my love," he said. "If you would have me clear-headed enough to get us out of this, make me come. . . ."

Rhiannon wiped the tears from her cheeks, then began opening Gideon's eel skin. The look of her, so terrified, still trembling from her ordeal in the water, touched him so deeply he reached and pulled her into his arms. Burying his hands in her hair, he took her lips in a tender kiss, tasting the salt of her tears, and deepened it, coaxing her tongue into his mouth. Rhiannon melted against him, clinging to him for dear life as he stroked and caressed her. How completely she responded to the tenderness she had evoked in him, despite the volatile emotions the curse brought to bear. How totally his she was, an extension of himself, the love in her palpable as he fed from her sweet essence, tasting her deeply, laving the soft insides of her cheeks and underside of her pointed tongue. She was giving him all of herself—all of her passion, all of her very soul in that deep, penetrating kiss.

Beyond the point of no return, Gideon tugged at the eel-skin suit until it gave, releasing his throbbing cock. Rhiannon gripped his shaft, fondling the soft skin, like satin, stretched over hot steel, the purple veins throbbing a steady rhythm. Free of its restraints, his engorged penis mushroomed into a gargantuan erection, an anxious force to be reckoned with. She gasped, and he swallowed the sound, taking it deep inside him, savoring the hum like a starving beggar at a banquet.

They'd been stripped of everything but each other—distilled into something pure. She was part of him now, as she never had been before, so totally that they seemed to breathe each other's breath and their hearts seemed to beat as one. This was the power of a passion that transcended lust, a power that commanded need, desire, and longing. It was what Gideon had been searching for since time out of mind, a love that knew no bounds, the innocent abandon of one yielding to a single kiss.

Rhiannon's cool hand riding his shaft made his heart race. Being made love to lying on his back was a luxury he had never afforded himself. For one thing, the weight of his body upon the traitorous wings alone created such a lustful onslaught of sexual energy it bordered on bestial. For another, it made rising awkward, especially when wounded. He longed for the carved-out niche in the cave that was no more, where he'd slept standing, longed for the soothing mineral spring, and the soft, peaceful twilight steeped in velvet darkness of a life that seemed to have belonged to someone else. Only once before in all his eons abandoned by the gods had he lain thus, and ever since he'd longed for the sweet agony the position promised. It was only fitting that he know such bittersweet ecstasy in Rhiannon's arms. This was hardly the time or place, however, but longing cancelled common sense, and he groaned as she straddled him, guiding his magnificence to the folds of her entrance, where she hovered, her gentle hands gripping his bare shoulders.

He could feel the crackle of her passion through her fingertips as the hands slid lower, her palms pressing against the hard pucker of his sensitive nipples. If he let himself, he could come in a heartbeat, but no, this was something to be savored, something to be prolonged, where he teetered upon the edge of sanity before letting go and opening up these long locked floodgates that would empty him completely. Yes, sanity was involved, for with the privilege of such a dangerous coupling for him came a visit to the brink of sheer madness, which is what gripped him now, as he arched himself against the moist nether lips that tortured him with their exquisite promise.

Just when he thought he could bear no more, she took him inside her one fold at a time, gliding on her juices. Gideon shut his eyes, imagining the dark mystery of her sex as it gripped him, plunging him deeper inside her until she'd taken him from mushroom tip to the root of his thick hardness. Grinding her clitoris against the base of his shaft, Rhiannon threw her head back, and her long hair cascaded down her back, teasing his thighs. Her undulations became more urgent as she rocked back and forth, taking him deeper and deeper into her velvet mystery—deeper than he'd ever gone before, until her womb, the very seat of her sexuality, caressed the sensitive head of his cock.

Groaning her name, Gideon reached for her breasts and cupped them, his thumbs grazing her tall, hard nipples. When had her shift fallen away? Slowly, he slid his hands along her sides, following the curvaceous indentation of her waist and the full, soft mounds of her hips as she straddled him. Tightening his grip, he raised and lowered her on his shaft. The motion put pressure on his wings, and a riot of drenching fire ripped through his loins. He'd forgotten the intensity of such a climax. It rippled through his body like a firestorm, wave upon wave of pulsating heat that threatened to consume him in an orgasmic explosion as she milked him dry.

How silky hot she was inside as her tightness gripped his penis, the thick folds of her sex expanding and contracting with each throb as she came. He could feel her juices release. He could feel their wetness flowing into his come as she released again. She touched his wings and his hips jerked forward, thrusting his penis into the pulsating depths of her again and again. It was as if his body had become a machine over which he had no control, an unstoppable mechanism of runaway energy pistoning into her, triggering multiple orgasms in them both that knew no bounds.

Yes, he had forgotten the exquisite agony, the unworldly ecstasy of coupling with a woman on his back. The forbidden position for one winged as he was. The posture that transcended mortal or immortal love and made it a passion fit only for the gods. This was something to which he was not entitled, something for which he would pay dearly as decreed by the terms of the curse that was his perpetual torment. But for this brief blink in time's eye, as he lay helpless in Rhiannon's sultry embrace riddled with carnal euphoria, he knew something worth dying for . . . a purity of sexual abandon like no other, and he wanted more, so much more.

It seemed to go on forever before they lay in each other's arms, sated at last. It would be so easy to fall asleep as he was, lying on his back with his soul mate in his arms, to wake and doze, and take her again and again in that forbidden position. He couldn't remember when he'd last slept. It seemed an eternity ago. The pain of the weight of his sexually charged wings notwithstanding, he longed—just once—to lie thus and sleep. The notion had plagued him like a splinter under his skin since time out of mind, for he had never done. It was time.

The mysterious perpetual darkness was closing in upon them. Only the marsh lights bobbing innocently on the mire shone through the blackness. All was still around them, and there wasn't a soul or animal to be seen. That in itself was suspect, but Gideon didn't care. He'd begun to doze when Rhiannon's soft voice broke the silence.

"I don't like this place, Gideon," she murmured. "It frightens me. Do you think the watchers will have gone by now?"

"Not likely," Gideon said, settling her closer in the crook of his arm. "I do not like this place any more than you do, but I like the prospect of lightning bolts even less. They are inevitable on the other side of that gateway back there, but I need to heal the wounds I have before I beg for more. Rest, Rhiannon, while we have the opportunity; then we will take our chances with the watchers."

She sighed, moving in his arms. He was hard again, and trying to ignore it, but the soft music of her gentle voice made an
end to that.

"What are those?" she asked, pointing toward the bobbing
lights dancing over the breast of the bog.

"Marsh lights," Gideon said. "Will-o'-the-Wisps they are
called in the astral. They are mischief makers—pranksters,
whose pranks are not always harmless. I wonder what evil
deeds got them banished here."

Rhiannon got to her feet. "Look, I think they want us to follow. . . ."

Gideon gripped her arm. "No!" he cautioned. "Never follow the marsh lights. They will lead you astray. You see? They
work their magic even from their distance. They would seduce
you into quicksand! Come . . . lie with me and stay by me. I
haven't slept, and I need to rest if I'm going to heal. I will try to
stay awake, but in case I don't, you need to stay by me."

Rhiannon visibly shook off the lure of the marsh lights and
rushed into his arms. Gideon groaned as her breasts flattened
against his bare chest, and her pubic mound leaned into his
erection. Sleep was a myth while her soft, eager flesh was
pressed against his hardness. He would reach for her again and
again before the strange, dark morning, eclipsing night and day,
cast its murky spell.

18

We should have interfered, the vaguely remembered voice ghosted across Gideon's mind. *If we had, none of this would be.*

The other breathed a gusty sigh. It seemed his mantra. *He made that rather difficult*, he said. *And now he pays the price. He could end it in a trice were he to let the girl go.*

The first voice took a defensive tone. *He will never do that.*

He is tested soon. Then we shall see. He has lost much, and he has just made a decision that will cost him even more.

The first speaker, still defensive, said, *He still has one question left and two feathers to redeem.*

He does, said the other. *Let us hope he uses them wisely. He has never stood at this crossroads before. . . .*

Gideon stirred with a groan. His thick member was swollen with arousal, and the pain of sleeping in the coveted position had taken its toll. Agonizing waves of excruciating pain rushed through his limbs, his wings, his sex. The effect was dizzying. White pinpoints of blinding light starred his vision. When his eyes finally focused, all that met them was a bleak black fog.

He groped for Rhiannon, but she was not in his arms, and he called out her name. The sound echoed back at him slurred and distorted. There came no reply, and a riveting barrage of cold chills gripped his spine, knitting the bones rigid. He called out again, but still no answer came, and he tried to struggle erect, finally realizing the folly of living his fantasy. It was next to impossible on the first attempt, for all his extraordinary strength. Sleeping on his back had all but crippled him.

The desperation of his third unanswered call set him in motion. Grinding his teeth as he ground out a bestial roar, he surged to his feet only to be jerked back down to his knees in the snarl of scrub and vines and nettles that had been his bed. He was tethered. Groping his throat, he found the cause. A thick iron band was clamped around his neck. From it, a heavy chain stretched into the fog and disappeared.

Something had hold of the other end of the chain, for it was in motion, going taut then slack, as if whatever hand had custody of it was demonstrating its power. Gideon's first instinct was to grab the chain and wrest it from his captor, but the minute his fist clamped around the links, smoke rose from his grip, and the stench of burnt flesh—his flesh—rushed up his nostrils. He dropped it, soothing his burned fingers.

"Who are you?" he demanded. "Where is Rhiannon? What have you done with her?"

"We meet at last!" said a deep, sultry baritone voice from the fog. "I have long wished it. Forgive the rude awakening. Unfortunately, it is necessary until we've talked. You have the advantage of wings, Lord of the Dark, and I, alas, do not."

"Where is Rhiannon?" Gideon demanded. "What have you done with her?"

"Done with her?" the voice in the fog said. "Curious question. We are not murderers here. Whatever fate those that enter through those gates have earned for themselves, they have done so on their own. We are simply . . . administrators here."

"Enforcers, you mean!" Gideon corrected. "They hardly mete out their own torture, Ravelle."

"You know me then," the demon said. "I am impressed."

"I know of you," Gideon said. "All of Arcus knows of Ravelle, the keeper of Outer Darkness, and his cruelties. You have me. Let Rhiannon go. She has done nothing to earn admittance to the Netherworld. The watchers put her here to punish me."

"Umm, yes, I know of your . . . punishments. There are those who would deem perpetual arousal a blessing of the gods. You'll find no sympathy for that here."

"Show yourself!" Gideon charged. "And loose me of this tether. I will not go anywhere without Rhiannon. Unchain me!"

"You are lord of your domain, Gideon, but you are at my mercy here," Ravelle reminded him. "You would do well to take another tack with me."

The demon's sugar-coated voice had suddenly turned dark and threatening. Gideon took stock. He needed all his wits about him to best this creature. He thought of the last question the rune caster owed him, and the two feathers. He also remembered the disembodied voices' words warning that he choose wisely. Desperately, he strained his ears to hear those voices again, but all was still. He was on his own, his focus on one thing only: He needed to find Rhiannon and leave Outer Darkness.

"Very well," he said. "I would appreciate that you return Rhiannon to me. She is an innocent in this, and—"

"Ahh, but the innocents are the most succulent," the demon interrupted. "I found her especially so."

Gideon stiffened, straining at the tether. "What have you done to her?" he seethed.

"Taken better care than you have, Lord of the Dark," Ravelle chortled. "For one thing, I clothed her, else she be fighting off all my subjects. Take ease, I haven't touched her . . . yet. I was referring to observation only. You are quite the stud, my friend, and *she* . . . well, there are no words."

Gideon's posture clenched again. So they had been watched. It would not be easy having her back from the demon now that he'd seen Rhiannon naked, in the throes of ecstasy. This was to be a battle of wits, and he prayed to the gods that had forsaken him to give him the power to win.

"What do you want of me?" he said, still searching the drifting fog for sight of the creature.

"I want you to remain here, with me," Ravelle said. "We have much in common, winged one. Just think of the power we would command were we to join forces. I have long dreamed of it. You have nothing left in your world. You are hunted like an animal. Here, you would be like a god, and we could rule together. Thanks to the corruption of humankind, Outer Darkness has grown too vast for one alone to govern. Think of it! Think of the power the two of us could command!"

"And Rhiannon . . . what of her?" Gideon hedged. The demon still hadn't shown himself. He needed to see the creature to strategize how to best it.

"We would share in all things equally," Ravelle said, "even your Rhiannon."

"Show yourself!" Gideon said, hoping his tone wasn't as abrasive as it sounded. "I make no bargains with wraiths in the mist."

There was a long silence before the mist parted and the creature pranced into view. Ravelle was much as he had been described, a horned, cloven-hoofed satyr, goatlike from the waist down, his upper body that of a human, muscular and magnificent, hairless but for an arrow-straight strip of hair that pointed to the bulge below his waist that two airborne sylphs were addressing.

"Have one," the demon offered, gesturing toward the winged females. "Avail yourself. I offer as a gesture of good faith. Take your pick . . . or would you rather a catamite? My stables are at your disposal, dark one. There, you will find a bedmate for every taste, a creature for every appetite. I would have thought such a one as these—winged as you are—would be the perfect enticement, which is why I summoned them."

"I want only Rhiannon," Gideon said, watching for a reaction.

The demon's reptilian eyes narrowed. The look in them chilled Gideon to the marrow. "How mundane," the creature said. "Denial of a good will offering is not an option. Even here there is such a thing as hospitality. You would do well to observe it."

"Another time," Gideon said steadily. "Rhiannon is my mate, Ravelle. It is she whom I hunger for. That is not to say that at another time one of these lovelies mightn't suit . . ." he quickly added. It would not do to anger the creature.

"In due time," the demon said. "Once we have settled our . . . business."

Gideon nodded. "Then let us get on with it, eh?"

Despite his refusal, one of the sylphs left Ravelle and descended upon Gideon. She wore no garment, only a fine silver chain about her waist. Her breasts, perfect and firm, grazed his shoulder, the nipples steely hard scraping against his moist skin. She touched his wings and they unfurled, nearly knocking her over.

"Do not touch my wings!" he warned, twisting away

A cold light flared in the demon's eyes, and a smile creased his sensuous lips that did not reach that lecherous gaze. He waved his hand. "Away!" he commanded the sylphs. Cowering, they faded into the mist, and Ravelle jerked the chain attached to Gideon's collar leading him away from the bog, to a clearing not far distant. On his guard, Gideon let the demon lead him, fully aware that no move the creature made could be trusted.

"I see you are still skeptical," Ravelle purred. He cocked his head, a sly glimmer in his snakelike eyes. He flicked a crooked finger toward Gideon's wings, then recoiled it slowly, resting the knuckle on his lower lip. "Must be a ghastly nuisance that," he said. "Even the touch of the wind ruffling your feathers gets you hard, um?"

Ravelle had made no move to touch them, but Gideon furled his wings regardless, and made no reply.

The demon laughed outright. "Don't worry, dark one," he said. "I'm not going to torture you, quite the contrary . . . if you will allow a little demonstration?"

"What kind of demonstration?" Gideon said, skeptically. He'd lived too long to trust a demon lord of Outer Darkness.

"This kind," said Ravelle, blowing upon Gideon's wings.

The issue from the demon's puffed out cheeks was blue, like the volcanic gasses that issued from the Fire Isle that warmed the bathing pools throughout the archipelago. It stung Gideon's eyes and rushed up his nostrils, making him grimace. Gideon shrank from it, but it clung stubbornly like a blue halo about his furled wings.

"What is that?" he choked.

"My demonstration," Ravelle said. "Unfurl your wings."

Gideon hesitated.

"Oh, come, come, dark one!" Ravelle snapped. "If I wanted you dead, you'd have been so long since. It is a nuisance ending the life of an immortal, too tedious. Besides, you are of more use to me alive, but you are stubborn, and a skeptic. You are of a sort that must be shown, and so I am showing you, plain and simple. Now, unfurl those wings!"

Gideon did as Ravelle bade him, and the demon came closer, his cloven hooves hidden in the mist, though their clopping chilled Gideon to the bone.

The demon reached toward him. "May I?" he said, his intent to stroke Gideon's feathers.

Gideon backpedaled pulling the chain taut. Clearly out of patience, Ravelle gave the chain a sharp tug, jerking Gideon to a standstill, and stroked the feathers on his left wing. To Gideon's great surprise, there was no arousal, no crippling surge of libidinous lust that always riddled him with unstoppable waves of carnal desire. He reached with his own hands and ran them over his wings. Nothing. No feeling at all. Could it be? His wings had been sexually charged since his fall from grace. How could this be? Slack-jawed, he stared at the smug-faced demon watching, arms akimbo.

"Well?" Ravelle said. "How long has it been, um?"

"I . . . I don't understand . . ." Gideon said.

The demon laughed. "How would you like your wings to stay thus? How would you like to soar through the sky like the sylphs do? How would you like to glide again with the cool wind soothing your feathers, not igniting the perpetual lust of the gods you still champion so—despite that they have condemned you to suffer such cruel torments? I can do that for you, just as I've done it now. Remain here with me. Rule with me, Prince of the Night. You *belong* here—in the dark. Together, what a team we would make. But I see you need more convincing . . ."

Inhaling, the demon sucked back the blue aura that had clung to Gideon's wings. The sudden drainage left Gideon weak and he swayed, wings shuddering as the lust returned a thousand-fold, and he groaned for the pressure of his hard cock swelling against the seam of his eel-skin suit, drawing his hand there, and dropped to his knees.

"Yes," the demon crooned, "it had been difficult for you, but it need not remain so. All you need do is join forces with me. You have no idea of the power I command, and of course there is your Rhiannon . . ."

Gideon's head was spinning. Just those few moments of relief were like heaven, but only to have it snatched away again was the cruelest kind of torture. Ravelle was a dangerous entity. He had honed in upon Gideon's greatest weakness and used it against him in the most vicious way, made more so by the syrupy manner in which the proposal was put forth. Gideon had seen through the demon's clever seduction, but still . . . oh, but *still*, that one brief moment of blessed relief . . . If only it could continue . . .

All at once a racket of noise hit his brain like cannon fire—raised voices, yelling,arguing, demanding to be heard . . .

I told you we should have intervened! one was shouting.

It's too late, the other said.

He cannot succumb! Do something!

He has free will. There is nothing to be done.

Then shout! Shout at the top of your voice and pray he hears you!

A garbled static of ear-splitting noise banged around in Gideon's brain. Two speakers were causing it. What were they saying? It sounded so urgent. What did it all mean?

Gideon was too dazed to make it out. He couldn't concentrate upon that. He needed all his wits about him to withstand the demon's seduction, for it was his greatest test yet. Shaking himself like a dog, he tried to rise. The voices were screaming inside his skull. Who were they? What did they want?

"Rhiannon," he murmured. "Take me to Rhiannon. . . ."

"Ah, yes, Rhiannon," the demon said, her name rolling off his tongue with a flourish. It sounded obscene when he spoke it. "You aren't ready. You need to rest and order yourself. You need time to mull over my little proposition first." He bent, secured the chain in his hand to something hidden in the ground-creeping fog, then stood and began to strut, preening like a dandy. "You will find this place much more comfortable than the bramble mire where I found you. Stretch out and . . . relax. Relieve yourself." He gestured toward the obvious. "That there is crying for attention. I honestly do not know how you've stood it all these years, but you needn't much longer. One word from you and all that will end. Join with me, and you shall have control of your body again . . . and your Rhiannon. Meanwhile, I shall entertain her. I've neglected her shamefully since your arrival, and that won't do. Innocents are such a rarity here. But have no fear. I shall see to it personally that *all* her needs are met . . . while you decide, um?"

"And if I decline your invitation?" Gideon asked.

"I think you know the answer to that, Lord of the Dark. Now then! Take all the time you need. Rest assured that while you wrestle with your answer, your Rhiannon is in good hands, um?"

Gideon got to his feet and staggered to the end of his tether. It jerked him to a standstill, and he grabbed the chain, only to cry out as it seared his hands again. The odor of burnt flesh rushed up his nostrils from his smoking palms, and he threw the chain down.

"Ravelle, wait!" he called out. "*Wait,* damn you!"

"Too late for that!" the demon twittered. "Think carefully before you decide. It shouldn't take you long, considering. Meanwhile, I'll see that our Rhiannon isn't bored, hm?"

Gideon called out again, but there was no answer from the thick, milling fog. Ravelle was gone.

19

Rhiannon crouched in a dark corner of the chamber where Ravelle had left her. It was well appointed, part of a castle-like complex that she assumed to be his stronghold. Why had she fallen asleep in Gideon's arms? Why hadn't she remained vigilant? The demon had taken her captive so easily. What was he doing to Gideon? She had screamed until her throat was hoarse and pounded on the chamber door until she'd scraped her knuckles raw, but there was no answer. She was alone, in a strange, dark, and evil place at the mercy of the keeper of Outer Darkness, and she was terrified.

She fingered the filmy gown the demon had given her. It was coal black like the atmosphere, spun of some anonymous stuff that sparkled like black diamonds and hid none of her charms. Strange little creatures, neither male nor female, like those carved in the stone of the cold hearth holding up the mantel, stripped away the old tattered shift the dryads had spun for her in the astral and helped her into the dusky frock. The winged imps dressed her hair with a wreath of petrified berries and blackened twigs that shot out from its circumference like rain glancing off a spinning wheel. A gauze veil that matched her frock fell from the circlet over the loose plait the creatures had fashioned in her hair that nearly reached the hem of the garment. Rhiannon detested the veil. It reminded her of a macabre bridal headdress. She hadn't missed the lecherous gleam in the satyr's reptilian eyes as he took her into his charge. Those eyes had undressed her, lingering expectantly upon her naked breasts. His lascivious gaze had chilled her so severely her nipples had hardened. Could he have taken the reaction as arousal? If he had, he was a fool, for she recoiled from his very presence. It was afterward that he'd summoned the imps, their pudgy arms loaded down with the makings of her present toilette, and she hadn't missed the lustful look he'd given the rest of her, raking her from head to toe, those glowing eyes lingering upon her pubic mound.

After they'd dressed her, the imps had locked her inside the vast chamber and left her, disappearing into the shadows. That was some time ago, and her terror that something horrible was happening to Gideon had nearly driven her mad.

The rasp of a key turning in the door lock spun her toward it, and she snatched a silver candle branch from the table and held it at the ready, her breath suspended as the door slowly opened.

"Do not throw that," Ravelle's velvet voice warned as he entered. "You cannot hurt me, and you will only hurt yourself . . . in more ways than one."

"Let me out of here!" Rhiannon demanded. "Where is Gideon? What have you done with him?"

"He is resting," the demon said, coming nearer, his cloven hooves ringing on the slate floor. "I've made him a very enticing proposition, and given him time to mull it over. There's no question, really, but just in case he doesn't realize that, I may need you to help me convince him."

"I won't help you with anything!" Rhiannon shrilled, brandishing the candle branch. "Come no nearer! I'm warning you, I have true aim!"

The demon breathed a gusty sigh. "How tiresome!" he said. "My lady, I cannot be killed. I cannot even be seriously injured, least of all by that! You look the fool in that ritual toilette wielding a candle branch." He glanced toward the table she'd snatched it from. Great silver salvers and bowls were set there heaped with food—all sorts of exotic fruit bursting with sweet juices. There were slabs of creamy cheese set out on great dewy leaves, joints of beef and mutton, platters of larded fowl and potted meats, as well as warm, crusty bread and crystal decanters filled with rich, red wine. Rhiannon had touched none of it, and the demon's eyebrow lifted. "You must be starving," he said. "Why have you not availed yourself?"

"I . . . I want none of your food," Rhiannon said. "Stand back, I say!"

The demon chuckled. "Silly chit," he warbled. "Eating my food can't harm you. This isn't the astral, where the fay capture with food. This is *Outer Darkness!* The worst has already happened to you, my dear. It doesn't matter what you eat anymore."

"I want nothing from you . . . nothing but Gideon. Take me to him at once!"

Ravelle had come close enough to wrest the candle branch from her, and he did so with flourish, and set it down upon the table. "Have done!" he snapped. "I mean only to tell you what I've told him . . . in case he needs persuading. If convincing is in order that might be best coming from you than me, that's all."

Rhiannon gave it thought, but she wasn't ready to take Ravelle at his word. She'd heard too many tales of Outer Darkness to trust its keeper, despite his syrupy voice and seemingly innocent, albeit frightening, demeanor.

"If Gideon is not convinced of whatever you've proposed on his own my opinion won't sway him, nor should it. He is lord in these matters. You waste your time with me."

"Well, it's my time to waste, and you are a captive audience, so you may as well indulge me. I have asked your Gideon to join forces and rule jointly with me here, you, of course, would be part of that equation."

"And he refused you?" Rhiannon said buoyantly. "I knew he would. He would *never* consent to rule here with you."

"One must never say never, my lady. I told you I made him an enticing proposal. I even gave him a little demonstration."

Rhiannon's curiosity was piqued. She couldn't imagine what Ravelle had offered Gideon that he would have to contemplate. "What sort of demonstration?" she asked.

"I simply showed him how it would be if his wings no longer plunged him into unstoppable lust when touched. I gave him a moment of freedom from the curse that has damned him to live with perpetual arousal. I have the power to do that . . . and so much more."

He sauntered closer. How grotesque he was with his goat-like body covered with fur from the waist down, and muscular torso roped with sinewy bands. He was clean shaven, his hair curling about his earlobes, accentuating a face all angles and planes, and eyes coal black, like onyx chips, with vertical pupils the color of saffron. Lights from a hearth fire gleamed off his horns. When had a fire been lit? She gasped. The carved imps that had stood mute, their plump arms holding up the mantel, had come to life. She gasped again. They were chucking more wood on the fire and stirring old embers to life with pokers. Cold chills riddled her spine. She hadn't been alone at all. They had been there watching her all the while!

More appeared. They had formed a ring around her. Some were poking and probing like curious children, others were lifting the skirt of her frock, ducking their heads beneath. Still others were playing with her long, plaited hair. When one of the creatures slid its hand up the inside of her thigh and grabbed her pubic curls, she screamed and swatted it away.

Ravelle seized the imp by its tail and flung it across the room. A roar like nothing she had ever heard dispersed the others. Seeing her chance, Rhiannon bolted. Streaking past the roaring demon, past the imps swarming every which way, she careened into the eerie, perpetual darkness.

She hadn't gone far when the satyr's hand fisted in her plaited hair jerked her to a standstill. "I'm losing my patience!" he snapped close in her ear. "Where do you think you could get to that I—the ruler of this place—could not find you, eh? Foolish chit! You would do well to cooperate. You will not like the consequences of rebellion, my lady!"

"If you want my cooperation, needs must you earn it!" she snapped back. "Keep those . . . those creatures away from me!"

"That was regrettable," the demon said in retrospect. "They are what they are, but no more precocious than curious children. There are many such . . . creatures here. Unfortunately, they rarely see one such as you. Once Gideon becomes my partner and you are established as our consort, they will remain in their place."

" 'Our' consort?" Rhiannon breathed. "Is that part of your proposition?"

The demon spun her around in his arms and cupped her breast, the long, talon-like nail on his thumb plucking her nipple. "Yes," he hissed, "it is. Why else would I have robed you in wedding attire? We will share you. You will have the best of both worlds. All that remains is to convince the Lord of the Dark of the benefits of an alliance with me."

Rhiannon gripped her headdress and flung it to the ground. "I would rather be dead!" she cried, twisting in his arms. He was aroused, his huge member terrifying in its length and breadth as he forced it against her.

The demon laughed at her reaction. "Nature provides the goat, the horse, and other of her beasts with anatomy equal to the challenge their lack of agility in coitus denies them. The extra length makes rogering a female possible. Magnificent, is it not?"

Rhiannon twisted away, but the demon held her fast, forcing her hand against his erection. "Let me go!" she shrilled, resisting.

Ravelle jerked her to a standstill. "Another demonstration," he said, as the penis he'd forced against her hand went flaccid. "Unlike your Gideon, I am able to control my urges, which sets me apart from animals of his ilk."

"Gideon is not an animal!" Rhiannon defended.

"He is the animal the gods have made of him. Compared with mine, his powers are weak now, but an alliance with me will change all that. Once we are joined, you will have the best we each have to offer, and he will have freedom from the curse that has crippled him since time out of mind. Then his gifts will be as they were before he fell from grace, and together we will be invincible!"

"You are mad!" Rhiannon shrilled, trying to break free.

He paid no mind, dragging her along a dark path through what looked like trees that had been burned. "I cannot fly," he said. "He will be my eyes aloft to travel the length and breadth of Outer Darkness. Others would usurp me. They hatch plots against me, but with his eyes keeping watch where I cannot, all that will cease. Meanwhile, I will keep vigil in places where his wings prohibit him entrance. It is a perfect plan, and you . . . oh, you, my lovely, you are the prize to keep us both sated!" He shoved her hand against his groin again. "You have no idea what pleasures this fine cock will give you!"

Rhiannon wrenched her hand free and dug in her heels. "Let go!" she cried. "I want to see Gideon! What have you done with him? *No!* Where are you taking me?"

"You waste your breath. You will see your Gideon, but first, a revel to get you in the mood while he mulls over my proposition."

But Rhiannon refused to go quietly to whatever a *revel* was by this creature's standards, and the satyr soon had enough sparing. Hoisting her over his shoulder, he ignored her kicking feet and pummeling fists, and strode along fondling her buttocks through the flimsy gown.

He gave a throaty chuckle. "You were far better off on two feet, weren't you?" he chided. "Umm, I like a round, firm ass." Hoisting her skirt, he reached beneath and stroked her bare behind. "Soft as a rose petal," he crooned, running his hand over one globe and the crack between. "Has he rutted you yet?" he queried, spreading her legs apart and plunging his forefinger the length of her slit. "Ah, yes! So he has, and saved me the trouble. Breaching maidenheads is a tiresome business. I used to enjoy the conquest, but alas, no more. Patience ebbs away with time. Besides, whomever I take is like a virgin whether she has been rutted or no, for considering my size, it will be as if I draw first blood in any case reaming that tight little quim. Ah, yes, indeed! My cock will find a happy home in you, my lady. If you must play the martyr, as you females are so often wont to do, justify our union, yours and mine, as a means to end your Gideon's torment, for once we align—all three—he will be set free of the curse of libidinous lust that holds him captive now."

Rhiannon didn't speak, nor did she fight him then, not while his taloned finger was probing her nether lips from clitoris to anus. Thus far it was an absent probing. His thoughts seemed to be elsewhere. He had not penetrated her. To anger him now might cause what horror she could barely imagine, and so she scarcely breathed as he strode on through the darkness, his cloven hooves clopping on the ground that seemed more mire than solid path.

It wasn't long before they reached a vast pavilion wreathed with tents where revelers were indulging in all manner of decadent activities. The satyr took her into the Great Hall, where wine flowed from fountains connected to great vats housed along a gallery below the domed ceiling. There, an elaborate skylight filled the span. Tables set about were heaped with food to overflowing with the mundane, such as joints of beef and roast mutton and lamb, to the exotic specimens of braised dormouse, hummingbird's tongues in aspic, and steamed elvers, which she could never abide as creatures much less food, to name but a few. She shuddered. The air was putrid with the stench of old fermentation, cooking grease, urine, and stale come. Rhiannon gagged, and the demon lifted her down, with a firm grip on her long, plaited hair, and led her into the thick of what appeared to be an orgy in progress.

Naked and half-naked men and women, imps, satyrs, and all manner of species, one more hideous than the next, were coupled in a ménage of entwined bodies impossible to define by gender. There was no modesty here. Males whose naked members were at different stages of arousal prowled the throngs in search of females not already engaged with one or more partners, while screams of pleasure and pain rang from the rafters.

Ravelle gave the reins he'd made of Rhiannon's long plait to an idle imp reclining upon sumptuous pillows in the center of the room. "Hold on to this," he charged the creature. "You may look, but do not touch."

The pudgy little creature wound her hair around his hand and began to snap it as a coachman would snap his ribbons driving his team.

"I told you to keep these creatures away from me!" Rhiannon cried.

"It's that or join in," said the satyr. "Which would you prefer? Your time is coming, but first I have my subjects to tend to."

He had scarcely let her go when females swarmed over him. A dark-haired sylph led the pack, her wings giving her the advantage, and quickly seized his penis, bringing him erect. A dryad and a human female then crowded out the rest and stood by awaiting their turn to be serviced by their lord and master.

Rhiannon tried to look away, but everywhere she looked a similar coupling was taking place. Terror made her heart race, and the sexual energy in that hall, to her horror, made her hot. The demon knew it would. That was why he'd brought her there, and why he'd left her tethered to the imp. He wanted her to watch. Realizing that almost put her in a panic, but that she dared not risk. She needed all her wits about her if she were to be reunited with Gideon.

Across the way, the sylph had brought Ravelle fully erect. Rhiannon was unable to look away and yet repulsed at the sight of his enormous penis. Her father had kept farm animals, and she had seen the beasts mate, but on a creature half human in appearance, such a member was beyond grotesque. The thought that she was next in line to suffer it threatened to drain her consciousness.

The sylph's outcry was more of pain than pleasure as the satyr bent her over at the waist and thrust its thick purple shaft into her to the root. A roar from the demon's lips as it came inside the winged sylph resonated through the gathering, and a mad frenzy of unbridled lust broke out among their number. Naked bodies became a living quilt of writhing flesh, reminding Rhiannon of a wriggling snarl of eels she'd once seen crawling on the mud flats of home what seemed a lifetime ago. She stiffened, ready to bolt before the creature turned its attention to her, but the imp tethering her by the hair gave the plait a sharp jerk as if he anticipated her next move, and she froze, for fear of calling attention to herself.

The odious creature had straddled a bolster behind her and

was rubbing itself against the rough fabric until it came, and came again. All the while, it whipped her plaited hair like the reins of a carriage horse as it bounced ever closer to her buttocks, inching along the bolster. Rhiannon whipped her head around and hissed at the imp, elbowing it hard in the belly. It squealed, but continued its obscene gyrations, and a dry sob left her lips. Her terror was palpable. If she cried out, it would surely catch the satyr's attention, the last thing she wanted, when he was in a euphoric state of carnal aberration, but the mere thought of that hideous imp anywhere near her body had nearly driven her mad.

Having had his fill of the sylph, Ravelle lowered his head and pitched her aside with his horns. She landed in the midst of a threesome that took her eagerly into their embrace. She became no more than another wrinkle in the living quilt of writhing bodies carpeting the Great Hall floor.

Rhiannon held her breath, terrified that her turn had come. The satyr was still aroused, his thick, dark shaft slick with come. He glanced about, but the demonstration wasn't over. He seized the human female by the hair, who had elbowed her way into position to be next, spun her around, and pistoned into her as he had the sylph, while others crowded close, stroking and laving and grinding their bodies into every inch of their master's undulating body.

Rhiannon could see the demon's dark aura radiating from him like heat radiates from a raging fire. It was the color of dried blood, more black than red. His stamina wasn't flagging as she'd hoped it would before her turn came. He was getting stronger. His shuttered eyes were shining like live coals, and drool was running down his chin. Where was Gideon? She would never escape without him. The revelers had formed a circle all around the spectacle taking place so close beside her she could almost reach out and touch the satyr. They were cheering him on, but instead of looking at the female he'd impaled upon his member, Ravelle's salacious gaze had fallen upon Rhiannon instead.

"See how they want me?" the satyr said, his voice like the roar of a lion bouncing off the walls of the pavilion. "They cannot get enough of me. Once you have had me, you won't be able to slake your appetite, either. That is just the way of it, 'my lady.' "

All at once a flesh-tearing wind rushed down from above, as Gideon plunged through the skylight feetfirst swinging a length of heavy chain in his hand, with little regard for who—or what—he struck with it descending. Feathers and glass shards sifted down like rain over the revelers, whose screams had reached fever pitch by the time Gideon had flown low enough to reach the satyr, still coupled with the human female.

Snapping the chain over his head like a whip, Gideon brought it down upon the satyr full force, driving him to the floor. He snapped the chain a second time and struck the roaring demon again. Ravelle writhed at his feet, his fist raised as the chain descended a third time, striking others as they fled as well. The naked ménage of undulating bodies was moving to a different rhythm now as they scurried every which way in a mad scramble to reach safety out of harm's way.

"You have my answer, Ravelle!" Gideon thundered, striking the imp tethering Rhiannon by the hair. Squealing, it scampered away.

Rhiannon screamed. She had never seen Gideon in a rage. His eyes were aglow, flickering like tongues of fire. The chain had come so close, the metallic odor of blood on the links rushed up her nostrils, and she screamed again as Gideon's arm, like steel, encircled her waist and lifted her into his arms.

Ravelle laughed, wiping blood from his eyes. "You cannot kill me, dark one!" he said. "I, like yourself, am immortal! And you cannot escape from Outer Darkness. Sooner or later, you are mine—both of you. This was a very foolish move."

Gideon wasted no more words on the demon. Soaring upward, he clutched Rhiannon to him so tightly she feared her spine would snap as he streaked back through the broken skylight into the night.

"Hold on to me!" he charged as they cleared the Great Hall.

"You are bleeding!" Rhiannon cried. His hands looked burned. They were covered with blood. His left wing was streaked with blood as well. Instinctively, she reached to stroke it to assess the damage, and he stiffened.

"Do not touch my wings!" he said through clenched teeth.

Rhiannon sobbed and threw her arms around his neck, burying her face in his shoulder as he flew straight for the phallic columns that marked the entrance to Outer Darkness. Of course she must not touch his wings. He was aroused. What torments had he suffered breaking free of the chain that still dangled from a crude iron collar around his neck? She dared not ask him then. His rage was like a separate entity. He seemed about to explode with it, though it wasn't directed toward her. His hands holding her were warm, his caresses filled with relief and longing.

"Have they harmed you?" he gritted through clenched teeth.

"No, but if you hadn't come when you did . . . Oh, Gideon . . . !"

"Hold fast!" he cried. "There's the gate. I'll soon have you out of here, but look sharp! There will be watchers once we leave this place."

The gateway loomed before them, and Rhiannon clung to Gideon with all her strength as they glided low over the ribbon of dark water where he had so recently rescued her from drowning. As he slowed to pass through, cautious of watchers, Rhiannon closed her eyes. They were perfectly aligned to pass through the gate, but when Gideon turned to soar through it was as if he'd hit a stone wall.

Rhiannon's eyes snapped open, Gideon's outcry ringing in her ears, as instead of passing through the gate, they bounced back from the invisible shield that jerked them to a standstill and sent them plummeting down, down into the black lake below.

20

Rhiannon screamed as Gideon cocooned her within his wings to absorb the shock of impact. The weight of the chain around his neck was pulling him down. Rhiannon was floundering; the dark water flooding her throat stifled her screams. Foremost in Gideon's mind was escape, but more important was keeping Rhiannon alive until he could see her to safety.

They had just gone under for the third time, when a hand plunged in after them. It closed around Gideon's chain and gave a sharp tug—just enough to force him to rally—while the hand moved on and fisted in the neck of Rhiannon's frock, hoisting her above the surface of the water. It dropped her into the punt without ceremony and moved on to seize Gideon's collar.

"I am in your debt, old friend," Gideon said to the ferry-man, as the specter gave the collar a jerk, sending it and the chain to the bottom of the lake.

The ferryman made no reply. He never spoke. Though Gideon's response was verbal, their understanding was mental, very deep, inaudible to any other, and eons old.

Gideon soothed his neck where the collar had chafed him. "Is there another way out?" he asked the specter. "No, I thought not . . . I will find a way. If you ever have need of me . . . Why won't I be? Anything—name it, old friend . . . I will try. . . ."

Gideon rose from the water and lifted Rhiannon out of the punt into his arms. "Hail and farewell," he called to the robed figure in the boat as he lifted off and soared skyward.

"What did he say?" Rhiannon asked as they streaked through the darkness away from the gate.

"There is no other exit," Gideon replied.

"More than that, I think . . ."

"Yes, I told him that if he ever had need of me to return the favor in kind, he had but to call upon me. . . . But he said something curious, that if things went well I would not be in a position where I could rally for him."

"There was more," Rhiannon persisted.

"Nothing significant," Gideon lied. He couldn't tell her the ferryman's final warning. He didn't want to worry her. He couldn't tell her that death's alter ego had warned him not to forfeit his immortality, because after all that had gone between them over the ages, he could not bear the task of ferrying the Lord of the Dark into the Netherworld. He didn't want her to know such a thing was possible if the gods were angered enough, though the thought of it haunted him and had for eons.

"Does that creature have a name?" Rhiannon asked.

"He needs no name," said Gideon. "It matters not what he is called. In this incarnation he is most dreaded, taking the condemned to their eternal torment. His other self is kinder."

"How can one befriend *Death*?" Rhiannon murmured. "It is beyond my understanding."

Gideon smiled sadly. "Immortals have no fear of death, Rhiannon," he said. "That is what makes the friendship possible . . . and treasured. Imagine his loneliness. But enough! He cannot help us further; we are on our own. I need to touch down in a place relatively safe from Ravelle, while I decide what to do next. But Ravelle is not the only danger here. I will not sleep again until I've gotten us to safety."

Here, Gideon's wings gave him the advantage. He could travel great distances in a brief space of time that it would take the satyr much longer to cover in his two-legged body. Wracking his brain for every scrap of lore he'd ever heard about the Netherworld of Outer Darkness, Gideon touched down in a forest glade and took Rhiannon in his arms.

"I thought I'd lost you," he murmured against her hair. "I never should have slept, and on my *back*! Madness! I will get us out of this."

"Have you asked your final question of the rune caster, or called back your feathers finding me?"

Gideon shook his head. "Not yet," he said. "I had no need of magic to find you. Once I broke my bonds, my wings made that possible. Ravelle is easily tracked. I found you quickly enough. There is great advantage in being able to view the land from the air. That is why he is so anxious that we join forces. I need to use the gifts Lavilia has given me wisely, and I needed to speak with you first, since what I do affects us both, Rhiannon."

"All this is my fault," Rhiannon said. "Whatever you must do, Gideon, just do it."

She was trembling, and Gideon soothed her with gentle hands, holding her close, his hardness leaning heavily against her belly. "I have to call back one of my feathers from the rune caster to get us out of here," he said. "There is no other way. We are fugitives on the other side of that gate. The watchers will be waiting once we cross back over. You know how much I want you . . . how much I long to make love to you, and you remember how it was the last time. They will attack if I try to love you. We are spared that here, but the dangers are far worse in this place."

"We have no choice," she said. "We must go back—now, before that awful creature finds us again."

"There has to be someplace where we can be together in peace," Gideon said. "I will find that place, and rebuild a stronghold where we will be safe, but we will need to be very careful while I accomplish it. The watcher's lightning bolts are nothing to be taken lightly. I wouldn't put it past them to try to kill you with one. You are expendable. The cowards banished you here knowing what would happen to you in Ravelle's hands as a punishment for *me*. They are relentless now, and they still wait by that gate back there. Are you willing to take the risk?"

"Yes, oh, yes!" Rhiannon cried, throwing her arms around his neck.

He found her lips with a hungry mouth and tasted her deeply, laving the warm honey of her essence from her tongue. How sweet she was. How soft and supple in his arms as he traced her curves through the filmy gown, grazing her hardened nipples with his thumbs.

All at once her posture clenched and he held her away. "What is it?" he asked, cupping her face in his hand.

"Ravelle," she said. "Can he . . . is he able to cross over into Arcus? Oh, Gideon!"

He heaved a sigh. "That is something you should ask Marius," he said. "Yes, I'm afraid he can."

"Why Marius?"

"Marius and Ravelle are arch rivals—immortal enemies. It is not a pretty story. Eons ago, Ravelle stole Marius's mate. The demon is a great seducer. He often prowls the archipelago in search of whom he may corrupt. Reva, that was her name, fell under Ravelle's spell and he stole her away and took her for his consort. After he bedded her, she took her own life."

"How terrible for Marius," Rhiannon murmured.

"It will not happen to us," Gideon assured her. "I will make us a place where it cannot happen. He has his strengths, but so have I mine."

"We will go now, then?" she urged. "I do not want to see that creature again."

Gideon hesitated, his hands caressing her. "In the past, the watchers have never attacked unless I attempted to make love to you. We shall have to choose our moments carefully once we return, and may have to . . . abstain until it is safe. I want to make love to you once more here, where we are safe from the watchers. We are safe from Ravelle also. I dealt him a staggering blow with that chain, and he cannot travel as swiftly as we can aloft." He opened his eel skin, took her hand, and crimped her fingers around his penis. How hot and hard it was. The events of the past few hours had left him ravenous for sex. He knew she must be also, come fresh from an orgy, despite the terror she must have felt at the demon's mercy.

This time, he would not lie down on his back, on his wings—never again. His one delicious moment of fantasy come to life had nearly cost them both more than they could afford to lose. He would not make that mistake again. Passion and the urgency of unbridled lust ruled him then. In his arms, she was pure sex, not just her body, her ravishing beauty, her exotic hair, so long and lustrous challenging the hem of her gown. Her heart beat with an erotic rhythm in his embrace; she came alive to it. He had awakened that rhythm in her when he opened the petals of the exquisite flower she was. He had created her, turned her childlike curiosity into a flaming passion that made her his alone. And now he had the best of both mysterious incarnations in this enigmatic beauty. He had always marveled at the innocence and fierce passion that lived in her side by side. Which one was she this time, the innocent or the tigress? How many women was she? He wondered if even she knew. He

longed to keep peeling the layers away until he had exposed
and claimed them all. It was like taking a virgin each time they
made love.

Her fingers played his shaft like a virtuoso plays a treasured
instrument. It was the reverencing that so totally captivated
him. She held it as if it were more precious than gold—more
valuable than all the treasures under the moon and stars. He
had never been reverenced before Rhiannon. He had never
been truly loved; he knew that now.

Gideon's breath caught as she traced the purple veins in bold
relief along his shaft. His wings unfurled halfway. His heart
nearly stopped as her dainty fingers felt for the pulse of the
blood thrumming through those veins from root to mushroom
tip. He groaned. Exquisite agony.

He could bear no more. Slipping the dark gown from her
shoulders, he let it fall at her feet, drew in his wings, and knelt
before her, seeking the pleasure spot beneath her pubic curls
with his tongue. Cupping her buttocks in his hands, he drew
her nearer, laving her steely nub, probing her folds, the sultry
heat beyond her nether lips as his tongue plunged inside, tasting her juices, gliding on the honey-sweet musk of her arousal.

Rhiannon moaned his name as she gripped his shoulders.
Her hands inched upward finding the pulse in the distended
veins at the base of his neck. They crept higher, until she cupped
his face and moved on, lacing her fingers through his hair. They
fisted in the long, dark waves, holding his head against her pubic
mound as he sucked, and laved, and nipped at her sex until she
cried out.

A thick, ground-creeping mist had begun drifting over the
copse, and the little mall where they stood half buried in it. Bewitched, Gideon savored every inch of her with his hands, with
his lips, with his body, until he could bear no more and finally
laid her down in the ghosting fog that hid the ground and covered them like a cool, soft blanket.

Gripping her buttocks, he raised her hips, guiding her legs around his waist, and plunged into her with a long, lingering moan. He needed to savor this. If they were anywhere on Arcus, the watchers would be firing their missiles by now. He had to make the euphoria last. The gods alone knew when they'd get another opportunity to love each other without fear of reprisal, but oh, what her tiny hands were doing to his resolve. When they left his neck and gripped his buttocks, gooseflesh riddled the length of his spine and he was undone.

His cock began to throb with orgasmic contractions made more urgent by the walls of her vagina gripping him as he thrust into her. His hips jerked forward, plunging him deeper into the sultry heat of her, deeper still, until the head of his penis nudged her womb, wrenching a guttural cry of carnal euphoria from her parted lips.

Clearly lost in the throes of carnal oblivion, Rhiannon fisted her hands in the mulch beneath them in an obvious attempt to keep from stroking his wings, and froze in his arms. She gasped, groping the forest floor again and screamed. "Gideon, the ground . . . it's *moving* . . . something slimy!" She fished her shift out of the mist and screamed again, dropping it as if it were live coals. It was covered with wriggling elvers.

Gideon was crouching knee-deep in the squirming young eels; he scooped Rhiannon into his arms and plowed through them deeper into the fog. "They cannot hurt you," he soothed. "It is just Netherworld glamour. The demons mine your thoughts for that which frightens you. You must have thought of elvers since you entered Outer Darkness. That is what exists here, all men's terrors plaguing them in perpetual torment. It is real only if you let it be."

When they'd gone some distance, he set her down again, but still the eels writhed beneath the mist, and she screamed again. "They are real enough for me, Gideon! Take me away from here. . . . I cannot bear it!"

Again, he moved some distance into the fog, and for a moment, the ground beneath them seemed firm. Again, he knelt to take her, but he had scarcely entered her when the firm ground beneath them became a writhing, squishing nest of elvers just as it had before. This time, laughter boomed through the quiet, deep, guttural explosions echoing from the mist. Gideon's posture clenched as he withdrew himself, scanning the drifting vapors for the demon to materialize. It was Ravelle's lecherous laughter. There was no mistaking that bloodcurdling sound, but there was no sign of him, and how could there be? There was no way the satyr could have followed them so quickly.

"You cannot escape me," Ravelle's voice tittered. "This is only the beginning, Lord of the Dark. You have made a formidable enemy alienating me."

Gideon gathered Rhiannon into his arms and flew to the opposite side of the thicket, but when he touched down it was the same, the ground beneath their feet was crawling with elvers, and the laughter came again.

"You see?" the satyr's voice rumbled through the dank, still air amplified by the mist. "It will be thus wherever you set your foot down in my world. So flee if you must. There is nowhere you can go that I cannot find you, and I do so enjoy a quest. We will meet again, dark one, when you least expect it. You will rue the day you turned down an offer from Ravelle, the Lord of Outer Darkness!"

The hideous laughter came and went like ocean waves, mingled with Rhiannon's hysterical shrieks, for the elvers were wriggling up her naked legs to her thighs, and her terror was palpable as they approached her pubic mound.

"Gideon, *please*! Call back the feather, I beg you!" she shrilled, burying her face in his shoulder as she clung to him, her rigid fingers digging into his muscles through the eel-skin suit.

Lifting off, Gideon soared upward, shaking the demon's

glamour free. One by one, the eels fell away, and he heaved a ragged sigh. "Ravelle has dominion over the land in his domain, but I have dominion over the sky wherever my wings take me. Let me show you. . . ." Twining her legs around his waist, he plunged into her in flight. "Creatures in the astral mate thus," he murmured in her ear, taking her deeper. "Hold on to me and you will know pleasures you never dreamed existed. . . . You will know what it is to be taken by the wind. . . ."

Gideon had longed to take her in flight since he'd first set eyes upon her in his pool; it was his most secret fantasy, but he'd dared not risk it with the watchers hovering. Seizing her buttocks, he drove into her, gliding on her juices, moving in and out of her folds one by one in excruciatingly slow increments, feeding upon her pleasure moans as they glided on zephyrs in the starlit darkness high above the ugly forest floor.

Like peeling back the petals from a rose, he entered her slowly, savoring each delicious layer, moving on to the next, leaving no velvety mystery unexplored, no hot, silky crevice unprobed. He was Lord of the Air, and she had made him so, for she clung to him, her hands clasped around his neck, in total abandon.

Gideon soared higher, creating the wind that tortured his feathers. "Hold tight! I won't let you fall. . . ." he panted. Letting go of her buttocks, he slid his hands along her curves until they cupped her breasts. The nipples had hardened like steel against his thumbs as they strummed the dark puckered buds.

Groaning, Rhiannon tightened her grip on his waist with her legs and arched her back, pulling his head down until his lips closed over one turgid nubbin and tugged, sucking deeply. Bewitched by the sultry moans leaking from her throat as he suckled, his skilled fingers pinched and rubbed and scraped against the other bud until she cried out for mercy, calling his name.

Darkness enveloped them like a glove, as he soared higher

still, creating more wind to whip through his feathers, making him harder, bringing him to the brink of rapture unlike any he had ever known. He could feel her come—feel the orgasmic contractions—the hot juices of her release as they laved his aching cock, and he wanted it to go on forever.

Convulsed in an unstoppable frenzy of carnal oblivion, he brought her to the brink again, undulating against her, grinding the root of his shaft into her clitoris as he hammered into her again and again, finding the secret place at the seat of her sex that riddled her with drenching fire. He could feel the scorching heat of that fire as her hips lurched forward, and her deep folds gripped him relentlessly. He could hold back no longer, and crushing her close, he rotated his hips spiraling into her, a deep-throated moan escaping his parched lungs.

"Hold tight, my love," he murmured. "I will take you to heights you've never imagined."

He hadn't broken his stride, hadn't changed the friction as he spiraled into her, keeping her just at the edge of climax. Soaring higher still, he felt her posture clench around his rigid cock, felt it grip him on the verge of coming. It was time.

High above the clouds, he paused in flight and, in a split second, dove downward at a heart-stopping speed, while filling her with his sex from root to ridged mushroom tip. Riding the wind, he clasped her fast as he pounded into her streaking through the air in a spiraling tailspin, fueled by her rapturous moans. Her climax riddled him like cannon fire, triggering his own release. It was as if his bones were melting as she milked him dry, the soft, hot walls of her vagina squeezing out every last drop of his come until it overflowed, as they soared down, down through the dark night sky, joined to the soul.

Gideon pulled out of the spin just short of touching down, and found her lips in a fiery kiss as they hovered above the thicket. "You have seduced the wind, my love, and it has loved you well," he murmured, when their lips parted. "I have longed to take you thus since first we met, to come inside you in the air—*my* air, for I am lord of it. It is the greatest gift that I could give you."

Ravelle's laughter came again, hideous and cold. "How touching," the satyr said. "Enjoy her while you may. Soon, she is mine to enjoy, dark one, just like that pitiable centaur's mate was once mine also."

Rhiannon began to tremble in Gideon's arms, and he soothed her gently. Beneath them, the mist had begun to dissipate, giving glimpses of the ground crawling with elvers.

"Don't put me down!" she cried, her pinching fingers digging into his neck. "The eels . . . they are *everywhere!*"

Ravelle's laughter echoed through the twisted trees. It rumbled through the shadow-steeped undergrowth alive with crawling elvers in the inky midnight darkness. "The feather . . ." Rhiannon reminded him. "Gideon, I beg you, please . . . call back the feather . . . Take me away from here!"

"Do not listen to him," Gideon soothed. "He makes a clever demonstration, but he is not here in the flesh. Do not let his evil glamour spoil what we have just shared. Mine is the greatest power . . . even here."

"If that is so, why do you hesitate?" she cried. "You cannot be having second thoughts about joining with him?"

That was the farthest thing from Gideon's mind, but how could he confide his real fears—that the watchers would kill her if he took her back? Wasn't that what they had in mind when they banished her to Outer Darkness? She had no idea of the danger she was in, or how close she had already come to death.

Gideon soothed her with gentle hands. "Of course not!" he said. "That was never an option. I wanted to prepare, to form some sort of plan before we go. There is great danger in returning, you know that."

"There is greater danger here. You know what he meant to

do with me. He wanted me to convince you to join forces with him here, and I was to be consort to you both! I won't stand his hands on me again. I'd rather be dead!"

Gideon's posture clenched, airborne though he was. "You said you hadn't been harmed," he reminded her, searching her eyes deeply.

"I wasn't 'harmed' in the way you mean," she returned, "but he put his hands on me—examined me to see if you had taken me . . ."

Gideon's mind was racing. Rage set the muscles along his rigid jaw ticking. There was nothing for it. Though he was hesitant for fear of wasting the feathers, for he had no idea what lay ahead, she was right, he had to call one back.

"Hold on to me," he said through clenched teeth. Closing his eyes, he called Lavilia with his mind, begging back the feather that would return them to Arcus.

The mantra was scarcely chanted when the disembodied demon laughter came again. All at once, the mist was gone and firm ground as far as the eye could see had become a writhing sea of elvers, eels, and snakes.

Rhiannon screamed as the squirming landscape undulated closer, and Gideon flew higher. "Why doesn't the rune caster answer?" she cried. "Didn't she hear your call? Suppose she doesn't respond! Such creatures as she should never be trusted, even I know that!"

Gideon smiled, folding her closer in his arms as he hovered above the ground that was still crawling with reptiles. "Look!" he said, pointing upward, where a single white feather was drifting down.

"Do you have to catch it?" Rhiannon asked.

"It will return to me, watch, but the minute I touch it we will be out of here and I have no idea where we will find ourselves, so steel yourself and look sharp. Be alert for watchers. My wings will protect you, but you must hold fast to me, Rhiannon, no matter what occurs. If you should fall and I am struck . . . well, I think you see what I'm trying to tell you."

The feather drifted lower, and a familiar voice echoed across his mind. *Look sharp,* it said. *Watchers abound. You have not been gone long enough. They have not tired of the vigil.*

"Where are you taking us?" Gideon queried.

You won't like where you're going, Lavilia replied. *It is only temporary, but it is what must be for the destiny to play out. You'll know soon enough, and you have no choice.*

"Ye gods, Lavilia! You had a suggestion for me when I was in too much of a hurry to hear it. This is *not* my final question. You owe me this, and it is the second time I've begged you . . . will you tell now what you wanted to tell me then?"

I didn't have a 'suggestion,' Lavilia said. *I had the solution, but you changed all that with your impetuous nature, Lord of the Dark. The window of opportunity has closed upon that avenue for now. I tell you this much for free: When it opens to you again, take it, for it is your last hope, yours and your lady's. . . .*

"Wait!" Gideon shouted, for the feather had nearly drifted into his hand, and the rune caster's voice had grown distant. "Tell me now! In the name of the gods, do not send me into battle unarmed!"

But the rune caster made no reply. Ravelle's distant laughter ghosting through the darkness was the only sound as the feather crossed Gideon's palm.

21

Gideon plunged down feetfirst through a barrage of the watcher's chain lightning into another dark forest, with a whoosh of sighing leaves and clacking branches. An irate murmur buzzed among the trees, awakened so rudely, and Gideon groaned when recognizing his surroundings.

"Where are we?" Rhiannon said, still clinging to him.

"Lavilia was right," Gideon replied, "we're in the last place I want to be with Ravelle on the rampage . . . Marius's Forest Isle."

"The lightning . . . can it reach us here, underneath these trees? I always thought it was dangerous to seek shelter under trees in lightning."

Gideon shook his head. "No, the watcher's missiles are not ordinary lightning. They will not harm the Ancient Ones," he said, "but the minute we step beyond these trees . . ."

"We can't stay here . . . not after what you told me about Marius and Ravelle."

"Come the dawn, I will perform a little test."

"What kind of test?"

"I will attempt to leave on my own," Gideon said. "If I can get through without an attack, we'll be able to figure a way to go about separately if needs must. I want to have a look at my isle. I'm told it sank into the sea. If there is *anything* left of it that can be rebuilt—"

"Don't leave me here, Gideon!" Rhiannon cried. "How could you even think to after what happened last time?"

"That won't happen again," he assured her. "I don't mean to go far, just to see if I can get past them without you in tow. If I can't, then the rules have been changed. We have to know this, Rhiannon. I'm trying to protect you."

An ancient oak alongside lowered a heavy bough to Gideon's head almost knocking him over, and Rhiannon stiffened in Gideon's arms. "I don't want to stay here!" she cried. "These trees bound me while those evil nymphs had their way with me, while they violated me! I never wanted to set eyes on these trees again. They are evil!"

"Not evil," Gideon corrected her. "Ancient spirits inhabit these trees. Many forest dwellers have come and gone over time, but the Ancient Ones remain, guardians of this place. They hold no loyalties to humankind, or the fay, or any entity, come to that. Their judgments are for the good of Nature and the forest, and are doled out at their own discretion. We may not always agree, but they are the nobility of the Forest Isle, and we pay homage and give respect. There are stone basins set about throughout the forest for offerings—herbs and flowers, seeds especially, they love those because they symbolize new birth. Such tributes are very prized, and the giver is rewarded in accordance with the gift. The Ancient Ones' magic is very powerful."

"Oh, so it was all right for them to bind me while the nymphs abused me because they are old spirits," Rhiannon snapped.

"No," Gideon said. "The nymphs evidently gifted them

well, and so they did their bidding and bound you. I gave them no tribute when we disturbed their sleep so rudely just now, which is why this stalwart fellow chastised me."

"You defend them?" she marveled.

"I respect them," he said. "And they will help us."

A rustling sound close by made Gideon curb his tongue, and he fell silent, pricking his ears in the direction of the sound. Rhiannon cried out as the great oak alongside seized her with its branches, covering her charms with its lush leaves. After a moment, the foliage parted and Marius appeared, longbow at the ready. Gideon's posture collapsed, and he bowed to the Lord of the Forest.

"We shan't stay," he said. "Ravelle is on our heels. I won't bring that down upon you. We'll be gone in the morning."

"You may stay as long as you like. I told you that before," Marius said, handing a hooded mantle he had looped over his arm to Rhiannon, who was peeking out from behind a curtain of oak leaves. "I do not fear Ravelle. Our day is coming, his and mine, but it is not yet. Come! You have the stink of Outer Darkness upon you. My bathing pool is at your disposal. Then we shall talk."

Rustling oak leaves turned them both toward Rhiannon, who was struggling with the mantle Marius had given her, while the great tree petted her with its leaf-laden branches. It seemed to be ordering her hair, while she slapped at the leaves.

A bemused smile creased Marius's handsome lips. "He means you no harm, lady," he said. "He only wants you to hide your hair beneath the cowl. We must go into the open to reach my lodge. The watchers are hovering. They will spot that magnificent mane of yours a mile away. He means only to protect you."

"Yes, well, I can only go by past experiences," Rhiannon snapped. "The last time I encountered this . . . creature it was not so inclined." She whipped her long plait around and stuffed it inside the mantle, then tugged the hood down over her head hiding her face. "There," she said. "Will this do?"

Marius nodded, as the great tree hugged her with its branches and petted her head as one pets a faithful dog. "He thinks so," he said, clearly suppressing a chuckle.

Rhiannon halfheartedly stroked the leafy branch caressing her with a cursory pat, wriggled free of the tree's embrace, and rushed to Gideon's side.

"No, lady," Marius said. "You will walk with me. The watchers are no fools, but neither are they possessed of sage wisdom. We confuse them, um?" He turned to Gideon. "Make your test now," he said. "I will see to your lady. We are right behind you and my bow is at the ready."

Rhiannon cast a pleading glance in Gideon's direction, and he returned it with what he hoped was a look of reassurance. "Do as he says," he said. "You are perfectly safe in Marius's keeping."

The look she returned clearly said she wasn't so safe the last time he'd left her in the forest lord's care. How he loved her when anger lifted her chin, courting shadows about the dimple set there, and sparks flashed in her doelike eyes. He loved the way color blazed in the apples of her cheeks when such a mood struck her, as if an artist had stroked it on at random. He longed to take her in his arms and lay all her fears to rest, but he dared not then. Instead, he strode into the clearing that stretched between the wood and the rambling lodge at the forefront of the forest lord's compound.

Marius's plan was sound, and all three reached the cottage despite the watchers circling overhead. Once inside, the forest lord led them to a rear chamber, past the faun, Sy, who was tethered to the hearthstone performing his chores at the end of a long chain. Pulsating warmth scented with pine tar and rosemary rushed at them, rising from the sunken mineral pool Marius had promised.

"It's even warmer since Vane's volcano erupted," the forest lord explained. "All of the pools in the archipelago are. It happens every time the lava flows."

"Are the pools still all connected?" Gideon asked.

Marius nodded. "All except yours, of course," he said. "That sank back into the sea with the Dark Isle, Gideon. I know you were hoping, but you may as well know the Dark Isle no longer exists."

Gideon nodded. "I assumed as much. Still, I was hoping . . ."

"There are other options," Marius said. "Go, refresh yourselves. I will see if I can find a suitable garment for your lady." He bowed toward Rhiannon and left them, melting into the shadows.

Rhiannon turned to Gideon. "You're going to leave me here," she accused. "You heard what Ravelle said. He will follow us, and this is the first place he will look!"

"You make it seem as if I mean to abandon you," Gideon responded. "My punishment has changed. I need to see how far I can go on my own without dodging lightning bolts before I attempt to take you with me if we are to dupe the watchers. I will not see you put to the hazard because of me, Rhiannon. I would not be able to live with myself if harm came to you and it was my fault."

"Well, you saw. You made your little test just now, thanks to Marius for suggesting it. So why must you go?"

"I need to consult with the rune caster. I have one feather yet to be redeemed and one question."

"Accepted. Why can I not go with you?"

Gideon hesitated. Taking Rhiannon with him was not an option considering what happened on his last visit to the rune caster's isle. He had no idea what payment Lavilia would extract for another consultation now. "You, my love, are a colossal distraction!" he said. "I cannot think clearly with you in my arms. Look at me! I am aroused just imagining it. Besides, I can make better time alone, and in case things have changed more drastically, I will not go about with you openly until I am absolutely certain it is safe."

"Is that so? Well, look where you've taken me!" she snapped back. "I hardly call this place 'safe,' where trees take liberties—fondle, restrain, and fornicate—and nymphs seduce and lure those who mean them no harm into danger. *Safe*, indeed! I do not like this place!"

"That, my love, is because you've had a bad experience here. Can you not try to put that behind you and trust in me? I know this place for eons, and I would trust Marius with my life—and yours. He is beyond reproach. The nymphs have been banished from the forest, and Sy is now tethered to the chimney corner—just as you saw him when we entered—when Marius is not in residence. I want to see the place where the Dark Isle stood for myself. There is another place I want to see, the Isle of Mists, a long-forgotten spit of land that remained when the Shaman's Isle fell."

"And I cannot accompany you while you see these places—places that you hope to share with me?" She spun away haughtily and began to pace.

Gideon reached her in one stride, turned her back to face him, and shook her gently. "No," he said. "You cannot—not until I'm absolutely certain it is safe for you to do so. I know it is hard for a mortal to understand immortality, but you must try to grasp this, Rhiannon." He hesitated, waiting while she processed what he was saying, her brows knit in a frown. "The watchers' lightning bolts hurt me, they weaken and daze me for a time, but they cannot kill me because I am *immortal*, you are *not*. To them, you are expendable. To punish me, they would think nothing of ending your life. They nearly did when they banished you to Outer Darkness. You were not supposed to come back from that alive, as a punishment for *me*. If one of their lightning bolts were to strike you it could *kill* you, and certainly would if it hit a vital spot. I do not want to frighten you, and I cannot make it any plainer. I can only do so much to prevent such a tragedy in the air. You must respect my judgment in this . . . for both our sakes."

Rhiannon stared, her eyes sparkling with unshed tears in the torchlight flickering about the pool. Gideon almost winced. He hated the stricken look of her then. She looked like a wounded doe, and he was the one who had struck the blow that brought her down. He had avoided bringing up the issue of immortality, though it nagged him under the surface every waking hour and sullied his dreams. He had avoided it, because he had no answer for it. That was one of the things he wanted to take up with Lavilia, and another reason why he could not take Rhiannon with him. Considering his curse, which was immutable in view of his station and the gravity of his offense, it did not bode well for a happy outcome.

He would give up his immortality in a heartbeat for Rhiannon; there was no question, if only the curse would allow it, but his sentence was eternal, and he knew of no way for her to achieve immortality, though it had happened for others. It had happened for Simeon, Lord of the Deep, and his Megaleen, but those were extraordinary circumstances, and he had none to offer her. Still . . . if he were to speak with Simeon, perhaps his old friend might have some glimmer of hope to impart. As it was, they were fugitives, and would be as long as they lived where watchers could chastise them.

If only Rhiannon wouldn't look at him like that. If only those tears would dry and she would smile at him again. How he missed that smile. He hadn't seen it in some time . . . a very long time. There was no hope of that smile coming now to erase her sorrow and cause dawn to break over his soul. Instead, tears swam in those doe eyes. One spilled over onto her reddened cheek rolling off her lower lashes, and he groaned, folding her in his arms. He felt as if he were drowning in that tear.

It was no use. His wings unfurled halfway, his hot hardness leaned against her belly challenging the seam in his eel-skin suit and he was undone. There was no question. She finally understood.

When she tore herself out of his arms, she rent a tear in his heart as well. He could have sworn he heard it rip. "Rhiannon, wait!" he called, bolting after her as she burst back through the door to the lodge cottage proper.

"Leave me be a while," she sobbed from the threshold. "Don't worry . . . I shan't go far. It works both ways. Like yourself, I just need to go off on my own for a bit. . . ."

He was about to follow after her in any case, when his field of vision shifted to Marius coming into the main room of the lodge with a frock looped over his arm. Their eyes met. The forest lord's gaze told him it was safe to let her go. Both he and Rhiannon needed time apart to order their thoughts, and after an agonizing hesitation, Gideon stepped back into the pool chamber and closed the door.

No sooner had the latch clicked, when the water in the pool began to roil and bubble until the surface churned with white water. From the center of the vortex being created, a man emerged, rivulets of water sliding down his eel-skin suit similar to Gideon's. His handsome face, all angles and planes, bathed in mineral water shone in the torchlight, as did his long hair, bound with ropes of braided seaweed.

It was Simeon, Lord of the Deep.

"Well met, old friend," Gideon said, as Simeon spun around in the water and faced him.

"I do not know that we are," Simeon returned. "I am offended, dark one. Why have you not come to me with your trouble, um? Have I not burdened you with mine more times than I can count in the past?"

"I was just thinking of calling upon you," Gideon said.

"I know," said Simeon. "You haven't been alone in this. Pio, my summoner, has been monitoring your progress whenever you were near water. He read your thoughts, and here I am."

"That beloved swordfish of yours is relentless," Gideon said. "The gods bless him. I would have come to you myself, but there is nothing you can do."

"Probably not, but you might have given me a chance to try."

"You are a good friend, Simeon, and I know you would give us sanctuary, but Rhiannon would never stand living beneath the waves. She isn't a strong swimmer."

"There are many air-filled pockets and caves beneath the waves, Gideon. She would not need to swim once she reached such a plateau."

"She would never make it there, and truthfully neither would I. I am a creature of the air, Simeon. I need to soar. Imagine yourself in the air instead of the sea. We are what we are."

Gideon reached out his hand to help Simeon out of the water, but Simeon declined. "Like you say . . . we are what we are, my friend. Is there anything I can do? You have only to speak it."

"Perhaps you can answer a question."

"Ask it."

"If you had wanted to give up your immortality in order to keep Megaleen, you could have done it, but you didn't; Megaleen gained hers instead. I would give up my immortality for Rhiannon in a blink in time's eye, but I cannot. My curse is irreversible and eternal. Is there a way for Rhiannon to gain immortality, like Megaleen did?"

Simeon gave it thought. "Megaleen's immortality was a gift

from one who had it to give. It was a selfless gifting—the greatest sacrifice one being could give for another. I do not think either one of you has someone willing to give such a gift."

"No, we do not. Is there any other way that you know of for a human to gain life immortal?"

"Outer Darkness was a way, but it is not worth the price. Damnation comes too dear, my friend, and immortality gotten thus would be a living hell. I do know one thing, though . . ."

"Tell it!"

"You will not find the answer anywhere in the twelve hemispheres of Arcus."

"How can you be so certain?" Gideon asked.

"Because I exhausted every one in my search," Simeon said. "I'm sorry, old friend, but else it be by magic, as it was in my case, or a gift of the gods, there is no way that I know of for a mortal in our world to achieve the longevity that we immortals know."

22

Rhiannon ran past the faun, past Marius, whom she hadn't seen entering the main room from the side, and rushed sobbing into the darkness. Overhead, the moon had risen, cold and white and round, and stars blinked down innocently. How such beauty could exist in a land so fraught with mystery and danger was beyond her comprehension.

Now and then a shadow streaked across the moon. Watchers! She pulled the hood close around her face and melted into the shadows at the edge of the lodge. She glanced toward the forest across the clearing. It looked unreal with the moon glow silvering the Ancient Ones' leaves and branches. It softened the deceitful pine needles that looked so silky and lush from a distance only to become prickly in the harsh reality of close proximity.

How still it all was. No breath of a breeze disturbed a branch or fluttered a leaf. An eerie pall had fallen over the isle. It was unnatural. She glanced up at the indigo vault. Dark, scudding clouds racing across the moon had suddenly obscured the watchers. There wasn't much comfort in that. Rhiannon knew they were there whether she could see them or not, and the cloud cover would force them to hover lower for a clearer view.

Rhiannon shuddered. The homespun mantle Marius had given her was rough and scratchy against her tender, naked skin. Gooseflesh and the coarsely spun fabric scraping against her nipples had brought them erect. She soothed them absently, a close eye upon the heavens, half expecting lightning bolts to come hurtling at her.

Sculptured hedges lined the path between the lodge and the paddock behind, and she backed into the thick foliage in an attempt to make herself invisible. She should go back inside, but she wasn't ready to face Gideon yet, not until she could mask some of the fear he'd planted in her mind—fear that he was going to remain young and virile and live on eternally, while she would grow old and die according to her species. That hadn't really sunken in before he'd made a point of spelling it out. There had to be a way for them to be together—there *had* to be. She was wracking her brain over that when a rustling noise behind stopped her in her tracks, her heart pounding against her ribs, but the sound ceased also.

She glanced about but saw nothing, and after a moment, she started to walk again, her feet crunching on the gravel underfoot. She was in the open along that path. She would have been safer in the woods, but nothing could persuade her to take that direction, not after what had occurred there before. Instead, she continued on her present course, knowing she should go back, and wondering why Gideon hadn't come after her.

All at once, dry lightning speared down in the near distance, and she cried out in spite of herself at sight of the blinding, snakelike shaft of ethereal light. The night sky all around had taken on a shrouded hue of a sudden, ominous and pale. The rustling had begun again. Adrenaline surged in her, crippling her where she stood. Terror froze her stiff, stifling the scream building at the back of her throat as a hand clamped tight over her mouth jerked her to a standstill. A soft whisper in her ear fluttered the tendrils that clung to her cheeks.

"Do not scream," Marius murmured. "It is I. Turn slowly, and stay close to the hedge. We are not alone, lady. I need to get you back to the lodge."

"Where is Gideon?" Rhiannon begged.

"He is safe, and he will have my head if any more harm comes to you in my keeping. Quickly now, and stick to the shadows. It's only a few steps. Your bath awaits, and I've found a fine kirtle for you."

"He's gone, isn't he?" Rhiannon knew. "He's gone and left me here! That lightning I just saw. The watchers! It was, wasn't it! They've struck him again! The nymphs will come and 'minister' to him as they did before. . . ."

It was beyond bearing. Jealousy roiled in her at the thought of the beautiful forest mavens having their way with him—making him come—relieving him as only they possessed the skills to do, as they'd done to *her*. How well she knew the power of their seductions.

The nymphs were immortal, and she was not. They would still be young and beautiful, and ready to serve his lusts long after she had withered and died and gone to her grave. In spite of Marius's warning, she groaned aloud at the prospect, and he clamped his hand over her mouth again.

"Keep still!" he warned. "I do not mean to frighten you, but look at the forest!"

Rhiannon gazed in the direction of the ancient trees. They seemed unchanged from before, silent sentinels seemingly frozen in place. It was almost as if all the animated spirits that lived inside the giant trees had vacated them.

"What is it?" she said. "Why are they so still?"

"It is an evil presence that calls the spirits inward. If they awaken here now there will be a reckoning. There are some things not even my longbow can save. Quicken your step. Do you not feel it?"

"Feel what?" Rhiannon murmured.

Without replying, Marius rushed her into the lodge and bolted the door behind them. "I do not know," he said. "A tremor, a current in the air, a vibration beneath our feet. Whatever it is, it has distracted the watchers, and allowed Gideon to escape safely."

"*Escape?*" she cried. The connotations of the word had paralyzed her mind with fear.

"Escape the watchers, yes," Marius clarified. "Gideon has not left you, lady—never that. He has gone to seek the answer to your future. Whatever this is, it began the minute he left. It evidently fears him."

"Ravelle!" Rhiannon breathed.

"The keeper of Outer Darkness is able to project his magic far and wide," Marius said. "It is how he procures his victims. Many years ago, those woods out there were filled with sprites and nymphs and sylphs, creatures of the astral who took refuge here among the Ancient Ones . . . and me from time to time; all gone now. The last were banished after what they did to you."

Rhiannon could feel the hot blood rise to her temples. She always knew when she was blushing. The heat in her cheeks always narrowed her vision. It was happening now. That he knew what the nymphs had done to her was too embarrassing to bear. It brought it all back—the clever creatures' cunning assault upon her body, while the trees held her at their mercy. She moaned in mortification, recalling their probing fingers entering her, spreading her juices, exploring her every crevice, every orifice until they'd brought her to a riveting climax. That she'd had no control over their magic, no defense against their sexual skills, mattered not a whit. It had happened, and Marius, Lord of the Forest, knew of it. She wanted the polished wood floor of the lodge to open up and swallow her.

"I can only imagine the humiliations you must have suffered, knowing that lot," Marius quickly said. The gods bless
the man! He'd evidently read her thoughts and meant to put
her at her ease. She longed to throw her arms around his neck
in a gesture of appreciation but had the good sense to resist the
temptation. There was an aura of lonely sadness about the Lord
of the Forest that was best left untampered with, for fear of
rousing something it would have been cruel to awaken, even
with the most innocent of gestures. "I have been haunted with
guilt over what happened to you here upon your last visit,
lady," he concluded.

"I do not like to remember what occurred then," she said
demurely. "But please, there was no fault in you, or Sy, either,
come to that. The fault was all mine. I disobeyed your directive
and duped poor Sy into disobeying his, because I was jealous
over what I feared the nymphs were doing with Gideon."

"Well, they are here no more. Because of what they did to
you, they are banished, and from what I understand, the astral
has banned them also. You must not question Gideon's devo-
tion, lady. He worships you. I have never seen him so taken before. You must understand the needs, if you will, his curse
imposes upon him. The nymphs' ministrations were purely
therapeutical . . . at least on his part. He wasn't even conscious
during what took place. So, you see, there was nothing to be
jealous of."

That was easy for him to say. She could not erase the visions
of those nymphs caressing Gideon, laying their skilled hands—
far more skilled than hers—upon his shaft until they'd brought
it fully erect—taking their turn upon it until they'd made him
come, and come again! She had taken him inside her—given
him her virtue—pleasured him on land and in the *air*, of all un-
heard of things, in her clumsy, inexperienced way. How could
it ever be enough? How could *she* ever be enough? She had
never felt so dismally inadequate, especially since, for all of

that, her "ministrations" would be temporary. They would only last the length of days of a human life—a blink in the eye of time—and then other immortals like himself would pleasure him once again. She wished he hadn't made it plain. She wished he'd let her muddle through in blessed ignorance of the cold reality that would all too soon separate them, but he had not and her heart was breaking.

"You will be safe as long as you remain inside the lodge," Marius said. "I cannot. I am custodian of the Ancient Ones, and I must be certain they are safe from any danger. Can I trust you to remain inside these walls while I do that?"

"Lord Marius, where has Gideon gone?" she asked, avoiding the question. She had to know.

The forest lord leaked a throaty chuckle. "The gods alone know what's come knocking at our door, and that is all that worries you, um? You two are well-matched, lady."

Rhiannon felt the fingers of a blush crawl up her cheeks again and lowered her eyes.

Marius smiled. "He is to be envied," he observed. "He has gone to seek out the rune caster to see what her magic can do to help you."

"This is all my fault," Rhiannon despaired. "He asked me to stay inside the cave—only that. But the day was sunny and warm, and I saw no harm in a stroll about the isle in broad daylight, when I could clearly see the pitfalls and dangers he was so concerned about. He didn't tell me about the watchers. If I'd only known . . ."

"He does not blame you. He is driven to put things to rights—obsessed with it. Granted, he erred eons ago, when all this began. He fell from the gods' graces. Now, he has been stripped of everything—his fine castle, his humble cave, his island, even his right to enjoy the pleasures of his own body. All he has left is you, and now he fears he will lose you, also—"

"Never!" Rhiannon interrupted.

Marius smiled sadly. "No, not your love, lady . . . He fears the watchers will kill you as a final retaliation for him—a final breaking of his willful spirit. It is a fear he can taste. It is why he went after you into Outer Darkness, why he was ready to condemn himself to an eternity in the hell of mortals if that was the only way to have you. Unfortunately, I believe he has brought some of that hell back with him. I believe it is here, on my isle, in my forest, as we speak, threatening the Ancient Ones and helpless creatures I am duty bound to protect."

"Forgive me," she murmured. "A personal question . . . You are so kind to your creatures. You treat them with such reverence. What crime did you commit that cursed you to walk in the body of the centaur when the moon waxes full?"

"I killed one," Marius said flatly.

"A-purpose?"

He nodded. "Quite so, but that was very long ago . . . so long now it seems as though it happened to someone else. The whole of it is lost in the mists of time, I fear, but no matter. I've grown quite accustomed to my four-legged incarnation."

"I did not mean to bring back sad memories," Rhiannon said, pained by his stricken expression. Whatever it was, it wasn't lost in the mists of time as he would have her believe, and she was wise enough to probe him no further.

"Think nothing of it," Marius said. "Ravelle casts his glamour before him to intimidate. I think that is what is occurring here now. Just help me to help Gideon by staying safe in my care while he is abroad. Do not begrudge him his mission, for if it fails, we all fail with it, and there will be a reckoning unlike any ever recorded in this world or any other where immortals live out their eternity."

Rhiannon was silent apace. She gave his words deep thought. All at once her eyes widened. Tears stung them, blurring his handsome image. *In this world or any other* . . . the Forest Lord's words struck her like cannon fire. Of course! Why hadn't she seen it before? Why hadn't she realized it when Gideon made it all so clear? She was too close to the situation—and Gideon—to see it. It had taken this sage guardian of the wood, who shared his body with a creature he had once killed to open her eyes, and he didn't even realize he'd given her the key.

She stifled an exhilarated cry in her excitement. Why hadn't it occurred to her before? She was tempted to blurt it out, but this was not for Marius's ears. She hardly knew him well enough. This was something for Gideon's ears. *He didn't need this mission*, her mind was screaming. *Gods above, I have the answer! I know! I know what must be done to save us all . . .*

23

Gideon opened the front of his eel-skin suit and freed his bursting penis to the night wind. So many times the wind had taken him thus, stroking his hot shaft and tight sac with cool breezes. He had almost given the wind substance, like the artists' renditions of buxom maidens drawn in the legends of old maps, their cheeks puffed out as they blew the painted ships about upon their painted oceans. Somehow, giving his seducer an image seemed less lonesome than the cold reality of mating with thin air. But there was no relief in it any longer, not since he'd had his Rhiannon in flight, and soared with her to the brink of Paradise.

Thinking about Rhiannon as the wind took him made the climax more acute. He came quickly, aided by the approaching storm and the risen wind that chased the roiling clouds overhead obscuring the moon. It was the storm that had saved him a more serious blow by the watcher's missile as he took to the air earlier. He had suffered only a graze instead of the direct hit the odious creature had intended, and spiraled out of their reach.

It was a cold wind for a warm night caressing him now, soothing the fever in his hot, sore flesh, cooling the thrumming veins along his shaft as the blood pounded through them rushing to the hard head of his penis, slick with pre-come. He had the wind to thank for such an erection, and now there was the memory of Rhiannon's soft, caressing fingers and the silken feel of her thighs gripping his waist. Closing his eyes, he imagined her long hair lashing him like a whip as they plummeted toward land for the final climax. Her scent rushed up his nostrils, softly floral, sweet clover laced with the heated musk of sex. His hips jerked forward, his shaft seeking the sultry comfort of her petal-like folds, searching for the thick walls to grip him, milking him dry. It was empty air that took him instead, and he groaned as the seed of his body rushed out of him spurt after involuntary spurt, carried off on the wind that seduced him.

The rune caster's cottage loomed up before him veiled as it always was in mist. The watchers gave Lavilia no truck. They had never bothered him when he visited her isle, but things were changing, and he couldn't be too careful. The odious harpies attacked him at random now, where they hadn't ever attacked him before unless he was in the arms of a woman. That being the case, anything was possible, and he could ill afford to suffer a lightning strike now.

He touched down upon the strand and moved with caution through the mist. Lavilia was near. He could feel her presence. How would she present herself this time? He had only to ask to know.

"Show yourself, Lavilia," he said. "I haven't much time."

"Come to settle your accounts, have you, dark one?" she replied from deep in the foggy mist. It beaded upon Gideon's feathers in liquefied droplets, casting an aura of rainbow shimmer about them in the reflected moonlight.

"You know what I need," he replied. He did not want to

waste the remaining gifts. If he could trick her into telling him what he needed to know . . . it was worth a try.

"The knowledge you need, you have had all the while, impetuous one, if you were not too blinded by love madness you would have seen it."

"I dislike conversing with the fog," Gideon said. "Show yourself and have done! I tire of tilting with shadows."

"In due time," she tittered. "I do not trust your mood, dark one. The desperate oftentimes do . . . foolish things. I would prefer not to become a victim of your current madness."

"You have not begun to see my 'madness' if you presume to cheat me, old one."

"Have I not served you well in the past?"

"You have," Gideon replied, "and you know my needs."

"Oh, aye, I know them!" she was quick to interject. "Is it your final question you have come to ask, or your last feather? I wouldn't squander that if I were you."

"I asked the question closest to my heart on a previous visit," he said. "Your answer was unclear."

"How is that?"

"You said it was possible for Rhiannon and I to be together, but not the way I expected, or words to that effect."

"You asked if you could keep your lady, and I told you yes, but not as you wished. That should have been enough right there for you to figure out the rest, but you were too besotted, and still are, I'll wager."

"Why must you always speak in riddles?" Gideon snapped. "Can you not tell it plain?"

"All augur comes in riddles. The oracle I summon with the runes is no different from the necromancer's spirit guides, or the sorcerer's ploys."

"Why is that?" Gideon wondered, thinking out loud. He was genuinely curious.

"Because the truth behind it is all too often too terrible to bear spoken plain . . . like now," Lavilia said. "You want me to elaborate upon an answer I have already given you. Is it my fault that you are too dense to see the answer staring you in the face? I think not, dark one. You need to take stock. Your sight has grown narrow these days. Love does that to a body."

"I've never had 'sight.' That is why I come to you."

"You come to me because you have no other alternative," she chortled. "You've made a grand muck of things blundering about on your own."

"Then enlighten me!" Gideon thundered, his voice echoing repeatedly, amplified by the fog. "Come out! Show yourself and let me look into your eyes."

After a moment, the mist parted and Lavilia stepped out of the writhing whorls of mystic vapor naked, her long gray hair barely covering her faded nipples. "Do not worry," she said, sauntering closer. "I want none of you this time; it is our last time, and I would remember our coupling as it was upon your last visit. I have something else in mind."

"She is with Marius. Is she safe on the Forest Isle until I resolve this?"

"Is that your last question?" Lavilia asked. "Think carefully, you only have one."

Gideon already knew he and Rhiannon could be together, just not as he wished. That much he'd tricked her into telling, so he wouldn't waste a question on that. He'd already wasted one when the nightmare began. He could ill afford to lose another.

"Yes," he finally said. "Is she safe where I have left her?"

"Not for long," said the crone. "You have angered the guardian of Outer Darkness, and none upon the Forest Isle are safe from that one's wrath."

Gideon gave a start. "Why did you send us back there then?"

"I didn't send you anywhere, dark one," Lavilia defended. "I got you out of hell to play out your destiny. That it is to happen on the Forest Isle is none of my doing. I haven't the power to dictate destiny, only to reveal it. *You* set this course in motion when you struck out on your own without hearing what you needed to know that would have prevented all of this, impetuous one. Lay no blame for that blunder upon me!"

"And thrice now I have begged you to tell me the rest of that augur. You *owe* me!"

"Do I? Take care, dark one. You can ill afford to anger me now. I do not need to tell you what you were in too great a hurry to hear. Someone else will do that for me. But this much I tell you for free . . . You will not find your safe haven anywhere within the reaches, tracks, and climbs of Arcus. Waste no time seeking sanctuary here or *anywhere* that the watchers can gain admittance. They are relentless."

"I have nothing left to lose," Gideon ground out through clenched teeth.

"Nothing except Rhiannon," Lavilia reminded him. "And your soul."

Gideon gave it thought. There was no time to waste, but he was down to his last feather in her keeping. He needed to be certain. When he didn't speak, Lavilia took the initiative.

"I can tell you no more," she said. "Take great care calling back your last feather. That is all the free advice I can give you, and I've said it before. I will not cheat you, dark one, but I am bound by the oracle I've summoned to do your bidding in this, and if you do not choose wisely . . ."

"I understand."

"I wonder that you do," she said on a gusty sigh. "But no matter. It will play out as it is designed. Come! Embrace me . . ."

"I thought you said—"

"I am not asking you to put that grand magnificence inside

me, there isn't time for that. I ask only that you give it me in spirit. When I touch that body, it becomes a living memory, dark one, a vision imprinted in my mind that I might call up whenever I will to bring your image to me as if you've come in the flesh. Let me have my playthings. It will not hurt you, and it will bring comfort to a tired old succubus on dark and lonely winter nights."

Gideon almost pitied her as she sauntered close, cupping his face with her wrinkled hands.

"I will miss you," she said, sliding her crippled fingers down his neck. She was like a blind person seeing by touch.

Gideon took a closer look, and his breath caught in his throat. She *was* blind. Why had she never showed him this before? "You cannot see!" he cried. "How is it in all these years I have never noticed?"

"I am illusion, dark one, remember? You have seen what I have wished you to see. I need no eyes for the kind of sight the gods have bestowed upon me. It was my sacrifice eons ago in trade for my second sight. My third eye sees far more clearly than the two dead orbs you gaze into now, dark one. I see you with my spirit through these old fingers, and your image will forever live behind these sightless eyes."

She continued to follow the contours of his shoulders, then traced his broad chest through the eel-skin suit. Spreading it wide, she reached inside and found the small, hard buds of his nipples set like gems in his pectoral muscles above the sleek, roped torso. When she fondled his penis, his posture clenched. She was making a mental image of every muscle, every crevice. He was already aroused when she began, as he always was after he'd flown. When she cupped his testicles, his hips jerked forward, and his shaft lengthened, the distended veins thrumming, straining the sensitive skin.

Gideon groaned and shut his eyes. He'd steeled himself

against this very thing before he ever touched down, and convinced himself that whatever sexual favors she extracted from him were no worse than the Ancient Ones' ministrations in Marius's forest. His cock had needed milking since the watchers' lightning strike as he set out. The wind hadn't been enough to slake the need the lightning awakened, that was why the nymphs had always serviced him when they were near. Without release, the pain would be excruciating. Resigned, he opened his eyes and gave a lurch. Lavilia had shapeshifted into the young and buxom creature he had taken on his last visit.

"You will have to finish what you've started there," he said, his voice husky with lust. "The lightning strike I suffered coming here needs purging."

" 'Twas my intent, dark one," Lavilia said. "But you will not have to suffer putting this fine shaft I am holding inside of me this time. I need to hold it thus when you come to make the memory that will live in the legends of the Arcan Isles for all eternity. For soon, you come this way no more, Gideon, Lord of the Dark, but your legend will live on for all who will come after you through the mists of time. I will see to it."

Cold chills raced the length of Gideon's spine. "You make it sound as if I am about to die, old one," he said, as cheerfully as her cryptic augur would allow.

"There is no death for an immortal, no matter what his plane of existence, you know that. Just as Simeon's penis was once preserved at the height of its splendor for all to witness down through the ages, so will your magnificence be preserved at the moment of ejaculation. So it shall be with all the lords of Arcus before my days are done. It is my gift to the posterity of the archipelago, so that whatever occurs, all who tread these isles will know the greatness that once reigned here."

Gideon gave an incredulous grunt. He'd seen Simeon's phallus before Simeon consigned it to the deep by way of a tide pool on the Isle of Mists before he wedded his Megaleen.

"*You* sculpted that phallus of Simeon?" he blurted.

She nodded. "With my third eye, just as I sculpt you now. Yours will be my greatest work, dark one. Stand still! I feel the blood pumping through those rigid veins; how hard the head is, yet how silken soft the skin that sheaths that hardness. No marble mined of any quarry could ever really do it justice. Without my magic, it could not be done."

"Touch my wings," Gideon got out, trying to hurry the process. His need was such that he could bear no more without pain.

"Not . . . quite . . . yet . . ." she said, pumping his shaft with her hand in a circular motion from root to ridged tip, avoiding the smooth, domed head that had begun to leak pre-come. His penis was so engorged it looked purple in the eerie light, as he watched her skilled fingers masturbate him.

"Mica's teeth!" he seethed. "Have done! My wings! Stroke my wings and set me free from this torture . . . It is enough!"

Her deep, tantalizing revolutions pumping him steadily made him shiver with each thrust of her hand. Like any temperamental artist, she would not cease until she'd gotten the aspect just so. Finally, he could bear no more. He was ready to let his penis decide for her, when she stroked his wings working his shaft hard in rapid tugs, and Gideon groaned as he climaxed, his seed spewing out of him in a steady stream until she had pumped him dry.

Gideon closed his eyes as the rush of orgasmic fire overwhelmed him. When he opened them again, Lavilia had melted into the mist.

"Wait! Don't go!" he cried. "Our business is not yet concluded!"

"Oh, aye, it is, dark one," she replied. "Your phallus will be a grand tribute to your time among us. You are a living legend, dark one. All Arcus will hear your tale. Bards will sing your song. None will ever forget the Lord of the Dark. I shall see to that."

"I care for none of it. I only want to live in peace with Rhiannon."

"Then call back your last feather wisely."

"Why can't you give it now and send us where we need to go, Lavilia?"

"Because, for one thing, you do not yet know where that is, and for another, though I *do* know, were I to do as you ask, you would be leaving a loyal friend at the mercy of a reckoning that you have created. Eternal happiness cannot be bought with betrayal. You must live out the destiny you have created for yourself and others before you can be free. Remember . . . all of this could have been avoided but for your impetuous nature. There is no room for such as that here now."

She spoke of Marius, of course, and she was right. He could not leave his friend, the Ancient Ones, and all the helpless creatures of the Forest Isle at the mercy of Ravelle.

"I must get back," he knew, bolting toward the strand.

"*Wait!*" she shrilled. "What have I just told you of impetuousness? Have you not heard one word I've said? Take one more step before I've finished with you, and I will call back the contract and let you flounder on your own—you and your Rhiannon—to sink or swim as you will!"

"Then please be brief," he sallied. "You were the one who said Rhiannon isn't safe there for long."

"Rhiannon is your soul mate, Gideon," she said. "The female that began this nightmare with you eons ago was not. Had you not fallen, Rhiannon would have had lovers, but she would have walked through her life never knowing she had another half who would make her whole. You get only one soul mate for all eternity. All other romantic partnerships you engage in involve kindred spirits. These are souls attracted to your sphere, souls that through one similarity or another attach themselves to your aura. Hangers-on blinded by your light. They can be very intense relationships, like the one that damned you, dark one, but no other save this one—your Rhiannon—is your true soul mate. Think back . . . You knew it the minute you set eyes upon her, didn't you? You knew this one was different."

"Yes, but how can that be? I am . . . I *was* an angel created to serve the Arcan gods. How can I even have a soul?"

"Ah, but you do—a gift of the gods along with the gift of free will that has damned you. The gods expected you to obey the spirit side in you. Instead, you turned to the flesh, which is why the gods pursue you so relentlessly. It wasn't so much the woman, as it was that you betrayed their trust. This they will not abide. And so they cursed you and sent the watchers to enforce your punishment. I will tell you one last thing for free. It is something that you know already if you've been paying attention, so it is no hardship, but something you haven't really taken deep enough to heart . . . You will have no peace until you free yourself of the watchers. They, too, are eternal, but of a lower form. Unlike you, they are possessed of neither soul nor conscience, which makes them very dangerous."

Gideon was beginning to think he'd asked the wrong question. She was right. Much of this he knew, but it had never really sunken in the way she presented it now.

It seemed to be her parting gift. There was wisdom to be gained in it somewhere, if only he could see it. Oddly, there was some comfort in what she'd said even if he didn't fully understand it.

"Hail and farewell, old friend," Gideon said. "If you are through with me, needs must that I return to the Forest Isle. I left without letting Rhiannon know in order to avoid a confrontation. If we are under siege, she will be frightened, and Marius will have need of me."

"Then go, dark one. We will not meet again. Call back your feather when you will, and then our days are done."

24

It had to be the longest night Rhiannon had ever spent. Not wanting to leave her alone at the lodge while he made his rounds, Marius had unchained Sy from the chimney corner and sent the faun on the errand instead. That had been hours ago, and Sy hadn't returned. It was still several hours before dawn, and Marius had grown restless. It was plain he was concerned about the faun's tardiness. He needed to go and look for him himself, but he dared not leave her alone long enough to do so, though she pleaded for it.

"If you want to go, please do so," she urged him. "I am quite capable of fending on my own. I shan't go off like I did the last time, I assure you. Believe me I have no desire to meet whatever we felt out there earlier."

"I gave Gideon my word that I would not let you out of my sight until he returned," Marius said. "We do not know what we are facing here, but I do know Ravelle, and he is a force to be reckoned with. I cannot leave you on your own to deal with that. I wouldn't even if I hadn't given Gideon my word."

"But what of Sy?" she persisted. "He should have been back

long before now, you said so yourself. Suppose something has happened to him?"

"Sy is a simple creature, easily distracted. I am hoping that is all this is. I am worried about the Ancient Ones. I do not like that they have gone inside themselves. I have only seen this twice before, the *silence of the forest*, and on both occasions catastrophe followed."

"I do not understand it," Rhiannon said. "Can you not call them back?"

"Folk tend to dismiss the Ancient Ones as mere trees, plants that grow and mature, and are cut down for firewood and for other creature comforts to serve man. They are so much more than that. Inside those aged tree trunks live spirits that are eons old, male and female, possessed of sage wisdom and compassion for all living things. Think of them as gods of the wood. The watchers will not harm them—not even to chastise Gideon. Their magic is great and inexhaustible. You've seen their shrines. They are to be respected, not terrorized and driven inward. They are gentle, harmless creatures for the most part, though I have met my fair share of those who have become disgruntled for one reason or another, and vindictive. These matters are usually handled amongst themselves, however. I rarely need to interfere. But such as these are vulnerable to the dark forces that lurk on every plane of existence since time began, and in their weakness, fall prey to such entities as Ravelle and his ilk. This is what worries me."

"There has to be something we can do," Rhiannon said.

Marius studied her for a moment. "You are a fearless sort," he said. "I envy Gideon. You are well-matched."

"I do not know if I am fearless or just foolhardy," she said, "but I would follow him no matter where his footsteps lead. Did he not follow me into Outer Darkness? Could I do less? Whatever this is that we have brought down upon you is my fault, and I will do all within my power to set it to rights."

"It was not your fault that the watchers cast you into hell, lady," Marius said. "Fault doesn't enter into it. Ravelle needs no provocation to set his sites upon me. We are old adversaries. He seeks out his victim's most vulnerable spot to attack—never the victim himself. This way the wounding is crueler. In my case, it is my charges here—the Ancient Ones and creatures of the wood that I am duty bound to protect. I know each and every one of those trees in that forest on a personal level. Over time, they have become part of me, and I have become part of them. It is as if we have become one entity. I know no better way to explain it. He knows that whatever he does to them will pain me more than if he dealt a direct blow to me. I fear that is what is happening here now."

"Is there nothing we can do?"

"We wait until Ravelle makes his next move. Then we shall see."

Rhiannon said no more. She didn't understand the demon's glamour. Was Ravelle among them in the physical sense? It had certainly seemed that way when Marius had led her back to the lodge earlier, or had the demon merely projected his image into their midst?

She sipped the sassafras tea Marius had brewed, and nibbled at the hearty little breakfast cakes made of unborn grains, whole wheat, and honey that were a staple on the isle, and waited. But when the fish-gray streamers of first light finally broke over the forest, and the silence that had fallen over the trees like a pall hadn't lifted, she knew that whatever the mystery surrounding the demon's glamour was, there would be a reckoning.

By midmorning, the storm clouds hovering overhead were so dense and threatening, Rhiannon was having difficulty justifying that night had given way to morning. Marius went often to the threshold, shielding his eyes from the dusky glare that promised a deluge, searching the air for some sign of Gideon's winged profile in bold relief against the roiling clouds. But it was nearly high noon before that image plummeted through the clouds dodging lightning bolts and disappeared inside the canopy of still branches bearing motionless leaves.

Marius seized his quiver and slung it over his shoulder. Snatching his longbow, he hesitated in the open doorway. "Remain here," he said. "He needs my arrows, and I cannot be distracted over you if I would prevent calamity here."

She had given up trying to make the sky give birth to Gideon, and Marius had seen Gideon before she did. She ran to his side. "Marius, please . . ." she pleaded, wanting to go with him.

The forest lord's posture clenched, and he showed her a side of his nature she had never seen and wished never to see again. His dark eyes smoldered like live coals, and his jaw muscles began to tick in a steady rhythm. There was murder in those eyes. They were immutable, their message unequivocal. In spite of herself, she gasped.

"Lady, *stay!*" he demanded. "Do not think to defy me. The watchers no longer care to wait for him to enter a woman to strike. They are not only after blood, they hunger for his very soul! Distract me now and they surely will have it! Now, do not cross this threshold."

Well, well, the Lord of the Forest has a temper, she realized, but the thought was scarcely out when Marius, loosing a string of expletives, stripped off the quiver, tossed down the bow, and began tearing at his clothes, ripping them off and flinging them every which way. It was almost as if he was compelled to strip naked before her. There was no shred of modesty in him. It was as if she wasn't even there.

It took Rhiannon a moment to realize what was happening. Marius had become like a man possessed in the throes of the strange frenzy that had left him standing before her in all his erect magnificence, his body, like burnished bronze gleaming in the glow of rushlights set about in sconces on the roughly hewn walls. Her breath caught in her throat and she backed up apace, for the last boot had scarcely sailed through the air when a blinding streak of white-hot silver light, like liquid mercury, surged around the naked forest lord before her, lifting him into the air.

"Mica on his throne!" Marius gritted out through clenched teeth as he came down not as a man, but as the centaur. "Now see what you've done!" he seethed.

Snatching the quiver and bow he'd hurled down when the transformation began, he burst through the lodge door that was barely wide enough to accommodate his bulk, knocking over a chair and trestle table in his path, and galloped out into the jaundiced midday twilight, a roar like nothing human Rhiannon had ever heard echoing after him.

She staggered to the open doorway and leaned against the jamb. The arrows left Marius's longbow in rapid succession so swiftly she saw only the blur of their motion as he disappeared into the forest. She could scarcely believe her eyes. How had that happened? How had he shapeshifted into the centaur when it wasn't moon dark? Whatever the phenomenon, after what she'd seen in Marius's eyes, she would not leave the lodge, though she ached to run to Gideon, to see for herself that he'd come through the watcher's barrage unharmed. She longed to tell him what had occurred to her as the perfect solution to their dilemma, but what she had just witnessed with Marius had rooted her to the spot.

Rhiannon sank to her knees in the doorway. Outside, the lightning flashed in snakelike columns streaking across the clearing, illuminating the stiff-limbed trees standing in their unnatural aspects. Neither a branch, nor twig, nor leaf moved in the deathly stillness that had fallen over the forest, as the heavens opened, dumping torrents of rain upon them—oak and pine, rowan, ash, and whitethorn alike.

She shut her eyes against the blue-white glare, and the next thing she knew she was in Gideon's arms. Raising her up, he crushed her close, then held her away, his wild eyes raking her from head to toe. They hadn't missed Marius's clothing strewn about. He cast a hard eye toward the disheveled pile of buckskins and cambric, then turned his dark gaze upon her.

"What happened here?" he said, shaking her gently. "What did you do to bring out the centaur?"

"What did *I* do?" Rhiannon cried, twisting in his arms.

"Aside from during the dark of the moon, Marius does not shapeshift unless he is sexually or emotionally challenged. What set him off?"

"Well, it certainly wasn't sexual," Rhiannon defended. "He's been agitated since you left. A strange silence fell over the forest. He wouldn't leave me because you asked him not to, so he sent Sy to make his rounds for him. When Sy didn't return he became edgy. Then when you finally did return and he set out to help you, he told me not to leave the lodge. I didn't want him to leave me alone. I was about to ask him to take me to you with him, and he . . . he . . . I don't know. I've never seen anything like what happened! He threw off his clothes, and the next thing I knew the centaur charged out of here all but knocking that door off its hinges. What is going on?"

"I do not know," Gideon said, raking his hands through his hair. "I only wish I did."

"Where is Marius now?" Rhiannon asked.

"I do not know that either," said Gideon. "He stomped off into the wood like a madman after he fired on the watchers. Sy is nowhere to be found, and the silence of the trees can only mean calamity. He suspects Ravelle, as do I, and I know we must leave here. We've brought enough down upon Marius, but the rune caster was right, I cannot abandon him now, when he needs me, especially since I've caused this nightmare."

"Gideon, we need to talk. I think I've figured out a way for us."

He took her by the arm and led her to the pool chamber. "That will have to wait," he said. "I have to find Marius and see what's to be done out there. If it is Ravelle that we're dealing with, we need to send him back to Outer Darkness where he belongs. Marius cannot do that on his own, neither can I, but maybe together . . . At any rate, I need to help him, and I cannot do that with you underfoot. I want you to stay here, where you are safe, while I see to it. Will you do as I ask, or must I lock you in? Never mind. I think I will lock you in, in any case. Ravelle is able to shapeshift as well. He takes many forms. He is very clever at it. Remember what happened in the astral, when you thought that creature was me. Ravelle is able to do the same magic. If he were to get hold of you now and spirit you back into Outer Darkness . . . No! I will lock you in until I settle this. You haven't slept. While I am gone, refresh yourself in the pool and rest. We can ill afford to take chances now. I have but one feather left to call back, and we will need that to buy our freedom when needs must."

"There has to be some way that I could distinguish between you," Rhiannon pleaded. The thought of being locked away in the pool chamber terrified her. What if the catastrophe both Gideon and Marius feared came to pass and neither of them returned? She would be trapped. There was no rear exit to the pool chamber except underwater, and she had no idea how long a stretch it was to reach another air pocket, or where it would take her even if she did.

"There would be no physical difference," Gideon responded. "Demeanor is the only way, just as it was in the astral, when you finally knew that entity was not me. Ask a question—something only I would know, but it will not come to that."

He crushed her close in a smothering embrace, cocooning

her in his wings. She could feel the pent-up sexual energy flowing through his dynamic body. She could feel it in the pressure of his hard roped torso, in the tightness of the corded muscles in his biceps and well-turned thighs. Their oaken circumference was so perfectly sculpted it was as if they had been turned on a lathe, every sinew, every ligament a conduit for the sexual stream flowing between them in their oneness.

The bruising hardness of his erect penis leaned heavily against her pubic mound as he drew her closer still, finding her lips with his warm, searching mouth. His hands roamed over her body through the fine homespun shift Marius had provided, lingering upon the turgid peaks of her nipples poking through the fabric.

"Gods above, but you are beautiful," he murmured, working the hard nubbin on one breast between his thumb and forefinger.

"Gideon, please don't lock me in here," she pleaded. "Lock the outer doors if you must, but do not leave me trapped in this pool chamber."

"Were you and Marius both out of the lodge at the same time earlier, no matter how briefly?"

"I went for a walk and he came to fetch me back when the trees went silent," she replied.

"Was that before or after Sy went missing?"

"After, why?"

"Then no," he said. "I cannot take chances with your safety. Ravelle could have slipped inside while you two were out. It's best that I lock you in here now, just in case."

"Gideon, Ravelle projected his image in the Outer Darkness forest and brought the elvers to terrorize us—and yes, I did think of my abhorrence of those creatures when I saw them as an entrée on his banquet table. If he could do that, mine my thoughts to extract my fears, and you know he did, what lock will bar him from this pool?"

"What other choice have we?" Gideon argued.

"You could take me with you," she suggested.

"That I will not do!" he said. "I have no idea what we are facing in that forest out there. I have only seen this phenomenon twice before in all my years. Many trees were lost on both occasions. More loss must be prevented at all costs. Have you ever seen a tree spirit die? No? Well, I have. It is a gut-wrenching experience to watch an ancient entity writhe screaming—tethered in its deathbed by its own roots—its flaming branches pleading toward the heavens while the fire consumes it utterly. Marius has seen this also. By the gods, angst over that is no doubt what set him off and caused him to transform into the centaur. He doubtless feared that a stray watcher's missile would strike one of those trees, trapping the spirit inside and causing a holocaust such as what has occurred in the past. I will not take you into the midst of such as that."

"Then give me a means of escape if needs must." Gideon hesitated, and she twisted free of his embrace. "You do not trust me!" she cried.

"I do not trust his magic!" he corrected her. "I do not know the depth of it, and when I fell I lost what powers I possessed that might have matched it, elsewise I would not need to consult with the rune caster."

Seizing her in his arms again, he took her lips in a fiery kiss that drained her senses, his hot tongue teasing, thrusting into her, igniting fires at the core of her sex that started her juices flowing.

"I do not want to leave you," he panted, thrusting his hand between her thighs, gliding his finger along her slit, riding her wetness.

Rhiannon groaned as he probed deeper, penetrating her swollen folds one at a time, opening the petals of her sex as he delved deeper, feeling the hot, moist walls of her vagina, reaching into the narrow void beyond for the womb his fingers were not long enough to touch.

Rhiannon groaned, leaning into his embrace, trying to take the probing fingers deeper. There was a glimmer of finality in his fondling, a facet of desperation that hit her as hard as if he'd actually struck her. That was more terrifying than her fear of Ravelle. His sudden bone-crushing embrace punctuated her fears, and she gripped his arms as he tore himself away.

"Gideon . . . don't leave me!" she shrilled.

But it was too late. A cold, damp wind rushed at her, filling the space where his warm body had been. He didn't answer. She blinked, and he was no more than a blur streaking through the pool chamber door.

The rasp of a key turning in the lock echoed over the warm, steamy water rising from the pool, then nothing. Except for the shrill reverberation of her pleading sobs and the dull thud of her tiny fists pounding on the ancient wood, there wasn't another sound.

25

Locking Rhiannon away in the pool chamber against her will was the hardest thing Gideon had ever done, but he needed his wits about him, and the only way he could hope to do everything in his power to keep her out of harm's way while he was about the business at hand.

Adrenaline surged through every fiber of his body, charged with the inevitability of the reckoning he feared, and the raw carnal need Rhiannon's soft, willing flesh had ignited pumping through his veins. His need was acute, but there wasn't time to address it. With Rhiannon's pleadings ringing in his ears, he snatched up a handful of the oat cakes heaped on a plate in the middle of the table and burst out into the rain-swept midday semidarkness.

The rain had begun to slack by the time he reached the forest, sprinting across the clearing rather than taking to the air. Mercifully, the deluge had kept the watchers at bay until then. That it was slacking was not a good sign. He had hoped for more saturation in case of fire. His head was spinning. The peace of mind he'd hoped locking Rhiannon away out of danger would bring hadn't come. In fact, he was more worried than ever. She had touched upon several valid points in her argument, and he wished he knew more of the demon's capabilities. Making matters worse, the disembodied voices were ghosting across his mind again. He strained his ears to hear what they were saying, but it was for the most part garbled, though some sentences did come through. If only he knew what it all meant . . .

Surely, we can reveal ourselves now, the first speaker said. *She knows!*

The other uttered an exasperated grunt. *Doesn't matter a whit what she knows, it's what he accepts that's going to do it . . . if it can be done.*

The first speaker sighed. *And you do not think he will accept it?*

He's a reckless sort, your Lord of the Dark, the second speaker hedged. *I do not think we dare take that for granted. She tried to tell him. He wouldn't even listen. He is too long a creature of habit in his own realm. I fear so vast a change may be too great for him to bear.*

The first speaker sputtered. *Be fair*, he said. *What's happening in that forest is the greater press.* The other didn't answer, and the first speaker went on quickly, *All right, if you won't reveal our identity, will you at least agree to call for reinforcements . . . if not for Gideon, for the Lord of the Forest . . . ?*

The voices trailed off to mumbling then. Gideon pricked up his ears to hear more, but the words were reduced to mumbling, like the droning of a thousand bees buzzing around in his head. He didn't like that they'd brought Rhiannon into their conversation. They had never done that before. But there was no time to dwell on that then. The forest loomed before him, tall and silent. It was as if all the spirits of the Ancient Ones had already vacated their host trees. He almost wished that was the case, staring up at the lifeless branches dripping water as if it were the sad things' tears.

Jolted back to the grim present, he beat back the strange voices' message and made his way between the trees. Breaking up the oat cakes he'd taken from the lodge, he crumbled some in each of the stone basin shrines he passed to pay tribute as he moved through the wood, pausing at each in hopes of a response, but there was none. The trees remained unchanged, their aspects dismal and still. It was as if the pulse of the forest had ceased to beat.

Dry lightning speared down as he made his way among the trees. He assumed it was natural lightning, for he had never known the watchers to jeopardize the Ancient Ones before. Ravelle, on the other hand, would have no such consideration, and Gideon took a chill recalling a past devastation that the demon had caused.

Dropping to his knees before one of the larger stone basins, he left his tribute, and prayed. "Ancient One, what must I do to forestall whatever calamity it is that threatens here?" he murmured, gazing into the great pine's still branches. What he wouldn't give to feel those fragrant needles stroking him now—any response from the tree would be welcome. He was even willing to suffer a cuffing, but the tree remained motionless, its fragrance the only evidence of life.

"It is no use," a voice said close beside him.

Gideon whipped around and surged to his feet to face Marius, whose restless hooves were tearing up the mulch underfoot, lifting pollen spores that had been held down by the rain until it looked like snow was falling all around them.

"Mica's toenails! Where have you been?" Gideon blurted out.

"Trying to purge a very embarrassing incident," the forest lord said.

"I know. I've been to the lodge," Gideon said.

"Let us just say I was distressed over all this and trying to keep my word to you . . . and something snapped. Where is she?"

"I locked her in the pool chamber while we settle this. She wasn't too receptive to that, but I need her safe until we settle this. What is happening here? I've left tributes in every basin I've passed hoping for a response, but it's as if the spirits have all vacated their trees."

"It is the same throughout the island," Marius said. "That's where I've been, checking the others, hoping we weren't having a repeat of what happened the last time Ravelle was on the rampage. It does not bode well, Gideon. Unless I miss my guess, we are under siege here. The Ancient Ones know it too."

"Have they vacated?"

"No," Marius said. "Where are they to go? It is an ancient spiritual rite they perform. You cannot reach them now—no one can, not even myself. They prepare for death, for their journey to the afterlife."

"This is not the watchers' doing," Gideon confirmed. "As insidious as they are, I cannot fathom them risking the Ancient Ones in such a way."

"No, they are out for your blood, my friend, but they will not put the Ancient Ones to the hazard to get it. This is Ravelle. I just wish I knew if it was merely Outer Darkness glamour that has turned these old sentinels in upon themselves, or if that demon is actually among us."

"What can we do?"

"There is nothing we can do," Marius returned, "until it begins."

Rhiannon leaned against the locked pool chamber door, touching the ancient wood. She was hoarse from calling out. It was no use anymore. She'd heard the lodge door slam shut outside. Gideon was gone, and there was nothing to do but wait for him to return.

Across the chamber, rising steam from the pool, rich in minerals, wafted toward her. Should she accept the invitation? Gideon had told her to refresh herself in the pool. She hadn't purged the stink of Outer Darkness from her nostrils, she wondered if she ever would. A good soaking in that heavenly water silkened with minerals and rosemary was so appealing she couldn't resist venturing closer.

Walking around the pool, she looked into the water lit by torches in their brackets on the wall, seeking the shallow end, where the color would appear lighter and hopefully would allow her to see the bottom. She needn't have bothered. When she reached it, the shallow end was marked by a pile of cushions and fluffy towels, which she assumed Marius had set there for her convenience. Kneeling down, she fingered the fabric and tested the softness. Eiderdown. Of course they would be plumped with the gleanings from local birds. Nature was represented everywhere on the Forest Isle kindly and reverently.

The pool was inviting, but exhaustion won out. Rhiannon sank lower into the cushions and closed her eyes, listening to the soft lapping of the ripples on the breast of the water echoing musically. Sleep took her quickly, but it was a restless sleep fraught with strange murmurings and shadowy dreams that wouldn't come clear except to project their eerie essence. She had no idea how long she had slept, or what wrenched her suddenly awake. Whatever it was, her breath was coming short and her heart was racing. Supposing it was due to the anxiety of worrying over what was happening in the forest, she swallowed her rapid heartbeat and struggled to a sitting position, wiping the sleep from her eyes. Beads of cold perspiration had broken out over her brow. It ran in rivulets between her breasts and down her spine. She was drenched in sweat, suffering strange recollections of Gideon's hands upon her, petting her—arousing her.

Rhiannon scrambled to her feet and padded around the cir-

cumference of the little pool to the door. Frantically, she tried
the latch handle, but it wouldn't budge. The door was still
locked. Gideon hadn't returned. She was hoping that the sultry
dreams charging her sex hadn't all been dreams, hoping that
Gideon had returned after all.

Still hopeful, she called out to him, but no answer came, and
her posture collapsed as she returned to the shallow end of the
pool, where writhing tufts of fragrant steam were rising from
the water. She had slept, but she hadn't rested. Her body ached
from ordeal and exhaustion. How good it would feel to slip
into that pool of silky water perfumed with pine tar and rosemary—scents of the wood, of the forest, heady and mysterious,
so soothing to sore, tired flesh and aching muscles. Without
giving it a second thought, she stripped off the wheat-colored
homespun kirtle and stretched naked, like a lazy cat, at the edge
of the pool. Then taking a deep breath, she submerged herself
to the neck in the soothing flux of gentle ripples and drifting
vapors in a desperate attempt to purge the stench of Outer
Darkness from her nostrils.

The weight of her long hair pulled her down in the water.
Adrenaline surged and she quickly felt for the bottom. It was
there, and she breathed a sigh of relief as she began to tread the
smooth rocky floor, feeling for the drop off. Being natural, this
pool was carved out of the reefs that formed the understructure
of the islands just like the others. No two were alike. She could
feel the pull from the deep end, where the water flowed on,
eventually finding its way to other pools and air pockets and
levels of existence beneath the sea.

Mineral salt lines, ringing the inside edge of the pool, were
visible where the rising and ebbing tide changed the level of the
water. She was mindful of that in her explorations, judging
from the residue that the tide must be rising now, and she swam
back to the shallow end just to be sure. There, beside the cushions she found a shell holding a slab of soap that smelled of pine

tar oil and a natural sea sponge. She raised the soap to her nose and inhaled deeply. It was a clean, crisp masculine scent, a testimony to the loneliness of the forest lord, whose bathing chamber she had invaded. No fripperies here, no feminine accessories or exotic oils, just subtle whispers of the forest, of the land, of Marius's world. She took up the sponge and made a rich creamy lather with the soap that slid along her forearms as it burst into a profusion of tingling bubbles.

Her tiny feet dancing on the floor of the pool, she began soaping herself in concentric circles starting at the base of her throat, then over her chest and full, round breasts. The gentle roughness of the sea sponge delivering the lather scraped her nipples, bringing them erect. The dusky rose nubbins grew hard as she lingered over them until the areolae puckered, making them taller still. The craters and crevices in the soapy sponge stimulating the sensitive buds set off a firestorm at the epicenter of her sex, calling warm pulsations to radiate throughout her belly and turgid thighs. Rhiannon moaned softly as she moved the sponge lower, following the contours of her torso, caressing her narrow waist and the curvaceous shape of her hips.

Creating new lather, she soaped her belly, leisurely ringing the little hollow of her navel, as more riveting waves of sensation rippled through her sex. No crevice, no fissure would be left untouched by the wonderfully rich lather. Reaching behind, she concentrated upon the globes of her buttocks, gliding the sponge along the crease between, lingering over the dimples at the base of her spine. Soft murmurs leaked from her lips as she touched pleasure spots she'd all but forgotten, erogenous regions that Gideon had awakened for the first time, like the soft skin on the inside of her thighs, and the delicate creases behind her knees. Her toilette had become a sentient experience extraordinaire. She'd become totally enraptured. But why wouldn't it chase the stench of Outer Darkness still clinging so stubbornly to her nostrils?

All around her, a ring of soapsuds defined her shape in the water, nudging her in little caresses as she soaped the sponge again and slid it lower, squeezing the lather through the little thatch of pubic curls over her mound and uncovering the hardened bud beneath. Spreading her legs, she probed deeper, sliding the sponge the length of her nether lips seeking her folds, swollen with arousal, from steely clitoris to the tight pucker of her anus.

The soap was rectangular in shape, a chunk evidently carved from a larger slab, its corners rounded from use. Rhiannon spread her nether lips and slipped it inside her, gripping it with the walls of her vagina, just as she had gripped Gideon's penis when he was at the height of his climax. Again and again she tugged at it with her thickened folds, while sliding it in and out of her to the rhythmic demands of her need, until she lost her grip upon the slippery phallus it had become and drifted to the floor of the pool.

She could still touch bottom, and she held her breath and dove beneath the surface to retrieve it, groping the pool floor. The soap escaped her twice before she captured it successfully. In the silt she'd stirred up at the bottom, she saw motion. The image wouldn't come clear through the dark fog of underwater debris, but it looked like another pair of feet was padding toward her. Her heart leaped inside, and she surged upward. Had Gideon returned after all?

As she broke the surface, he spun her around facing away from him and tied a silk scarf over her eyes. "Shhh," he whispered huskily, "let me . . ."

His hands were hot and skilled as he cupped her breasts from behind, his fingers working her nipples as he thrust himself against her, his hard penis riding the fissure between her buttocks. He began to undulate, grinding his body against her in the slippery water. When she reached to remove the silk blindfold, he spun her around facing him.

"Shhh," he murmured, when she started to speak. He grabbed her hands and lifted them to his lips as she tried again to remove the scarf over her eyes. "Let me love you . . ."

His words were husky with desire as he crushed her close. He was holding her so tight against his erection, against the hard, roped torso, she could scarcely breathe. The air seemed thick of a sudden. The steam stung her nostrils. No . . . not steam—*smoke!* Where was it coming from?

Rhiannon resisted, pressing her open palms against his chest. "Wait, Gideon!" she cried. "I smell smoke . . . Something is burning!"

"Don't touch my wings!" he gritted out as her hands groped for them.

She paid him no mind. Something was wrong. Her hands making wild circles in the air searched for his wings just the same, but there were none, and she tore at the blindfold until she'd ripped it off despite his strong hands fisted around her wrists trying to prevent her.

She screamed.

It wasn't Gideon at all. It was *Ravelle,* his horned head thrown back in riotous laughter. He'd evidently meant to prolong the deception as long as possible, but he hadn't fooled her. She was far too clever for that.

Across the way the pool chamber door was still latched, only now thick tufts of smoke were seeping in under the door sill. Rhiannon screamed again, calling Gideon at the top of her voice, but Ravelle's blood-chilling laughter was her only answer. He was trying to drag her toward the deep end of the pool, where her terror of it would make her dependent upon him. He had nearly succeeded, when the water all around them began to roil and bubble, forming a vortex. When the swordfish leaped through the well of swirling water and stood dancing on its tail, menacing Ravelle, the demon let Rhiannon go just long enough for another figure to rise up from the whirlpool and seize her. It was Simeon, Lord of the Deep.

"Do not be frightened, my lady," he said. "I am simply repaying an old debt."

Rhiannon opened her mouth to scream again, but the sound froze in her throat for the suddenness of what was happening all around her. Thick smoke had all but obscured the swordfish jabbing at the demon with its long, razor-sharp sword as Simeon pulled her into the vortex.

"Hold tight!" he charged.

Rhiannon opened her mouth again to scream, for she was in mortal terror of the deep water that offered no safe bottom to her kicking and reaching feet, trying desperately to find it.

Simeon paid her no mind. Swooping down, he blew his warm, salty breath into her nose and mouth, as he plunged with her in a rush of silvery phosphorescence deep beneath the surface of the water, the swordfish spiraling triumphantly after them into the abyss.

26

Enough! a familiar voice shouted in Gideon's mind. *I've yielded to you long enough. I'll not stand by and wait till all hope is gone. He needs to know now, before it's too late to help him.*

The other speaker Gideon had come to know as the argumentative one sighed. *He is an entity to be reckoned with, your Lord of the Dark. I just want to be sure we aren't offering something we will regret.*

The first speaker grunted. *And what has she done, pray, that you would risk her life with the demons of Outer Darkness rather than bring him home?*

The other snorted. *You know what invitation brings to bear,* he said. *Immortality is not something doled out lightly. He is larger than life, this fallen angel of the gods, and she . . . well . . .*

You would rather see her damned to Outer Darkness than bring peace and comfort to this prince of the air? One more mortal in our midst can hardly signify, considering all those that have crossed over since time out of mind. I say again, enough! We need him, 'tis time!

They argued further, but Gideon couldn't make out their speech. If only he knew what it all meant. There wasn't time to think about it now. The rain had ceased, but a stiff wind had risen, and still the trees were silent. It was the strangest thing Gideon had ever seen. Trees that should be bent at the crotch, their branches sweeping the ground, stood motionless, while the howling gusts ruffled his long hair and narrowed his eyes to slits.

"What is it?" Marius said, as they moved through the forest. "I know that look. What ails you?"

"I do not know," Gideon replied. "Voices . . . I hear them sometimes. They seem to be talking about me, but I cannot make out all that they say. What I can understand makes no sense, and yet . . . it seems so important that I hear it. Sometimes I think I'm going mad, and now that there is Rhiannon, it seems vital that I do hear their message. Then, there is *this* . . . this whatever it is that has driven the Ancient Ones in on themselves. I like it not."

"It is a reckoning," Marius said flatly. "We've seen it before, the silence of the trees. Ravelle caused the last one, too, and many were lost—burned alive in their ancient hosts, laid to waste at the whim of a demon from the depths of Outer Darkness. Sacrilege!"

"*Can* he be defeated?" Gideon asked, almost afraid of the answer, and with good cause judging from the expression upon the centaur's face at the question.

"No, he is immortal, even as you and I, but he can be driven back and kept in his place. Please the gods we can manage that before this sanctuary is ravaged again."

Gideon was about to reply when one of the voices in his mind spoke again—this time, it spoke to *him*. It had never done that before, and he stopped in his tracks and listened.

Gideon, Ruler of the Dark, Prince of the Air, it thundered in his ears. *Get you back to the lodge! That is where it has begun, your reckoning. . . .*

There! The voice said to the other. *Does that satisfy you? I will help him, but the choice will still be his.*

Gideon didn't wait for the other's reply. His extraordinary sense of smell raised his head into the wind and he inhaled deeply.

"*Smoke!*" he cried. "Marius . . . the lodge!"

The centaur pranced to a standstill. "Climb up!" he charged. Extending his arm, he pulled Gideon up on his back. "Hold on!"

Galloping among the motionless trees with the wind whipping tears in their eyes was an experience that chilled Gideon to the bone. Of all the enchantments the archipelago had to offer, this phenomenon was by far the most bizarre, and the most blood-chilling. He clung to the centaur's back with both hands fisted in the coarse pelt and prayed they weren't too late. He could reach the lodge in record speed if he was to take to the air, but the watchers were still hovering, and he dared not risk it. A bolt of lightning gone astray like they were often wont to do would be catastrophic should it hit the trees.

The smoke grew thicker the closer they came to the clearing. When it loomed up before them, the sight of the lodge engulfed in flames all but stopped Gideon's heart.

"*Rhiannon . . . !*" he cried, his voice trailing off on the wind. He slid off the centaur's back and ran toward the writhing tower of flames, but a lightning bolt speared down in his path preventing him. In his haste to reach the lodge, he had forgotten about the watchers circling overhead. One was set to hurl another missile, when the whirr of an arrow in flight whizzed past Gideon's ear on its way to its mark. It struck the watcher in the shoulder, catching him off balance as he hurled his missile down, and the bolt of deadly lightning spiraled off and missed its target striking a stile at the edge of the clearing instead.

Marius put himself in Gideon's path as he reloaded his bow. "You can't!" he thundered. "The lodge is gone, Gideon. You cannot save that! It's too late!"

"But . . . Rhiannon!" Gideon cried. "I left her locked in the pool chamber. She didn't want me to lock her in!"

"There is nothing you can do!" Marius insisted. "That blaze will consume you." Another arrow left his bow so swiftly Gideon didn't even see him load it, then another, and another, but still the watchers hovered.

Gideon raised both his fists to the heavens and let loose a string of blasphemies at the winged creatures that began hurling chain lightning down in all directions.

She is not there, the voice shouted across Gideon's beleaguered mind, for it was numb. Tears stung his eyes, and he spun in circles, pleading with the smoke-filled sky to give birth to the speaker.

"Who are you!" he demanded. "*What* are you? Show yourself, or I will let these vile henchmen of the gods have their way with me at last. I do not want to live without Rhiannon!"

"Gideon? Have you gone mad?" Marius hollered, his raised voice carried on the wind. "It's only demon glamour. There is no one there!"

"No!" Gideon insisted, holding his reeling head as if he meant to keep it from spiraling off into the storm. "The voice I told you about . . . it says she isn't here." He spun around again, his wild eyes dilated like a madman's, and yelled into the wind, "Where is she, then?" he insisted of the disembodied voice. "Help me . . . *tell me!*"

Seek her among the labyrinths of the deep, said the speaker. *She is with Simeon.*

"What is it?" Marius called out, clearly nonplussed. "Get

hold of yourself! That fire is spreading. We must dig a trench to stop it or the forest is lost!"

"Simeon has her," Gideon said.

"You don't know that," Marius insisted. "Ye gods! I do believe you have gone mad!"

Gideon reeled like a castaway lord. Ahead the lodge was nothing more than a fiery column reaching into the roiling clouds. Overhead, the watchers were closing in. He had never seen so many at one time dodging Marius's arrows. The forest lord was right. The fire had to be stopped before it reached the Ancient Ones. Ravelle's mocking laughter riding the wind underscored that. That they couldn't see the demon by no means minimized the danger. Mere glamour or no, Ravelle was among them. He had to be driven back to Outer Darkness, and it had to be now, before more harm came to the isle.

He had to believe that the voice had told the truth, that Rhiannon was safe in Simeon's care. The alternative was too terrible to contemplate, that her spirit had risen with the belching plumes of fire and ash spitting sparks into the noonday twilight called by the storm, lost to him forever.

Behind, a strange droning sound was coming from the forest. Had the trees found their voices? What did it mean? Overwhelmed, Gideon groaned. The wind whipping through his feathers had aroused him beyond the point of no return. His hard shaft strained against the seam of his eel-skin suit until he feared the seams would burst, and he loosed a cry he scarcely recognized as his own voice into the traitorous wind, as he came in involuntary spasms only to grow hard again as soon as the seed left his body.

Help comes, the voice he'd been hearing called out over the din of frantic thoughts banging around in his brain. *Do what needs must, then go to her and bring her home. . . .*

Home? Gideon groaned. He had no home. "Who *are* you?" he demanded.

There was a palpable silence before the voice came again. *Your savior,* it said, and said no more, though he called out to it again and again until his deep baritone voice broke, hoarse and breathless, and his heart felt as if it were about to burst through his chest.

"Gideon, look!" Marius said, bringing him back from the brink of what could only be sheer madness.

Dazed and disoriented, Gideon stared toward the forest, where a creature was emerging, one that he'd heard of but never seen, a huge white stag with eyes so human-like they were shocking in an animal—the *Great White Stag,* ruler of the Arcan astral, protector of all forests and the Ancient Ones that dwelled within them. It was said that only the righteous could look into its eyes, and yet Gideon was, meeting its enigmatic gaze relentlessly.

"Did you call it?" Marius asked.

"No . . . I don't know . . ." Gideon stammered. Was this the help the voice had promised? "The voice I hear, it said that help would come."

"Listen . . . listen to the trees. It may have saved them. You evidently have friends in high places."

Gideon stared. The droning became louder. It was as if the trees heaved a collective sigh. One among them moved, not just to stretch and spread its branches. Its roots were not immersed in the ground. Instead, they trailed after it as it lumbered into the clearing, the huge white stag at its side.

Marius bent his centaur forelegs at the knee joint and genuflected before the two strange entities, whipped by the wind, approaching. "Pay homage!" Marius spat out in a hoarse whisper. "These are astral creatures—Otherworldly royalty . . . bow down!"

Gideon sketched a bow. "What's happening?" he asked.

"I am not certain," Marius said, rising from his bow. "This has never happened before. It appears that the mantra the trees were humming has brought their lord and mentor from the astral. See? Now *all* the trees move, Gideon!"

But they did not just move their boughs and branches. Their roots, too, came out of the ground and carried them back from the encroaching flames, for the fire was eating its way across the clearing before the risen wind.

Pandemonium had risen over the howl of the gale as Ravelle's chilling laughter rose over the racket. His image danced in the flames approaching. "You cannot destroy me," the demon tittered. "I am not here in the flesh, and even if I were, your pitiful magic has no dominion over me! Just look at what I've done with glamour alone!" He swept his fiery arms wide. "See what I have wrought, Lord of the Dark, and you, Marius, our day will come. . . ."

The satyr's laughter rang in Gideon's ears, as the Great White Stag pranced forward, rocking him back on his heels as it entered the flames as well. Its red eyes shooting fire, the stag advancing backed the demon deeper into the writhing column of flames that consumed it, laughter and all, though the hideous sound echoed after it.

The stag then emerged from the flames unscathed and joined the great spreading oak that had led the other trees to safety. Seeming to sigh again collectively, the Ancient Ones returned their roots to the ground and settled into their new beds downwind of the flames that threatened no more, and Gideon took to the air, while Marius covered his ascent.

"Is it over?" Gideon called out over the wail of the wind.

"Not over," Marius said, "postponed for now. Like Ravelle said, our day will come, his and mine, and it will be a reckoning like no other. Our issues are as old as eons. Thank you, my friend!"

"If you have this in hand, I must say good-bye, Lord of the Forest," Gideon shouted. "I must find Rhiannon." No matter what the disembodied voice proclaimed, he would not take an easy breath until he held her in his arms again.

"Hail and farewell, certainly, but never good-bye between friends, brother prince."

Gideon smiled sadly. Conversing thus, while Marius's arrows deflected the watchers' thunderbolts was bizarre at best. "I may not come this way again," he said. "But if you ever have need of me, somehow I will find a way. . . ."

"The gods go with you!" Marius called after him.

Gideon laughed outright as he soared off into the clouds. "Do not wish that upon me!" he chided. "Else I have to take these loathsome harpies with me. Unless I miss my guess, where I am going they cannot follow. Farewell, old friend . . . until the fates decree we meet again . . ."

27

"She did not make the journey well," Simeon said. He had taken Rhiannon to a vast pool chamber at the Pavilion, where she lay in a sumptuous bed heaped with quilts of woven lemongrass and seaweed. "I had no choice," he went on. "The compound is understaffed now, and I needed the sprites to tend her. She fought me the whole distance and then collapsed as you see her now. They haven't been able to revive her."

Gideon's heart felt like lead in his breast. With Simeon's help, he'd just made the journey underwater to escape the watchers. It was difficult for a winged creature of the air to surrender to breathing beneath the waves. He could only imagine Rhiannon's terror in such a situation, considering her fear of deep water. Sinking down on the bed beside her, he gathered her into his arms and rocked her gently.

Across the way, the quiet murmur of ripples lapping in the pool caught his eye, as Pio broke the surface, danced on his tail, and plunged down again, his head bobbing in and out of the water. If ever a fish could be anxious, this fish was anxious now.

"Pio is quite taken with your lady," Simeon said. "He hasn't left her side since I brought her here. I had her in my own guest apartments at first where Megaleen could easily spell the sprites tending her, but Pio raised such a ruckus I had to bring here, where he could monitor her progress. I have never seen my summoner so distressed. It was he who brought me, when the demon threatened her in Marius's pool. Poor Pio, I do not know how we shall all fare when you take her away. He won't be fit to live with, I fear, for being smitten with the arrows of love."

Gideon smiled in spite of himself, watching the swordfish's antics in the pool. "Be sure that he is amply rewarded," he said. "I am in his debt." Gazing down at Rhiannon's still face, his smile dissolved. "Is there nothing to be done to wake her?"

"It is shock. She should rally soon. My healers have been and gone. That isn't what worries me, Gideon."

"What, then?"

"I was in hopes that you and your lady could stay here, beneath the waves, but her terror of it is so great, I fear it would not work, my friend. She would have to travel underwater from time to time to reach our different halls and compounds. She would never make it. Fear closes the breathing passages. It cancels the effect my breath in one's nostrils imposes upon a body to allow them to breathe underwater temporarily. I did it to you just now without ill effect, because you did not fear. Her terror was such that she might have died if the journey had been longer. I'm sorry, my friend."

"It is just as well," Gideon said. "I would not bring my trouble upon you. My curse has brought enough catastrophe upon the Arcan Archipelago. The Dark Isle is gone, Vane's volcano has erupted because of me, Marius has lost his lodge, nearly lost his forest, and we still have no idea what has become of Sy. He went off to make Marius's rounds and hasn't been seen since."

"I wouldn't worry about the faun. He is a simple sort, and though a lower form, he is immortal. He will wander back in time, or not if he finds greener pastures elsewhere."

"No matter what, I will not put you to the hazard too," Gideon said. "It's here already—at your very doorstep. The watchers are swarming out there. As soon as Rhiannon is able, I will go, but I can never thank you enough for what you've done. She would have burned to death in that pool chamber but for you. I shan't ever forget it, my friend."

"Thank Pio there, not me," Simeon said. "Why did you lock her in there in the first place?"

"I knew Ravelle was among us. He was stalking her. I feared she would wander about while I went to Marius's aid and come to harm—that he might spirit her back to Outer Darkness. My only thought was to keep her safe. I underestimated that demon's power. I shan't again."

"Please the gods you are well rid of him! Where will you go?"

"I am not quite certain. An Otherworldly voice is guiding me. It told me Rhiannon was here with you. I will listen, and decide."

Marius was about to speak again, when Rhiannon stirred in Gideon's arms. The Lord of the Deep surged to his feet and gripped Gideon's shoulder. "I will leave you to your lady," he said. "Pio will carry any message you have for me. I am only a heartbeat away, old friend. Do not hesitate . . ."

He left them then, in a blink, though Pio remained, keeping watch from the pool. Gideon brushed the long hair back from Rhiannon's brow and murmured her name. But her mind was still doing battle with the sea, and she stiffened in his arms, resisting, her tiny fists beating him about the head and shoulders.

Seizing her wrists, he shook her gently. "It is I, Gideon!" he said. "Don't! You are safe, Rhiannon!"

But she continued to pummel him with her fists. "I begged you not to lock me in that chamber!" she shrilled.

Gideon had no defense. He let her work out her anger until she collapsed sobbing in his arms, her wet face against his breast. She was naked beneath the quilts, and he reached for the warmth of her, for the soft roundness of her breasts, strumming her nipples erect, sliding his hands over her belly and thighs like a man possessed. He could hardly believe he held her, for he truly feared he'd lost her, hardly believe she was responding to his caresses as vehemently as she had pummeled him. It set off a charge of sexual energy that built to a ravenous explosion of unstoppable lust. His need was inexhaustible.

Tossing the quilts aside, he tore off his eel-skin suit and raised her to her feet, pulling her into a steamy embrace of sensual skin-to-skin exploration. He was touching her as if it was for the first time, and the last time, his fingers seeking every orifice, every crevice. It was as if he was trying to memorize every pore in that satiny skin.

Her hands on his body were driving him mad. They flew over his naked skin, riding the sexual stream that flowed between them, making them one in body, mind, and spirit. It was a fiery orgasm of the soul, a throbbing that tugged at the very center of their beings, a riveting battery of little deaths that built until they'd been plunged into a state of carnal oblivion. Then, nothing else mattered but the moment that had run away with their passion, nothing entered their minds, not their surroundings, their issues—their future, hanging by a tenuous thread, for there was no future except in each other's arms.

The facet of desperation that ignited Gideon's passion lifted him out of himself. It was as if he were floating above the chamber looking down upon what they were doing to each other. He could see and feel her need, like a palpable aura surrounding her. She was malleable in his hands, and ready for the riveting climax her abandon promised. There was only one way to do such a coupling justice, and that was in the pool, the way they had made love when he took her virginity, the way for him it would always be as if he were taking her virtue for the first time.

Just thinking about it, his wings unfurled halfway. His eyes, dilated with desire, focused upon her face, blushed like the dewy petals of a rose in the rushlight glow. Scooping her up in a tender embrace as though he feared she'd break, he carried her toward the pool, but her posture clenched and she resisted, squirming in his arms.

"No!" she cried. "Not in the water . . . Gideon, no!"

He shook her gently. "There is nothing to fear," he said. "We have this brief time together before we make a decision that will change our lives as we know them forever, Rhiannon. I want to love you as I loved you the very first time. There are no demons in this pool . . . only ghosts of the past—our past. I want to raise those ghosts to chase the other specters that are haunting you."

"Please," she sobbed. "I beg you not! I will see that demon in the water until I die!"

"That is why I must," Gideon argued. "Haven't you heard me? I will not let Ravelle steal this from us. There will be water where we go, and you *will* make love in it with me, just as you will in the air. These are our pleasures. I've been robbed of everything else. I will not let evil rob us of these as well."

With no more said, he jumped into the fragrant steamy water with her in his arms and set her on her feet. No sooner had he done so then Pio broke the surface, his intent plain as he rubbed his long, iridescent body of shimmering blue scales against Rhiannon's shoulder, his sword a definite threat to Gideon, who burst into laughter in spite of himself and the inveterate need that cursed him.

"You have made a conquest, my love," he said, stroking the

swordfish's sleek skin. "Now tell him to go away, because I am about to do things to you that will make that fine blue skin of his blush pink. . . ."

Gripping the globes of her buttocks, he lifted her, guiding her legs around his waist, and opened her nether lips. "Hold on to me, Rhiannon," he murmured, pushing past her folds one by one, savoring each pleasure moan that marked the petal-like contours of her sex.

The walls of her vagina, swollen with arousal, gripped his penis fiercely, just as her legs gripped his waist. Her terror of the water was like a separate entity then. He could feel it in her clenched muscles, in her runaway heartbeat hammering against his pectorals, and in her sweet breath coming short as it puffed against his skin. This was not an abandon to carnal lust, it was sheer fright, the very thing that needed to be purged.

Determined to gain back what had been lost from their love-making, he raised her legs to rest against his chest and eased her back in the water, his hands splayed out underneath her but-tocks, supporting her as he took her deeply.

"Relax and float in the water," he said. "Surrender to me, Rhiannon, like you did that first time in my pool. Open to me and let me make you come. . . ."

It was no idle request, for she had steeled herself so well her vagina had clamped shut so tightly around his penis he was afraid to move for fear of hurting her. She'd become as brittle as glass, and he feared she'd shatter if he moved inside her the way his throbbing member demanded of him.

"Stretch your arms out in the water and let them float on the surface," he charged. "I have you completely. You will not sink. You must trust me, Rhiannon. There is nothing to fear"—he chuckled—"your little friend here will skewer me through with that deadly sword of his if I fail you." She did as he bade her, and he began to sway gently inside her, a close eye upon her pubic mound, upon his penis moving in and out of her, for it was low tide and her mons area was at the level of the water. It laved them as he took her, the tiny ripples his ardor created touching just the right spot to drive her mad. But still she resisted, and when he changed his rhythm, she lost what balance she'd gained and her arms flew around his neck, raising her out of the water, causing crystalline droplets to rain down into the pool from her hair and naked skin.

"There is nothing to fear," he soothed. "Lay back, Rhiannon. You are frightening Pio. He thinks I'm hurting you, and I have no desire to have that sword of his make a eunuch of me."

It was not said in jest. The summoner had begun to swim around them in frantic circles, his sword coming nearer with each nervous revolution. But for the demands of the curse, Gideon would have been hard put to maintain an erection. Nevertheless, his cock was bursting. Watching it glide in and out of Rhiannon's sex past the silken pubic curls in slow, spiraling thrusts had him on the brink of climax. But he wanted to prolong the ecstasy until he was absolutely certain she'd lost her fear of the water.

Pio wasn't making Gideon's task any easier, and he shot the swordfish a withering look, but the summoner gave as good as he got with a display that brooked no interference. Narrowing his circles, the great fish began slapping and thrashing about in the water, with little regard as to where he flung his tail, which more than once slapped Gideon's buttocks none too gently.

Gideon had been put on notice—called out by a *fish*. If the situation wasn't so grave, he would have blurted out a hearty guffaw. As it was, he was not amused, and he gave Pio a scathing mental message to the effect that it had been far too long since he'd had a tasty swordfish steak, which sharply curtailed the summoner's antics.

That was the charm. When Gideon looked back to Rhiannon again after delivering his warning, she giggled, and dawn broke over his soul.

"Oh, Gideon," she tittered, "you should see your face!"

He didn't speak. His massive wings unfurled halfway at the sound of her musical laughter. Gathering her into his arms, he set her on her feet and rushed her against the smooth side of the pool. Tears blurred her image as he crushed her close, murmuring her name as he took her deeply. Groaning himself, he swallowed her pleasure moans as her hips jerked forward, and she reached for him, grinding her sex against him until the tip of his engorged penis nudged her womb.

Lifting her into his arms, he guided her legs around his waist and staggered back from the wall of the pool, his shaft deep inside her. "Don't be afraid," he murmured against her hair. "Hold on to me . . . I want us to come together. . . ."

Before she could answer, he plunged into deeper water with her, his groans echoing in the steamy air, ringing in his ears as the water laved his wings, taking him beyond the point of no return.

Grinding the root of his shaft into her clitoris, he took her and took her as she leaned into his embrace. Her climax was riveting. He could feel the orgasmic contractions rush through her as the walls of her vagina gripped him, milking him, draining him of every drop as the ejaculate rushed out of him. It overflowed her tight sex, swollen from arousal that had made her tighter still, leaving a hot, pearly trail in the water as he came.

Nestling his head in the hollow of her throat, she sighed as his wings closed around her like a cocoon. She was his—all his. There was no fear in her now, only the bliss of pure rapture of the soul.

After a moment, Gideon gathered her up and carried her out of the pool. Wrapping her in one of the soft lemongrass towels heaped about, he carried her to the bed and set her down upon the sumptuous feather down quilts. How beautiful she was with the pink glow of sex staining her cheeks, and her dreamy eyes still dilated with the dregs of desire.

Splashing in the pool behind called their eyes there, where Pio had broken the surface again, dancing on his tail at the edge of the vortex his antics had created, before he plunged into the curl of the spiral and disappeared.

Gideon smiled. "Poor Pio," he said. "I fear you have quite captured his heart."

"I shall miss him," she replied, "but we cannot stay here, Gideon! I will die beneath the waves—I *will*! I am in terror of the deep. I could never bear it. But I think I have stumbled upon the answer for us. It's what I've been trying to tell you. Something Marius said reminded me of something you said once . . . about worlds where we could live in peace. Can the watchers enter the astral?"

Gideon stared, trying to wrap his mind around what she was saying. The same thing had occurred to him, when the astral royalty came to Marius's aid in the forest. He didn't know the answer. Dared he hope?

No, they cannot, my lord Gideon, said the disembodied voice parting the confusion in his mind. *The only two regions in our universe that bar the watchers are Outer Darkness and the astral plane. You have tried the one, will you try the other? You would rule there as Prince of the Air, your rightful title, dark one, with dominion over all the winged ones in the Arcan Astral. And while the curse upon you cannot be entirely lifted, you would have more control of your urges without threat of the watchers' lightning bolts, and there would be . . . concessions . . .*

Gideon rocked back on his heels trying to digest what the mysterious speaker who had been with him all the while was saying. *Who are you?* he asked.

My name is of no consequence, the speaker said. *Suffice it to say that I am an astral elder, with full authority to make the offer, though I should warn you that it is not unanimous among us. Your impetuous nature is rather daunting to some. You will have to prove yourself, of course, but I have no doubt that my faith in you is justified.*

Gideon's head was reeling. Could the astral be a safe haven for them both? Was it too much to hope for? There was one thing he needed to know before he would even consider it. *Rhiannon?* he asked. *What of Rhiannon?*

All mortals who cross over and become our . . . guests gain immortality among us.

Gideon's heart leaped. *What must I do?* he begged the speaker.

Call back your final feather and embrace your destiny, the voice said.

"Gideon?" Rhiannon prompted. "Have you heard me? Can the watchers follow us into the astral plane?"

Gideon hesitated. What little experience he had with the astral realm was hardly enough to determine whether he could exist among the fay forever. He was a creature of habit, a solitary soul accustomed to his own private world among the princes of Arcus. How would he fare as ruler of the winged beings of the Arcan Astral? He was accustomed to his cave, his mineral pool, his freedom to soar however and whenever he wished—accustomed to his very existence, for it was all he'd ever known since the fall that cursed him so many eons ago. It was a moment before he realized all that was already gone. The watchers had plucked him clean clear to the soul, but they hadn't crippled his spirit. He had been stripped of his existence as he knew it—of his home, of his isle, of his cave, of his privilege, of his freedom to soar without the threat of lightning bolts, but when all was tallied, they hadn't been able to strip him of his heart. He was still an angel of the gods, whether they wanted him or not. Could this be what Lavilia meant, when she'd said that he could live out his eternity with his Rhiannon, but not as he wished?

He drew a ragged breath. "No, the watchers cannot cross over," he said. "But we can . . . with my last feather from Lavilia, if that is what you want. You may as well know it won't be easy. It would be an entirely different life than either of us has ever known. You need to know that now, because once we cross over, there is no turning back."

"What about me?" she asked. There was fear in her voice again. He could bear anything but her fear.

"You would be as I am, but in a whole new plane of existence," he said. "No one returns from the astral. It is an immortal plane. That is why I hesitate. It is a mammoth decision for both of us. All mortals who are crossed over—whether they are taken or go voluntarily—gain immortality; unfortunately, captivity is the price."

"There is no question," Rhiannon said. "We must go, Gideon. Whatever comes we will face it together."

Gideon took her in his arms. It was more than he'd dared hope for, but the alternative was too terrible to contemplate, for if they were to stay, he would surely bring catastrophe down upon his friends and fellow princes, and most grievous of all, upon Rhiannon herself. He had already had a foretaste of that, and he found her lips with a hungry mouth that joined them—mind and body—soul to soul.

When their lips parted, he looked her in the eyes, though when he spoke it was to the rune caster. "*Lavilia!*" he called out, ignoring Rhiannon's gasp. "It is time."

The reply came almost at once. "You are certain, dark one?" the rune caster said.

"Yes, we are certain," Gideon said, his adoring gaze, so full of promise, riveted to Rhiannon's face, radiant with hope, as he cautioned her to keep silent during the rune caster's disembodied discourse. "We shall go into the astral together."

"So now you know what I was trying to tell you when you flew off in such a mad rush the last time you traveled there."

"You were trying to tell me that it is where we belong?" Gideon queried.

"Love madness has scrambled your brains, Gideon, Prince of the Air!" Lavilia's voice boomed. "I was trying to tell you, you should have *stayed* there with your lady then, where you would have been safe and where you would have avoided all that has occurred since!"

Gideon groaned.

"However," Lavilia went on, "you were not ready to hear sage advice then, and the game needed to be played out as destiny designed. The gods are a fickle lot, and all things are relative in Nature, dark one, as you will soon find out in your new domain."

"We will not meet again," Gideon said, answering his own question.

"I would not say never," she said, "but not in the near future, no, we will not."

"The feather, then!" Gideon said. "We are ready!"

"One thing I tell you for free," Lavilia said. "You must catch this feather when it falls and keep it in a safe place. One day you will have need of it."

"In what respect?"

"You need not know that now," Lavilia said. "You will know when the time comes, but that is another story, and not entirely yours. Fare thee well, dark one! I send you to your destiny. Your lives have just begun. Hold on to your lady . . . until we meet again."

Epilogue

---

*The Arcan Astral West Country, Region of Perpetual Spring
One month later*

Gideon rose from his sleeping niche early. Rhiannon was still sleeping soundly in her hammock woven of woodbine and honeysuckle vines. It was suspended between the two great oaks, Ancient Ones that rose through the airy bedchamber skylight. The room had neither roof nor ceiling but for the canopy of leafy boughs the oaks formed swaying gently overhead. How beautiful she was sleeping so soundly, so peacefully in her new surroundings, her breast rising and falling beneath the silky sheet, her lustrous lashes casting long shadows upon her cheeks.

Aroused, he nodded toward the shadows, and a troop of tiny winged creatures flew near and took hold of the coverlet gently, peeling it back for him to view her as she slept. She was naked, for nudity was the height of fashion in the astral realm. Except for filmy garments spun by silkworms and spiders so fine they hid nothing, nakedness was the norm.

A wave of his hand dismissed the creatures, and he knelt down, toying with a lock of Rhiannon's long hair waiting for her to awaken to him. It was a good life. No watchers hurled their missiles. No demons marred the sanctity of dreams—one more erotic than the next—that filled their nights with carnal ecstasy.

The elder who had spoken to him for so long was right. Though the curse could not be broken, there were concessions. His tender wings would always be sensitive to touch, but he had his Rhiannon for comfort without reprisal, beloved captive of the realm that had given them sanctuary. He had his freedom to soar the length and breadth of the astral in his pursuit of order among the winged classes. It would take time, but he had found a home among those who needed him, reverenced and respected him, and most important of all, he had the woman he loved.

Rhiannon had been given Maribelle, the gruagach, as her personal attendant, when she wasn't tending the livestock, and their compound often overflowed with cows and goats and sheep for the woman's tenacity. But now, they were alone, except for the tiny creatures always hovering nearby to do their bidding, and Gideon was hard against the seam of the glittering skintight astral suit the elders had provided to replace his tattered eel skin on formal occasions, like now, when he would shortly be making his rounds.

How would he make love to Rhiannon today . . . in the rock pool that flowed from a natural spring that wound its way through the surrounding forest? Or would he take her in flight, soaring through cloudless cerulean skies, his wings unfurled for the wind to stroke and caress and ruffle, bringing him to climax like no other? Or would he do both?

Soon, dawn would break, and the couplings would begin. The sweet springtime air would be filled with male and female creatures mating in plain view. There was no modesty among the fay. Public mating, Gideon soon found, was a common occurrence, shocking at first, especially for Rhiannon, with her mortal morality, but they both soon fell into the rituals as if they were born to them, delighting in the pure uninhibited joy of their sexuality. Just thinking about it made him harder. Bending, he kissed Rhiannon awake, and lifting her into his arms, he carried her into the forest.

The minute she left the hammock, the trees that supported it bent and swayed and reached with their leafy branches to order it. Smoothing the honeysuckle that had cradled Rhiannon through the night scenting her skin, they discarded any crushed blooms and made the hammock bed with fresh rose petals liberally sprinkled about. It was a labor of love, Gideon thought looking on, for every creature, like Pio, had become enamored of Rhiannon, seduced by her beauty, bewitched by her charm.

The tide that fed the rock pool was running high. He stepped into the warm water and floated on his back as Rhiannon straddled him. The first rays of dappled sunlight filtering through the trees tinted her skin shades of saffron and rose as he opened his skintight suit in front and lifted her onto his penis, taking her deeply.

Shafts of fractured sunlight breaking through the trees showed him others who had come to the pool to couple in celebration of the morning, climbing up and down the sun beams as if they were ladders. The air was filled with mating fay. Watching them engaged in the sex act excited him, made him harder still, and when her thick folds tugged at his penis, he groaned and let her take him, let the power of her passion slake his hunger—fill his need, for it was only the beginning.

The climax was riveting, wrenching a groan like nothing human from his throat as he surrendered to her skills, the skills he had awakened in her, skills that made her his alone. After a moment, he surged to his feet in the water still inside her and wrapped her legs around his waist.

"Hold on," he murmured in her ear.

Purring like a cat, Rhiannon clung to him as he soared through the trees into the cloudless sky, high above the astral forest buzzing with carnal excitement below. He was hard inside her again as he took her lips in a fiery kiss that weakened his knees and wrenched another guttural moan from her throat. He could feel the blood throbbing in the folds of her vagina, as he ground the root of his cock against her swollen sex. His wings fluttered in and out of furl as they carried him up, up, gliding on a zephyr, as if they had a will of their own.

"Are you happy, my love?" he murmured in her ear.

Rhiannon reached to stroke his face, and he leaned into the caress. "How could you even ask?" she murmured.

Gideon kissed her fingers. Drawing one into his mouth, he laved it seductively with his warm tongue, igniting fresh fire in his loins. It was time, and he furled his wings around her and plummeted down, down toward the misty world they now called home, where creatures of the fay mated in public, trees made their beds with honeysuckle and rose petals, and springtime sunlight never ceased to beam down upon the land.

Yes, it was good. Gideon, Lord of the Dark, Prince of the Air, hurtled toward the Astral forest with his Rhiannon in his arms. They came together in shuddering spurts before his wings snapped open slowing their approach. Taken by the wind, they plummeted into the morning mist through clouds of mating fay under the spell of carnal oblivion to begin another day on their journey to forever.

Turn the page and you'll be
ADDICTED!

From Lydia Parks,
coming soon from Aphrodisia!

1

Jake Brand tipped his chair back on two legs, wrapped his hand around a glass of whiskey, and took in the sights as if he had all the time in the world. In a way, he did. At least, in the foreseeable future, he had a decent shot at eternity.

The young blonde leaning over a table, shaking her backside in his direction, was another matter. In a few short years, her firm breasts would start to sag and her tight ass would droop. If she were lucky, some lonely trucker would offer her his life savings and a ranch-style home in the outskirts of Albuquerque before that happened.

But tonight, Jake planned to entertain the sweet young thing in exchange for dinner.

"You sure are taking your time with that drink," the blonde said, frowning at the five-dollar bill on his table.

Jake plucked a folded fifty from his shirt pocket and dropped it on top of the five. "I've got nothing but time, darlin'."

The young woman's eyes widened and her red, full lips

stretched into a greedy smile. She snatched the bill from the table and stuffed it into the back pocket of her denim miniskirt.

She winked at him. "I'll be back for you in just a minute."

"I'll be right here," he said, grinning. He watched her hurry to the bar, toss her towel under it, and whisper something to the bartender.

The burly redheaded bartender glanced over at Jake and nodded, and the blonde started back for Jake's table, swinging her hips as she tapped out the background song's rhythm with her high heels. He liked the way the shoes made her legs look a mile long. The thought of those legs wrapped around him caused a pleasant reaction, and he moved to adjust his tightening jeans.

She didn't stop at his table, but continued forward until she stood straddling his thighs, her hands locked behind his neck as she swayed back and forth in time with the music. "My name's Candy," she said, her voice soft in his ear. "You like candy, don't you?"

"Hmm," he said, inhaling her scent, weeding out vanilla shampoo, cheap perfume, stale cigarettes, whiskey fumes, and sweat. Yes, he definitely had the right dinner partner. "I can eat candy all night long."

"Oh, baby," she whispered, "You make me hot."

He chuckled at the insincerity of her words. Undoubtedly, few of her many customers cared if she meant them or not, and he didn't, either. Before the night was over, he'd get the truth from her, and she'd be more than just *hot*.

Jake ran the tips of his fingers up the backs of her exposed thighs.

She stepped back to frown down at him. "No touching. That's house rules."

He grinned again, enjoying the way her simple emotions played across her face.

He lowered his voice a notch. "I could bring you to a quivering climax without touching you, but it wouldn't be nearly as much fun."

One corner of her mouth curled up in cynical amusement. "You think so?"

"I know so." Jake used the Touch to retrace the paths of his fingers with his thoughts, remembering the warmth, the smoothness, the soft hairs on her upper thighs.

"*Hey.*" She took another step back and stared into his eyes.

Jake pushed a simple concept into her simple mind. *Pleasure like you've never known.*

She swallowed hard, hesitated, and then moved forward to straddle his thighs again. He could smell her excitement as she sat on his legs and wrapped her arms around his shoulders. "I don't know how you did that," she said softly. "And I don't really care. You wanna go in the back room?"

"I think we should go up to my room."

She nodded, then turned her head to kiss him. Her warm breath caressed his skin before her lips met his, and he closed his eyes to enjoy the heated tenderness of her mouth. Her tongue slid across his lips, moving precariously close to the razor-sharp points of his teeth. Jake let a groan escape as he enjoyed the way her heat enveloped his growing erection, in spite of the clothes between them.

Candy ended the kiss and stood, drawing Jake after her with her small hand in his, leading him upstairs. The noise of the saloon-turned-strip joint faded below them as they climbed, leaving only a bass vibration in its wake.

"Which room?"

He nodded toward the door at the end of the small hallway. "Six."

"The best." She raised one eyebrow. "You rich or something?"

"Something."

"Oh, I see." She tossed her head, sending her blond waves into a dance around her shoulders. Candy knew exactly how attractive she was. "So, you're a man of mystery. Your name isn't *John*, is it?"

"No, it's Jake." He withdrew the key from his pocket, unlocked the door and pushed it open, then stepped aside as his young visitor entered. She didn't look around; she'd seen the room before.

"Jake." She turned in the middle of the room and smiled as she surveyed him from head to toe. "You know your fifty bucks don't buy you much. You want a blow job, or straight sex?"

Jake laughed then. "How do you know I'm not a peace officer?"

"A cop?" Candy grinned. "I know cops. Half the force comes in here after their shift. You're different, but you ain't no cop."

He nodded as he crossed the room and sat on the foot of the bed. "You're right about that. I'm different."

Candy tugged at the hem of her shirt, her head cocked seductively. "For twenty more, I take off my clothes just for you, baby."

Jake pulled off his boots and dropped them onto the floor. "I've got a better idea. How about a wager?"

The young woman straightened and narrowed her eyes. "You tryin' to tell me you ain't got no more money?"

He withdrew a hundred from his pocket and dropped it onto the bed. When she reached for it, he covered her hand with his own. "Not so fast there, sweet thing. Don't you want to hear my proposal?"

"*Proposal?*"

"For a wager."

Candy withdrew her hand slowly, then folded her arms across her chest. "I'm listening."

Jake stretched out on his side, studying the girl. "How long have you been at this?"

"At what?"

"Hooking."

Candy frowned. "You ain't some kind of preacher or something, are you? If you think you're gonna convert me—"

Jake silenced her by raising one hand. "You've got me all wrong, sweetheart. I'm definitely not a preacher."

She waited, her hands now on her hips.

"I'm willing to bet you one hundred dollars that I can bring you to a screaming climax in the next half hour."

Her eyebrows shot up and then she burst out laughing.

Jake watched her, enjoying her amusement.

"Right," she said between guffaws. "A *screaming* climax?"

He nodded.

When she managed to regain control of herself, she dropped down onto the edge of the bed, extending her hand. "You're on, Jake."

He took her hand in his, enjoying the warmth. Then he sat up and raised her hand to his lips.

"But you gotta wear a rubber."

Jake looked into her blue eyes. "Do I?"

Candy nodded. "Safe sex or no sex, that's how I stay alive."

"I promise we will run no risk of infecting you with anything."

Jake rose and drew Candy up to stand in front of him. Watching her face, he ran his palms slowly up her sides, peeling her shirt off over her head.

She stared at him with calm resolve, but goose bumps rose on her skin where he'd touched her. "Your hands are cold," she said.

"You'll just have to warm them up for me, darlin'."

He unsnapped her skirt and pushed it off in the same manner, sliding his palms over her rounded buttocks and down the backs of her thighs. As she stood before him in her high heels, he stepped back to drink in the sight of her.

Her breasts were full and firm, with large, dark areolae. As he studied them, her nipples puckered, and he knew she liked to be watched.

Her waist, narrow with youth, led his gaze down to her partially shaved pubic mound, the line of dark brown hair giving away her true color.

Then there were those legs. Damn, they were long.

"Oh, yeah," he said, aloud but to himself. "This will be fun."

Jake stepped closer and eased his hands down from her shoulders to her breasts, memorizing the shape and warmth of them, twisting the nipples playfully before moving on to her waist and then her ass. *Nice.* He nuzzled her neck to get more of her scent, then pressed his lips to the top of her shoulder. The sound of her heart beating drowned out the hum of the room's air conditioner, and he let himself enjoy it for a few moments before turning back to the task at hand.

He moved his mouth to hers, covering her lips with his own as he eased one hand into her soft blond hair. His other hand he slid down her back to the smallest point and pulled her gently to him.

Her hands rose to his chest for balance.

He opened her mouth then, and ran his tongue around hers, catching the taste of whiskey and tobacco, as he moved his hand around her hip and eased it between her legs. Her swollen vulva parted for his fingers as he slid them back and forth, hinting at entering her, stirring her juices.

Her hands flattened against his chest.

Jake eased one finger deeper, stroking her clit, and her fingers curled. She drew on his tongue, and he continued to stroke, enjoying the way her hot little bud swelled.

Candy tore her mouth from his. "You said . . . a *screaming* climax."

"Yes, I did," he said, his mouth near her ear.

Her hips began to rock to the rhythm of his hand, and she gripped the front of his shirt in her fists. "Damn, you're good," she said, "but I don't scream for no man."

Jake chuckled as he slid his hand out from between her thighs. "Good, darlin', 'cause I don't want this to be too easy."

Candy rubbed against the front of his bulging pants. "Even if I ain't screaming, you don't have to stop."

"Don't worry, sweet thing, I'm not about to stop." He reached down with both hands, cradled her ass, and lifted her from the floor.

She wrapped her legs around his hips and her arms around his neck.

Jake carried her to the bed and eased her down as he kissed her. The girl knew how to kiss, and he felt his erection hardening to the point of discomfort. He unbuttoned his pants to relieve some of the pressure, then he withdrew from her.

Her eyes blazed as she looked up at him, partly with passion and partly from whiskey, no doubt.

Jake parted her legs, knelt at the edge of the bed, and kissed the insides of her thighs as he drew her to his mouth.

Her cunt was hot, salty, and wet, and he slowly licked the length of her, savoring the taste. Her legs opened more in response, and her ass tightened. He continued with long, slow laps as he listened to her suck air between her teeth, and he enjoyed her quickening heartbeat. Not long now, and he'd have her ready, sweetened, primed for him.

Jake pushed his tongue between her cunt lips and lashed at her clit, then drew it carefully between his teeth and sucked.

Candy's back arched, and she moaned as she neared an orgasm.

He moved away, nibbling at her thighs.

She grunted in frustration and he smiled.

Closing his eyes, Jake pushed his thoughts out then, moving the Touch up the length of her body like a hundred butterfly wings, caressing every part of her at once, flitting across her nipples and stomach, as he slid his fingers into her cunt.

Her hips rose up off the bed and she cried out in joy. "Oh . . . God . . . that's good," she said between panted breaths.

She clamped down on his fingers and flooded them with her juices as he moved in and out of her, traveling across her damp skin with his thoughts, feeling the conditioned air blow across her breasts, finding her pulse in a hundred spots at once.

His burgeoning cock emerged from the front of his pants as he enjoyed Candy, pulling her to the edge of her resistance, then pushing her away.

She cooed, and then groaned, and then growled with disappointment.

Continuing the Touch, Jake rose and removed his clothes. He loved the feel of heated flesh against his own when he drank. Letting the Touch drift lower now, he stretched out on top of Candy and kissed her neck, her jaw, and her shoulders.

She wriggled under him as the treatment intensified. His thoughts rolled over her cunt, then dipped in and out.

"Fuck me," she said, digging her fingers into his back. "Please. I'm on fire."

"Yes," he whispered, easing his cock between her legs.

She thrust up into him, taking him into her all at once, and he almost lost her.

"Oh, no, you don't," he said, drawing back.

She locked her legs around him before he could withdraw.

"Good lord, get on with it."

Jake glanced over his shoulder, surprised to find Thomas Skidmore standing beside the bed, pale hands fisted on his narrow hips.

"Go away," Jake said.

"Why do you insist on doing it this way?" Skidmore waved dramatically with one arm, his style mimicking the British theater of years gone by. "I've never known anyone who felt they had to get permission. You are strange, dear boy."

Jake returned his attention to Candy, rocking against her in time with her growing need. She hadn't noticed the intrusion.

"Just hurry. We have places to go." Skidmore closed the door behind him as he left.

"Oh, God," she said, louder now. "Don't stop. Fuck me. Harder."

Jake turned his head to speak softly into her ear. "I need more than your cunt, sweet thing. I need your blood."

He felt her tense as fear crept into her fevered excitement.

"I won't hurt you," he said. "We'll come together."

After a moment of hesitation, she turned her head, offering her neck to him as she writhed in anticipation, her hands fisted against his back.

Jake pressed his lips to her neck, thrilling to the pulse rising and falling beneath the surface. He let loose of the reins then, thrusting into her sizzling cunt as his cock hardened to steel, pushing deeper, needing release nearly as much as he needed to feed.

His fangs lengthened, and he opened his mouth. Trying to hold back, savoring the anticipation, he smelled her approaching climax. Yes, she was ready.

Jake pressed his fangs into her neck and she screamed. He closed his eyes as her orgasm flooded him, first biting down on his pulsing cock, then flowing through his veins and exploding in his brain. He drew hard as he pumped his seed into her, letting her fill him with need, fulfillment, dreams, wants, desires.

He knew her arousal as she danced for hungry eyes, her smug disgust as sweaty men humped her for money, her euphoria as she lay alone at night with a vibrating orgasm rolling through her narcotic haze. And he felt her ecstasy as his own. She came again as he thrust harder, longer, until he'd taken all he could, and given all he had.

Jake held his mouth to her neck for a moment to stop the flow, then moved it away and slowed his thrusts to nice, easy strokes.

Her grip changed to a shaky hold on his shoulders, and her cries softened to weak groans.

He stilled, then withdrew and rolled onto his back to enjoy the sensations of nerves popping and firing through his entire system, waking from a long sleep. After more than a century and a half, he still loved the vibration, especially when sweetened with orgasms.

"You win."

Jake turned his head to find Candy lying with her eyes closed and her arms at her sides, her body glistening with a fine sheen of sweat. Already, the small wounds on her neck were nearly healed, and her heart rate had begun to slow.

He grinned.

If not for Skidmore waiting impatiently outside somewhere, Jake might have spent a few more hours with his little morsel. But the old man was right; they had places to go.

After getting dressed, he dropped the bill onto Candy's bare stomach, then leaned over and kissed her soundly.

She hadn't moved much, and smiled up at him. "You come back anytime, Jake."

He winked at her, then tossed the room key onto the bed beside her before leaving his dinner guest and the air conditioner's buzz behind.

Downstairs, he found the tall, thin vampire in an out-of-place purple velvet suit, standing in the shadows near the door, and Jake made his way through the maze of tables, young strippers, and horny old men.

"It's about time," Skidmore said, wrinkling his nose with disapproval.

"Some things shouldn't be rushed." Jake picked up his black felt Stetson from a hook by the door and slipped it on as he stepped into the New Mexico night. Warm, clean air swept over him as if he were no more than another jackrabbit making his way across the desert, and a star-filled sky opened above as Jake strolled across the parking lot to the convertible parked near the exit.

"Will you please get a move on?" Skidmore hurried ahead, hopping effortlessly into the passenger's seat. "I refuse to spend another day trapped in the boot of this wretched beast. It'll take at least four hours to get to the mine, and that's thirty minutes more than we have."

"Don't sweat it," Jake said, trying not to get annoyed with his fellow traveler. Skidmore tended to get on his nerves after a month or two of whining. "We'll be there in three."

Jake started the Impala and pulled out onto the narrow highway, turning north. With no one else around, he easily pushed the car to ninety and they roared through the darkness.

"Oh, I nearly forgot to tell you what I heard," Skidmore said.

It was a lie; the older vampire never forgot anything. Jake waited, but Skidmore just smiled.

"What?"

"A very special friend of yours will be at the meeting. If we get there early enough, perhaps you'll have time to get reacquainted."

"Katie?" Jake glanced over at his companion, whose face seemed to glow in the starlight.

Skidmore grinned and ignored his question.